THE
LAST TIME
WE
SAW HER

ALSO BY JACLYN GOLDIS

The Safari
The Main Character
The Chateau
When We Were Young

PRAISE FOR THE NOVELS OF JACLYN GOLDIS

"Rollicking good fun."

—*The Wall Street Journal*

"Tense and twisty."

—Julie Clark, *New York Times* bestselling author of *The Ghostwriter*

"Will have you up all night hungrily hunting the pages for stealthily laid clues. A must-read!"

—Heather Gudenkauf, *New York Times* bestselling author of *The Overnight Guest* and *The Perfect Hosts*

"A twisty, well-paced murder mystery that never fully lets go—readers will gasp, even at the final page. Brilliantly done."

—Sarah Penner, *New York Times* bestselling author of *The Lost Apothecary*

"An intense, intricate puzzle box I couldn't put down."

—Julia Bartz, *New York Times* bestselling author of *The Writing Retreat*

"Will surprise even the most eagle-eyed reader. Goldis has mixed the family drama of *Knives Out* with the locked-room atmosphere of *Murder on the Orient Express* and the resulting cocktail is like an Aperol on a hot summer's day: perfect."

—Katy Hays, *New York Times* bestselling author of *The Cloisters*

"Enormously entertaining . . . a transporting page-turner with surprises around every corner. I couldn't put it down."

—Luke Dumas, *USA Today* bestselling author of *The Paleontologist* and *A History of Fear*

"Unputdownable."

—*Woman's World*

"The perfect literary treat for readers who like matching wits with an author while doing a bit of armchair traveling . . . Goldis once again deftly tips her literary cap to the Queen of Crime, Agatha Christie, in another cleverly constructed puzzler that brings all the delights of classic Golden Age mysteries into the twenty-first century."

—*Library Journal* (starred review)

"Delicious tension and drama."

—*Kirkus Reviews*

THE LAST TIME WE SAW HER

A NOVEL

JACLYN GOLDIS

EMILY BESTLER BOOKS

ATRIA

New York   Amsterdam/Antwerp   London
Toronto   Sydney/Melbourne   New Delhi

ATRIA

An Imprint of Simon & Schuster, LLC
1230 Avenue of the Americas
New York, NY 10020

First Emily Bestler Books/Atria Paperback edition June 2026

EMILY BESTLER BOOKS/ATRIA PAPERBACK and colophon are registered trademarks of Simon & Schuster, LLC

Simon & Schuster strongly believes in freedom of expression and stands against censorship in all its forms. For more information, visit BooksBelong.com.

For information about special discounts for bulk purchases, please contact Simon & Schuster Special Sales at 1-866-506-1949 or business@simonandschuster.com.

The Simon & Schuster Speakers Bureau can bring authors to your live event. For more information or to book an event, contact the Simon & Schuster Speakers Bureau at 1-866-248-3049 or visit our website at www.simonspeakers.com.

Interior design by Davina Mock-Maniscalco

Manufactured in the United States of America

1 3 5 7 9 10 8 6 4 2

Library of Congress Cataloging-in-Publication Data has been applied for.

ISBN 978-1-6680-6701-7 (pbk)
ISBN 978-1-6680-6703-1 (ebook)

Scan here to get book recommendations, exclusive offers, and more delivered to your inbox.

For the authors whose books I've loved,
your stories have brought me so much joy

But it was not [the size of the tree] that now impressed my companions; it was the knowledge that seven hundred thousand pounds in gold lay somewhere buried below its spreading shadow. The thought of the money, as they drew nearer, swallowed up their previous terrors. Their eyes burned in their heads; their feet grew speedier and lighter; their whole soul was bound up in that fortune, that whole lifetime of extravagance and pleasure, that lay waiting there for each of them.

—Robert Louis Stevenson, *Treasure Island*

CHAPTER ONE

Sydney

Ten Years Before

WE'RE GOING ON *a treasure hunt*

X marks the spot

You sit behind me, tracing a circle on my back, representing São Miguel Island. Though the island isn't actually a circle, but the shape of a dragon plopped smack in the middle of the Atlantic. And right now, we're in the belly of the dragon. We've been exploring the island, camping in tents upon its rocky ground each night, nearly five weeks now.

You slash the *X* on my back. The location of the treasure.

I shiver because it's ironic: I do know where the treasure is, but you don't. And I need to keep it that way until I figure out what to do next. Because finding the treasure—it changes everything. My heart does a literal backflip. I don't freaking know what to do. I don't—

Spiders crawling up your back

Your fingers creep up my back, over the still-fresh scratch wounds on my shoulder blade, across toward my hairline. A gust slithers in from the cove, teasing goose bumps from my skin. I tuck the little front braids I always wear behind my ears, then adjust my white beaded necklace, returning its silver heart pendant to the center.

It's not the first time we've played this game, said this familiar camp rhyme. Not the first time your fingers have wandered my back. But it's different now, because of everything that has happened this summer. I'm not the same girl as when I arrived in the Azores, desperate to escape the medical charts and doctors, and to explore this place where distant ancestors of ours landed, escaping persecution, and made their lives and fortunes.

And I wanted to have some fun: that's what the summer was supposed to be about. Fun was indeed had—my lips curl into a sly smile, then quickly flatline. Because the past few days, I've watched my life literally face-plant. Like, in no time things went from mildly shitty to apocalyptic.

I stare ahead toward the mouth of the cave with ferns overhanging, whipping in the wind, and not far beyond, waves foaming onto the black sand of the cove. The air is crisp, with the clean, mineral scent of rocks wet from the ocean spray and the slightly musty smell of moss creeping alongside the cave walls. My flashlight slices through the dark, revealing twitching shadows at the threshold. The ocean crescendos in my ears, and I lick my lips, tasting salt from my earlier swim. I fight the impulse to look around. Definitely not toward the hole in the cave floor roughly four feet to our right, which I've covered with my backpack.

Spiders crawling down your back

You whisper it, tapping your fingers down my spine, and then you press closer, so I feel the heat of you settle against me.

"Sydney," you say, your breath against the nape of my neck, "I'm really glad I came here now."

I part my lips to speak, but no sound comes out. My chest jitters with a quiet, rising panic.

I still can't believe you're here. We campers are supposed to be alone, separated in our assigned spots on the island for our twenty-four-hour solo missions, but I spotted you walking toward the cave. And good thing I had my head in the game to hide the treasure.

I shift on the hard floor. My heart beats frenetically and feels almost painful, like it's being shoved around inside a mosh pit. And I'm a bizarre kind of exhausted that's shot with adrenaline. Unsurprising, as it's not yet dawn, but you didn't exactly wake me up. I slept tossing and turning, like I was back in the hospital again and aware of every nurse coming in, every beep, ache, and flicker—including the flicker that turned out to be you. And now, finding the treasure and dealing with your arrival have sucked out all my energy and sent every single red flag waving. The sun hasn't come up yet but I can tell by the receding darkness that it's not far off. In a few hours, I'll have to start packing up. Figure out what to do—about all of it. They'll wonder where we are. But that stuff is intellectual, I realize, because even without a rational explanation of what's going on, every molecule of me is screaming that something here is totally off.

But I'm kinda scared to ask you to leave because of . . . I don't know what, exactly. You? That feels ridiculous. But still. The vibes don't lie.

I don't know what to do. I don't—

Knife in your back

Blood gushing down

You pound your fist between my shoulder blades and suddenly I'm done. It's too much, this trip, this treasure hunt sprung to life. All the values Camp Zahav has drip-drip-dripped into us our whole lives, of teamwork and Jewish traditions and *tzedakah* and good deeds and pride in our culture and living off the land, have gone in a flash. We've all been possessed, it feels like, by the promise of riches and having all our problems alchemized into gold.

I try to twist around because I don't want to play this game anymore, but you grip my shoulders with strength that startles me. It feels like you almost trap me in place.

Knife in your back

Blood gushing down

You pound your fist against my back again so hard that I lurch forward. I don't like your voice. It's strange, not playful now. Not like the rhyme is supposed to be. I'm about to lose it and just tell you to get the hell out when—

Knife in your back

Blood gushing down

No—that's wrong. That's a stanza too many. I'm supposed to feel your breath on my neck by now, followed by your whisper: *Cool breeze, tight squeeze, now you've got the—now you've got the—chilllllllls.*

I already feel chills. But it's too soon. You've gone off script.

Knife in your back

Blood gushing down

A sharp, curdling pain between my shoulder blades, but this time it's not your fist. It's—

It's—

A knife, I realize in horror, as excruciating pain spikes through me. I scream. Keel over.

No—this can't be—how—you of all people—you—you couldn't—

My vision blurs. A scream tries to claw its way out, but my throat locks up tight. I crumple to the ground and watch you stand, not even glancing back at me.

You walk right toward the treasure. And I realize too late that you knew it all along.

X marks the spot.

CHAPTER TWO

Olivia

FOR A LONG time, I figured that if I ever set foot on this island again it would be in handcuffs. But surprise, surprise. Hello again, São Miguel. Here I am. The Sister Killer.

I cross Rua dos Mercadores and the cheesemonger peers at me with craggy blue eyes, like he knows exactly who I am. Well, of course he does; it would be the rare islander to whom I'm anonymous. I slow, take in the window display of waxy orange Azorean cheeses, which, though beloved by locals, frankly taste exactly like the meadows on this island smell—of pungent cow manure. I prefer my cheese less authentic, closer to the detectable chemicals-in-a-can sprayed orange goop. I nod at the old man but he stares back stoically, almost like he knows what I am capable of. What I'm here ten years later to finish.

I quicken down the cobblestone street, one of the main ways in central Ponta Delgada. The locals call it PD and it's a place I know with deep familiarity—partly because I spent that summer here ten years ago and partly because of all my research from afar for my bestselling young adult novels set on this island.

Octopi crafted from sea-green crepe paper dangle above. I puzzle over them as I walk, their haphazard and amateur vibes clashing with the old-world architecture, until I spy a banner declaring that they are citywide installations made by school-children to celebrate one of the summer's many festivals. I continue on, past the three basaltic stone arches of the Portas da Cidade, yielding sweeping views of the old city up through the port. The basaltic stone is an omnipresent feature of the island: dark gray and black rock formed from the rapid cooling of volcanic lava, sometimes polished by wind and water and thus smooth to the touch, and other times rough and porous. You see it and step upon it everywhere here. As I walk, I weave my fingers in the gnarled-on-purpose edge of my jacket sleeve, knowing that my father would prefer I greet him wearing some-thing refined and synagogue-appropriate. Plus, I'm late—Dad hates when I'm late.

The anticipation of his displeasure makes me smile my first genuine smile of the day.

I walk down a street of papier-mâché crabs, then cross the plaza to the street parallel, where guppy fish encircle the lamp-posts. I pass the massive fort with its—wait for it—basaltic stone, then dip a right. I'm almost there, and my ribs squeeze in, like I'm bracing for impact.

The same tense anxiety thrums in my veins whenever I'm about to see Dad. Suddenly I don't want to go up to the syna-gogue. How is any of it going to lead to closure? I don't actually want to do the documentary—and why did I tell Jules I'd—

I feel the itching sensation of a person behind me. I swivel, and an elfin blond woman lurches forward. "Are you . . . Olivia Azulay?"

Oh, fuck. I exhale deeply and feel my armor slip on. "Yes?"

"I knew it!" The woman has the grace to blush. So probably a fan over a hater. Or a fan-slash-hater. There are lots of those. She's clearly not Azorean; she sounds Canadian.

"You're prettier than your pictures," she says. "You've grown into a beautiful woman," she clarifies, making clear exactly what she means, what she's seen. The photos of me at seventeen, the ones beneath which the label Sister Killer is emblazoned. A lanky and awkward girl, with stringy dishwater hair. A girl who didn't really wear anything other than baggy cargos and oversize camp-themed T-shirts that said things like "I live nine months for three."

"Sorry, I don't mean to make you uncomfortable! You probably get people stopping you all the time. I just—our daughter—Adeline is her name—Adeline would *die* that I got to meet Olivia Azulay. Wouldn't she, Gene?" The woman glances back at the tall man with an auburn goatee who is grabbing her elbow, eyes batting apologetically as he tries to tug her along.

"Adeline loves your books. She'll be so upset she missed you. *So* upset. It's why we're even here in the first place. She wants to do the Lagoa do Fogo loop like the kids in *X Marks the Spot*. And today she went to Vila . . ." Her nose wrinkles. "Vila something about a camp?" When I don't answer, she adds, "It's from your book."

"Vila Franca do Campo," I finally say.

The area where Sydney disappeared. But I don't add that.

"There's a cove, isn't there?" the woman asks. "That Addie wanted to—"

"Yes. Well, many places on this island appear in my books. But listen . . ." I check my phone, then feign surprise at the time. "I've gotta get going."

"Oh! I'm sorry, really sorry, to keep you," she says, not sounding sorry at all. "But since we've met—here of all places—and our daughter is really your number one fan, can you sign—Gene," she says sharply. "Do we have a napkin or something?"

He sighs and gives up his grip on her elbow, then riffles around in their backpack. "No. No napkin."

"*Gene*," she says in that tight, icicle voice I used to hear my mother use with my father.

"There's nothing to sign, Laura." He also has the resigned

voice of my father, before Sydney and then my mother died in one fell swoop, leaving him free to marry young, hot Daniella and slot into his ready-made new family.

"Rip out a page from your war book!"

"It's not a war book," he protests. "It's by Daniel Silva, quite good in fact, about the head of—"

"Gene," she says again, still icicle cold. "If you want Addie to ever speak to you again, rip out a page." She rolls her eyes at me, as if I'm about to commiserate. "I told him it was ridiculous to bring that heavy book with us, but he insisted. He'd rather be in foreign worlds. Never the one right there in front of him."

I recognize the words of a long-suffering wife. It's a pattern I observed in my own parents. When one partner is constantly trying to slip away, the other inevitably transforms to a predator. And then only two options present: either predator devours prey, or prey escapes for its life.

A ripped cream book page is proffered to me. It feels wrong to accept it, wrong that it's been ripped out of something that used to be whole. Back when I was a kid, the pages inside books felt like they cocooned me in imaginary homes. Books don't do that for me anymore. They aren't home. Now I write them. They represent financial security—and a place to put my rage.

I place the paper on my thigh and accept the pen that Laura pushes toward me as well.

"Make it out to—"

"Adeline. Yeah, got that."

I scrawl out my standard message. *Dear Adeline, Maybe you'll be the one to find the treasure. Don't forget, X marks the spot! Olivia Azulay*

Then I doodle the thing I always do, what's become my symbol of sorts. It's a pair of lips open wide, with three lines emanating out from between. At fleeting glance it looks like a kiss, like the xxx marks Europeans add to texts.

But it's not, and only I know: it's my version of a silent scream.

I hand the paper back to Laura. She scans it, looking pleased, aware this will buy her cool parent cred. But then she crinkles her nose. "What's that drawing? It's on the spine of all your books, but it's not a kiss, is it? It's like a scream or something. Is it a reference to your sister? You're angry that she died? Or angry that you . . ."

"It's fiction," I tell her, something hot flaring in my throat. No one's ever figured it out before. Figured a part of me out. And I don't owe it to this stranger to explain that, in general, I am obsessed with angry women. That my apartment has sketches of women in various poses and manifestations of fury. A psychiatrist would have a field day. Probably Superintendent Flores on this very island would as well. She tried so hard after that summer to prove my guilt, to amass enough evidence for my arrest. I'm glad the island is big enough that my chances of running into her these next few days are low. Though I have a lifelong habit of being in the wrong place at the right time.

"Is there really a treasure still out there?" I'm jolted back, surprised but not surprised that this annoying woman is still standing before me. Not taking the hint.

"You never know. But I have to—"

"Is it true what they say?" she presses on eagerly. "That the books have clues to the real killer—I mean, the real person who killed your sister?"

I shrug. "Well, that assumes the killer isn't me now, doesn't it? Because it's unlikely I'd incriminate myself in my own books, right?"

I almost laugh at the abject shock on her face. But come on, I've been called the Sister Killer for ten years now. My publishers have capitalized on it. Millions of readers are riveted by the rumors of clues—to both Sydney's disappearance and to the phantom treasure—residing within my pages. The police have parsed my words over and over again, to naught.

I was never charged. And as I finally leave Laura standing there wide-mouthed, and I hurry along, I feel a burning in my chest, the familiar urge to add, "Fuck you, lady. Stop treating me like an animal at the zoo. I don't exist for your viewing pleasure."

But I do, don't I? I didn't ask to be infamous, but I've accepted— capitalized on, really—the fact that I am.

Sydney once said in her taunting way that deep down I wanted her to die so I could finally get out of her shadow.

Well, certainly no one would argue that I haven't emerged quite squarely from my sister's shadow.

———

Dad is waiting for me outside the synagogue, his tall, impeccably dressed frame leaning against the red brick, his still-thick, now fully gray hair lit by a shard of sunlight spilling onto his face and making him squint.

"Dad," I say, coming close enough that I smell his woodsy cologne.

"Livvie."

We hug, our usual thin embrace, over as quickly as a rubber band snaps back.

He scrutinizes me with his blazing blue eyes, the ones that I noticed as a child could wink just so to make any waitress or service person bowl over to serve him. "You look beautiful."

I glance down at my baggy bleached overalls over a striped blue button-down, white Salomons, and green jacket with patch- work quilt sunbursts that Tomika affectionately calls grandma core. Even though I'm no longer gawky, even though my baggy clothes and nineties bob with curtain bangs are currently fash- ionable, there's no way Dad actually thinks I look beautiful. Especially considering his definition of beauty means Sydney—

my curvy, tanned, loved-to-dress-up sister—and Daniella, the most turned-out, stereotypically plastic Barbie trophy wife.

Not that I've set eyes on my stepmother in ten years. Dad I see occasionally, when he returns to Boston for work trips and swings down to meet me in Brooklyn for pizza, making irritating jokes about how far outside Manhattan I live, as if Crown Heights is the boonies. At the beginning it's always awkward silences and resentments, but then we ease back into us, and for a couple hours it's almost like when I was a kid, when we liked and understood each other. We'll talk about politics and climate change and abortion, about how antisemitism is skyrocketing and whether it's safe to wear a Star of David anymore, subjects that rouse our mutual passions. You wouldn't look at Dad and be, like, that guy is a feminist and social justice warrior. And I mean, he's not one hundred percent feminist, let's be honest; he does have several blind spots, my stepmother being a giant one. Sure, on the surface he's a staid businessman, and in a traditional marriage in a Portuguese culture where the man is still considered the king, but he's also a progressive in many ways. Mom was a social worker, even though she was wealthy enough from her family inheritance not to need to work. But Daniella no longer works; she lives between Lisbon and the island, supporting her daughter Cass's Olympic training. Those dinners in Brooklyn with Dad—I enjoy them more than perhaps I let on. He might have betrayed me, but he's not a bad person. Not in his core. But now he's with Daniella. So who knows how thoroughly her influence has permeated.

God, even the fleeting thought of Daniella brings a sour taste to my mouth. For ten years I've managed to avoid her, and now I'll have to face her this weekend. Along with the rest of my "new family," or "second family," or whatever people call it when your sister disappeared in the most horrific, high-profile way, and then your mother killed herself, and your father married someone new and has a whole new life with people you'd rather spend the rest of yours dodging.

Except Reuben, my stepbrother. He's mostly fine.

"Really, you look so wonderful," Dad says.

"Mmm. Right," I say, batting off his compliment. We both know he's only saying it obligatorily, because Sydney was the one he always called beautiful, beautiful, beautiful, in his melodic voice, with my admittedly beautiful sister lapping it up. Frankly, I wasn't the daughter with the looks, the vocal cords, or the athleticism. Being a talented writer was never a thing Dad doled out top marks for.

"How's . . . Tobiko?" Dad asks.

"Tomika, Dad. God. My girlfriend is not a sushi condiment."

Dad reddens. "Sorry, gosh. Tomika. Of course, I know that. She's a wonderful girl, Tomika."

"She's a woman," I say through gritted teeth. "Please don't infantilize her."

"Sorry." His cheeks color deeper. "You're right. How is Tomika?"

"She's fine," I finally say, because it's what we're both good at, after all, burying things.

"Great." Dad clears his throat and nods his head toward the entry. "Well, shall we?"

"Guess so."

We walk into the tiny building where a security guard sits in the alcove. His eyes flash in recognition at Dad. "*Boa tarde*, Senhor Azulay!" They zoom off into a flurry of Portuguese, bits of which I pick up. Not because of the summer I spent here, or because my father now lives here full-time, but because of book research, of course. I know, for instance, that *mesa* means desk, which the non-Jewish guard uses incorrectly to describe the bimah Dad has funded in Sydney's honor, the reason behind this memorial weekend for which we've all gathered. And I know that the guard's accent is different than mainland Portuguese. Azoreans use front-rounded vowels—sounds more readily found in French and German; I gleaned that factoid from some article I read to help give my characters color. I can recognize it now, the way the guard just offered Dad *fruta* from the bowl on the welcome desk, with the *u* more pronounced. It's funny; my readers think I'm native Azorean and lived the things I write. But I'm not, and I don't, not completely at least. I guess I've always been talented at the smoke and mirrors.

Eventually the small talk ceases and the guard leads us past the plexiglass markers that represent the mikvah, the ancient purification baths. Then we ascend the stairs to the upper floor, where the small museum documenting the Jews of São Miguel greets us. Dad played a huge part in the restoration of the synagogue and the museum, and it is indeed lovely and moving. The room is flooded with natural light, and glass cases of ancient artifacts abound. There are old Torahs and bronze Seder plates and Kiddush cups, relics of the Jews who escaped the Inquisition in both Portugal and Morocco and landed on this island. My distant ancestors—and unlike Sydney, who was on our heritage trip exclusively for the boys and the fun, I've always been sentimental about this place. The island has felt like an invisible bruise on my body, even before my sister disappeared. The bruise is only part of what I know to be a deep reservoir of pain—the cries of my ancestors who were forced to convert, who were exiled, accused, and persecuted for simply being Jewish. Ironic how none of that persecution exists anymore but still feels incredibly alive in my bones.

It sucks to be so sensitive, though admittedly it's an asset to a writer. Syd was sensitive, too, but more outwardly so. She didn't keep things inside, like me, but instead screamed and cried and sometimes used her fingernails and fists. As kids, I often wished

I were more like her. Stronger. Louder. Willing to risk actually being seen, instead of just pouring my feelings into fictional stories.

The guard ushers us past the towering glass cases with more artifacts. I pause, my eyes fixed on the bottom row, where handkerchiefs are rolled up, and talitim, too, the shawls men don when they are praying. They're not pristine; the cloths are visibly worn. Soiled. And something in that makes my heart clench. I avert my eyes and walk into the sanctuary, where the Jews of this island used to pray. The walls are painted a cheery sky blue and the cherrywood bimah is located in the center in the Sephardic way, surrounded by ornate pews.

Dad goes immediately to the bimah. Sydney's bimah, as we've now come to call it. The synagogue restoration project was immense, and because there wasn't enough money to do it all at once, certain things had to be done piecemeal. So while the museum was completed years ago, the synagogue took longer. The bimah is the final piece, the memorial to Sydney. It's a fitting tribute to my sister because Dad used to be a volunteer cantor for our local synagogue in Boston, and Sydney was part of the children's choir. I can still picture the two of them, singing "Avinu Malkeinu" over the High Holidays. Sydney, the pride of the whole synagogue, the apple of our parents' eyes.

But many things have changed since then, and this bimah isn't only paid for with Dad's dollars. His guilt, I suspect, has seeped into the wood.

"What do you think?" Dad asks.

"She'd love it."

"You think?"

"Yeah," I say honestly. "I do."

After all, what wouldn't my sister love about all of this? Everyone making the trip back here, a party of sorts in her honor. The bimah in the center of this room dedicated to Sydney, the star.

Surrounded by longing and regret and remonstrations. The only thing she wouldn't love is that she isn't here to bask in it all right along with us.

"I'm going to make a speech," Dad says. "Maybe you'll take a look at my notes?"

"I'm sure whatever you wrote is nice," I say, hoping he'll read between the lines. I don't want to edit his speech to my dead sister. I draw the line at that.

"Maybe you'll give a speech too?"

"I think that would draw attention we don't want. The local media will be there. You know how they'll pounce on anything I have to say." I don't add that whatever I have to say I'll save for the documentary.

"I suppose. I just want it to be perfect for her."

Dad stares longingly at the bimah, as if somehow it might open up and resurrect Sydney. Like she'll beam out and slide into her white choir robe, singing "Lecha Dodi," angel wings sprouting from her back.

"I should be going," I finally say. "I need to get up north, settle in before dinner."

"Right. To the Ananda, yes?" I nod. "It's nice of Eli to put you all up."

"Yeah." Even though I could well afford the hotel's pricey tab, I know some people can't. Jules and Aiden. Maybe Reuben as well, despite the outward markers of his success.

"I'll see you later then," Dad adds.

"Oh. You're coming to dinner?"

Dad nods. "With Daniella and Cass. Eli invited us. Reuben is in town, too, as you know. Not so often we get all the kids home."

"Oh." I take in that unexpected information. I thought dinner would only be us former friends and counselors.

"So will you be staying to film the documentary after?" I ask, knowing I'm only saying it to goad him, because obviously he isn't. "You realize dinner isn't going to be some long-drawn-out thing. It's passed appetizers, a simple reunion. Jules wants to start filming after dinner since we're all only here for a few days."

Jules was our counselor on the Azores summer trip, with Aiden, our supervisor. They were both sixish years older than us, twenty-three to our seventeen then, but let's just say—boundaries were crossed. The age differential wasn't a barrier to . . . well, a lot of things. Aiden played to type, a real-life Brad Pitt, with a mysterious, literary, bad-boy vibe. It was all but guaranteed that Sydney would fall for him. Jules was more innocuous; she was a bit insecure, but genuinely sweet, capable of deep listening and compassion, of becoming an indispensable, unthreatening ally. To me. We got close. And I felt . . . well, I felt a lot of things toward her. Which Sydney resented. So of course she had to threaten us in the end. Threaten our bond. I'm curious if Jules is going to bring up *that* in the documentary.

Maybe I'm just jealous, even after all these years. It's what everyone has said, ever since I was thirteen months old, when Sydney made her grand arrival. Sometimes it doesn't matter what the truth is. The truth becomes the thing everyone says and believes, by virtue of it being said and believed over and over again. A well-trodden path that stamps out any vestiges of the real truth that existed before something shiny and artificial was imposed in its place.

Anyway, Jules dabbles in filmmaking; she dabbles in a lot of things, none of which have made her much money. She pleaded with us all to participate in her documentary, dangling platitudes like *closure* and *teasing out the truth at last* and *the world's insatiable appetite for the truth of Sydney's story*. Said that the documentary will be powerful, that she's the only one who can do it true justice. Then she appealed to base emotions—pity. Saying she's down on her luck, that she's in massive debt. But I know Jules has deeper motives still. I've felt resentful, to be honest, that

Jules hasn't much cared to stay in touch over the past decade but comes running back all friendly and trying to get in my good graces to get me to sign on the documentary dotted line. The rest of them all dropped out of touch, too; it's not like I was invited to Lexa and Eli's "wedding of the century." Well, understandable, I guess. The Sister Killer comes with a certain level of repulsion, and I sort of lost it that summer, even before Syd disappeared.

But being back here—and for the documentary—I have a stake in it too. And I vacillate between fear—what Jules will expose, what all of us will—and relief. Hope, even, that maybe the truth will come out and it will all be over at last.

"You can't be serious." For the first time today, Dad looks at me. Really looks at me with his oceanic eyes. Identical to Sydney's. "Livvie, tell me you didn't agree to do the documentary."

I launch my shoulders back. "I did. And you should too. You were there; you were also on the island when she disappeared." The police investigated everyone who had an opportunity, of course—including Dad and Daniella—but they were cleared early on.

"For work! I was working. I had nothing to do with—"

"I'm not implying that you did. But it's time, Dad. Ten years later . . . it's time for the truth to come out. I can't live like this anymore."

"The truth," Dad hisses, coming so close to me that his spit lands in my eye. "The truth is my family was destroyed. My daughter is gone. A documentary isn't going to bring her back or change any of what happened after. And I can tell you one thing for sure: I will not participate in the documentary. In my opinion, it's a colossal . . . *problem* for you to help with it."

"Yes, your *daughter* is gone. And apparently, I did it. So who better to talk about what happened the day Sydney disappeared than me? The Sister Killer. God forbid you'd want to try to exonerate *me*!"

Dad's eyes dart around, like the security guard might have

caught that. "Please don't say that," he pleads. "Please don't call yourself that."

"It's the only way to take the power back. They can't weaponize a phrase that I call myself." I hear the feigned lightness in my voice, but my chest betrays how turbulent I am, how much of my energy it still takes to keep myself so tightly bound.

"The documentary is a horrible idea. Livvie, promise me that you're not going to say . . ."

I stare at him defiantly, daring him to continue. But Dad breaks the eye contact first. Looks off toward the plaque that I know talks about the doctor who was burned at the stake in the 1800s for being Jewish.

"You know Reuben is doing the documentary too," I say pointedly. Reuben—my stepbrother, and my fellow camper on the trip from hell.

Dad opens his mouth, then closes it. I almost hate the flood of satisfaction I feel, that I've knocked Dad off-kilter. "No, you're not serious. What a stupid thing to agree to. This is dangerous, Livvie. You don't know what you're starting. Both of you."

From the limited view to which I've been privy, Reuben and my father have an antagonistic relationship. Like mine with Daniella. Though it's a bit more nuanced.

"Is Daniella doing it too?" I continue on, though I know the answer. I'm not proud of it, but goading him feels like some sort of salve now, with everything hanging in the balance on this trip.

That woman is dangerous. Sydney said it to me offhand about Daniella, a few days before she died. One of my biggest regrets in life is that I didn't press her on it. Because I remember the look in Sydney's eyes, and it was off. Something was so hugely off.

"Don't start, Olivia." At the mention of my stepmother, Dad's eyes flicker with fury. Suddenly he's so close to me I can smell his sour post-coffee breath. "I mean it. Stop with all of this. Daniella and Cass aren't doing the documentary. I can promise you that."

Of course. Of course, they wouldn't. Dad would forbid it. Though technically speaking, both were there that summer. Daniella led us on a few remote hikes that required a local's expertise, and my stepsister, Cass, who was eleven at the time, would sometimes tag along. Cass is an Olympic medalist gymnast now. A champion. The threat of bad press and dropped endorsements would be an easy out not to agree to the documentary. Still, Jules would want her in; no doubt Casia Bensabat would be an added attraction. A guaranteed way to make sure it would be a smashing success—and rake in all the money. Jules needs money, desperately. I do know that.

"They were there that summer," I finally settle on saying, deliberately agitating him further. "I'm only asking. I know Jules wants you all to participate."

His defiant eyes stare back at me, mirrors of my own, and I am aware we are both keeping a lot back from this conversation.

I was on antianxiety medicine that summer. I'm still on it now. Before our Azores trip then, I was having panic attacks and endless intrusive thoughts about my sister being sick and dying—and also my fears of coming out. I was being bullied, by my sister, too, which is hard to admit. And I didn't know then that during high-stress moments, the medication can lead to confusion and even blackouts. Can make you wonder whether events actually took place or if you imagined them. The police found it convenient that I didn't remember a lot from when Sydney disappeared.

In fact, I did have some memories, hazy ones, which I chose not to share with the authorities. They were choppy. Flashes, really. I've never known if they were real or by-products of the medication. The only person with whom I shared them, once, was my father. Once was more than enough.

"What the hell do I care what it would mean to Jules? We have our own family to worry about, and for our family, it would mean rehashing things that we've tried to put to rest."

"Well, I'm glad you've managed to put things to rest," I say hotly. "Because I haven't."

Finally, Dad's tanned face softens, flattening out his deep worry lines, and he says in a hoarse voice, "I haven't gotten over my daughter's disappearance, if that's what you're implying. I only want to honor Sydney, Livvie. She deserves that much from us." His *us* cuts me, makes me certain he still thinks I did it. "This documentary, it stomps on her memory. It makes a mockery of her death. I've forgiven. I want you to know—" He grips my forearm with strength that startles me. "I want you to know that I've forgiven whoever killed her. You have to do that. You have to forgive yourse—the *killer*. Otherwise, the guilt, the anger, it eats you alive."

I register his slip, of course. Nailing the point home. But I just stare back at my father, all the guilt and anger indeed churning in me. He's right—fucking hell. It is. It's all been eating me alive. The success, the wonderful girlfriend. None of it really matters, does it? I'm still frozen in time from the summer Sydney died.

"I have to go, Dad." I feel tears threatening, but I force them back.

Dad releases my arm. His features rearrange themselves again into his greatest acting role—concerned, loving father. "Seat belt on tight, okay?" I roll my eyes. "I'll see you tonight then."

"Right. Okay." I turn then and flea, barrel down the stairs, mumbling a goodbye to the guard before ducking back out into the day.

As I bake again in the cool summer sun and look around for a cab to take me north, all the emotion is constricting in my throat. I replay my conversation with Dad, and what it could mean. So he's not going to participate in the documentary? Not exactly surprising. He's always been private, holding things close to the vest. And of course, he'd have told Daniella and Cass not to participate either. Instructed them, as the head of their household. Still, I feel a tiny bubble of relief that I've told him my plans. The beginnings of them, at least.

After all, it's my first time back on the island since Sydney died. But I didn't come to research a new book, or even for my sister's memorial, for which this camp reunion has presumably been organized.

Truth is, I loved my sister, no matter what happened. No matter what anyone thinks. We might have fought, we might have hated each other at times, but we could also send each other the perfect GIF to punctuate an awkward family moment. And sometimes one of our parents would do something ridiculous, like how Dad would walk backward on the treadmill because he claimed it was good for his calves, and we'd catch eyes and both keel over laughing. Laughing so hard I could no longer breathe.

For ten years, I've had no one to laugh with like that. Not much in the world that's felt very laughable at all. And so I came here for the documentary—and everything I hope will finally domino from that.

———

I'm in a cab, turning past the stone archway on Rua do Brum, when I catch a glimpse of my sister. In the decade since Sydney disappeared, I've thought I spotted her a million times. But this— this is different.

I tell the cabbie to stop, undo my seat belt, and slide across the seat toward the window from which I spotted her, pressing my face up against the glass. Her honey blond hair is long and in loose, flowing waves, and she's wearing heart-shaped sunglasses and a flouncy white sundress. But that's not all. I swear I can make out little braids in the front of her hair, just like Sydney used to have.

"*Pare! Agora, por favor!*" I urge as the cab finally slows.

I watch my sister veer down a side street, pulling out a phone from her tan studded bag, and that's when I catch a glimpse of a familiar white beaded necklace. I squint, questioning my own sanity. But it looks like . . . it could really be . . . Sydney's *exact* necklace she was wearing the last time I saw her.

"*Pare! Por favor,*" I say with more urgency. I riffle in my wallet for a few bills, then jiggle at the door handle, but the child lock is still on.

By the time I've managed to pry open the door, I run and search and scream her name until I'm hoarse. But Sydney is gone. Again.

CHAPTER THREE

Lexa

I BURST THROUGH the eco-chic suite, all the bamboo and blond wood and cryptomeria, I think, is what the cedar wood is called. The manager said it, spouting off facts about the terrain when he drove us in a golf cart through the expansive, manicured property of the Ananda to get here. The edge of the world, it feels like, journeying from the airport toward Ribeira Grande across the rural island, in whose expanse you see far more cows than people.

The hotel grounds are enormous; they once were home to a precursor hotel, now abandoned a bit inland, with shattered windows and an eerily empty swimming pool. The locals refer to it as the Ghost Hotel. The Ghost Hotel is a funny amalgamation of being an eyesore and also a teen make-out spot, and we haven't torn it down because it's far enough removed that it doesn't mar the Ananda's perfect ocean views. It's rugged coastline up here, cleaved by ancient volcanic forces, with towering rock faces that plunge into the Atlantic. The southern coast is the gentler one, more protected, with rolling hills that gradually descend to the sea. Ironic, as the southern coast is where Sydney died. Or should I technically say—*disappeared.*

The infinity pool is riotous in the wind, sloshing onto the teak deck, and beyond it the verdant green landscape slopes down toward the black sand beach, the ocean roiling as far out as I can see. I've been on islands before, of course, but none as remote as the nine-island Azores archipelago. They've been called the most strategic islands in the world, poised midway between North America and mainland Portugal. A thousand miles from the mainland. I remember how claustrophobic and small it made me feel, and alternately how powerful, the summer I spent here ten years ago.

That summer changed everything for me.

Jules once told me that she spent the entire year longing to get out of the Azores for our summer at camp in New England, and then while at camp, she spent the entire summer longing to be back here. I get it. I do.

I stop at the edge of the pool. "I'd forgotten how unreal the view is up here."

The Ananda is the most luxurious hotel in the Da Costa Group portfolio—the company owned by the wealthiest family on the island. The family I married into three months ago.

It hasn't gotten old yet, signing Alexandra da Costa on all the paperwork. Hearing the trill of "Mrs. da Costa." The shining faces wanting to meet my every need because I'm both the chief marketing officer and the wife of the heir of the company that employs them.

"My view is the unreal one," Eli says, wrapping his arms around my waist. I sigh and turn my head to stare at him. My gorgeous husband. He's been mine for nearly ten years now, but only a few months officially so, in the eyes of the law. His wispy, light brown hair sticks out in tufts beneath his baseball cap, and his left eyebrow is almost an upturned *v*, higher than the right, giving him a look of perpetual mischief. I reach out to graze my fingers across his cheek, up toward his ears with their slightly pointy tips. Then I face forward again and lean back against his chest.

"I love it here. This place is amazing. Almost makes up for what we have to do this weekend."

"I love how excited you get about nice hotels. Even after all this time."

A twinge in my chest—but then his arms, his cozy warmth, the sweeping nature. I relax. "Oh, is that—" I crane my neck. "The pool extends next door?" With creeping unease, I take in the plexiglass divider and verify that on our right, the pool isn't edged in the same basalt stone that borders it on the left.

"Yeah, all five junior suites share the pool. I booked the rest of the group into the adjacent rooms—give 'em a little treat, you know?" I hear the pleasure in his tone; Eli loves nothing more than playing Santa Claus. "Aiden, Jules, Liv—"

"And Reuben?" I feel my stress mount. "You put Reuben in with us too?"

"Yeah. Reuben too."

I take that in. "I thought we had a private pool. Not a shared one. There's not a presidential suite we can move to?"

"It was booked out apparently."

"We *own* the hotel!" I try to sound light about it, but it carries a bite. Normally I'd have taken charge of the reservations, but Eli insisted on handling things because of all the work stuff I've had on my plate. What a fucking help—though what's the point in getting angry now?

"Well, doesn't mean we're going to cancel a paid reservation. I think we can slum it in a junior suite for three nights, don't you think?"

"But—people can swim over and spy on us."

Eli laughs. "I don't think anyone's going to be looking at us. What are you so afraid of—"

"They're all coming here, E," I say sharply. "I don't want—"

"Lex," Eli says calmly. "Everything's going to be fine."

Nothing infuriates me more than a person painting over a

bad situation with indifferent calm. My husband rubs his chin; he's perpetually trying to grow a beard, but all that ever results in are a couple patchy spots. He's at it again on this trip; I'm going to have to ask him to shave, one of the few things he really pushes back on. He's tried some new hair growth supplement that targets beards, apparently, and the only actual argument we got in before our wedding was about whether a supplement could even target a beard. Honestly, I'm right; how do your cells know that you want the pill shuttled to your chin, and not to your leg hair?

"Nothing's fine," I tell him. "And the fires I'm putting out at work, I—"

"You're working way too hard. You've been texting nonstop since we got here. I thought we agreed we'd actually take a break and delegate stuff."

"It's the Toronto launch. People are fucking things up left and right! Honestly, I should be there now. Not here."

"Want me to talk to my dad?"

"No, I don't want you to talk to your dad," I erupt, then take a deep breath. None of this is actually on Eli. "Sorry. Work stress is the stress I can deal with. It's a known quantity. It's this . . . reunion. Far too many unknowns."

"Oh. Well, I think you're worried for nothing. It's gonna be fun."

He flips his navy hat backward, which only adds to his boyish vibe. Normally I find all this exceedingly cute. Adorable, really. Because I've basically been an adult since I turned six. I don't even remember what it was like to be a child without cares, and yet Eli has lived that way his entire life. The differences between us normally endear me to my husband. Like how I wake at five thirty, but he sleeps in another two hours. He's the calm to my restless. The happy to marinate in the status quo to my deepseated ambition. The slightly messy to my militantly ordered. The nerdy-adjacent to my chic. But today I resent Eli's cavalier, lighthearted ways. I wish he had a full beard. I wish he hovered heads above me, on the lookout for any falling objects. I wish he could be the one to take everything on his shoulders. I inhale sharply. Instead of me.

I finally allow my husband a smile. "Sorry, I'm wound tight. It's just . . . being back here after so long. It's trippy. And seeing everyone again. It's going to be, I don't know—"

"Bizarre."

"More than bizarre. You know it's way bigger than bizarre," I say pointedly. "Last time we were here—"

"Sydney was alive," he fills in.

I grimace. "Not only that."

A flash in my brain, which I never invite but shows up for the party nonetheless. Syd dancing with Eli around the campfire, their hands finding each other's again and again like some sinuous dance. Another flash—her telling me, ordering me, really—to come join a game of euchre. I see myself walk over all robotic, automated to follow her commands. Later, when Syd and Eli lose against me and Jules, Syd says she's not feeling well, but I suspect she's just feigning it to avoid losing another round. She grabs her journal and hunches over with a flashlight, scribbling furiously. When I come behind here to pat her back, to make sure we're still okay, she flinches and jerks away, blocking her words so she's sure I don't see.

I blink back to now. "The last time we were all together, you were Syd's boyfriend," I finally say, not making eye contact with Eli.

His face pinches, pain in those innocent, teddy-bear eyes. When Eli emotes, it's written all over his face. He can be sensitive, prone to emotional outbursts, but he has this inexplicable skill of quickly getting himself back to his baseline Happy Baby mode. I coined the descriptor when we first started dating, nine and a half years ago. Six months after that nightmare summer. We do yoga together, and I always tease him that he's a real-life Happy Baby, the state of which is reserved for the point-one percent. Those lucky souls endowed with the absolute belief that all their needs will always be swiftly taken care of. The men, in particular, who women love taking care of. Even when Eli should be concerned about something, freaking out like me, he adopts a carefree attitude I can only assume is characteristic of the born-with-a-silver-spoon set. He figures snafus will work out. With endless money, there is usually a way.

Eli's face eases back to Happy Baby. "I was Sydney's boyfriend a lifetime ago, Lex. You were with Reuben."

"I know." Reuben is everything Eli isn't—brash, self-centered, and a bit cold. Dodged a bullet there. I remember hugging him, and how thin the embrace felt, the way he'd quickly set me back into place, protective of his borders. Reuben kept himself so closely held, whereas Eli is open and easy. His hugs are tight. We could stay wrapped together an entire night, if I'd let him. And Eli needs me. I like being needed, it turns out. Reuben could always fend for himself.

"People grow up," Eli says, and I realize he's still talking about him and Sydney. "Realize what they truly want."

"Or someone dies. Forces their hand." It's a dark thing to say, but I'm feeling exceptionally dark. Suddenly doubting whether we should have come here at all. Certainly, whether Eli should have paid for everyone's hotel stay, thereby encouraging some people to show up who might not otherwise have. We didn't invite them all to our wedding, certainly not Reuben, or even Olivia. Only Aiden and Jules, our former counselors with whom we've kept in perhaps unlikely touch. This reunion is different; we didn't control the guest list.

"Stop." His tone is light, but I can tell that I'm veering into territory he doesn't feel like retreading. "We're not going down this road. It goes nowhere good. We've been together nearly ten years. Everything else is ancient history. We've said our *vows*, Lex. You know that I only want you."

He's right. We did just say our vows, in Provence. But I don't tell Eli that even then, Sydney's ghost was right there with us under the chuppah. I'm not usually insecure, at least not anymore. But when it comes to Sydney, I always feel dragged back to who I was as a teenager. Chasing after the popular girls, ever in Sydney's shadow.

Still, I loved her. I really did love her. And I've lived with a longing—and no shortage of regret and guilt—ever since she disappeared.

"Don't worry. Really, honey. Everything's going to be fine. We got this." Eli's back to sunny, back to a person who lives in an incontrovertibly benevolent world.

I nod and smile, because my husband needs me to.

"Maybe we shouldn't do the documentary though," I say, rehashing a topic we've discussed ad nauseum.

"We're doing it for Jules," he reminds me. "She needs it. And we didn't kill Sydney. We don't have anything to worry about. Plus, it will look suspicious if we're the only holdouts."

"Who cares if it looks suspicious? We're public-facing. The company has shareholders to answer to. We can say it's not prudent to be involved. And I want to do this for Jules, too, but . . ."

"If we don't do it," he finally says, "we won't be there when they record it. We won't know what's said. We won't be able to manage it if things crop up."

Silence, because I know he's right. Even if he doesn't understand how right. "Better to be involved and know what we're up against." I try to smile.

"We aren't up against anything," Eli says. "We didn't do anything wrong."

I cock my head at my sweet husband and think what a luxury it must be to walk through the world with such naivete. He opens his arms, like it's all done and good, and I sigh and wedge myself into his shoulder crook. It requires me to contort a bit, fold down, because I'm actually two inches taller than Eli, five eleven to his five nine.

I notice he's staring at his phone around my back. "What?" I ask.

"Nothing. My dad." But his voice has a scowl wrapped around it.

"Oh. Anything important?" Eli runs his family's charitable foundation. His father would have loved for Eli to want to rise in the company ranks, take things over one day, but that's never been his path. He always says that he's happy for his wife to run the empire, while he makes the world a better place.

"Ever an emergency with him." He says it lightly, but father-son tension percolates beneath it. Eli's father can certainly be demanding, exacting. A hard act to follow as a kid, I'm sure, but as a daughter-in-law, I've felt like I've won the lottery. Maybe it's that my own father was mostly absent after my parents divorced. It's been nice to have a dad again in some way. And Eli's father epitomizes a stable, secure dad. The kind who takes charge, the kind you can rely on. The kind who believes in me enough that last year, he promoted me to CMO.

"What should I wear to dinner?" I ask, my voice muffled in Eli's navy tee that smells of the intoxicating Le Labo Thé Noir 29 I got him for our wedding. "My brown midi dress with the cutouts at the waist, or maybe baggy jeans and that off-shoulder—"

"The cutouts." He perks up. I stand up straight so we're looking at each other more or less straight on, and I watch Eli's hazel eyes torch with interest. "I vote for the cutouts."

I smile, feeling relief that something in my life, in this trip, is predictable. In my twenty-seven years, I've learned that men are fairly base creatures. Unpredictable in some elements, but quite predictable in most.

I head back into the room, riffle through my suitcase, and find the Staud dress rolled in the packing cube in which I placed all my midi dresses. Invariably Eli makes fun of me when we pack for trips—how I need four suitcases and thirty packing cubes, how particularly I roll and fold up my clothes. But I grew up in chaos—fights and creditors and my mom's tchotchkes strewn in every corner. Eli can joke that I'm the Clean Machine all he wants, but there is a method to my madness. I simply like things orderly and neat. I like to be prepared. I don't leave things to chance. In real life, plans don't simply sail off into the sunset. They move seamlessly because your ducks are all accounted for and in an orderly row.

The dress is a bit wrinkled from the plane, but nothing steam from the shower can't smooth out. The maid had already offered to unpack my suitcase. She'd reached for my overnight bag, atop which I'd tossed my phone, but I snatched it away from her, rushing out a perhaps overly harsh *I've got that*. Eli had arched an eyebrow at me, understandable because normally I'm all for the maid steaming and pressing my clothes while I fling myself onto the terrace with my laptop, then return to a closet that looks pleasingly like a Paris atelier. But not today.

I grab my phone and spot a message on the home screen. The message does something to my nervous system that my body has become accustomed to, a constricting feeling. I grab the dress and tuck my phone inside it.

Eli is unpacking his suitcase, sliding his jeans into one of the dresser drawers. Then he holds up Azul.

"Brought it, in case we have time."

We're a board game couple: Rummikub, Catan, now Azul. We love playing in the evening, splitting a bottle of wine, a fire roaring.

Since the wedding, during our game times, Eli's been talking kids—when we'll have them, how our girls will look like me.

Girls. As in assuming my vagina would be delighted to push out multiples. I haven't had the energy to say what I actually feel, which is that I'm not ready for kids. Not anywhere in the near future. Maybe not ever. Finally, things are almost perfect in my life. It took so long—so much work—to get here. After this trip, the struggle will all be over, the dangling threads finally snipped. And then all I want is to enjoy this life that I sculpted. The thing no one says about kids is that no matter how much help I will be able to afford, kids mean signing up a huge chunk of the rest of your life for a wild card. Who will these little people be? Will you enjoy being a mom or not? Doesn't matter. You get off birth control and spread your legs and then the rest of your life goes up for grabs.

To a person like me, who thrives on being in control, that sounds entirely unappealing.

"We're not going to have time for games this weekend." I laugh off my anxiety. "The schedule is packed tight."

"You're afraid because I'm on a winning streak."

"Okay then, tonight after the documentary stuff, you're on, da Costa. And I like how confident you are. It will make it so much more fun when I destroy you." I laugh and find myself feeling lighter, despite everything.

In the bathroom, the lightness dissipates. I run the shower, then hang the dress over the glass. I open my phone and draw a deep breath, then scroll to the last page of my apps to Signal. I open it and see a series of messages from him. *You got this. Love you.* Followed by a red heart emoji.

My heart pounds as I write back and then quickly exit the app.

Everything's going to be fine, Eli said moments ago.

And it is, I swear to myself. It's going to be fine, because this trip I'm going to make it fine.

I stare at myself in the mirror as the steam fogs it up. I force myself to smile with teeth, a reassuring smile that might look a bit deranged if an onlooker—or Eli—were to walk in. Thing is, when I was a teenager, I pretty much never smiled with teeth. I had crooked teeth and an overbite and those things were low on the priority list of where to allocate our limited money. A couple years after Eli and I got together, he surprised me with veneers for my birthday. He said he actually loved my natural smile, which he only ever saw when I laughed involuntarily, a thing he was always trying to make me do. But he said if I wanted them, then he wanted to make all my dreams come true. I've had a perfect smile for years, but smiling still doesn't come entirely naturally.

My smile fades, but I keep my eyes locked on myself, and a warrior appears before me. A warrior who has proven herself adept at winning.

Winning the man. The riches. The C-suite role. The fairy-tale life.

I didn't know what I was getting into when I joined Eli's family. But now I'm in too deep to turn back. There's another battle up ahead.

And this trip, I know: Winner takes all.

CHAPTER FOUR

Jules

I PAUSE BEFORE stepping out onto the terrace to jiggle the bustier portion of my emerald dress and make sure my boobs are secure. I wince as something hard pokes my ribs. I'd bet a lot of money that it was a man who invented boning.

"You look great," Maria says to me in Portuguese. "Green with your red hair, chef's kiss. You should wear it more."

Yes, my whole life I've had people coming up to me to touch and marvel at my hair and inform me of the color palette that would better suit it. My hair isn't dark brown the way everyone else's is on the island, not even dyed blond like the ritzy few. Apparently, my father had red hair like me; he was Irish, simply passing through the island on a backpacking trip with friends when he met my mother. The only thing he ever gave me was half of my genetic makeup.

"I swear this dress was looser in the store. And I feel ridiculous. Like I'm in a pageant."

"That's just because your normal style is Jessica Fletcher in coastal Maine circa 1992."

I laugh. "How long have you kept that skewering insight inside?"

She smiles smugly. "I pinpointed you the moment I saw you,

Silva. And by the way, Jessica Fletcher dresses up for balls and galas."

"But this material is so . . . shiny. I don't look too . . . like I'm trying too hard?"

"You look perfect. Plus, it sets the right tone."

I finally sigh and accept that this is what I'm wearing tonight, because I don't have another option. Still, Maria's opinion isn't exactly reassuring. We have wildly different tastes. She's always in flowing midi dresses with tight bodices, and I hardly ever wear dresses. I'm a denim and collared-shirt girl, more likely to be found trekking through a meadow with cow poop embedded in my soles than at a swanky hotel, in heels pinching my toes. And usually, I have one of my grandmother's cardigans that she knit for me somewhere nearby. I touch the sleeve of the cream cardigan poking out of my tote. So what if it's a security blanket? I need it tonight. But I acknowledge that Maria's right, that tonight I need to be seen as strong and trustworthy and powerful. That's why I chose a dress with enough cleavage to knock the men a bit off-kilter, but not too much that they won't still find me capable.

I hope.

"You'll get behind-the-scene shots, right?" I ask, satisfied my chest has attained the ideal midpoint of locked in place, with tasteful cleavage. "They've already signed releases. That was a struggle in itself. So if you see a few of them huddling off in a corner, try to get as close as you can and film. They're not going to tell us everything when they're sitting down and conscious of the camera. I already know that. But don't be intrusive. I want them to trust us. To be comfortable. To let their guards down—oh, and remember, none of them speak Portuguese, other than Reuben. So you'll have to explain everything in English. All these years later and all their bullshit about their Portuguese heritage—and they never even bothered to learn the language. And, oh, remember that—"

"I know. Really, we've gone over it all so many times. The documentary is gonna be fantastic. Guaranteed." Maria smiles reassuringly, her wide winning smile and short dark hair that makes her look like Audrey Hepburn. But a fiercer Audrey, with her trademark ruby red lipstick that matches her patent red heels. Maria always wears red lipstick and red shoes (ballet flats, Mary Janes, even cowboy boots); it's her thing. Along with a silver hoop piercing in her nose. And so she stands out amid the rest of the islanders, who typically lag at least a couple decades behind the trends in the States. It's what first drew me to Maria when we met in a film class this past year at University of the Azores. She just looked cool. And I've always been an insecure kid at my core, I guess. Chasing after the cool girls. Wanting—needing—them to accept me. Like Sydney and Lexa that summer. Lexa was once the same way before securing the prize of her friendship with Sydney; it's something we've since bonded over.

Maria is an actual student, near graduation, and I was auditing the course as part of my grandmother's dying wishes. But we didn't become close until a couple months ago, when we worked together on our final project and discovered an unlikely connection harking back to that fateful Azores summer when Sydney disappeared.

"It has to work, it has to," I whisper, aware it's become my mantra. The thing cycling through my mind when I wake in the middle of the night in a cold sweat.

"It will, Jules."

I catch a glimpse of the patio. All the fancy passed appetizers and then a swoosh of thick golden hair that makes my heart constrict. "It can't fail. I'm banking everything on this." My chest continues to throb. It's him, or this fucking dress that doesn't fit my breasts, or just all the stress tunneling at me.

Bottom line, I need this. And Maria needs to know how much I need this. How much is riding on this, for me and for her. I even gave her a stake in the proceeds. Well, her contribution is already substantial. If the documentary hits big, if we sell it to Netflix or Hulu and make it the sensation I know we can, then we both win. I just wish I had so much more to show for this past decade when I see everyone—wish I could rock out there with an aura of "I fucking love myself and look how far I've come, bitches." Instead of the sad, piddling, desperate reality.

"Are you going to reveal it tonight, or wait?" Maria asks.

"Not tonight. *Devagar, devagar.* We have to be careful with everything. We need them more than they need us. Until things start to come out . . . then hopefully it will be a runaway train . . ."

"Everyone will finally tell the truth. What if we find out that Sydney's still alive or something?" Maria lights up with that enthusiasm I used to have when I was her age too. Twenty-three—ten years ago—a lifetime, really. Life didn't feel like a wasteland then, like a swamp I was muddling through, trying to avoid being swallowed alive. "Imagine if Sydney's hiding somewhere around here, come back for her own memorial." Maria's arms sweep open, up toward the volcanic rock in the distance, jutting up from the skeins of thick fog. "You always said she liked a grand entrance. Maybe the reason there was no body is—"

"No." I put a hand out, because I need her to stop talking. "Listen to me, that's not—the documentary isn't going there. We've talked about this. Sydney's not gonna poof, pop out from nowhere." I haven't been able to tell Maria everything, but I do need to implore her to accept this on my word. I finish fidgeting with my bodice, try to puff myself up to the level of confidence I once marveled that Sydney Azulay was able to maintain.

"Sydney's blood was in the cave," I remind her, and my heart crimps. "There's no chance she's alive."

Maria shrugs, her face still sparkling with the possibilities, far enough removed from the actual events to find this whole thing almost like a treasure hunt. "But she could have cut herself, accidentally or intentionally. Really, there are so many possibilities. Who *knows* what happened to Sydney!"

Anger pulses through me, because Maria wasn't there. She didn't know Sydney. And she's acting like this is a case on the news rather than a nightmare I'm still enduring. For ten years, I've felt guilty about what I suspected, what I withheld. Justice for Sydney: that's the real goal of this documentary, the goal I've felt as a hollow pit in my stomach. That I'll reveal the murderer. The one I've long suspected, but now even more so. No matter how it will directly affect me and my future. My stomach tumbles over itself.

"Listen to me, Maria, and listen good." I open the door to the terrace, sucking in the fresh air. "Sydney is dead. She was murdered ten years ago. No matter what comes out this weekend, I'm positive of that."

———

I sweep into the reunion with as much confidence as I can project, trying to shove away the mean thoughts my brain is currently spewing, that this much cleavage was a misstep. I step out onto the grand patio with its panoramic island view and breathe in the soothing aromatics of rosemary and thyme from the property's garden, trying to sync my breath to the rhythmic ocean pulse.

My eyes lock onto all the familiar faces, and I have to remind myself that a decade has passed. That I'm not back inside that weird, wonderful, awful summer again. That I'm not the same meek girl-adult ostensibly in charge, but really desperate for everyone's approval. For friendship. Love. Especially *his*.

Sure, they all look slightly older, but still with that sheen of youth. The glow of your twenties, when you don't actually need an Instagram filter. I'm six years older than them—and I feel it on my face. The stress of recent events has burrowed grooves into my forehead and spackled spindly wheel spokes around my eyes. I spot Reuben first, mouth full of canapes, talking to—my gosh, that's Olivia. I've seen recent pictures of her, of course, but none quite do her justice. She's a casual goddess, looking like all those cool Scandi influencer girls I follow on TikTok. Hair lush, eyebrows—laminated? Of course, people grow up, but it's jarring. She used to be so . . . plain.

"Jazz!" I forgot that was Reuben's nickname for me. Because when I'm happy, I can veer theatrical, with the tendency to declare my excitement by using jazz hands.

I've known Reuben since we were kids. I'm older, of course, but I was a camper just like the rest of them before the heritage trip. My grandmother's parents knew the camp founders. Even my mother went to camp as a young girl, on scholarship. Camp Zahav is in my blood, and my summers there always felt exotic, with these Americans whose lives seemed so much grander than my small island existence. I felt wrapped up in their big dreams and even bigger beliefs that those dreams could actually come true. And then I was no longer a camper and had risen through the main camp staff ranks until I pretty much aged out, and I muddled through the first few years of my early twenties until the opportunity arose to staff the pinnacle of it all, the summer heritage trip. With Aiden, to boot. Suddenly, life acquired this pink, youthful glow again, where anything was possible. Until it all crashed and burned, of course.

I walk over to them, though Aiden's swish of golden hair is still, always, in my line of sight. I can see him over by the pool, nursing a drink, staring out at the sea, doing his typical loner thing. No. I'm not being detoured by Aiden this time.

"Hi, Reub." I give him a hug and whistle. "You clean up nice." It's an understatement; Reuben has always been polished, movie-star handsome, the bold, flashy, designer version of Aiden's easy, threadbare swagger.

"Thanks, Jazz. Try not to fall in love with me tonight." He winks, and I laugh. Reuben has always been an asshole, but a fun one, quick with quips and easy on the eyes. And, boy, does life seem to roll out the red carpet for fun asshole men, amiright? My gaze skims over Reuben, taking him fully in, how his curly dark hair is peppered with a few gray strands at the front that wouldn't be noticeable to most people, but I'm perceptive.

"It will be hard to restrain myself," I tell him, smiling. "Seriously, you look good. Older." His face falls at the "older" bit, and I remember that Reuben is very vain. Even though he's only twenty-seven, still on the sweet side of thirty. But thankfully for him he's a man; going gray will only make him distinguished. Aside from the hair, his face is bright and tanned, and it's like no time has passed. I can almost feel we're back there—Reub with a walking stick in hand, striking out at the front, like he's trying to prove something. His leadership and superior physical strength. Or else to be the first one to find the treasure. He was the most treasure-hungry of us all.

"Well, it has been ten years."

"You're young still! Younger than me at least." I shade, thinking I sound elderly.

He laughs, a bit forced. "Can you believe it's been a decade? So much has happened."

"Yeah?"

I realize it's jealousy I feel. Truth is, though I wouldn't admit it to Reuben, but aside from my grandmother's death, hardly anything monumental has happened in my life in the decade since that summer. The same sitting on the couch with my grandmother before she passed away, watching romantic classics and marveling at other people's happily-ever-afters. My grandparents had an epic love story, and she always told me I'd have the same. I believed in it once, before that summer, optimism oozing out my pores. I was the girl who always fast-forwarded through the part in the romantic comedy toward the end, when whatever misunderstanding or fight happened and the couple seemed furthest apart, like they'd never close the gap. I couldn't watch it; I needed to leap forward into the happily-ever-after.

I thought once—well, I thought Aiden could be the exalted "The One." An embarrassing admission now, even to myself. That summer was the happiest and most naive time of my life. Though Aiden and I weren't together, because we'd decided early on it wouldn't be appropriate, I thought he wanted me and things would change at summer's end. And in the interim, I befriended the campers, considered them true friends. They respected and admired me, at least at first, and that felt intoxicating.

That summer was the peak of my life, a pathetic fact to face. But then Sydney disappeared, and the magic swiftly met its end. I realized I didn't have Sydney's charisma, Eli's wealth, Lexa's determination, Reuben's confidence, Aiden's passion, or Olivia's talent. I was me—plain, nothing-special me—broken by Sydney's disappearance, blaming myself, feeling abandoned by almost everyone, acutely cognizant of life's hard, unfair, unlucky parts. Eventually, when the publicity receded, I returned almost anticlimactically to my ordinary life on the island. And there waiting for me were the same small-town Azores folk, the same cow smell, and leading tours to the same wide-eyed tourists. The same gambling, hoping to make it big but always losing more than I had, my accounts persistently in the red. The same dreams of being a filmmaker, of saving up enough money to go try my hand in Hollywood. The same people smiling and nodding kindly at those dreams. No one truly believing I'd ever achieve them.

"Olivia." We hug, too, this tall stunning creature in a pale green midi slip dress with a tan oversize blazer atop, and it surprises me to see a thin ghost of Sydney somewhere inside her— her bushy eyebrows and dirty blond hair, and those sage-green eyes, different from her sister's startling ice blue. I always liked Olivia. I saw myself in her, maybe. The two outcasts. But for that very reason, as the summer progressed, I subconsciously avoided her too. I gravitated toward her sister. Sydney, as bright as the sun if you stared at her straight on. So full of life, so vivacious, like the more I crept toward her, the more of her sun I could pocket for myself.

"Hey, Jules. It's good to see you. It's been forever." After we hug and part, her eyes dart around the patio distractedly, reminding me of ten years prior. How anxious and on edge she always was.

"Forever," I agree. I remember the last time exactly, even though it's an ugly memory to dip inside—what happened *after* Sydney disappeared, after the police had descended and found traces of Sydney's blood in the cave, and that old man had come forward, claiming he saw someone throw a heavy-looking black trash bag off the cliff near the cove the morning Sydney disappeared and then, moments later, spotted Olivia coming up off that path.

The police were convinced Olivia had done it, murdered her sister and disposed of her off the cliff, but there was the matter of proof. All the campers, and Aiden and I, were scattered close to one another on the southern part of the island for the camp's annual Azores summer twenty-four-hour Survival Day. We'd dropped Olivia off a mile from her sister, each of the campers to hack it in the wilderness, alone. Aiden and I spent the night in separate tents, located smack-dab in the middle of everyone. None of them had their phones—otherwise they would have spent the entire time on social media—but they each had a map demarcating everyone's locations. Civilization was basically right at their doorstep. Sure, back then the island was more sparsely populated, and tourists hadn't yet descended in droves. But the campers weren't in the middle of nowhere, but rather close to town, some of them next to the sea. They all knew how to get to help if need be.

Plus, they had radios to be used in the event of an emergency. That was a stipulation owing directly to Sydney. With her kidney disease, we initially intended to exclude her from Survival Day. But right beforehand, Sydney convinced her dad that she should get to be treated like every other camper. And so Isaac made the call to cajole the heads of camp. With the caveat that she be given an emergency radio, which we eventually distributed to them all. None was ever used.

For months the police dug for proof that Olivia was there, that she'd gone to Sydney's spot by the cove. That she'd murdered and disposed of her sister.

Proof such as my bracelet that I'm now twisting on my wrist. The silver bracelet with the cross and the dozen arrow-tipped arms dangling beneath.

It's a family heirloom. I never take it off, not since my grandmother gave it to me when I was twelve. The cross was to protect my ancestors because they were crypto-Jews, or Marranos, forced to convert during the Inquisition. In fact, many of my family traditions are Catholic in nature, but I know I'm Jewish. And the bracelet reminds me of my heritage. After Sydney disappeared, in all the craziness, when I realized I'd lost my bracelet and began hyperventilating even more, Aiden told me that Sydney had found it. That he'd seen her put it on her wrist so she wouldn't tangle it or lose it. That she was wearing it when he dropped her off for Survival Day. That she told him she'd give it back to me next time she saw me.

After Sydney disappeared, I resigned myself to the fact that my bracelet was gone. That it had disappeared right along with her. Until I spotted it on Olivia's wrist a day later. I still remember how my heart halted. Olivia turned uncharacteristically crimson as she removed it, fumbling with the clasp. She said she'd found the bracelet in the cove, after we all convened there when Sydney didn't return back to the meeting point.

But the police had gotten there before us. They'd scoured the cove first. I knew there was no way Olivia had simply found it after the fact.

The only explanation was that Olivia had gone to the cove. She'd seen Sydney before she disappeared.

Olivia asked if I was going to tell anyone, and I considered it. But eventually I said no. I worried the evidence could have put things over the edge. Olivia and I were close on the trip. And she was so clearly troubled that summer—fidgeting and restless, saying "sorry" all the time as her default word (though not to her sister), always pulling her sleeves down over her hands. As her counselor, I knew she was on antianxiety medicine, and her preliminary forms and medical evaluations had elaborated on her fragile state. I also knew she had a crush on me back then, that she was struggling with coming out. And I didn't want to impede further on her precarious place when I wasn't completely certain she'd done something wrong. I felt there was no way that she'd killed her sister. Those two might have fought about ridiculous shit, but they loved each other. And if I spilled about the bracelet, which when added to the testimony of the man who claimed he saw Olivia in the area after a heavy trash bag went over the side of the cliff, it could have provided the police with a full-blown case against her. Plus, if I told the police about the bracelet, then rightfully, I would have to tell them everything else I knew and suspected. And ten years ago, I didn't. I chickened out.

And now I'm even more certain. Olivia didn't kill her sister.

"You're in New York, right?" I ask Olivia after we lightly hug.

"Yeah. Brooklyn. Crown Heights?"

I shake my head, feeling foolish that I've never heard of it. "I've only been to New York once, to visit Lexa and Eli, but that was Manhattan." I don't add that I could hardly afford a New York trip without Lexa paying for it. A trip anywhere, really. I mean, I can barely make my car payments. Until the documentary gets picked up by a streamer—then all will be golden.

I realize I'm still tapping my bracelet, my nervous tic where I run my forefinger over each of the dozen arrows in turn, counting to myself.

"And you're still living on the island?" Olivia asks in a friendly way, though it makes me swell with shame. Like I've stayed a nothing while they've gone off to lead such big, successful lives.

"Still here," I say, wincing at my obvious false cheer. "Leading tours and doing some agricultural stuff. So many more tourists than when you were here last."

"There were none back then. It felt so . . . wild and raw. Sometimes like we were the only people in existence." She fiddles with the charm on her bag and continues to dart her eyes around, like a tourist lost in a bad part of town.

I nod. "I almost forget what it was like before Sky Azores started direct flights to the East Coast."

Olivia nods, too, and I remember she's in the loop about this; her dad is high up at the airline. He used to commute between here and Boston for work, but now he lives on the island full-time.

"And what about you—you're a world-famous author! I've heard people say you're more successful than J.K. Rowling!"

"Oh man." She laughs. "Not true. I mean, don't I wish."

"Well, you wouldn't believe how many teenage girls come here wanting to do the *X Marks the Spot* tour." I don't say that I've started a tour called precisely that. It's my biggest moneymaker. It feels embarrassing, pathetic really, to admit it.

"I know." Olivia makes a wry face. "To be honest, the books have made me successful, and I've loved writing them, but it's getting a bit . . . tired now. Coming up with more adventures and mysteries and murders for kids who stay forever seventeen. They never leave that one summer on São Miguel. One endless summer. I didn't envision *that* when I started writing ten years ago, that's for sure."

"Mmmm, I can imagine," I say, even though I can't, not the huge money she's raking in, nor the creative dilemmas. But I do remember her poring over her journals, writing fiendishly, on the outskirts after dinner, as the rest chattered and joked and played euchre around the bonfire.

"And what about you, Reub?" I ask, because he's been quiet. I follow his gaze to the side of the patio toward . . . Lexa.

Of course. Tall, statuesque Lexa with ramrod-straight posture, wearing a rich brown dress that perfectly sets off her glimmering olive skin. The dress has a trendy rose applique and cutouts that somehow veer elegant over sleazy; it probably costs more than a year's rental of my shoebox apartment. She was a beanpole on the summer trip with lanky dark hair and those big amber eyes. Pretty and smart and scrappy, but not a shapely, standout star like Sydney. But now she's ravishing. I'm actually close with Lexa; I've already stopped by to greet and hug her and Eli. You wouldn't necessarily pluck Lexa and me from the candidates on the trip to become besties, but unlikely, over all these years we have. Lexa has a quiet magnetism to her, and away from Sydney's blinding sun, Lexa's own gravity took hold. Before she left São Miguel when the police released her, I remember how she gripped my hand and said if I needed her, to call.

So I called. I was drowning after everyone left the island—Aiden, our campers, and the police and press too. Guilt, shame, and fear were my only reliable bedfellows. At first, we bonded over losing Sydney, I suppose. Over the trauma of Syd's disappearance and our shared experience of the aftermath. Cataclysmic worldwide fame, for all the wrong reasons. We used to have hours-long phone conversations, and slowly we opened up about things outside the black hole of Sydney. I was there for her, too, when she first started seeing Eli as a romantic option and I felt how she craved my seal of approval, my reassurance that she wasn't pond scum for co-opting her best friend's guy. We've been real, true friends for a decade.

But the sight of Lexa now, in this scene, has me jumpy, almost as if Sydney's about to pop out. Even though I know better. Just, those two were the best of friends, but decidedly different. Syd dominated—well, she did with most everyone. Even with me and Aiden; sometimes it felt like Sydney was running the show. If she wasn't informing everyone to wash their smelly feet at the end of the day's hike or they weren't allowed into her tent, then she was announcing who was substituting for her on the Round Robin schedule of dinner and cleanup duty. Sydney was expert-level at weaseling out of shit.

I remember observing Syd and Lexa and feeling like Lexa was holding her true self back. Well, high school kids did that all the time. Lexa worshipped Sydney; it was obvious in all the ways she catered to her, saving her a seat on the bus, asking her to sing for everyone, because Sydney reveled in that spotlight and reveled even more at her wingwoman rolling out the red carpet toward said spotlight. Lexa wasn't popular their freshman year, and Sydney took her under her wing into her popular friend group at school. Made Lexa her project. But it was more than that, I think, that caused Lexa to adhere herself to Sydney's orbit. Lexa's family wasn't privileged like Syd's; she was a scholarship kid like me. And Sydney would let Lexa borrow her clothes sometimes, or her silk scrunchie. The way Lexa looked at that girl sometimes, it was like she wanted to consume her. Become her.

Look, I adore Lexa, and she's grown up a lot since that summer. She's ambitious, but also kind. She goes to her great-aunt's assisted living home every week to lead the residents in bingo. She's worked her way up at Eli's family's hotel group, from lowly marketing assistant to recently being named CMO. A huge role for someone not even thirty! Even though she could easily take Eli's money and be a lady who lunches and plays pickleball, or launch a dime-a-dozen skin care line, she's a hard worker. Eli brags that she's brilliant and also complains that her phone is nonstop tethered to her hand.

But Reuben, as far as I know, has had zero relationship with Lexa for the last ten years. Reuben was in love with her during our summer on the island. Thing was, I thought she was in love with him too. I mean, she was enamored with Eli, of course, who wouldn't be—he had the witty, sweet, heir-to-an-empire thing going on. But Eli was taken—by Sydney—and anyway, I thought that Lexa really liked Reuben. Respected him, at least. Enjoyed him. Found him outrageously hot. That boy adored her and was harmless if a bit loud, but Eli was always the shiny trophy, I guess.

Young love, though, is ultimately a fantasy. I know that intimately.

Reuben thrusts his shoulders back and adjusts his cuff links. He's quite possibly the only local who wears anything as formal as cuff links. Other than his stepfather. Liv is still distractedly looking around and clearly not paying attention anymore, so Reuben says in Portuguese to me, "The sunset is so gorgeous here. I always forget it."

Reuben's mother tongue is English; he was born in the States, but he moved here as a kid right before lower secondary school so his Portuguese is excellent, if a bit accented. We were among the only campers at Camp Zahav actually coming from the island.

"Not always. In the winter, it's fogged over a lot," I say, switching to English. I don't want anyone to come up to us and think I'm talking behind their backs. Everything has to feel aboveboard so no one backs out of the documentary. "How's San Francisco?" I ask him.

"Oh, it's good. Totally good. Though I've been out of town

a lot." His face sparks, animating his dark eyes and long, curly lashes.

"I saw—the wineries in . . ."

"Bilbao. Basque country." He grins.

"Looked epic. I live vicariously through you on Instagram."

"And weren't you in Vietnam?" Olivia asks, snapping back to the conversation.

"Yep! Over New Year's. Have you guys been? I stayed at the Six Senses on Ninh Van Bay. Private island. Completely over-the-top."

Olivia nods politely. "Sounds bougie."

"It was. Highly recommend," Reuben replies.

I nod, and a silence thickens among us. I grapple around for a conversation topic. I've always felt uncomfortable with silence.

Olivia fills the void for me. "Still walking around with crystals in your pockets, Reub?"

"Totally!" He laughs and pulls one out, a small stone, translucent and brown. "Smoky quartz. To absorb negative energy. Which means it's gonna be working overtime this weekend."

"Oh, well—yeah." I laugh louder than called for. "I should get some myself."

"Right, Jazz? This weekend feels like a black hole of funky vibes. I can intro you to my crystal buyer, Krystal. That's actually her name, if you can believe it. Krystal with a K though, thank god for her. And I'll tell you, Krystal is legit. She only takes payment in cash, gold, or *favors from the universe*. I never ask what that means."

"I feel like you're a cash guy. Probably got some fancy money clip situation in your pocket," I tease.

"Indeed." But he frowns. "The universe is being stingy with its favors lately."

"Oh really?" I say vaguely, wondering if Reuben will ask about either of us. He was always one to babble on about himself, even though he genuinely does care beneath all the bluster. I got the sense that he was so in his head, so preoccupied with his own worries that he couldn't go there with anyone else.

"I still love my crystals from Krystal, but lately I've also gotten super into meditation. Either of you meditate?"

"Meditate?" I ask uncertainly, eyeing Olivia, who is back to darting her eyes around the patio. I wonder what that's about. "Uh . . ."

"Like, you must've heard of Joe Dispenza." He animates, like that will suddenly evoke an *aha*. "Really? You must've come across him, he does crazy heart-coherence meditations? These workshops last a week, it's like . . . a religion. The new ayahuasca, I swear you get high off the energy of just meditating. Actually, it occurred to me, with us together again, we could do some of it."

"This weekend?" I'm confused. "Meditate?"

"I mean, after Syd was . . . after she . . . We're reuniting after all that . . . toxicity—"

My eyes dart over to Olivia, to see if she's activated by the portrayal of her being the number one suspect in her sister's disappearance as toxic. But she's tapping her nails against her wineglass and staring out at the sea. I say to Reuben, "You're suggesting we all sit down to meditate together?"

Reuben laughs. "Only a thought. Now that I think about it more, I don't see Lexa and Eli going for it."

I try to seem intrigued, but really? Meditating? It's the kind of obtuse and ridiculous thing we locals would scoff at, something for people who have money and a lot of time on their hands and capital T traumas that they spend a lot of time talking about, in and out of therapy. (I know Americans, even if I'm not one. Hollywood is a great educator, plus all the summers I spent at Camp Zahav.) No one I know here meditates, unless you can count the time they spend in quiet with their sheep.

"Maybe instead we could do a barefoot walk tomorrow

morning on the beach," Reuben suggests. "I try to get my feet in the earth every day. For the negative ions."

"You're a real California hippie now," I say politely and watch Olivia stifle a giggle. Reuben is a character. I'm remembering that now.

"Well, it's all about optimizing my energy. Biohacking, but, like, for the soul. And you know what they say, don't you? What the real IPO is?"

Olivia and I look at each other and I feel like we're speaking telepathically. We simultaneously shake our heads, then shrug.

"Inner Peace Optimization." My smile freezes in a sort of rictus grin. It's so ridiculous, but he seems earnest.

"So where did you guys travel to last?" Reuben asks us, seeming to get that a conversation segue is needed.

"South of France," I say, after a beat. "For Lexa and Eli's wedding."

"Oh, that's—oh. How was it?"

"Gorgeous," I say quietly. "Unreal."

To diffuse the awkward vibe, Olivia offers, "I don't much leave Crown Heights these days."

Reuben nods, deflates. He rakes a hand through his tousled curls and returns his crystal to his pocket. "Well, travel is great, but it doesn't exactly pay the bills, does it?" He laughs with an unmistakable note of rancor. "You're on a roll, Liv. I've read a couple of your books. They're really good. Suspenseful. Even though I was there, I was still riveted."

"It's not like they're true." Her brow furrows. "They're fiction."

"Right." He shrugs. "Superimpressive though."

"Thanks. And Dad says you're killing it in venture capital."

He nods. "I'm raising half a billion for my new fund, and it's going well. The opportunity is fire, really. If either of you knows anyone who wants to invest—"

"I don't," I admit.

"Oh, sure." He smiles ruefully. "It's a different world here." He gestures vaguely around.

"But you've taken the US by storm, clearly." I point at him, at his short-sleeve brown floral shirt that isn't my ideal-man style but looks expensive, and dark pressed jeans that exude wealthy techy. "Your mom told me you drive a Porsche. Fully surpassed us Azoreans, haven't you? The Camp Zahav crew is crushing the game."

I say it cheerfully, though I feel a stab in my chest I recognize is jealousy.

"Oh." Reuben winces, like he's embarrassed, but I discern pride there too. "My mom can't help herself from bragging."

"Well, she has reason to be proud." It's an understatement: Reuben's family is São Miguel's version of the Kardashians. His younger sister, Cass, won Olympic silver in gymnastics all-around two years ago. She's the darling of the island, the pinnacle of Portuguese pride. And Reuben has made it in San Francisco, the São Miguel dream. In certain subsets, at least. Many islanders are content with their lot. But some of us have bigger aspirations.

No one ever talks about how Reuben made it, though. But there are rumors, of course there are, that he found the treasure that summer.

The treasure hunt. God. After Eli came out with the clue in his great-grandfather's papers, we all got infected with treasure fever. Me, too. I remember all the plans I had, how I was going to help my family and give myself a real fighting chance in life. I could practically feel the gold coins streaming through my fingers. We all said we'd split it, but I've long wondered how much any of us truly meant that. Maybe Reuben did really find it and keep it all for himself. How else to explain that after that summer, he suddenly bought a Range Rover, had all the nicest clothes and sneakers, enough funds to study abroad in France, and then seed money for his first company that he started in college? Not that the Bensabats are poor or anything—they had a normal house on the south coast, in Vila Franca do Campo—but Daniella, his mother, was a single parent and didn't come from money. Aside from Eli's family, most of us on this island are working-class.

"It's weird, isn't it?" Reuben asks, a murky expression on his face as he watches Lexa and Eli chatting with Aiden. "Everyone back here."

"It's so fucking weird to all be . . . I don't know if you can call this *together*, but like . . . convened," Olivia agrees.

"You're gonna go easy on us, right, Jazz?" Reuben asks, eyes snapping back to our trio. His voice is friendly but carries a bite.

"Easy on you? Oh . . . the documentary?"

"I just want to know—we all want to help you. But this is a vacation, right? It's such a grind in SF. Eli promised a fun—"

"We're here for Sydney's memorial," Olivia says quietly. "Not for fun."

"Well, obviously." Reuben straightens. He pulls his phone out of his pocket and his eyes darken at a row of texts that are blurry to my view. He turns slightly and stabs out a terse response. I can tell by the no-nonsense set of his jaw that he's back in business mode. "I need to know what I'm getting myself into, Jazz. I'm having second thoughts, to be honest, about the documentary."

"We spoke about this, Reub," I say carefully, thinking back to our several phone conversations. To the tailor-made sales pitch I gave to each of them. Spinning this as a full-circle moment, and a way to help me succeed in my filmmaking aspirations. Maybe I leaned a little too much on the poor-me angle, but honestly, I didn't say anything untrue. Even before my grandmother died earlier this year, the past decade I've been rather unmotivated. Lethargic. Depressed. After Sydney was gone, and the summer ended, no more Aiden, no more any of them, it was like my balloon got popped and all my hope leaked steadily out over the years.

I'm reminded of my last conversation with my grandmother,

six months ago before she died. A scene that presses on a sore place in my chest: Vovó eating ice cream, the only thing she could manage to get down in the end. Tub in her lap, propped up in her bed with the lovely pink blanket she patiently crocheted herself, she didn't mince words. She knew she didn't have long, and she told me she'd coddled me. She hadn't pushed me off the couch, out of the house. That maybe she'd enjoyed it, having me close. That we were too similar, she and I. Both grew up without fathers, both afraid of leaping lest we fall. But she said she didn't want me to be like her. That she wanted me to reach for the bigger, riskier life. To go after my dreams with all my verve.

She said that people like the da Costas don't need luck because they have money to function as their luck. But people like us, we need to make our own luck.

And she told me that I could do it, that I could have the bigger life I've always dreamt of. That life was about grabbing opportunities. I told her my opportunities had passed—Camp Zahav and that summer trip. I could have networked with those wealthy American campers and their parents better, accepted the au pair jobs offered to me. I could have told Aiden how I really felt back then. And I didn't do any of it. But Vovó laughed and said that opportunities weren't finite. Another would come along soon. And all I needed to do was pay attention. Grab the opportunity where I could make my own luck.

This documentary, I am certain, is that opportunity.

"I don't have any underhanded intentions," I finally tell Reuben.

"What's your angle then?"

"My angle?"

"Yeah, Jazz. Like, the documentary isn't going to be neutral. You're going to have a person you suspect of having done it. And you're going to be steering us all in that direction."

"I don't have an angle," I tell him, but that's not entirely true.

I have certain suspicions, Reuben included, but nothing conclusive. I'm banking on the documentary proceeding like one of the crossword puzzles Vovó and I used to do. As one clue fills in, others become clear.

"And are you going to be in it?" Olivia asks. "You'll be asking the questions, but are you going to be answering them too?"

I think again about getting Olivia alone. Taking her to the side and pooling what we both know. But can I trust her? I don't know for sure. I've never known, not since I discovered her with my bracelet and she provided an entirely unsatisfactory explanation as to how she got it. I believe that she's innocent, I always have, but maybe those are just my blinders on. It's hard to trust myself, recently more than ever.

"Oh." I gather my courage, try to project strength. "Yes, of course. I'll be answering the questions same as you guys. I have an assistant—Maria, she's around here—and she'll be moderating sometimes." I'd already decided on this. Besides, if things don't move, if people aren't forthcoming, we've strategized certain ways to press them along. I've held my cards to my vest for too long. Protecting people who perhaps didn't deserve it.

This reunion is about justice and peace. For me and for Sydney.

Reuben opens his mouth, like he's about to interrogate me further, and my itch of worry builds, coalescing all my fears that this documentary isn't ever going to get off the ground. That they're all going to band together, refuse to participate. We'll do the memorial and some lackluster reminiscing and exploring and then everyone will be on their merry way. They'll leave and I'll be poor, pathetic Jules again. No!

I'm sifting for how I'll cement their participation, because I need this. Everything has changed since Vovó died. And especially since I went to Eli and Lexa's wedding, an all-expenses-paid trip, every charge covered by them. Like this reunion too.

I *need* this documentary.

But then Reuben swivels at the sound of a baritone voice, and I exhale a shaky breath, relieved at the reprieve. We all watch Isaac Azulay emerge from the glass doors, accompanied by his second wife, Daniella Bensabat, Reuben's mom. And Cass, too, Reuben's sister. She's twenty-one now. The pride of the island—the Olympian. Isaac and Daniella got married seven or eight years ago, I think. After Sydney disappeared, and then Isaac's first wife died. The three of them pause beneath the awning, all dressed to the nines, stylish and refined. Like celebrities aware that without them the party hasn't yet begun. Soft jazz fuzzes through the speakers and my lungs seem to struggle for air. Even though we're outdoors, in the crisp Azorean breeze, their entrance feels like it's sucked up all the oxygen.

Olivia flinches as she watches them, which intrigues me. Then her face settles into something hard that I try to read. It's not fear, I realize, but a darker emotion. Anger. Hate, even.

"Hey!" I say, just realizing it. "You guys are stepsiblings now." I point between Olivia and Reuben. "That's—wow. Wild."

"Yeah," Reuben says, after a beat, eyes still on the trio, but unlike Olivia, I can't make heads or tails of his expression. "One big happy family now."

"One big happy family," Olivia echoes. Then her fierce expression slides back to impassive, and she turns from her father and his new family and stares back out toward the churning sea.

CHAPTER FIVE

Reuben

THERE ARE TWO reasons I hardly ever come home for a visit—Mom and *him*—but seeing Cass is the flip side of the coin. I adore my little sister. She's six years younger than me but has always been wise beyond her years. And not only is she a superstar athlete, the pride of the island, but she's a good person. A *much* better person than me. And let's be real: the only good egg of us all. Seeing my little sister makes this journey over almost worth it, despite the shit I'll need to wade through while I'm on this godforsaken island for three days. Which, to be clear, is three days too many.

"Cass!" My sister launches into my arms and I hug her tight, my tiny strong Olympian. Over her shoulder, I watch Olivia walk away, and I feel a surge of guilt.

"Reub! I've missed you so much."

Cass is wearing a lavender jumpsuit, quite different from her typical gym gear, but her biceps are, as usual, Michelangelo-sculpted caliber. "Been slacking on the workouts?" I tease.

Her blue-almost-purple eyes glimmer. "C'mon, it's offseason."

"So only eight hours a day of training instead of fourteen?"

She laughs her deep, throaty, almost baritone laugh that has always belied her youth, that aged her even when she was a kid.

It always makes me a little melancholic because it's a marker, of sorts, of how fast she had to grow up. I did, too, because our mother was basically a single parent. And Mom cared far more about having fun—about sucking the marrow out of life—than about being a present parent.

Cass's eyes narrow to slits. "Mom's on a rampage, be warned. They're both *very* pissed you're doing the documentary."

My heart folds in on itself in a way that is familiar. "How do they even know?"

"Dunno." She arches a caterpillar-resembling eyebrow that is inexplicably trendy now. "I think Olivia told him."

"Well, good," I say, even though it's the opposite of good. "Good that he knows."

"Reub, you're not going to say—"

"No. I'm not an idiot. I'm not going to say *that*." My heart beats fast, replaying the conversation I've been having with myself these past few weeks when I awake in the middle of the night in a full-blown sweat.

Cass looks doubtful. "Still, I don't know if—"

"There's my all-star son!" Mom swoops in for a heavily perfumed hug, and as ever, I think how strange it is that such a strong personality comes in such a small package. She's not muscly, like Cass, but the thin sort of petite; she stands on tiptoes to kiss her husband and, though I'm a few inches shorter than him, must also tip her head up to look at me. Her naturally dark hair has now gone gray, but you wouldn't know it on the surface; fifteen years ago, she began dyeing it a luxurious butter blond that suits her tanned, clear skin. Her big, dark eyes are framed by (false) fluttery lashes, and her face is what people have always called heart-shaped, which I don't really get—it's a face. She has a nice one, same kind of slightly jutty chin as Cass, but a heart? I don't see it. Maybe the heart is what people want to see because on the surface, Mom appears sweet and innocent. She looks like she needs taking care of, and men have always lined up to do so. But she doesn't need anyone—trust me, she doesn't. I am well aware that my mother is more than capable of obliterating any obstacle in her way.

I endure the three seconds of a hug to which I still feel obligated and then slip out. "Hey, Mom. You look good."

She's fifty-seven but can easily pass for a decade younger, with the facelift and subtle Botox and fillers that only thrice-a-year trips to her go-to girl in Boston can provide. She could get it done on the island—of course—but Mom likes her ritzy America trips. In that sense, I am my mother's son.

"Thanks, Reub," Mom says, smiling. "Think I can pass as your sister these days?"

A voice booms out, "Any younger and you'll be mistaken for his child."

Him. Isaac.

We nod at each other. He clears his throat. Steps forward for a hug. I brace myself and just do it. Hugging him is like entering a cold plunge, but minus the euphoria after the fact.

"Good to see you, Reub." He looks well, I have to admit. His white hair thick, almost coiffed, striking against his blue eyes and tan that's a touch too red. He's fit as ever—I know from Cass he's been doing CrossFit—and he's wearing a sharp navy Brunello Cucinelli suit. Business at the airline must be going well, then. Or else it's the reams of money he inherited from his first wife when she died. Quite conveniently, so he could marry my mother without having to first forsake his inheritance. I'd call him lucky, but given the tragedies he's endured, that would be callous, even for me.

"Mm-hmm," I manage to say.

"How long are you here?" Mom asks, threading her fingers into Isaac's hand and giving it a good squeeze, as if to fortify him for this encounter. "You know, I've been texting you, Reubie."

I cringe. "And I've called a couple times too." She tries not to sound excessively eager, though her stalker-level calls reveal her hand.

"I know. I've been busy." I look down at my Saint Laurent sneakers that I bought a couple months ago, which have probably already accrued an astounding amount of interest in my mounting credit card debt. The staggering numbers swim around my throat, and I cough.

"Well, will you come to the house, maybe stay over a few nights before you head back?" Mom's eyes are wide with hope, and I almost feel bad to let her down. Almost.

"I'll have to leave right after the weekend. Work is nuts."

"Really? But it's been so long, Reubie. I thought you'd stay with us, catch up a bit, and with Cass too. I can cook you my famous macaroni from a box." She smiles but I can't match it.

"I have to get back." I shuffle my feet and avoid her gaze.

"I know. I know you're busy, but we miss you."

I open my mouth to reciprocate, because she seems to really need me to, but the words don't queue up. I can't tell her I miss her back. Not after everything. And especially not now. "I just saw Cass," I point out, giving my sister a genuine smile. "We had the best time together."

"I love SF," Cass says. "I want to come back again soon. Maybe after World's. Before Olympics training really starts to heat up again."

"Spare bedroom's ready for you," I say cheerfully.

"Aka the crystal display room that you allow me to sleep in."

"They're my babies, what can I say?"

I just got a new one, in fact. A huge citrine geode that cost me $17,000. I don't share those specifics, of course, even with Cass. It was a ridiculous spend, especially given my current financial state, but I had to have it. Crystals make me inordinately happy— they have since I was a child. They come straight from the earth, with none of the toxicity we humans tend to add. They're pure and beautiful, with the potential to heal and protect you. Though I may not broadcast it on the outside, adulting is fucking brutal. Everyone always oohs and ahhs at my career successes, but frankly, it's not all success and none of it has made me happy. I still want success and wealth, can't deny it. If I can only figure things out, get out of the red, find a few more big investors, I'll be happier, guaranteed. But now I'm pursuing inner fulfillment too. Crystals are part of that, and I love mine more than the vast majority of the humans in my life.

"You're welcome back anytime," I add, not mentioning that if I don't get my financial situation squared away, I'm going to need *her* guest bedroom, and not the other way around.

"And what about me?" Mom asks. "Maybe I want to come visit my son too. Then do I also get to stay in the crystal room? Tell you what—I'll even book a hotel. And bring you a crystal. Is that the going price these days? Because I'm happy to pay it."

Before I can say snidely that I don't need or want her run-of-the-mill basic crystal quartz peace offering, I'm blessedly saved by the bell. By Isaac. He's made his way to the center of the patio, clinking his wineglass filled with something ruby red. The best wine you can get on the island, I presume, given that Eli's bankrolling the tab.

"Can I—can you all—I know this isn't a formal event. But, well, it feels significant for me that you've all made it here for this important weekend. If you'll indulge me, I'd like to make a brief toast." Conversation begins to peter out, and everyone moves inward toward Isaac. My eyes flit across the row of familiar faces. They all seem bizarrely the same, like they haven't iterated since high school. No new features, no bug fixes. I wind up standing beside Lexie. Or maybe I intentionally maneuver there.

"Hey," I say quietly. "You look gorgeous, Lexie." I throw a hand through my hair, self-conscious that I didn't make an appointment to dye it before I left. I've been plucking the grays, but they're spreading exponentially. And I fucking hate them. Figures that Eli still has his youthful brown hair, not a single gray strand in sight.

"Hey, Reub. It's Lexa now." She doesn't meet my eyes.

"Oh." I clear my throat. Of course, I've known it, that she'd decided Lexie was too childish. Jules told me that, ages ago. But she's Lexie to me. That won't change. "Sorry. Lexa. I'll try to get it right."

"Whatever." She shrugs, like it doesn't matter what I call her for this limited reunion, which elicits a stabbing sensation in my chest. Cass jostles against me, and I take the opportunity to accidentally-on-purpose brush up against Lexie. Skin of my arm against the skin of hers. I force myself to face forward as my heart slaps my chest. A memory rushes back—that summer, Lexie ahead of me on a hike, picking ginger lilies for us both, taking off the red parts on the stem and us eye to eye as we sucked up the sugar. Then me grabbing her hand to go faster. To be at the front, my preferred spot, though she often strayed back with Sydney and Eli.

Now Lexie breaks apart, leaving my skin tingling with phantom want. She whispers something in Eli's ear, and he looks over at me, extends a hand. I hesitate before shaking it briskly, maintaining a neutral expression, while inside I'm berating myself that my palm is sweaty. Goddamn sweaty palms; they've been afflicting me since I was a child. I force myself not to break our grip first because it would feel like an admission of shame, so when Eli finally does I'm grateful. He sidesteps back over to his wife, slipping an arm around her waist. Marking his territory, I suppose. I force a pleasant smile, but everything inside me is tense. This evening feels excruciatingly like hanging out with a bunch of out-of-date Facebook profiles that never got deleted.

Isaac clinks on his glass again. "I know this is Eli and Lexie's shindig, but as Sydney's father—Olivia's, too, of course—I want to welcome you all back to the island," he says, making eye contact with Aiden and smiling, then down the line at Jules, again with his wide, sales-y grin. Clearly contrived because there is no way he's happy about Jules's documentary plans. Which gives me a sick pleasure.

"I know I speak for my wife and me when I say that we are very touched you all made the trip. This week is exactly ten years from the day Sydney disappeared." His face gets a haunted, distant look to it that manages to rouse compassion in me. "Hard to believe, isn't it?"

Murmurs of agreement, but I'm quiet.

"It was important to me to mark the occasion with a memorial. The synagogue restoration project felt like the perfect vehicle. And I thought it'd be fitting to gather back here at the scene of where, well . . . where Sydney was happiest. With the people she loved most."

God, Isaac loves being the center of attention, just like Sydney did. If bullshit were a currency, he'd be a unicorn start-up.

Olivia is standing across from me, looking jittery and tense. Well, join the club.

"You are all extremely busy, and the fact that you flew across the ocean to our little island to commemorate Sydney means the world. And I would be remiss if I didn't express my appreciation to Eli and Lexie for hosting everyone at this beautiful hotel."

Despite no doubt feeling irritated at being referred to yet again by her now obsolete nickname, *Lexie* half smiles, like hosting everyone is no biggie, which I guess it's not—now that she's a da Costa, and also CMO of their hotel group. That wasn't on my Lexie bingo card when we were dating, to be frank. Though she always reeked of ambition.

Eli says, "It's our pleasure. We're not here for fun—this is a solemn occasion—but it's nice to all be together again."

"Well, I want to correct you on that," Isaac says, eyes misty, his expression heartfelt in a way that infuriates me. "I'd like to propose a toast to a fun weekend, in Sydney's honor."

My chest tightens as I think about the momentousness of this occasion. I mostly try not to go there. I've been trying not to go there for ten years. But I can't deny that I'm still living with the consequences of decisions I made that fateful day Sydney disappeared. Those decisions have pervaded every second, every hour, every day of my life. They've leeched out everything good. And I'm determined to put it all to bed on this trip.

"My daughter wouldn't have wanted everyone to sulk for her," Isaac is saying. "She'd want us to celebrate her life and she'd want you all to have a blast being back here in her memory."

I catch Olivia's eyes again, and she smiles wryly at me. I shoot her a rueful grin back. And I know we're both thinking the same thing:

Did this man even know his daughter? Because if Sydney didn't get to be included on the fun, then she certainly wouldn't want anyone else having it either.

CHAPTER SIX

Cass

AFTER DAD'S TOAST, waiters swirl around with appetizer trays, and everyone disperses to mingle among a few high tables by the pool. I grab some limpets served in their shells with a drizzle of oil atop, mini *prego* beef bites on cornbread, and *chicharros fritos*, the most delicious fried mackerel with *massa de pimentão*, this spicy red pepper paste. I contemplate grabbing chocolate and salted caramel *espécies*, but then I hear my coach in my ear, and I resist the temptation. Willpower has always been my strength.

I survey the tables. I spy my parents at one, talking, expressions tense. Pass. Reuben's at another, chatting with Jules. I start to head over to join them, but then I spot another table. Eli, sitting next to Aiden, with two empty chairs flanking them. I draw a breath, change course. I walk over and pull out the vacant chair beside Eli.

"Is this seat taken?"

Eli regards me with surprise. "Cass!" It takes a beat for me to realize that's good surprise on his face. "Wow! You look—wow! I didn't know you'd be here."

I take that as permission to sit, and I set my plate on the table and ease down. "Really? I was always planning to come tonight."

"But you're training on the mainland, aren't you? Isn't Lisbon home now?"

"Yeah, but I have a training spot and coach in town, as well. Reub's back here, which like, never happens, and I wouldn't miss the memorial. Sydney and I . . ."

Eli's face softens, and he places his hand on top of mine. To my surprise, his touch vaults through me, fast and electric, like the moment my feet leave the beam. His brown eyes meet mine, and I can tell he felt it too. He gingerly lifts his hand and returns it to his perspiring wineglass.

"I know," Eli says, taking a sip. "Sydney loved you like her little sister. I always forget you were here that summer."

I laugh, try to shrug that off. I had a huge crush on him back then, but he wouldn't know that. And I wouldn't have been so memorable. I was the eleven-year-old kid tagging along when my mom occasionally led their group on local tours or backcountry hiking trips that the counselors would have had difficulty navigating. It's not like I was really a part of their group that summer. I was mostly training anyway. But still, I can't deny it burns a little that Eli's memories of that summer don't include me whatsoever.

"I loved Sydney too," I say simply. "We had a special bond."

"You did," Aiden says, from my other side, and I regard him for the first time. Still hot, kinda boring. "Sydney used to braid your hair like hers and put—"

"Wildflowers in the braids!" I smile.

"And now you're our famous Olympian," Eli says.

I throw a hand out. "I wouldn't say famous." But I like the *our* he used.

"Oh, you're definitely famous," Aiden says. "And you deserve every bit of it. Your floor routine at Paris was unreal."

"Seriously," Eli says. "You deserved gold, not silver."

"Thanks, guys." I can't help beaming. Many people have said

the same, but to hear it from the two of them—men I idolized when I was a kid—means a lot.

"Wine?" A waiter hovers over my shoulder with a bottle of red. Always red in Portugal; white is looked down upon here, considered subpar.

"*Não, obrigada.* Just water for me."

"C'mon, have a glass with us," Eli says.

"Can't. Training."

"Wow, I admire your resolve. I can barely make it to the gym these days."

"Well, can't tell it," I say lightly, though my eyes can't help but graze Eli's muscly arm, then filter down to the silver band on the ring finger of his left hand.

"E?" a voice says from overhead, and I glance up to catch the frosty look on Lexa's face. "You didn't save me a seat?"

"Oh." Eli scrambles up to kiss her cheek. "No, I did." He points across the table. "But—"

"I'll move," I offer, but I wait a beat before standing.

"No, it's fine," Lexa says in her dry voice, which is as monotone and dismissive of me as it was ten years ago. She circles the table and takes the seat next to Aiden. "Who doesn't like a good game of musical chairs?" she says coolly. "Hey, Cass."

"Hey, Lexa," I say, using the name I know she prefers now. "Nice to see you."

She nods but doesn't reciprocate the sentiment. "You didn't want to sit with your mom and Isaac?"

"No, my parents are . . . in their own world." We all turn and indeed, they've switched from their tense discussion to hands interlinked and scooted close, decidedly in their love bubble.

"Your parents—that's nice that you think of Isaac as your father," Eli says.

"Oh." I shrug. "Well, my birth father left when I was a baby. I'm named after him, but that's about all I got from the man. Isaac married my mom when I was thirteen, and he's always been good to me. Treated me like his own daughter. Maybe after Sydney . . . he needed that or something. He's the only father I've ever had."

I look up to see Jules lingering by our table, her gaze on Aiden. I smile up at her, in case she wants to join us, but she quickly walks away. I wonder if my father comment triggered her. I don't think she has one.

"That's sweet," Lexa says, sounding anything but.

"It is really nice," Eli says, nodding at his wife as if to say, *Be supportive.* "Lexa has a relationship like that with my father. She calls him Dad too."

Something flickers across Lexa's face. Pain? Love? I'm not sure. "My father hasn't been in my life for a very long time, so when Eli and I started getting serious, it felt nice to have a father figure again," she finally says.

"I relate," I say, and I think a quiet mutual understanding passes between us.

A breeze whips in from the sea, flinging up my napkin. Aiden grabs it and hands it to me.

"Quick reflexes." I laugh.

"You need them when you're James Bond tagging sharks in the deep ocean." Eli playfully slaps Aiden's shoulder.

"Really? Is that what you're up to these days?"

"Yeah. Living on Terceira actually," Aiden says, naming one of our neighboring islands. "I was kind of floundering back when you last knew me but Sydney disappearing was a massive wake-up call. I got it together. Decided to try to do something meaningful with my life."

"You definitely did something," Eli says. "He's a marine biologist."

"Whoa." I'm admittedly shocked. "That's—"

"A stretch, I know." Aiden laughs. "I wouldn't have predicted it, either, back where I was then."

I'm quiet, because I know more than he thinks about how much he was floundering. The cocaine and stuff. Rumors circulate, but I'm not a gossip. I'm impressed though. He's certainly cleaned up his act. Even if he never seemed like that much of a mess to me, at least as an observant kid.

"Marine biologist sounds big-time," I finally say. "I have to admit, though, I hardly know what it means. I have a total block with anything scientific. Show me a picture of the periodic table, and I start to sweat."

"Says the Olympian! Think how we all feel when you get on the balance beam." But Aiden smiles, and I find myself smiling genuinely back.

"What a lovefest," Lexa says across the table, not smiling but her voice jarringly singsong. "Is my standing ovation next?"

"What's going on with you, Lexa?" I swivel toward her, trying to put her at ease, not to see me as a threat. "I understand mazels are in order."

"Oh." Her jaw relaxes its clench. "You're talking about . . . ?"

I point to the wedding ring on Eli's finger, and then to hers, to the massive rock that looks like it gives her left hand a built-in weight-lifting routine.

She regards her ring and smiles genuinely. "It's exciting. We're really happy."

"I'm sure. You guys live in New York?"

"Manhattan." She nods. "Upper West."

"Oh, cool. What do you do there?"

She pauses, and I realize she probably doesn't do much. She's married to Eli da Costa. But she surprises me by saying, "I'm CMO at the Da Costa Group. Chief marketing officer," she clarifies at my slack-jawed nonresponse.

"Wow," I finally manage. On the surface, she looks like a high-fashion girlie who, with Eli's funds, would be starting a vanity fashion brand or something. Or pop out a few kids and organize charity luncheons. Eli slings a proud arm around his wife, and they exchange an intimate glance that gives me a searing jolt of jealousy.

Suddenly Jules appears, wraps her arms around me and Eli. I gaze up into her fairly spectacular cleavage. "Hey, guys. Wanted to give a five-minute warning. We'll go in and start filming the documentary, okay?"

"Sure," Aiden says, but I notice Jules doesn't look at him, only stares at Lexa.

"Okay, Lex?"

"Okay," she finally says.

"Great! Sure you don't wanna join the documentary, Cass? You were there that summer. It would be awesome to catch any-thing you remember."

"Sorry, my dad—Isaac—would kill me," I tell her. "It was the worst time of his life . . . Sydney gone . . . Olivia accused. The memorial is one thing, but doing something for public consump-tion? He'd flip. He's pissed Olivia's doing it. And Reuben. I guess both of them can do what they want, but—"

"But you're the people-pleasing youngest?" Jules says. "Sorry, didn't mean that to sound rude."

"It's fine, you're right. Anyway, I was hardly with you guys. I was training like crazy that summer. Eleven is a make-or-break year. But yeah, I want to respect my dad's wishes."

"Okay, I understand. If you change your mind, we're here." Jules pats me on the shoulder. As she walks away, she calls, "I hope we'll see more of you, though, this weekend, Cass."

"Yeah, are you coming tomorrow?" Eli asks. "We're going canyoning in the morning."

"I can't. Training in PD. Otherwise, I'd love to. But I'll be at the memorial in the afternoon, of course."

"Then you have to come to Furnas with us tomorrow night, after the memorial," Aiden says. "We're having cozido and doing the hot springs. It'll be fun. A way to . . . decompress. After the ceremony. And to honor Sydney, of course. She loved cozido."

"Really?"

"Yeah, she was a big meat person." Aiden laughs. "Definitely not a vegan. I remember from when I was a counselor for her unit back at Camp Zahav. That tiny girl could pound a couple burgers."

"No, I meant—really you want me to come?"

"Yeah, of course we do," Eli says.

My eyes dart between both guys, who seem genuine. I'm surprised and warmed over, I have to admit. I know I'm famous, that people admire my drive and accomplishments, that they want to talk to me about the Olympics, but somehow I don't think that's why Aiden and Eli are asking me to join the Furnas night. Which is . . . surprising, to be honest. I'm twenty-one, but I've spent my whole life working toward something most people don't understand. I haven't had the time for romance. I've definitely never been in love.

I feel myself flush, like my thoughts have been exposed. I have to be up early every morning, but then I have Mom in my ear, how she's always saying I need to live more. Even my coach says it too. That I need more beyond training and hanging out with my parents. That having a fuller life will fuel my body too. Give it more power. "Okay," I say. "I'll come tomorrow night. Anyway, it will be nice to spend more time with Reub while he's in town. He's leaving the next morning."

"Great," Aiden says, flashing me a wide grin.

"Yeah. Amazing." Eli rubs his hands together. "Isn't that great, Lex?" he throws across the table, like an afterthought.

"Great," Lexa echoes. "Yep. Just . . . fabulous."

———

When we're all filtering out the patio, back toward the hotel lobby, I stop abruptly by the heavy glass doors that lead inside.

I'm the first one there, and it takes a few moments for my eyes to grasp what they're seeing.

"What is that?"

Reuben's behind me, and he whistles. "Holy shit." He crouches down beside this very strange sight—scattered gold coins.

"Are those real?" I ask.

He's streaming them through his fingers. "Nah. Fake. Maybe a kid left them here accidentally or something."

"That's—" Aiden's eyes darken. "So like . . . someone's referencing the treasure . . ."

Olivia whirls around. "What the hell? Is this someone's sick idea of a joke? Who did this?"

I turn, too, to catch Lexa's face, sheet white. Eli has his hand in the small of his wife's back, looking . . . I don't know . . . taken aback, but not angry like Lexa, or jolted like Olivia.

"That isn't cool," Eli says. "I don't really get it. Why would someone joke about the treasure now?"

"I'll speak to the hotel staff," he goes on, staring blankly at the coins. "See if anyone saw anything."

"We should check if there's video footage," Olivia says. She's jittery, as ever a bundle of nerves. Reminds me of the panic attack she had the day Mom and I hiked with them out by Pico da Vara. I'd never seen anyone unravel so fast.

"Good idea about the video feed," Reuben says, returning to a stand. "Because it's really not okay if someone here is fucking with the rest of us. We're here to honor Sydney."

"Not to start this treasure shit up again," Aiden says.

"There won't be video footage," Lexa says dryly, her face deadpan. "We don't do cameras at da Costa resorts. Our guests cherish their privacy."

One of the staff approaches, as if to see if we need assistance, but Lexa pins her down with a gaze and the girl walks away discreetly. I catch Dad staring at the fake coins, his eyes tearful, and

I try to smile reassuringly at him. Of course, the treasure would shoot him right back to Sydney. That's what everyone suspects led to her death, after all. The treasure hunt they were all obsessed with. I remember Reuben, really into deciphering the clue, but it's all vague in my head. I never got into the treasure; I was far more into showing them my gymnastics skills the few times I came around.

"Well," Jules finally says, cutting the silence. "Onward then? To filming, I mean. We have a room reserved for us. Though . . ." She points to the coins. "It's strange timing, this. Because the treasure started it all."

"That's—" Eli says, face puppy-dog sad. "I feel like I'm ultimately to blame for the treasure stuff."

"Come on, E," Lexa says wearily. "Save it for the camera, right, Jules?"

Jules's eyes blink faster. "Lex, you know my intention isn't to exploit anyth—"

"Sorry. I know. I'm just—" Lexa pulls her phone out of her purse. "Stressed. I need to go put out a work fire." Lexa strides off in the other direction from the room Jules had indicated.

"Wait, Lex?" Jules calls. "You're coming to film, right?"

Lexa turns. "I said I'd be there, J, so I'll be there. I'd do anything for you, I hope you know that by now. Just—don't make me regret it."

CHAPTER SEVEN

Vanished from the Cove

Documentary Transcript

Jules Silva (interviewer): Okay, so, to start, I'm going to make my big introduction about why we're all here, set the stage, yada yada yada. Maria, we'll fill this in later, but for now, let's just get into it! So . . . hi, everyone. Lexa, hi—okay if we start with you?

Lexa Levin da Costa: Hi, Jules. Sure. Gotta admit, this sort of feels like a *Real Housewives* reunion.

Jules: Oh. Does it? I don't really know if that's good or bad—you can cut that, Maria. So . . . Lexa, why don't you start us off by explaining a little bit about the annual summer trip to São Miguel. And how and why this group came together in the first place.

Lexa: Well, we all—I mean, Eli, Reuben, Olivia, Sydney, and me—we all went to camp together since we were in elementary school. Aiden and Jules too. Camp Zahav, it's in Kingston, Massachusetts, and it's a camp mainly for Sephardic Jews. Wait, do people know what Sephardic Jews even are? Basically, a broad misconception is that all Jews are Ashkenazi, aka Jews who are white and from European countries. It's definitely not so. Camp Zahav mostly attracts Sephardic

Jews, so Jews of North African descent, with ancestry traced back to medieval Spain and Portugal. But I mean, not all of us at camp are Sephardic. Like, I'm only half Sephardic. My mom's family is from Romania, and my father's family is originally from Spain but lived in Morocco for generations. I think all of us have some Sephardic ancestry, except Aiden is . . . fully Polish, I think?

Aiden Jacobs: Russian and Polish. Probably a sprinkling of Ukraine in there.

Lexa: Okay, but Ashkenazi. No connection at all to Portugal. So it's not a mandate at camp, all Jews are welcome and some Ashkenazis do attend, but the camp was started in the 1930s by Jews whose ancestors came specifically from this island. Eli's great-grandfather was a founder—he used to live on this island but then moved to Massachusetts. Anyway, that's the connection to this place. But basically, growing up, camp was just camp. There were probably like thirty of us in our age group, and it was such fun.

Olivia Azulay: *Such* fun. Every year when it ended, we'd look forward to the following June. It was, like, the highlight of my life.

Lexa: We did all the normal camp things—archery, swimming, *omanut*.

Olivia: *Omanut!* I got real good at making lanyards. Oh and—remember swamp walks?

Lexa: I hated swamp walks. I don't know how you guys didn't care getting so gross and dirty. And who knew what was lurking in all that mud . . .

Olivia: It was the best. And then getting out, and inevitably someone would have lost a shoe or something. And the counselors would give us Bug Juice—oh! And Shabbats, you have to talk about Shabbats. They were awesome. Special. We all wore white, and we'd do all the Kabbalat Shabbat songs. I loved those.

Lexa: Me too. But the pinnacle that Jules is trying to lead us to, I think, is the summer on São Miguel. Right, J?

Jules: Ding, ding. Thanks, Lex.

Lexa: It's for the oldest age group, sort of a heritage trip, to explore this place where our founders are from, but it's also supposed to be a rugged hiking trip. Like, only for the toughest campers. You had to apply for it, and the camp director had to approve of you attending. We camped in tents every night, we only showered once a week, we cooked all our own food. It's intense. It weeds out a certain kind of camper—the ones who can't hack it. Honestly, I'll be real, you might look at me now and think that I couldn't hack it. But I could. And I did. I'm scrappy. But only five of our age group signed up. And older camp alums can apply to lead the heritage expeditions, which is what Jules and Aiden did.

Aiden: I always knew I wanted to staff it. My own heritage trip when I was a camper was pivotal in my life, I think, looking back. It makes you grow up, to appreciate the world, and the privileges you have. I fell in love with the Azores, it's why I moved to the islands after college. But the trip isn't . . . cushy, put it that way, with cabins and mattresses and the camp chef. The Azores trip is more—

Lexa: Intense. Rugged. So that should tell you something about all of us who signed up. Trust me, it's not for the faint of heart, or people who like to shower often. So it was us five: Sydney and Liv are sisters, Sydney . . . was my best friend. Eli—well, he's my husband now, but he was Sydney's boyfriend back then. Sounds bad, I'll acknowledge that at the head, but it wasn't like that. Reuben was actually my boyfriend that summer. So . . . a bit of musical chairs, you could say. Reuben's from São Miguel, but he was born in Massachusetts like the rest of us. He used to come to camp every summer in the States. Anyway, that's us. The Fab Five. That's how it all began.

Jules: Thanks, Lexa. Great. That covers a lot of good ground. Olivia, do you want to pick up from there? Can you talk about why you decided to go on the trip, and why Sydney did, as well? And how you both ended up in the same age group, even though you are not twins?

Olivia: Syd and I are thirteen months apart. Irish twins. I'm older. But in kindergarten, I got held back, and so Sydney and I were always in the same grade. But . . . it's not like people mistook us for twins. We're—we *were*—really different. Sydney was . . . I don't know, the life of the party. A force. Everyone wanted to be around her—or be with her. Like, we had paper-plate awards every summer at camp—do you guys remember? Sydney always got Campfire Songbird or Most Likely to Be a Famous Movie Star.

Lexa: Paper-plate awards! I forgot about those. I was Camp Fashionista, I think. What were you, Liv? I feel like you were—

Olivia: I was Counselor's Sidekick. I remember that one. It sounded so Goody Two-shoes, but I guess I was always eager to please. And I'm just . . . quieter. When we were kids, Sydney was always singing around the house, and our parents were videoing her every move. I'm barely in any home movies. Because I was always in some corner writing my stories or staring off into the sky, daydreaming. And that's not exactly exciting to film. But anyway, when it came down to the São Miguel trip, we both wanted to go. I . . . well, I wanted to get out. I wanted to explore the world. And I had this idea, that I needed to be in some exotic place to write this great novel. I thought the island would inspire me. And it did—but not for the reasons I thought. And I guess, Sydney, for all her loving beauty and stuff—she was filming her beauty routine on Instagram before GRWMs were even a thing—Syd loved nature. She loved being outside. And she . . . well, she was sick. Her whole life, with chronic kidney disease. It was a genetic thing; her kidneys didn't function well. And so we lived with it in the background—her death, I guess. It sounds morbid. And it was, but it was also normal, somehow. It was horrible. Normal and horrible. Sydney was in constant pain, sometimes so much she could almost black out. And she always got nauseous and lightheaded. Sometimes her ankles would swell up, or her face, which of course she hated. Sydney had to take medicine and try to lower her stress, but the summer was supposed to be as destressing as it got. That's what sold our parents. Hiking, nature, sunlight. No social media. Good wholesome fun.

Reuben Bensabat: But the summer was stressful, let's be honest. For a carefree summer in a gorgeous place, we somehow made it pretty stressful.

Lexa: Well, you were stressed because you wanted to find the treasure so bad.

Reuben: And you didn't?

Lexa: Not nearly as much as you.

Reuben: If loving a good wholesome treasure hunt is wrong, I don't want to be right. And let's just say, you weren't—

Jules: Guys, please. Chill. We haven't even gotten to the treasure yet. Maria, make a note to cut that until we intro the treasure aspect. Let's get back to Syd, we were talking about her kidney disease.

Eli: But how relevant is her disease, really? In the end, that's not why Syd died.

Olivia: What are you implying? Are you not so subtly hinting that I killed my sister?

Eli: No, but I mean . . . you were the main suspect. That's just fact. I'm assuming we'll get to it.

Olivia: Oh, is it facts you guys want? I mean, then we might as well get all the cards on the table from the jump. It's what you're leading everyone toward revealing, isn't it, Jules? Eli played right into your hand, huh? Exposing that everyone has always thought I—that I killed my own sister. Just because my memories were patchy from that night. Not to mention how my medical privacy was breached. All those articles about my panic attacks, and the meds I was on. Like my anxiety disorder was evidence of me murdering my sister in and of itself!

Jules: Liv, please. Let's go step-by-step here. I know emotions are heightened, that's understandable, but we need to give context for all of this.

Aiden: I don't think anyone here is trying to pinpoint you, Liv. There are lots of things that could've happened. That's why you were never charged, and why we're even here. Like, Syd could have had a kidney complication that we didn't know about . . .

Jules: And then, what, disappear with no trace? Other than the blood in the cave?

Aiden: I don't know. I'm just—

Lexa: I for one don't think you killed Sydney, Liv. I'll say that on the record. We don't know each other well, not as adults, but I've always thought the police focused on the wrong person when they zeroed in on you. And I don't think it was fair how much the journalists eviscerated you. We all have our . . . mental health struggles. It sucked how yours were trotted out for public consumption.

Olivia: Oh. Well—thank you. I mean, we don't even know for sure if Syd . . . if she actually . . . I mean, she must have, it's been ten years, but—

Jules: There was never a body, of course. But assuming she did die, who do *you* think killed her, Lexa?

Lexa: Who killed Sydney? You want me to speculate? Well, I think you're asking the wrong question. I think you should say—*why* did someone kill her? And I'll tell you the answer:

for the gold. It was sitting right outside the terrace just now—the pile of fake coins.

Jules: Yes, okay, because we're doing this in real time, and we've all reunited for the first time in a decade, let's talk about that. Because it all started with the treasure, didn't it?

Lexa: *We're going on a treasure hunt. X marks the spot.* You guys remember that? Wow, it just came back to me. *We're going on a treasure hunt. X marks the spot.*

Everyone except Olivia and Aiden joins in: *Spiders crawling up your back, spiders crawling down your back. Spiders crawling up your back, spiders crawling down your back. Knife in your back, blood gushing down. Knife in your back, blood gushing down. Cool breeze, tight squeeze, now you've got the—now you've got the—chilllllllls.*

Jules: Man, that really takes me back. And we couldn't exactly do the hand motions while we're all sitting in a row here, but the game is meant to be played with two people, one sitting behind the other, the person behind doing the hand motions on the other's back. The rhyming lines were pure old-school camp, but I remember how much we played it that summer. It became our mantra or something, as we searched for the real treasure. But we should fill the viewers in that, as Lexa said, after we all just reunited for the first time in ten years, we found a pile of coins on the floor as we were about to head in here to film this documentary.

Eli: *Fake* coins.

Jules: Fake coins. Yes. Like someone was messing with us.

Lexa: One of us. Like someone in this *room* was messing with the rest of us.

Jules: In order for this to make sense to the viewers, let's start from the beginning. Eli, why don't you take this? Tell us about arriving on the island, and how the treasure hunt started.

Eli: Yeah, that was all me. I thought—I thought it would be fun. I couldn't have imagined how it would all end. Treasure hunt—you read it about as a kid, you know? Clues and adventure and pirates—

Olivia: No pirates, at least.

Eli: True. Well, what happened was, right before we were going on our trip, my great-grandfather died. My dad's grandfather, the guy who helped found Camp Zahav. His name was Vasco da Costa. He was really old and out of it since, like, my earliest memory. And I was sorting through his house with my dad and found this paper he'd left. It was in a really old file cabinet. My dad wanted to toss everything, but it felt cool to go through, a real, living museum. He had crazy ancient swords, and all these old letters. I've always loved that stuff, getting my dad to tell me all the stories from the Azores he'd learned from his dad. He didn't know much, but the stuff he did know was pretty sordid. Anyway, I found this paper that was all yellowed and written in Portuguese. Which was strange, because even though Great-grandfather Vasco was born on the island, he lived in America most of his life. Nothing else was in Portuguese.

Lexa: And remember that dark smudge on it? It was like . . . or we thought it could have been . . . blood.

Eli: Oh, yeah! The blood splatter. My dad once said one of my ancestors was actually murdered in his office, a letter opener stabbed in his neck, if you can believe it. Someone who worked for him was trying to steal his fortune. It was totally . . . spooky. The letter struck me as odd, because it had been cut off in the middle of a sentence. I had it translated, and the translation was the strangest thing. The letter was addressed to "my beloved." It said something like "come see me, you know where to go, but if something happens to me, you have all the answers." And then it said "Twelve tribes of Israel will point to Fortun . . ." F-O-R-T-U-N but then it trails off, like he meant to finish the sentence but got interrupted midwriting. *Fortuna* is the Portuguese word for fortune. I couldn't believe it! I was so excited. There's always been a local legend that Vasco's ancestors got their wealth because they found a treasure dating back to Inquisition times. It was supposedly gold bullion from a long-ago shipwreck. And there was this legend that the da Costas found that lost treasure and only took some of it to start our family company, but left the other half buried in case anyone in the family ever needed it. After my family found the treasure, as the story goes, everything in their lives turned to gold.

Jules: The treasure had healing powers, basically. That was the legend, right? And Eli, don't just nod; please say yes if something is correct.

Eli: Yes. I remember my dad telling me about it when I was a kid. After our ancestors found the treasure, an old sick woman, my great-great-great-great or something like that grandmother, spontaneously healed and lived many more years. A child in the family was missing, thought to have drowned, but then he miraculously reappeared. Marriages healed, feuds too. Beyond the riches, the treasure paved the way. Smoothed a lot of paths and situations. Apparently. I mean, all of this is lore.

Jules: But we used to talk about it around the firepit. Not only on the island, but at Camp Zahav. Everyone at camp knew about the treasure.

Eli: Yeah. That's why finding this paper right before the trip felt so . . . crazy. But, like, I showed my dad the treasure clue and what could be a blood splatter and he was, like, not into my speculations. He said that was a legend and to forget it. That Great-grandfather Vasco had already searched for the supposed remaining half of the treasure and found nothing. We had plenty of wealth and didn't need more, but like—I was going to the island. I mean, I'd been before, with my family, but this was going to be living off the land, in the place where my great-grandfather was born. So how couldn't I follow this up? It felt kind of like—destiny. But I never meant to do anything, to cause—I didn't have anything to do with Sydney disappearing . . .

Jules: Tell us what happened when you told everyone about the clue?

Eli: Well, it was the first day—you all remember. We were huddled around the campfire, we'd just made a delicious beef stew. We set up our tents—the guys' tent and the girls' one—and then Aiden and Jules had their two solo tents. The whole summer stretched out with . . . I don't know, I guess I'd call it promise. I don't think I've ever been happier than in that moment. I mean . . . not until now. My wedding and marriage and—you know what I mean.

Jules: Go on.

Eli: I—Syd and I were holding hands, sitting around the fire. And I told her I'd be right back and went into the tent to grab the paper from my backpack. I showed it to everyone. They all immediately got why I'd brought it, why I was so excited. I mean, we'd grown up with the legend of treasure. How many counselors used it to spin tales around campfires? I said if we found the treasure, we could all share in the wealth. We promised we'd all share it. We were so united then. Even Jules and Aiden too. It wasn't only a camper thing. It united all seven of us. Like we had one common goal. Like we were going to do right by each other. Finally find this treasure. Have the best summer ever—and get rich in the process.

Reuben: You were already rich. Rich as balls. Seventeen-year-old you already had more zeros than a Silicon Valley networking event.

Eli: I wasn't doing it for the money. But you can't deny the rest of you were.

Jules: What were everyone's motivations, do you think?

Eli: Really? You want me to speculate? I don't see how this is relevant to Sydney disappearing.

Jules: It's all relevant. The treasure is an anomaly in a summer of anomalies. Sydney disappearing. The treasure. It's not far-fetched to imagine they're linked.

Eli: Well, then, I mean, money. Who didn't need it? Reuben—I mean, look at him—he's wearing cashmere socks.

Reuben: Oh and what, are you telling me you're out here raw-dogging life in cotton? Now that's tragic.

Eli: But I didn't need money. I never have. I'm not trying to say it in a bragging way. Whenever it comes down to money, I always sound . . .

Reuben: Like an asshole.

Eli: Okay, you really want to know the unvarnished truth, Jules? Reuben was a scholarship kid. We all knew that. He was born in Boston, but his mother moved back to São Miguel when he was—

Reuben: Ten. And I can tell my own story. So what if I was a scholarship kid? The scholarship was there for a reason. To give poorer Sephardic kids the opportunity to experience camp. Lexa was a scholarship kid too. And Jules, you were also, if I'm not mistaken.

Jules: Yeah, my grandmother's parents knew the camp founders or something. My mom even went to Camp Zahav too.

Reuben: Right, so if being poor is a motive to murder—if that's what we're talking about here—then many of us had it. And most people on this island too. The people here are farmers. Fishermen. They make dairy products and herd cows. Anyone here would be lured by treasure.

Eli: But we're not talking about everyone on this island. We're talking about us. The original seven, including Sydney.

The only ones who knew about the treasure clue. And of all of us, you had the biggest dollar signs in your eyes, Reuben.

Reuben: Doesn't mean I found the treasure! Or that I did anything to Sydney!

Eli: I'm not saying it does. Anyway, as I said, the other part of the treasure lore was that it could turn your problems into gold. Like, heal you. Fix your life. I think all of us wanted that for some reason or another. But no one more than Syd, I'd say. She was sick. She truly thought the treasure could heal her.

Olivia: She really did think that. I remember. She was convinced that she was going to get rid of her illness once and for all.

Jules: Okay. We all wanted to find the treasure. I can vouch for that. So then what happened, Eli? After you showed us all the letter?

Eli: So then . . . the trip became like *Lord of the Flies*. The treasure made everyone go crazy.

CHAPTER EIGHT

Olivia

THE SUN IS just beginning to stir when I slip out of my suite and head down the white stone path toward the beach. I round the plunge pool bordering all our rooms, relieved no one appears to be in the vicinity. I bleat with a yawn and marinate in the solitude, eager for the jolt I'll feel when I dip into the sea. My soles crunch over a section of the path made of crushed shells as I quicken my pace. I didn't sleep much—so many turbulent thoughts. Not surprising given the circumstances of this trip— and seeing my sister yesterday.

It was Sydney, it wasn't Sydney. My thoughts have tangled up and I can't seem to unpick them. Can I trust my memories? Can I believe what my eyes seem to see? Ever since that summer, I'm constantly unsure of myself.

And so I haven't told anyone I spotted her. A woman who, I swear, could be adult Sydney. Those tiny braids . . . that white beaded necklace . . .

Maybe she's still alive, here, for some unknown reason . . .

If she is, it means there's finally proof I didn't murder her . . .

I think back to the documentary filming yesterday, and how defensive I got at the slightest implication of my guilt. Innocent people don't react that way, do they? I'm losing it again, is what it feels like. Once more, on a national stage, but this time by my own volition.

Now sufficient sunlight torches my way that I switch off the flashlight on my iPhone. The air is crisp and cool, with the earthy scent of drying seaweed and briny ocean tang. Palm trees shimmy in the breeze, and seagulls swoop down toward the cliffs' rocky outcrops. As I descend the last steps toward the black sand beach, the ocean seems to gather force and sound, and the sensation of my feet on the rough sand coalesces so many disparate parts of my life. I drop my bag atop a lounger and feel my feet drawn out like magnets toward the rollicking waves. Something old hardens in my throat, and I am suddenly a hundred different versions of myself.

Seven-year-old Olivia who won her big swimming competition, glancing toward the cheering contingent in the stands, but finding no familiar faces lurking there.

Ten-year-old Olivia bashing a stapler onto her knuckles to try to break her fingers, because she learned the only way to get attention in her family was to be in physical pain.

Seventeen-year-old Olivia who screamed at her sister that she wished she would die.

Then Sydney . . . dead on the cave floor . . .

Eighteen-year-old Olivia who sat in her dorm at Elmhurst while all the other girls were partying with insipid frat boys, alternately staring at pictures of her mother and sister, bringing them so close to her face that tears dripped onto the Polaroids. Crying, and then writing scenes set on beaches like this one for what became *X Marks the Spot*.

I wade out until the water is above my knees, then I turn around and stare back. From this vantage point I can see up the cliff face toward the imposing hotel. And then a bit to the right lies a canopy of wild trees, concealing the abandoned Ghost Hotel we visited on our summer trip, all graffitied walls and shattered windows. It was too creepy a place not to use for the *X Marks the Spot* books (the site of the murder in book three, to be exact). Syd and I laughed hysterically about something when we were there; I can't remember what now, only that I made a witty comment and she rewarded me with a bellowing laugh, radiating a bit of her sunlight my way. I always craved and luxuriated in my sister's validation. And when I didn't get it—agony. The memory is like an electrocution, the flash of her crooked smile, and I turn back to face the ocean and plunge under. The water isn't cold because of the Gulf Stream, but it's still a shock as I'm sucked right into a current. Then—bliss. I swim beneath the surface for a very long time, thrashed here and there, at one point pulled into something strong and viselike. When it finally releases me, I gasp for breath and break the surface, a part of me grateful for the oxygen. Another part wishing I hadn't surfaced at all.

When I emerge from the water, I see her again, up the path from the beach, wearing a white sundress, with those braids, those distinctive little braids.

My sister.

———

"Sydney!"

She's wearing those same sunglasses again, heart-shaped, and her face flickers toward me, but then she turns and walks quickly away, farther up the path.

"Sydney!" I scream and tear across the beach. Salt water blurs my vision, and I trip over a basalt rock, diving into the rough sand. When I right myself and scramble forward, I realize I no longer see her. She's gone—whatever I saw is now gone.

I make it to the path, still screaming her name, feeling insane in a way I've felt before at other times in my life. I keel over, crying by now, then crouch low on the path, hugging my arms around my legs. The air is brisk, and I'm shaking, choking with sobs. I consider telling someone what I've been seeing—but who? And more important, what? They'll think I'm certifiable—and maybe they'd be right.

Anyway, how could Syd possibly be alive after all this time? And even if she were, why would she be stalking me from afar, without coming close?

Eventually I calm myself somewhat and stagger back to the lounge chairs, detaching a rope of black seaweed from my hair. I am surprised to see Aiden, who apparently had the same early-morning swimming idea. He's slick with water, toweling off. In his short black swim shorts, I can tell he's even hotter than back when he was our supervisor. No surprise Sydney was so obsessed with him. On his lounge chair sits a copy of *East of Eden*. Which means he's branched off from the Russians; I remember how obsessed he was with Chekhov, quoting him often. Aiden and I were the readers on the trip; everyone else would be playing euchre or singing camp songs or strumming on the guitar Reuben brought, and we'd somehow find a lone spot on the outskirts, taking a beat to ourselves. We used to laugh, because Aiden had highbrow, classic literary taste, skewing Russian, whereas I was devouring *The Selection Series*, dystopian royal romances.

"Hey, Aid." I lower my shaky body down to my lounger, burrow into my towel. "Didn't even see you out there."

"Are you okay? I saw you running up there—"

"Yeah, fine. I thought I lost my earring. Diamonds, you know. On the path, I remember it being loose. But when I got up there, I realized it was in my ear." I rub an earring, trying to smile reassuringly and not like a psychopath.

"You know, it's dangerous to go swimming by yourself in these conditions."

"I like to live on the edge," I joke, but he doesn't laugh. "Anyway, looks like you were swimming too."

"I basically swim for a living. But you're right."

I glance back up toward the path, almost expecting to see her again—but nothing. So I spread out on the lounger for the sunrise, feeling sort of like I'm muddling through a dream, or a nightmare. Aiden reclines too. It's funny—as many times as I've described a sunrise or sunset in my books, all the pinks and oranges and purples in different conglomerations pulled from my memories and imagination, I'd forgotten they can be white like this. A ghost of a sunrise, subsumed by the infamous island fog. I grab my notebook from my bag and scrawl something to remind myself.

"Plotting your next bestseller?" Aiden asks.

"I want to remember that sunrises here can be foggy."

"Oh, yeah. The weather changes on a dime."

"Right." But I'm reminded that for the past ten years, though I've managed to write a series based on the islands, my grasp of them has been theoretical. My research has been fueled by travel books and, more recently, ChatGPT. YouTube videos too. I might have mined my memories for the first book—tried to work through the trauma of that summer in the only way I knew how—but at some point, I couldn't face the memories anymore, the flashes I wasn't even sure were real in the first place. And now I'm questioning my decision to come back here. And wondering what's waiting for me around the bend—Sydney, or an insane asylum.

"You're good?" I ask Aiden, trying to forget what I just saw, or thought I saw. "Like, doing good, I mean? Happy?"

"Oh." He looks surprised by my question. "I'm doing what I love, yeah. Tagging sharks."

"Sounds—"

"Scary?" He smiles.

"No, I was going to say fascinating. The sharks are endangered, right? Or is that the whales?"

His gray eyes spark. "Both. I'm in the water every day. It's— I love it. And I always felt more at home on the Azores than in the US."

I nod, I know this about him. He'd moved from New England to the Azores even before leading our summer trip, having caught the fever from his own experience as a camper. Though he was back and forth for a time because his mom was sick.

"Maybe it's feeling so far from civilization," Aiden says. "Like the whole world can nuke each other, but chances are they'll leave us out of it out here."

"Civilization is overrated." I laugh, though I realize the irony of my saying that when I live in bustling Brooklyn. But I think for me, the emptiness in the Azores would be too confronting. Even though I don't love socializing, and am certainly a homebody, I like the fact that there are people around me in New York. I like sitting in a coffee shop by myself, or with Tomika, and all the chatter and bustle around that distracts me for a little while from myself.

Aiden cocks his head to the side. "And what about you, Liv? Are you happy?"

"Happy enough," I say, trying to sound breezy, though I'm not sure I succeed. The words scrape my throat as I say them. I remember how excited I was ten years ago for the Azores trip, especially because Syd wasn't supposed to come. I booked it ahead of Sydney, but I didn't say so in the documentary. For years she'd said how awful the trip sounded—camping, showering once a week in gas stations. The abomination of hiking clothes. She loved nature, but in small, more glamping-inclined doses. Plus, she was sick. I never thought realistically she'd be allowed to come. I guess I wanted something that was my own. Somewhere I could shine too. Syd was far more bougie than me, but she couldn't stand that I'd be on a trip with her best friend and boyfriend. She couldn't stand being left out of anything.

"I've read your books," Aiden says, surprising me. "You're enormously talented."

"Wow, really? You have?" I'm touched. And honestly, surprised. "My books favor the teen girl demographic."

"I know. But I was curious."

"Curious to see if the Sister Killer incriminated herself?" I'm smiling, but my tone isn't jokey anymore.

He reddens. "No. I mean—"

"It's okay. Join the club, really. Want to ask me where I hid the treasure too? Because randos on the street do, so you should feel free to."

"The treasure?" He frowns. "C'mon, Liv. No one actually thinks you killed your sister for treasure."

"Oh, sure they do. And they have lots more theories where that came from. I'm glad the police weren't consulting with my readers when they opted not to prosecute."

"What are the theories?"

I tick off my fingers. "Treasure. Because Sydney found it and I wanted it. Or else because I was jealous of her. Because she was sick and sucking up all the attention. Because I was crazy, my innate cuckoo-ness needing to be medicated. Oh, or because I wanted Eli. To steal Eli from her, although that theory dissolved when I came out and started dating women. So then maybe it was just pure sisterly jealousy and hate. That's a safe catchall." I try to laugh, but it comes out lackluster.

Aiden doesn't respond, but he lets out a heavy sigh.

"What? Any motive I missed?"

He tents his fingers in thought. "No, I was remembering the coins outside last night."

"Oh. Yeah."

"Do you think someone put them there?"

"Someone, like one of us? Well . . . yeah. Who else would have done it?"

"But why? Why would anyone try to bring up the treasure now? All that is ten years in our rearview. We're back here for Sydney. The treasure stuff, to bring it up, feels . . . sick."

All of it churns in my chest. For a second, I think about

telling him what I saw—or thought I saw—twice now. Can I trust him? I don't know that I can. Aiden purses his lips, and I'm reminded of Aiden and Syd kissing, the night before Survival Day. Right beside a redwood tree by Sete Cidades. Lexa, Jules, and I were heading off to pee in the woods rather than use those gross Porta Potties for the zillionth time when we saw them.

"I don't think you killed her, Liv," Aiden says quietly, and the memory fizzes away from me. "I never thought you were capable of that. It just—it didn't fit. Even though . . ."

"Even though the fact that I don't remember a lot of it is . . . convenient. You can say it. Everyone else has."

"You were on antianxiety medicine."

"Still am."

"Well, that's not a crime, last I checked."

I stare out at the churning ocean, stymied for a response. Finally, I say, "Any second thoughts about agreeing to the documentary?"

"Yeah." He doesn't smile. "A million of them. Especially after the coins. It's feeling creepy. Like someone has a hidden agenda. And I don't like it."

"Yeah, me too." But I notice that neither of us says we're going to back out. I know why I'm not, but I wonder about Aiden's reasons. "Why did you agree to even do it?"

"For Jules," he says simply, arms outstretched, almost like surrendering something to the cosmos. "She needs it. And honestly, for Sydney too. I've always felt she deserves . . . deserved . . . the truth coming out. I'm surprised after this long that we still don't know."

"Even if somehow . . ." I think about how to say what I want to so that I don't scare him. Or reveal that I know things he doesn't think I do. "Even if somehow doing the documentary implicates you in the process?"

"That's a risk. But I've always been a risk-taker, I guess. You don't spend your days swimming with sharks otherwise." He leans back and crosses his arms over his chest. "I think Jules thinks I did it. Killed Sydney," he clarifies.

The waves roar in my ears, matching the quickened beat of my heart. "Really? Why?"

"Because of . . . you know, the fact that Syd and I—well, you know." He stares down at his hands.

"Oh. Your kiss." So he does know that I saw them. Which means he must have heard Sydney and me go at it.

"You heard us fight?" I ask him, feeling ashamed. I wish I could take back how I acted that morning before we split for Survival Day. Screaming *I hate you* at my sister. Her screaming it back. Not even speaking or making eye contact when we parted.

"I think most everyone heard you guys. Look, I'm not proud of my role, but I didn't kill your sister. The police knew that we kissed. I told them. Your father decided not to press charges. I've always felt grateful for that. And if it comes out in the documentary, so be it. Everyone probably knows anyhow, you know. Because of Casey and Roy." He smiles sheepishly.

"Oh. Right, sorry." He's referring to Casey, the girl who dies in book one, and her dalliance with her supervisor, Roy.

"Don't be," Aiden says. "I'm ashamed of it. Incredibly ashamed. It never should have happened. For the record, she kissed *me*, Liv. I never meant for it to happen. I wasn't trying to seduce her. Nothing like that. I was twenty-three. She was sixteen. And she came up to me—she leaned in. By the time I understood what was happening, she'd already . . . I don't know . . . gone in. I know it sounds like an excuse. I was in charge. I should have nicely but firmly pushed her away. But Sydney—"

". . . always got what she wanted."

"Still, it was an abuse of power. I must have—I don't know, given her some reason to try. It was—I was . . ."

I wait for him to finish, but he doesn't.

"What if other things come out?" I finally ask.

"What other things?"

All of a sudden, I'm so tired of all the lies. I almost let it all spill out to him. But what would it accomplish?

"I don't know. But all of us together feels like a bomb about to explode," I finally settle on. It's the truth, at least, even if only part of it.

He relaxes. "Yeah."

"Do you ever think she could still be alive?" I ask him, holding my breath.

To my surprise, he laughs. "Yeah. Honestly, sometimes I do. Or maybe I just hope it." He sounds wistful, sad. "I think about her every day, you know?"

"Do you?" That surprises me.

"Of course. I was in charge, Liv. You can't imagine the guilt. Or—" He stops, like realizing I could. "I couldn't stay in Boston after." He shakes his head. "I mean, I went back for periods for my mom, but I could never stand it. Everyone staring at you, like you're inside a fishbowl."

"I know."

"Oh shit. Obviously, you would. It—well, it changed the course of my whole life. Not to say—how it affected you was so much worse, Liv. Goes without saying. But honestly, sometimes I still feel it's eating me alive."

I nod, can't bring myself to speak.

"God, what I wouldn't give for her to poof, pop up back here. She did like a grand entrance, your sister."

"That she did."

And then we sit there as the wind whips into the beach grasses, and white gulls plunge down toward a tidal pool, and my heart drums in my chest, and I don't say anything more. Not the fact that I know Aiden was transporting cocaine on the island that summer. That I heard him on the phone, coordinating a drop, the week before Sydney disappeared. That I know he doesn't just feel guilty because he was supposed to be in charge but for deeper, more nefarious reasons.

Aiden—brooding but sweet, curls up with books, reliable and stalwart. That Aiden. A drug mule.

It doesn't matter though. I don't think that's why Sydney died, so why ruin Aiden's life too? Plus, the police didn't hold me long; if they had, if I'd gone to trial, probably my self-preservation instincts would have kicked in. I'd have thought twice about keeping what I knew to myself. But I feel similarly to what Aiden just said to me; it didn't fit, him as the murderer. But then who? Ten years is a long time to stew on things. To question your own judgment. *What-ifs* float in nonstop and bait me.

I've only ever told one other person what I think I remember— and that person will never speak a word of it. But with the documentary, I don't know, maybe there are other ways of handling things.

And now maybe Syd's actually alive. Something I've always hoped but suspected deeper down couldn't be true.

It shoots back to me again, like it always does in my nightmares. That page from Sydney's diary. Jules hasn't brought it up yet—Syd's diary. During the days, Sydney shone, always energetic and in the center of things, but at night, in our tent, she'd write in her diary with her flashlight. Or sometimes she'd slip outside, and I could see her flashlight bobbing through the thin tent wall. I knew she was writing, deep into the night. She always kept the diary with her, but I managed to sneak and read it a couple days before she disappeared. Finding her diary changed everything. I can still feel the fury, coiled and seething in my chest. Then more spliced-up memories—memories I'm not sure are even real. Me standing on a cliff above the cove, throwing Syd's diary and watching it tumble into the churning Atlantic.

I stare out at the ocean, and I wonder if Aiden feels it too. That we've all tempted fate by coming back here. After Sydney disappeared, and the police narrowed in on me as the sole suspect, I thought it was all over and I'd have to come fully clean. But then the investigation let up, and no charges were filed, and I slipped into my writing cocoon and finished my book, which doubled as my therapy. And then to my surprise, or maybe to the surprise of no one else given the publicity of Sydney's disappearance, the book easily garnered me an agent and a big publisher and became an instant bestseller.

Still, the past ten years have contained the hardest moments of my life. The things that happened—Sydney's disappearance, Mom committing suicide—you can't come out of them unscathed. I may not look bruised, but my insides tell a different story. The AS—After Sydney—Era, as I've privately thought of it, has been a slow process of trying to trust life again. I wouldn't say life and I are BFFs, but there's some tenuous level of appreciation going on now. But I only got here by protecting myself, crowding out everyone that was toxic, everything that was a memory of the past.

And now my career is cruising, and more important, I've found my soulmate in Tomika. The mere thought of her feels like peace flooding in. Tomika is kind and wonderful and somehow, though she's four years younger than me, she feels wiser, more solid. She's a safe landing place, and finally, I've allowed myself to settle in and land.

We're homebodies. Couch people, we call ourselves. We have this thing where we like to get each other original, limited-edition chips and snacks. Top Ramen Chicken–flavored Pringles. Frank's Red Hot goldfish. Wasabi KitKats. The more random and potentially disgusting, the better. Our favorite thing is then watching one of our shows with said limited-edition junk food, munching together side by side and ranking our favorites. Memories float back, making me surge with longing. Imbuing me with that distinctly Portuguese concept of *saudade*—aching want, desire tinged with melancholia—a word with which perhaps my whole life I've felt a kinship.

A few weeks ago, I found limited edition white chocolate cheesecake M&M's in a bodega and nearly sprinted the block home. Tomika is obsessed with cheesecake, and sure enough she devoured the package, telling me offhand that she didn't need diamonds; a steady supply of white cheesecake M&M's would suffice. Then she flushed and said, really, she didn't need diamonds or M&M's. Just me.

I didn't tell her, but I already have a ring. It's at home. I'm planning to propose after this trip. Tomika wanted to come here with me, but I couldn't bring her into this world. For me and for her, I can't let what happened bleed into my future.

When I was a kid, growing up with Sydney, I thought that to be loved I needed to be more like my sister. Carefree, extroverted, beautiful, popular, straight. But I wasn't like Syd, decidedly not. I was quiet, anxious. I remember when I was seven, I saw something on the news about how older people could die of heart attacks, and so I railed against having to get in the car with our grandfather, because I was scared he'd have a heart attack while driving us. But Sydney didn't back me; she said that was ridiculous, and I was a scaredy-cat, and so we had to drive with my grandfather. Every time I'd stare at him the whole way, planning what I'd do when he started to convulse. That was just me—always thinking ten steps ahead, brain whirling, afraid of the world. But it wasn't me who got sick, in the end; it was Sydney. And even that I envied in a warped way. The attention she got, the care, the fuss.

For the first seventeen years of my life, I wholly existed in relation to my sister. It was only once she was gone that I found—or was forced into—my new world that revolved around me. It's small but it's cozy, and these last ten years, despite everything, I've managed to be happy. To force myself to forget. To focus on only what I want in my awareness. That's the power of being a writer, I suppose—the ability to create my own storyline for the world I choose to live in, even if it's a world that actually omits the truth.

Coming back here was a mistake, I'm starting to suspect. Agreeing to do the documentary too. I should get on the next plane out of here. Back to Tomika, to our sweet, quiet life. If I had any real smarts, that's what I would do—convince myself that my eyes are playing tricks on me, that Sydney is goner than gone, and I need to stop this train while I still can. Before the inevitable crash.

"Your sister was amazing, Liv," Aiden says, snapping me back to the moment, to the waves churning against the rugged cliff and the coarse black basal sand electric beneath my feet. "Special is what I mean. I've been thinking about her a lot lately. Sydney was one of a kind."

"Yes," I say, my heart racing. "She really was."

CHAPTER NINE

Lexa

"THE FILMING LAST night wasn't bad, huh?" Eli spears his fork into a melon slice, his lips quirking in a satisfied smile. With his preppy, rich vibe and the island panorama behind him—complete with striped pool chairs—the scene feels ripe for Slim Aarons to pop in and snap the shot.

"What documentary filming were you at?" I sip on my Americano with almond milk, my omelet a sickening sort of glistening in the sun. My stomach churns, and I push the plate forward.

"What? It was harmless, Lex. It's not like Jules asked intrusive questions."

"Harmless, I'm not so sure. And it's a bit low rent, no? Like the whole production. Only one cameraperson. The lighting sucks. Where were the ring lights at least? Nothing is blurred, you'll see all my pores. I'm gonna look ugly."

Eli laughs. "You couldn't look ugly if you tried. Anyway, not everyone has our . . . I mean, Jules is doing this on spec, right? I'm kinda impressed she hired someone at all."

"I don't know if she hired Maria, probably only gave her a cut in the profits."

"Well, we love Jules. So let's be supportive."

I bristle at that, because I do love Jules, but love has nothing to do with anything right now. "Of course, I'm supportive. That's why I'm doing this whole thing. For her."

"Well, worst case it's a bust, but we helped out a friend. Best case, we find out what happened to Sydney. Right?"

I don't respond and instead stare out into paradise, our island, as Eli called it last night, as if we hold the entire deed. I guess we do, in a way.

A curdle of laughter bleats from the path down to the sea, and my eyes catch on Aiden and Olivia making their way up it, Aiden's laughing at least. As they get closer, I see Liv is smiling, but there's no light in her eyes, like her mind is a million miles away. *A duller* Anne of Green Gables, I wryly think back to Sydney's once less-than-flattering commentary of her sister. But truth is, I have dual memories of Olivia, most from before that summer, when she was a pure, sensitive spirit, always daydreaming and writing in her notebook. Our Azores summer, something changed—her panic attacks, for one. Certainly, much has been written about Liv's patchy memories from the time before and after Sydney disappeared, and whether or not she was faking her memory loss.

One thing was sure: Sydney had the power to bring her sister to the edge. Olivia once screamed at Syd that summer, "I fucking hate you," which shocked me, because if I hadn't heard it myself, I wouldn't have believed gentle Olivia could fling vitriol like that. But then Olivia would transform instantly back into the version of herself I recognized—quiet and smart, kind and perceptive. I remember that summer how patient she was with Cass. Actually, both the sisters were. I frankly thought it was irritating that a child was tagging along for some of our hikes. Like, couldn't Daniella have found a babysitter? But Syd would string Cass flower crowns, and Olivia would tell her fanciful, imagined stories. Even with Cass, the sisters were in an eternal competition.

Still, Syd was far from perfect. But her sister on the other hand? Perfect Olivia is how everyone always thought of her—until that summer.

I think about the coins outside the terrace yesterday, and I wonder.

"See you in a bit." Olivia gives a tentative wave at us, stopping at her suite, which I am reminded again is a stone's throw from ours.

"Yeah, see you." I wave back.

Olivia's teak door shuts behind her.

Eli asks, "How were your dreams last night?"

"Oh. Not great." I remember them in bits and blobs, but nothing concrete—a feeling of shame, then terror. Running past something geometric, tasting something nauseatingly sweet.

"Did you write them down?"

It's what my therapist advised me to do. But I've been having nightmares since I was a kid. I'm used to it, even if lately they've been the worst since Sydney disappeared. It didn't help that right before bed, I received another text from the person inspiring those nightmares.

"Nah. It makes me relive them. I still don't know why that's a good thing."

At Eli's turbulent face, I laugh. "Everyone has bad dreams, E."

"I don't."

"Well, that's the difference between us. It's why we're perfect together. You're running through fields of sunflowers and rainbows—"

"And you're the dark one." But he smiles. "I just hear you, Lex . . . tossing and turning."

"Like last night." My breath catches.

"Like last night."

I woke up in a sweat as if I were thirty years older and in menopause. I took a shower before the sun even broke, and that's how Eli woke to me, in my robe on a chair, staring at the blackness outside. He knew I'd showered because of the night terror, but we didn't talk about it then. I had climbed back into bed and curled up into him and our breathing synced up. He went back to sleep and I lay wrapped around him until the sun finally pierced the blinds and I accepted the day had begun.

Every night before we go to bed, Eli kisses me and says, "Sweet dreams." I find it unspeakably tender, albeit deluded. The first time he said it is when I really fell in love with him. Not Elias da Costa, the son of a billionaire, the popular but reserved guy I knew would look good on my arm. But *Eli*: a man who really saw and cherished me. I've never felt like I deserved a love this big, but god knows I'll fight to the end to keep it.

Eli stands and comes behinds me, begins massaging my shoulders. I immediately tense. "Lex." He laughs. "Come on, relax." His hands knead my neck, and my muscles begin to uncoil. A moan of pleasure bleats out of me. "There you go. Relax. This trip can be fun."

I smile, actually enjoying the feel of my muscles loosening. My eyes flutter closed. "Fun? Not how I'd describe it."

"What would you call it?"

"War. I'd call this trip war. Mmm, there. Yeah, wow. That's good, E."

"War? Come on."

"I mean it. It's like I'm suited up for battle." I feel my head lolling to the side. "God, Eli. Have you been hiding this talent from me all this time? I swear you've never massaged me this good."

"I watched a YouTube video," he admits.

"You did?" My head swivels to take him in. He's serious. "Really? Why?"

"I was going to surprise you for our anniversary."

"We just got married. Our anniversary isn't for another full year."

"Not that anniversary." His eyes meet mine meaningfully. "Our first one. Ten years since—"

"Our first kiss." I close my eyes, remembering. Searching for the sparks of that kiss—the want, the delight. But mostly what surfaces is the relief. That kiss felt like the period at the end of the longest run-on sentence in the history of the written word. The first thing I did when I got home that night was tell my mother. I remember how she broke out the good wine, the one she had saved from her wedding to my father, even though they'd split up. I'd only just turned eighteen; she said I could have a small glass as it was a special occasion. Eli doesn't know we did that, that my mother's reaction to us being together was celebration. But then after we'd toasted, she said that if I was about to embark on this big relationship, I needed to know some truths. And she said that the number one truth she wished to impart was that the strongest bonds are often built on the things we choose not to say. *A relationship, Lex, can survive a hidden truth better than a revealed lie.*

My mother was once a digger, and her prying into my father's secrets—of the female persuasion and gambling kind—set fire to our life. After their marriage fell apart, she wore her regret like a sad perfume. My father's absence in our life took up inordinate space. I started working tons—as a lifeguard, at American Eagle, at the small custom frame store my mother managed. They weren't the romantic kind of high school jobs, though I did enjoy working at the frame store. But I wasn't saving up money for clothes and makeup and a car. I was working to help my mom be able to keep our small house, so I wouldn't have to leave the school district.

My mother's early advice cemented my resolve. After Eli and I got together, I knew that I would do anything and everything to preserve us.

Eli and I don't tell anyone else about our first-kiss-iversary.

Stupid maybe, to celebrate it in any event. And it came in the shadow of Sydney's disappearance. Not even a month after we left the island without her. I'm not proud of that fact, but we were both grieving, and in a firestorm of media attention too. Sometimes loss brings people together. It did for us, with admittedly some steering of it that way on my part. It doesn't matter whether or not I wish I could change our origin story. The aftermath of Sydney disappearing is, for better or worse, how Eli and I sprouted into us. And genuinely, with every cell in my body, I love him.

People thought I gave up Reuben so easily—the media certainly had its fun labeling me a gold digger—but the truth is, Reub and I never fully meshed. We were long-distance except for the summers at camp; Reuben lived most of the year on the island. And it worked for me in a way I didn't much like to parse. I loved the validation of having a boyfriend, showing my friends his pictures and listening to them say how cute he was, but I didn't hate it that we didn't see each other often. I didn't long for him. In hindsight, it's telling.

Reub was the loud DJ, Mr. Front of the Pack, always asking me my favorite songs so he could play them—which was sweet, but I didn't have a favorite song. I barely knew the lyrics to anything, which made me feel hopelessly uncool. He would be dancing, with perfect rhythm, and I'd just be standing there, trying to move my hips in the same seductive way everyone else somehow seemed to know how to move them. Reuben was the life of the party back then, before he got all spiritual and Zen-like, and so was Sydney. I decidedly wasn't, and after hikes, after we'd cooked big dinners, Reub and Sydney would get everyone singing or playing games. We'd chant that childish treasure hunt rhyme, that old Camp Zahav mainstay. *We're going on a treasure hunt, X marks the spot.* Even the guys got into it our Azores summer. Maybe because we were treasure obsessed, and also bored; without our phones, there was a lot more space for play and silliness. But there was also a nostalgia as we repeated those familiar words, switching partners among one another. There was something sensual about the game too—an excuse for my fingers to trail up and down Eli's back, and his on mine, when ordinarily touch between us would be verboten. Sometimes, too, my eyes would meet Eli's across the sparking fire. He was calmer, not so grandiose. I'd always wanted Eli. Even before Sydney set her sights on him. Reuben had always been my second choice.

Would I love Eli without the money, without my access to his family's company? My girlfriends asked it at my bachelorette weekend on one of our drunken nights. I said, of course. And I like to hope it's true. Most of the time, I think it is. But inside I know it's not a fair question, because Eli and the money and my upward career trajectory are all inextricable.

He's still massaging me, and I say, "This is good, good work."

"Only the prequel."

"I thought it would be hard to top last year's present, but apparently I thought wrong." He built me a bench, like an actual bench, with wood from Home Depot. And on it he carved, *Let's Age Backward Together*. Eli loves that stuff; he's always tinkering on projects. And then he got down on one knee with my stunning engagement ring.

"Well, I'm always trying to improve." He chuckles. "And the massage is only the *amuse-bouche*, so don't worry, I'm not giving the whole celebration away. But I know you love massages, so I thought I'd learn."

"That's really sweet," I say, feeling genuinely touched. This is partnership, I'm realizing. Thinking of the other person in everything you do. Putting the entity of your coupledom first, above your individual whims and desires. We've been together for ten years, but it's only now that we're really being tested.

"Well, I love you." He drifts a languid hand down my back,

toward the curve at the top of my butt, and my body feels seismic with want.

"I'd love to." I rake my nails against his forearm, admiring them: painted clear, with silver stars on each one, my fingers adorned with a bevy of clunky silver rings. "But we don't have time now."

"I know, I know." He returns to PG massaging. "Another documentary sesh, and then canyoning. All before the memorial later, and then Furnas. Packed day. But we knew we'd have to cram it all in."

I nod, feeling the knots in my shoulders return. This trip is busy, yes, but the stressful part is beyond the jammed schedule.

"Cass grew up, huh?" I settle on as a new conversation topic. "She's stunning."

"Is she?" Eli asks. "I didn't notice."

"Oh, c'mon. You're married, not dead. You can admit she's supermodel-level gorgeous. And a freaking Olympian." He murmurs some sort of assent and digs his fingers into me with more zeal, clearly not wanting to take my bait. "She seemed into you."

"*Into* me?"

"I don't know . . . a little flirty." I try to sound breezy when I say it. My mother's voice whispers in my ear again. *The harder you push, the farther they drift.*

"You're worried about a twenty-one-year-old girl flirting with me? Reuben's sister? Come on, Lex. You're way more secure than that."

"I'm not worried, I'm just saying." But I am worried, aren't I? Or I was. The way she looked at him last night set me off-kilter. Ever since Sydney died, I've had Eli. I've been sure of us. And this trip of all times, I need that security. He's what I need to know I can rely on.

For the first time, I think my mom is wrong. That secrets

burn through everything good, no matter if anyone has figured them out or not.

"I love you, Lex. Cass is a kid to me, and she holds nothing on you. I'll always think about her tagging along like a little puppy. She's sweet, but she's a child still."

"She's an Olympian."

"So she's a successful child. And I'm a married man." Eli puts his hand in front of my face, the sun glinting off his wedding band. "Conversation over. Okay?"

"Okay."

Eli's fingers move in shockingly effective ways across my trapezius muscles. "Odd though, isn't it—Aiden and Jules?"

I settle. "Mmm?"

"Did you notice they're totally avoiding each other?"

"Are they?" The muscle release has traveled to my head, made all my thoughts blessedly woozy at last. "How can you tell?"

"They were cozy at our wedding, remember?"

"Totally. He was dipping her on the dance floor."

"Aiden is not a dipper."

"Unless he's Drunk Aiden. I've seen Drunk Aiden a time or two." He's visited us a couple times in New York, and he's more philosophical and chatty after a couple whiskeys. "I like Drunk Aiden," I clarify.

"They hooked up. Don't you think?"

"I don't know, E. I wasn't keeping tabs. It was our wedding."

"But—"

"Yeah, I bet they hooked up. Jules has always been in love with him. I wish for her that he felt the same way."

"All you girls were in love with him."

"Not me," I say quietly, and his hands pause, limp on my shoulder blades.

Finally, he does a few half-hearted chops that hark me back to his previously subpar massage skill set. Then he says "Finito" and returns to his chair opposite me, looking off into the distance.

"So Jules and Aiden—wouldn't it be amazing if he got his act together and went for it?" I say, trying to spark my husband back to his previous good cheer. "He couldn't do better than Jules."

Eli's gaze is still unusually stony. I can handle the ebbs and falls of my moods. I know how to pep talk myself up into the will to soldier on and take care of business. But I can't do the same for my husband. I need him sunny and supportive.

"They both seemed . . . I don't know, happy, when they were dancing at our wedding," Eli says. "I guess it's the contrast, why I'm thinking of it now. They were avoiding each other last night. When we walked in, they were the only ones in there, but they were sitting on opposite sides and not speaking. Aid looked up at us like he was a man on a deserted island, and we were bringing him fresh water."

"Weird." But of me and Eli, Eli loves love. He loves other people to be in love. Maybe because his parents aren't in love, and he sees their lack of love as the foundation of all their unhappiness. Whereas I see it differently. Only a rich person thinks love is the missing ingredient. Because my parents had love, and that didn't suffice. I'm aware that money on its own can do a whole damn lot.

"Does Jules seem happy?" Eli asks.

"Honestly, E, how about wondering about my happiness?" I grab a fist full of my hair in my palm and squeeze, relishing the burn.

It's the texts. They're driving me insane.

Immediately I regret my childish outburst. Eli's face falls, and I see the boy I fell in love with. The one who confided things around the campfire, who hung back on hikes with me because I was the slowest. Eli has always tended to the wounded ones. And I was a wounded one back then. I shouldn't be surprised that he's doing it now for Jules. I love Jules, too, of course, dearly, but the documentary—it's far beyond what I feel comfortable with. Especially with . . . everything. Eli's offered Jules money before, but she's always adamantly refused. So he's convinced me that our doing the documentary is a tangible way we can support our friend. That's Eli—the man I fell in love with. One of the reasons why I did, at least.

"I'm sorry. I'm finding this trip stressful, to be honest. And the coins. They're making me rethink whether we should even do the documentary."

"You don't need to worry about it, Lex. It doesn't have any-thing to do with us."

"Of course it does," I say slowly. "Someone is fucking with us."

"Could be a harmless kid who dropped the pieces of some game."

"It's not a harmless kid! It's—"

"Stop. You're spinning out, okay?" He stands like he always does when things get heavy. "I—I'm gonna go relax for a few."

I exhale slowly. "Okay." I know that means he's going in to play Minecraft on his phone.

He gives me a crinkled smile. "Maybe take a walk? You're a little high-strung. Fresh air could be good."

"We're sitting in fresh air," I point out, but not meanly.

"I'll meet you downstairs for the filming. It's going to be a good day, 'kay? I promise it will." He kisses my cheek and drifts inside.

I turn back toward the sea. Black clouds have descended now, hovering so low I could almost reach out and touch them. I forgot that, how the weather turns on a dime here. So many vari-ables to consider. It's hard to know how anything will turn out. I feel my lips flicker with a smile, because Eli promising it's going to be okay is the height of irony. But at least I have money and power stacked on my side this time around.

My eyes flutter closed and I picture the end result. What I want the world to look like after this weekend, when we leave this place. It's called manifesting—the process of bringing your ideal to fruition. Catching your dream life and anchoring it into place. Irony of all ironies, Reuben taught that to me. When he was first dipping his toe into spirituality ten years ago, quoting from his legions of Instagram gurus.

Now I envision that after this weekend, the bloodshed that started when Sydney disappeared and has been dripping for a decade will come to a resounding end.

CHAPTER TEN

Vanished from the Cove

Documentary Transcript

Jules: Let's get right back into it. We left off last time at the treasure, but before we go there, at the head, I want to begin with—no. Wait, starting over. Okay, so . . . Maria reminded me that we haven't covered the biggest pieces of evidence in Sydney's disappearance. I think she's right, we need to start there. First, the fact that an old man living in the area of the cove where Sydney had her Survival Day— Mr. Fortunato Sousa—testified to seeing a trash bag thrown over a cliff. He was talking about the cliff above the cove, a little to the west. He didn't see who threw it, but he did see a girl coming up the path immediately after. He identified Olivia. He—

Olivia: But Mr. Sousa had dementia, really severe dementia. His doctor confirmed it, so honestly, anything the man testified to doesn't hold weight.

Aiden: And didn't he just say he saw a girl roughly Liv's age with long brown hair? That could have feasibly been Lexa—

Lexa: My hair was shorter that summer, to my shoulders.

Aiden: But, like, guys don't notice that.

Reuben: It could have been Jules, too, maybe, in certain lights.

Jules: My hair is pretty flaming red.

Olivia: If we're getting into semantics, my hair is more dirty blond than brown. It was far off from where he was said to be sitting, and he didn't see well either. Look at the optometrist reports.

Lexa: He identified you from pictures, Liv. He said it was you. Sorry, but—also, we hadn't showered in almost a week at that point. Dirty blond hair looks brown when it hasn't been washed in forever. I'm not saying you did it, but . . . just to get the facts straight.

Olivia: He was basically blind! And like I said, advanced dementia. He was spouting off all sorts of crazy stuff, referring to Sydney as "the girl with the treasure." He recognized Sydney, from pictures shown to him, or seemed to, and kept saying that over and over again. "The girl with the treasure."

Lexa: True. That was weird. It's what all the conspiracy theorists and podcast detectives lean on.

Olivia: Well, knowing Sydney, she wasn't going to strictly observe Survival Day, and she must have ventured up from the cove toward the town. Maybe she saw him and they talked—Sydney didn't like being alone, or following rules, so I could see her going up the steps for some entertainment. She must have told him about the treasure hunt. But he literally gave nothing beyond that. He was babbling. Half the things he said didn't make sense. That's why him saying he saw me throw a trash bag over a cliff didn't hold. He was loony tunes. And I was never convicted. It's crazy that I have to keep reminding everyone of that. Maybe Syd's alive still! Maybe she made it out and—I don't know what exactly, but have any of you thought of that?

Aiden: You okay, Liv? This has gotta be—

Olivia: I'm fine. Fine.

Jules: We're only trying to get to the bottom of things, Liv. Not accusing you. I've never truly believed you killed your sister, but there's never been any other strong theory about what happened. I want to know what happened to Sydney as much as you do. Even if—sorry to say—I don't believe she's alive. And this is a piece of the puzzle, whether or not it's relevant in the end.

Olivia: You said two pieces of evidence. So get it over with already, get to the other one. The blood under my fingernails.

Jules: Yes. Sydney's blood.

Olivia: I scratched her shoulder. You all remember. We fought before Survival Day.

Jules: Yes. I saw. You were vicious.

Olivia: We both were. We were sisters. That's how we were with each other. She scratched me plenty of times too. And I didn't shower after. Days of not showering. Sydney must have gone for a swim at the cove, but I was in the meadow. So, yes, I scratched her shoulder and it drew blood, and so I had blood underneath my fingernails. But it wasn't fresh blood. I didn't kill my sister. I don't know how many times I have to say that.

Jules: You said *I fucking hate you* to her.

Olivia: My memories are a little hazy, but I'm sure she said it back! Anyway, those were just things we said. We didn't mean them. I know you're all thinking about my panic attacks. About the medication I was on. But the medication didn't make me violent, that's already been disproven. And yes, I was having a lot of anxiety about Sydney's kidney disease, and about coming out. Our relationship might have been volatile, but that doesn't mean I killed my sister.

Jules: True. But there was blood in the cave. Sydney's blood.

Olivia: Again, that doesn't prove I did anything to her. It doesn't even prove she's dead.

Jules: For the sake of accuracy here, some of your memories from the day Sydney disappeared were called inconsistent by the police.

Olivia: I already admitted to that. My sister disappeared! The stress of finding that out . . . of everything that followed . . . I can't describe it. One of the side effects of my antianxiety medication was blackouts, not remembering key details. So some things I said were inconsistent. Doesn't follow that I must have killed her! And the police respected that too. Otherwise, they would have charged me.

Jules: Okay, let's leave this for now. We'll go further into motives later. I wanna cover everyone's motives in one go. So let's circle back to the treasure. Okay, Liv?

Olivia: Whatever.

Jules: Everyone? Lex?

Lexa: Yeah, fine.

Jules: So we left off at the part how we all went treasure crazy after Eli showed us the letter he found in his great-grandfather's papers. Eli, can you talk about what happened from there?

Eli: Yeah, well, it's what I already said—everyone went nuts over the treasure. It's not like we had this clear clue. It was twelve tribes of Israel. I still don't know what it meant. If it even meant anything. But we didn't have our phones, we had to turn them in at the beginning of the Azores trip. That was part of the deal, living off the land and stuff. But Jules and Aiden had theirs. So they did some Wikipedia digging for us. Like the significance of the number twelve. There are twelve major volcanic craters on the island. That sort of overwhelmed us. We'd be going to some over the course of the trip, but not all. There are also twelve traditional festivals on the island. Right?

Lexa: Yeah. That's right. I forgot that.

Eli: But, like, the Jewish presence has long been gone from the island. Even in my great-grandfather's time—he was one of the last Jews to live here. Sure, some have moved back, like Daniella and Isaac and their family, and Jules is a Jewish islander, but that's pretty rare. There isn't a cohesive Jewish community. The festivals are all Christian ones. So why would some ancestor of mine have pegged the clue to a Christian festival? There are also twelve significant churches on the island. But we ruled that out for the same reason. And the crater connection seemed . . . tenuous.

Olivia: Wasn't there something about completeness too? That in Azorean folklore, twelve represents the hours on a clock. And the months in a year.

Eli: Sounds vaguely familiar. But none of that got us far. We were wandering the island noting every house that had a twelve in its address. We floated that there could be a celestial connection, or an agricultural one, but it all felt like reaching. We even went to look around my old family estate on the island. It's in disrepair now; no one lives in the house, but we still own the property, and my dad had given me the key to the gates, so we spent a couple hours exploring. We even looked inside the mansion.

Lexa: Wow, I'd forgotten that.

Eli: Yeah. Weird. My great-great-grandfather, José, used to live there. It was kind of cool, I remember, to see it. Like a time capsule. But we found nothing we could trace to the number twelve. No treasure.

Reuben: We brought shovels, didn't we? Even dug up a few spots. But it already looked like your family had dug up the garden, doing the same thing we were. Searching for the treasure.

Eli: Yeah. I mean, it's long been family lore that there was treasure still buried. Supposedly our ancestors kept it hidden in case another Inquisition came along, and we needed money to bribe people and escape. So at some point, I think after my great-great-grandfather José died, his son, Vasco, tore apart the grounds. But nada. No treasure, and not when we went looking decades later either. And no twelve anything, nothing to do with the tribes of Israel. We were all kind of bummed, but then Aiden had a new idea. He said that the synagogue on the island had fallen into disrepair. It was the oldest synagogue in the region, dating back to Inquisition times. For Jewish artifacts, that was the spot. And turns out there was a project in Boston with the funds to restore the synagogue, which gave us a way in. We thought that could be the most likely prospect. So we decided to forgo a hike one day and instead we offered to do some volunteering, help them sort through artifacts. Call it . . . *embracing* the Jewish element of the trip.

Jules: You thought your family's treasure could have been hidden in the synagogue?

Eli: Maybe not in the synagogue itself. But we all thought it was a good starting point. Like maybe we'd find a clue there.

Jules: And what happened?

Eli: You know what happened.

Jules: But the audience won't—

Lexa: We got kicked out. That's what happened. I don't really know exactly, but suddenly Olivia and Sydney were screaming at each other.

Jules: Liv, you want to take this?

Olivia: Do I want to take it? No, not particularly. It's not relevant.

Jules: Everything is relevant. That's the whole point of this. Especially if you want to clear your name.

Reuben: Can you stop tapping your foot?

Jules: Who are you talking to?

Reuben: Eli. Don't you all hear it? Stop shaking your foot, man, it's driving me mad.

Eli: I'm not. Chill.

Reuben: You are. Tap tap fucking tap! How does Lexa live with it? I'd jump off a bridge.

Eli: Feel free.

Jules: Okay. Simmer down, everyone. Eli's not trying to annoy you, Reub. And Reub, can you please chill? Great. Let's move on—Liv? Can we go back to your fight with Sydney at the synagogue?

Olivia: I mean, we fought a lot, you've already referenced it. I'm not claiming otherwise. That fight—I think it was because she was flirting with Aiden. She wanted him, and . . . I don't know now why it bothered me so much. But it did. She was doing it in front of Eli's face. She was putting lip gloss on in our tent, with a flashlight! Before we'd go out on one of those early morning hikes. We were using Porta Potties and squatting in a campsite, crisscrossing the island on a shitty school bus, and she's putting on her lip gloss. It wasn't for Eli. No offense.

Jules: I remember that. I didn't realize that's why you were fighting.

Aiden: I didn't either. And for the record, I wasn't flirting with Sydney. We were friends. I was friends with all of you. But I was also your supervisor. I maintained that boundary. Or—I really did try to.

Jules: You pulled her hair, Liv. I do remember that. Her—

Olivia: Braids. Yeah. She always wore those little front braids. I was so mad. I just yanked them. She was so pissed. That's when they kicked us out.

Lexa: Wait, I thought you fought for a different reason. Because . . .

Jules: Why?

Lexa: No. I don't know. Forget it.

Eli: Well, it doesn't matter anyway. The synagogue was a dead end. We never found anything there to connect us to the treasure.

Jules: Okay, let's take a beat, guys. Liv, you okay? Off the record, I mean.

Olivia: I'm fine. Let's keep going and get this over with.

Jules: All right, let's move on to something that might be . . . surprising to most of you. But not all of you. I said before there was one strong avenue of investigation in Sydney's disappearance—which had to do with Liv—but actually, there's another. For this we have to go back long before our trip, to June of 2001, when more than tens of millions of dollars' worth of pure cocaine began washing up on the shores of São Miguel Island.

Aiden: What does this have to do with anything?

Jules: I'll get there. Everyone here knows the story, I'm simply saying it for the sake of the filming.

Aiden: Say cheese for Maria, everyone, you mean. I don't want to do this anymore.

Jules: No need to be rude, Aid. I have a point. And trust me, you're going to want to be here for it. Anyway, as I was saying, fifteen years before we went on our summer trip, over one thousand pounds of pure cocaine started showing up on the island. What happened is that a sailor was navigating a yacht from Venezuela to mainland Spain with all this cocaine. But the crossing was rough, and storms thrashed the boat, damaging his rudder. He realized he wouldn't make it to Spain, so he charted a course toward São Miguel, which is the largest of the nine Azores islands. But he couldn't go directly into harbor. Obviously, he knew that if port authorities checked the yacht, they would discover all the cocaine, which he was ferrying for a gang based in the Balearic Islands. He had to get rid of the drugs temporarily, so he began searching for a place to stash them. He navigated the yacht toward a cave near Pilar da Bretanha, on the northwest tip of the island, not far from the Sete Cidades lakes. Now, the coastline is dotted with secluded grottoes and coves and—

Lexa: Is this going somewhere, Jules? Because we're supposed to be ready for canyoning soon. They're picking us up, and we'll need to finish in time to make the memorial. Today's a pretty tight schedule.

Jules: I'm wrapping it up soon. Ten more minutes, tops. Trust me, you'll want to stick around for it. So, as I was saying, the sailor started offloading the cocaine, which was bound in packages the size of bricks, wrapped in plastic and rubber. He secured it in fishing nets with chains and tied it to an anchor beneath the water. Then he kept on sailing south, intending to return to retrieve the contraband, but what he didn't count on was rough waves and a swell that pounded the inlet, releasing the cocaine from the net. It started to drift to shore. *Everywhere* across the island.

Lexa: They can watch the Netflix series for this. *Tides* something? We're doing a documentary about Sydney. Come on, Jules. That's why we're here. For Sydney. And for you.

Jules: *Turn of a Tide.* I'm almost to the point, Lex, I promise. And this *is* for Sydney. Because of this one event in June of 2001, the entire character of this island changed, and the domino effect continued on even to our summer trip fifteen years later. To Sydney.

Lexa: What are you getting at? I don't understand.

Jules: You will. So many islanders found packages of coke—

men, women, and children. And not all of them reported it to the authorities. The stories have become island lore at this point. That one man was selling so much of it from his car that his seats were coated in white powder. That someone paid a friend ten ounces of cocaine for the mere privilege of borrowing his phone charger. That housewives were battering their chicken cutlets in cocaine, thinking it was flour. The island became hooked. Addicted. Before the yacht arrived, islanders had seen little of the stuff. Cocaine was a drug of the elite. Until it wasn't. I know people—friends of my family—who consumed more than two pounds of coke in a month. People who went into drug-induced comas. The island has never recovered. We have the highest rates of drug addiction in Europe by far. We've become a hub for drug trafficking. And that's where Sydney comes in.

Reuben: I echo Lexie—Lexa. What does Sydney have to do with any of this, Jazz? This feels like a stretch.

Jules: What does this have to do with Sydney? Well, I'll tell you. It has to do with Sydney because Aiden was transporting cocaine that summer. What better cover for drug mule than summer camp supervisor? Maria can confirm it.

Aiden: *Maria?* What the fuck, Jules? *I* was transporting coke? That's ludicrous. Absolutely ludicrous. And defamatory. I could sue you. What are you guys trying to do here?

Jules: Maria, tell him the rest. I'll take the camera.

Maria: I know you were a mule, Aiden. I was only a kid, but I saw you in our house with my father, picking up a package.

Aiden: You saw me? That's convenient. You're much younger than us. How old were you even back then?

Maria: Twelve. And I know what I saw. And by the way, my father died four years ago of an overdose. His heart finally had enough and stopped.

Aiden: This is . . . ludicrous. Absolutely ludicrous. So not only am I being blamed for Sydney's disappearance—which is a vast bridge to leap—but you're blaming me for your father's death too?

Maria: No. I'm not blaming you for that. I'm simply saying, involving yourself in the cocaine trade on the island has consequences. If Sydney could talk, she would tell you that. And when Jules and I put two and two together, we knew we had to figure out a way to get justice.

Olivia: Please, before you invoke my sister's name, how did you even . . . how did you connect this to Sydney? And what do you mean, you put it together? Put *what* together?

Maria: Jules and I met in a film class. We got close in the last few months. We were working on our final project together. Jules had just gone to a wedding . . . now I know it was Eli and Lexa's. And she told me that something started up with her and this guy from her past. She'd always had a crush on him, but it had never amounted to anything. They'd reunited at the wedding, and he was living on Terceira. He wasn't a commitment kind of guy, so she didn't have high hopes, but she cared about him. She showed me a picture.

Olivia: Oh.

Maria: Aiden. I recognized him immediately. Of course, I hadn't known his name. But I remembered him picking up a package. I don't forget a face. I just don't. I don't care that I was a child. I know what I saw.

Aiden: Even if this is true, and I'm not saying it is, what the fuck does this have to do with anything? Is this why you never responded to my texts, Jules? This is why you froze me out? Because of some allegation by this . . . this . . . woman? That isn't even proven true? And what do you mean I'm not a commitment kind of guy?

Jules: Maria, I got this. Look, Aid, I put something together when Maria told me her story. I put together the backpacks.

Aiden: What about backpacks?

Jules: Survival Day. The campers were all in their separate spots, and after we'd dropped them off, you and I went for a beer in town. And then you went to get out your wallet from your backpack, and you realized you had Sydney's instead. That she'd taken yours.

Aiden: You know this. I didn't hide it from you. It took all of . . . an hour? Hour and a half, tops? You know I came right back. What—you think I killed Sydney and then came back? That's preposterous. I needed my backpack, and she needed hers. She had medications in hers. I couldn't not take them back.

Jules: It wasn't the fact that you guys had mistakenly swapped backpacks, it was the look on your face. The abject fear. It always stayed with me, felt kind of off. And your relief when you got back. It didn't track. But I could never place it, until Maria told her story and it clicked. You had cocaine in your backpack to do a drop. I should have reported it to the police, but I didn't want to get you into trouble for something you didn't do. She'd kissed you . . . I knew you'd reported that. But the backpack thing—the fact that you were the last one to possibly see her—that might raise suspicions. And I didn't want that for you. But then I found out about the cocaine, and it's been tearing me up inside. What happened, Aiden? Sydney threatened to turn you in? So you killed her?

Aiden: That's what you think? That's—absurd. You have no proof. Zero, Jules. The police already cleared me. What, you think they're going to take the ten-year-stale word of a child who might have seen me with her father?

Jules: Well, no, they're not. Because Maria already went to them and told them what she saw. And I backed her up. Told them about how much you were on the phone that summer.

Aiden: Arranging things! I was the fucking supervisor. Of course, I was always on the phone. Arranging things for the trip.

Jules: No. This was more than arranging. Talking in whispers. And then with the backpacks. I told them that too.

Aiden: Okay, so where's my arrest warrant then? If you've got it all figured out.

Jules: Look, I admit it, the case is stale. But don't think Superintendent Flores wasn't interested.

Aiden: Got it. So what is this documentary—help the police get the evidence to nail me?

Jules: I'm trying to get justice. And, yeah, maybe it is. And you're not going to lie your way out of it this time. It's not like you don't have a history of stealing.

Aiden: I don't. What are you talking about?

Jules: You told me. How you were arrested for stealing in high school. That you stole many times.

Aiden: Wow, Jules. Wow.

Jules: Am I wrong?

Aiden: I stole books. That's what you're talking about? We didn't have money for them, and I liked to read. So yeah, I did steal books. Once, not many times. And I got caught. The owner called the police. It's not like I'm proud of it.

Jules: It shows a pattern, Aiden. And I'm done ignoring it.

Aiden: So are you all my judge and jury then? Is that what this is?

Jules: Well, I told the police what I know. And Maria has done the same. But . . . they've said it's too tenuous to reopen the investigation over this. Even with the backpacks. They said there's no proof of it. Which . . . I should have reported it back then. They could have taken DNA off the backpacks. Of course, I wish now I had. I don't know why I was protecting you. Frankly, they still think it was Olivia. But they never had the evidence to prosecute her.

Aiden: Well, there you go then. I never asked you to protect me, Jules, and if they had taken DNA, by the way, none of it would have implicated me. You're trying to take me down—I really don't know why—but I don't have to stand here and take it.

Jules: It's not over. Because if you killed Sydney due to your own drug dealing, then I'm hoping someone here knows more information. A detail so the police will stand up and take action. So finally, you'll pay for what you did to Sydney.

Aiden: I didn't kill her. I don't care what you think. I didn't kill her. I don't know what happened to Sydney.

Jules: Anyone? Does any of this spark a memory in any of you?

Aiden: See? Nothing. You had to bring us all here for this bullshit? You know what? I'm done.

Jules: Put your mic back on, Aiden.

Aiden: No. I'm done here. I'm not going to stick around and be slandered and defamed.

Jules: Fine. Go. What about everyone else? Come on, guys, one of you must have seen something. Think back. Who was in the van with Aiden and Sydney during Survival Day drop-offs?

Olivia: I was. We dropped Sydney off at the cove first. I don't remember anything about a backpack mix-up. As far as cocaine . . . I want to solve this as much as anyone, but frankly, that seems off as far as a murder motive. The Aiden I know—even if he got mixed up in that, he wouldn't have killed my sister.

Aiden: Thank you. At least someone here knows me.

Lexa: I don't know about this cocaine thing, either—feels like an allegation out of a soap opera. Aiden—honestly, he was a good supervisor. He cared about us. I know he would never have done something to hurt Sydney. And I also know that if we keep on this train, we're going to be late for canyoning.

Reuben: Really? Do we have to go? I mean, if Eli can stop fucking tapping his foot. Because it feels like this is just getting good.

Aiden: Yeah? Well, enjoy then. Because I'm done here. I'm out.

CHAPTER ELEVEN

Jules

IT'S A SHORT drive inland toward Salto do Cabrito, where Eli and Lexa have planned for us all to go canyoning, rappelling into waterfalls like we did ten years ago. The van Eli hired cruises south, whizzing past the island's trademark blue-lavender pom-pom-puffed hydrangeas that line the roadsides, past the black-and-white dairy cows grazing in the pastures. We're nearing the fumaroles that are all over the island—the calderas that bubble and steam, proving volcanic activity here is still very much alive. I know the plan is a short twenty-minute hike, ending at the spectacular canyon overlooking the calderas from which we will rappel down a series of waterfalls. We canyoned several times ten years ago—teaching the kids all the safety protocols, then rappelling into the waterfalls—and they were a memorable highlight, if that summer is granted highlights. Sydney in particular loved it. I still remember the glee on her beautiful face. Even though she was sick—maybe *because* she was sick—Sydney didn't shy away from taking risks.

After our last canyoning experience, Sydney hugged me and told me that it was the most fun she ever had.

She always said stuff in that vein—this is the *most* fun!; you're the *most* beautiful!; I'm angrier than I've *ever* been; I hate you *so* fucking much. Sydney lived in extremes, and there was something intoxicating about being around that. Being the object of her fervor.

I asked Lexa to sit next to me on the van, to catch up. Frankly, confronting Aiden like that was fucking brutal, and I'm worried I went too far. I said it brightly to Lex, almost chirping, hating myself instantly for still trying to win her shiny friendship, even all these years later. There's been this stilted weirdness between us since she arrived on the island, and I need her—need my friend—more than ever right now. But she seemed almost irritated when I asked her to chat, said she has a thousand work emails to respond to, and can we talk later? She knows—*knows*—what a big deal it would be for me to accuse Aiden, and yet she didn't even acknowledge it. Just said after filming, *Wow, that was a doozy. You sure you know what you're doing with the documentary, J?*

No! No, I don't know what I'm fucking doing. I'm wading through this as blind as you, and there's so much I haven't told you, and was waiting to say in person. I need you. For once, we're not knee-deep in your wedding vendor travails and petty work complaints. For once, I'm the one with the issues, and you're too absorbed in yourself to notice!

No, of course, I didn't say any of that.

Maria plops into the chair beside me, and by her constant eye-flickering over at me, I can tell she's eager to unpack what happened while filming. But I don't feel close enough to her to unload; I've told her I need to zone out. I stare at the hydrangeas, which the farmers use as fences, bordering the pastures. The most beautiful prisons on earth. When the cows get close to the flowers, they smell a strong odor that repels them. So the farmers don't even need to use electric fences; the hydrangeas do the work just fine.

The cows choose their prison, like I chose this island as mine. But no longer.

I still can't believe no one backed me up about Aiden dealing cocaine that summer. After Maria told me about seeing Aiden with her father, it all clicked into place. The backpack exchange—why Aiden had been so desperate to switch them back.

Truth is, I've always tried to see Aiden's goodness. My mother was a therapist, and growing up, I felt like she was dissecting me and everyone else. People couldn't just be accepted as they were, but hung out to dry for their narcissist tendencies. If I had a dollar for every time she called a man avoidantly attached, I'd be a very rich woman. I know I picked it up, this tendency to see people's insecurities and foibles as things ripe to be changed. Especially in myself. Vovó always told me to be gentler with people. Gentler with myself. But I've built up a hard turtle shell. Aiden made it in through my hard exterior—at the beginning of our summer trip—and I regretted it after. It took me years to get over him. To get over something that never even was. Maybe in retrospect I never really did get over him.

I got sucked into the vortex of Aiden again at Lexa and Eli's wedding. And now Aiden's threatened to quit, which is a problem for my documentary, and for justice for Sydney. I knew confronting him in front of everyone, on camera, was a risk, but I decided it to be a worthy one. I counted on others chiming in with suspicions or clues, and Aiden being so caught off guard he'd be forced to admit what he'd done. But it didn't go that way. If I can't prove it was him, this whole thing is going to be for naught—and then what? I'll spiral again, and this time I won't be able to pick myself back up. This time there's no Vovó to sit beside me on the couch and rub my hand. No Vovó to keep me company sometimes while I take a bath, knowing that I like chattering and having someone close. No Vovó to listen to all my worries and insecurities and tell me how strong and lovable and capable I am.

I stare out the window as a buzzard soars by with its beautiful plumage. As a reluctant tour guide, I've learned minutiae about the bird species on the island. And of course, being a local, I know the embarrassing story of our flag. How Portuguese explorers first arrived on these islands and spotted birds they thought to be Azores birds. They named the islands accordingly. But later it turns out that the birds they spotted were kestrels, a different species resembling the Azores birds. But not the same.

I'm right, I tell myself, leaning my cheek against the cool glass and rubbing my arms as the overexuberant air-conditioning teases out my goose bumps. This isn't like the birds. I know I'm right. That Aiden killed Sydney because she found out about him transporting cocaine and threatened to report him to the police. Or maybe she even threw the cocaine into the ocean and Aiden's drug partners came for her. Aiden wasn't gone long enough for it to have been a drawn-out ordeal, but any number of scenarios could have ensued. It can't be a coincidence that Sydney disappeared right after. It all fits, and it's serendipity that my path crossed with Maria's, that she gave me the puzzle piece to slot things into place. It's the only explanation that makes sense, taking into account all the motives and opportunities. I knew in my gut Olivia didn't do it. I never thought her capable of it.

I never thought Aiden capable either.

My breath catches as I realize he's now hovering over me. His sandy hair falls alluringly into one eye, and I remember how my heart fled my chest when I saw him again at the wedding. "Can we talk?" he asks, calmer than I expect.

"No. Not now." I move my forefinger rhythmically over each of the arrows on my bracelet. I ratchet down the window and gulp in the crisp air, heady with the scent of azaleas and the zesty scent of citrus fruits from the nearby orchards.

"Please, Jules. I'm sorry I freaked out, but you caught me off guard. You owe me this conversation. I want to tell you the truth."

"I don't want to talk about this right now. I'm—this is too

much. Maybe I shouldn't have dropped it like a bomb in the documentary, but I was so sure someone else would corroborate." And so angry, but I don't add that. "You win. For now, at least. Okay?"

"I don't want to win. I want to finish the conversation you started in there. Please."

It's what I've wanted these last couple months, even as I avoided his rather lukewarm outreach since the wedding. If I confronted him on what I knew in person, he'd find a way to rationalize it. To convince me not to do the documentary. To convince me of his innocence. And I couldn't fall for it again. Just like I know deep down that now he's not going to give me any truth that matters. He's denied everything. Nothing has changed in half an hour. Or in ten years. Only now the stakes are higher than ever.

"Tell Maria your *truth*. She'll film you for the documentary. Or save it for when we film again later. Honestly, Aiden, I'm spent."

He's looking at me funny, brow furrowed, like trying to piece something together. "This isn't for the documentary! Fuck, Jules. I don't care about the documentary at all. I care about *you*. I care about you believing that I didn't do anything to Sydney. That I'd never hurt her. Or anyone."

"Sir." Our guide, Manuel, taps Aiden's shoulder amid an angry outburst in Portuguese from the driver. "Please sit down. You are distracting the driver."

"You care about *you*," I tell him, feeling the anger taking me over. "You've always cared number one about you. I knew it that summer, when you strung me along, and I know it now. I was stupid. The wedding was a stupid mistake. You don't even know how stupid. Just—go."

"Go," I repeat, even though I don't fully mean it. Deep down I want him to fight—with me—*for* me—which fills me with shame. He probably killed Sydney. I should be trying to put him behind bars, nail him in the documentary. But instead, my eyes linger on his lips, and despite myself, I fall inside the memory of kissing him. The two of us, coming together like a slow summer morning, where every movement is as languid as liquid honey. But it's false, that memory, I remind myself. We humans hate any separation; we're forever grasping for experiences that make us feel less alone. Aiden is my crutch, the thing I justify would make me happy, the longing I turn to when I'm lonely. And I've been so very lonely, ever since my grandmother died. It's no wonder I fell for him at the wedding, fell for his old lines.

I realize I'm emotional—spinning out—perhaps even over-reacting a tad. But I have reason to be.

"Leave it for now, Aiden," Lexa says from behind me. "Go."

And then he does. "*Desculpe*," he mutters to Manuel.

I don't watch him go; my ego is too strong for me to turn around and give him that satisfaction. But I've always had eyes in the back of my head, attuned to his tiniest of movements. For a decade I've been hung up on him; I've never gotten over him. We weren't even ever anything, not any definition that matters. But Aiden's always been good at walking away, and I've always been good at wishing things were different.

———

"Now the east part of the island is the oldest," Manuel says, leading us up a mildly inclined trail engulfed by leafy greenery. I catch a whiff of pleasant lavender, which shoots me back to the wedding weekend in Provence, to Aiden—memories I don't exactly want to let marinate. "Three to four million years old, to be precise. The east is the only part of the island that is an extinct volcano. But the rest of the island is between six hundred and seven hundred thousand years old."

"How old is it right here?" Reuben asks.

"I'm sorry?"

"Like, right in this patch of dirt I'm stepping on. How old do you think this dirt is?"

"Sure," Manuel says, pronouncing it in his thick accent as *showa*, and not at all gleaning Reuben's sarcasm. "Six hundred to seven hundred thousand years." Manuel is short, in the neighborhood of five foot six, with sweet, almost childlike blue eyes, and an earnest, eager demeanor.

"So you can only pinpoint it within a margin of error of a hundred thousand years?"

"For the love of . . . leave the guide alone, Reuben," Lexa mutters.

I swear I see Reuben smile. Like he only wanted to get a rise out of her.

Reuben falls quiet, and the rest of us hike along. I sip from my water, trying to stave off a wave of nausea that's been swelling in me since the car ride. All the tension has pooled in my brow, creating mini earthquakes in my eye sockets.

Manuel is talking about how there are no snakes, and no poisonous animals on the island, how there are no indigenous species—rather all the animals and fauna were imported. Facts I've recited myself to tourists, ad nauseum.

Finally, Eli says, "You know, Manuel, we appreciate all this, but I should have told you all of us met because we spent a summer here ten years ago. Jules and Aiden actually live in the Azores, plus Reuben's from here too. So we don't need the full tour."

"You spent summer here? Ah, this is how you know how to rappel. To do the advanced track."

"Yes, we did it a bunch of times back then."

"Okay, so I lead the way. My colleague has already set up the ropes and harnesses. Everything is waiting for you."

We continue on, past the elephant ear plants with taro root at their base and the camellia japonica trees. I observe them all in my head, like I'm about to dole the descriptions out to earnest tourists. But this time I'm not the guide. This time I'm trying to do something different with my life. Though it seems likely to be a flop.

"I forgot how much it smells like cow here," Olivia says, siding up to me.

"Sulfur too. You'll remember quick."

"That's the thing about writing a book series in a place you only spent a summer in when you were a kid. YouTube videos don't include smells."

"You could have come back here. You could always have stayed with me."

She shakes her head vigorously. "No. I couldn't."

I squeeze her arm, feeling instantly awkward, remembering that Olivia isn't a touchy-feely person. I draw my hand back, and she stares at her skin where my hand was but doesn't react.

"I'm really glad you came back here now," I eventually say. "I'm sorry if the documentary . . . if doing it is painful."

Olivia pulls the lip of her green baseball cap down, covering her eyes. "I needed to face it. For Sydney. But the stuff about Aiden, Jules . . ."

"Yeah?" I feel a surge of hope, that she knows something.

Her eyes dart to the side, like she glimpsed something, and then her shoulders sag. She's just as jumpy as she was that summer. "I truly don't think he killed her. I don't think Aiden could have done that."

"You remember all the calls, though?"

"Yeah. But even if he was some sort of drug mule like you think, it doesn't follow that he'd *kill* Sydney."

A pit of disappointment in my stomach, because if Olivia knew anything she would say it. She wouldn't protect Aiden. This is her chance to finally clear her name. Which means she must know nothing. And maybe that's synonymous for this whole documentary. A sign that it's going to end in a big, fat nothing.

I look up at Liv, and for the first time, I note what it says on her hat. *Favorite Daughter.*

"Your hat . . ."

"What?"

I motion to it, and she takes it off, stares at it. "Oh. Lexa lent it to me earlier. I didn't even notice what it said. Just—I burn, and the sun is strong here." She puts it back on and grimaces. "Well, that's ironic, isn't it?"

I try to laugh. "Yeah."

But she doesn't smile. "Trust me, if anyone is the favorite in my family, it's least of all me."

———

Manuel leads us past the calderas—the large circular depressions that formed in the wake of ancient volcanic eruptions—toward the lip of the canyon. I scramble ahead, past the laurel and juniper trees, toward the summit and all the bolted anchor places we'll use to rappel.

I'm first on the landing. "*Posso escolher o que eu quiser?*" I ask Manuel. *I can take whichever one I want?*

"*Sim.*" *Yes.*

I choose a station at the farthest point of the summit, near a thicket of trees abutting the canyon's edge. Maria's the only one of us who hasn't done this before, and I see Manuel walking her through the setup. She's put her camera away; I told her to get shots of everyone on the hike, and then to join us for the canyoning part, which doesn't lend itself to videoing simultaneously, especially when you're a novice. Plus, on the van ride over, Lexa, Reuben, and Liv all got into a collective venting session about the filming. I could tell that complaining was beginning to bond them, even the unlikely pair of Lexa and Reuben. Everyone needs a break from the cameras—and to be convinced I'm not trying to throw them all under the bus—if I don't want a mutiny on my hands. If I want this documentary made. Which I want, as much as the truth. Maybe even more. That thought digs into a sore place in me. I want justice the most, I remind myself, but I need the documentary to succeed too. I've put everything on the line for it.

Maria wiggles into the wet suit, then Manuel helps her into the harness, ensuring it's properly fitted. They've already fastened the ropes to the anchor points, I notice, which is good. Will hurry along this journey. If we get back with time to spare, and have enough intervening fun and laughs, sans filming, maybe everyone will even be open to an extra documentary session, before the memorial.

The rest of them file up top and begin to put on harnesses and helmets. The anchor points are all bolted into the canyon, so we'll all rappel down side by side into the waterfalls. When we first did this ten years ago, we rappelled the more beginners' way, all going down together on the same rope. But everyone's done it before, so this time we're on our own.

"Jules, can we please talk?"

I register Aiden occupying the station beside mine. I huff out a breath. "Can we try to enjoy the moment? And save your rebuttals for the documentary?"

His forearms tense, and my eyes linger on his tattoos—all of them birds in various stages of flight. My mind cycles in a loop that encompasses only flashes and shadows, his hands and thighs, then mine. Drawing the bedsheets around us—the highest thread count of damask cotton, I presume, courtesy of Lexa and Eli, after all. Him saying that this time he wasn't going to let me go.

"Please, J. Let's talk. Ever since the wedding I've been wanting to talk. And you've been shutting me out."

I cross my hands over my chest, feeling exposed, but no one's looking at us, getting into their own harnesses. "That's an interesting reframe. But please, I don't want to talk about us."

"Fine. Not about us. Not now, at least. You want to talk about the drugs? Okay, so this isn't easy to admit, but everything you said in there earlier about my being a mule that summer—it took me by surprise."

"Took you by surprise," I repeat, acting like I'm checking the ropes as my heart ping-pongs my chest.

"I needed time to process."

"To get your story straight."

"No. But it's something I've certainly buried. Tried to forget. You think I'm proud of it? I'm so ashamed. I was in deep, Jules. It was—that summer, you know what I was going through, with my mom . . ."

"Only what you shared. And that wasn't much. Before the campers came, when we had that week to ourselves planning and setting things up, we got close. *So* close," I say pointedly, so he'll fully catch my drift.

We had agreed it would be too messy to date that summer, or Aiden had decided it, and I'd agreed—because what else could I say? I knew he was going through family stuff, and he was right that being lovey-dovey in front of the campers would be unprofessional, with even more potential to be so if we were to split in the middle of the summer. But all that logic didn't manage to convince my heart. Now, given what I know, I realize I dodged a bullet. But it's still hard to do away with my anger and hurt at how fast he walked away from me, at how he kissed Sydney. Probably also killed her.

"You didn't talk much about your mom," I finally say.

"You knew she was sick. I told you about all the treatments, and fights with the insurance people—"

"With the insurance?" Something in that rings a bell.

"That's why I was on the phone so much," he says quietly. "They don't tell you that when you get your diagnosis. It's all very clinical. You have multiple sclerosis. Not—the treatments will require high deductibles and copayments. It's likely to bankrupt you. No, that's nowhere in the fine print."

His pain oozes to the surface in a way that makes me feel suffocated by my skin. "I didn't know . . ."

He gives me a tiny shrug, comes closer, pulls tighter on one of my harness straps. His proximity, his clean ginger smell, makes me feel lightheaded. "I didn't share. I wasn't good at sharing back then."

I force myself to inch back. "So share now. Tell me if I invented the whole backpack switcheroo. If Maria should have had her eyes checked when she was a kid. Tell me we've both concocted a story that isn't true."

"I can't." He places his palms up and out. Surrender. "I'm sorry I erupted. I was shocked that you brought it up on camera. I really thought—look, it didn't have to do with Sydney's disappearance, so I guess naively I figured I could let it rest. I was angry—"

"*You* were angry. That I told the truth."

"No, listen, J. Listen. You're right. I'm wrong. Okay, can we start there? I'm sorry for everything. You were right about why I switched the backpacks."

My heart beats faster. "And Maria? She was right too?" I think I knew it, from the moment it seemed to click, but I didn't want it to be true. I didn't want Aiden to be a drug dealer and a murderer.

"I got sucked in." He hangs his head. "I'm not proud of it. Look, I'd already moved here, before we staffed the trip. And— I mean, do you want to know exactly how it happened? How I became—"

"A mule? No, my imagination can fill it in. I mean, cocaine is still big business here. I only can't believe you got mixed up in it while you were leading the trip. You were supposed to be the example, Aiden. The example to all of us. Of integrity, of honor, of living off the land. Being proud Jews. I know it's cheesy, all the camp values, but it always meant something to me."

I think about it, how I grew up longing for those summers in America, at Camp Zahav. It was this random, special privilege—and god did I have fun. Those summers were a double-edged sword, though, because I learned there were things beyond simple island life. Maybe in a way those summers did me in, because my dreams ballooned as I witnessed these big, bold American lives. But I drank the Kool-Aid. I lived and breathed camp life and values. You had to, to be selected by the director to lead these trips. So I thought those values mattered to Aiden too.

"They meant something to me, too, Jules."

"Actions trump words. And all I know about you now is that you've repeatedly lied to me."

"About the drugs—I swear I only did a few runs that summer. Enough to make money to cover our debts. My mom needed treatments. You should have seen her. She could barely leave her bed. You know, my dad died when I was young. We didn't have a financial safety net. Her sister was taking care of her for the most part, but kept calling me, saying the money was running out. It all felt heavy on my shoulders. I couldn't—I had to do something."

I swallow a lump in my throat. Aiden's mom died a couple years after that summer. I went to the funeral, and I can still conjure the imprint of our hug. How tightly he gripped onto me.

"We were responsible for people's *lives*. We had five kids' lives in our hands. I know everything with your mom was horrific. I mean, I can't actually imagine. But that doesn't give you an excuse to . . ." All of a sudden, my peripheral vision flares, and I'm reminded that we're not alone. I catch Maria frowning—she knows we're having things out and is upset not to be catching it on camera. But suddenly this is bigger than the documentary. I need to know if Aiden—someone I've really loved, whether he deserves it or not—killed Sydney.

"Did you . . . did you hurt her? I need to know, Aiden. Please be honest with me."

"Did I hurt Sydney?" He shakes his head wildly. "God, no. I swear, Jules. I swear on my mother's life."

"She's gone, though."

"I swear to you on . . . your life then!"

"Um, please don't."

He sighs. "I was trying to think of someone else I care about."

"Me," I say flatly, not believing him.

"Yes, you." His gray eyes pool with emotion. "I didn't hurt Sydney. I didn't. I would never. When I got back, she'd gone for a swim. She was walking in from the sea . . ." He looks past me, at some orchid plants glistening with dew, and his face screws in memory.

"She was toweling off. She looked so—"

"Beautiful."

"*Vulnerable*. She was a kid, Jules. I always thought of her as a kid. And she was sick. We were supposed to protect her. To protect all of them."

Aiden sighs and looks away, clearly tormented, and it dawns on me that I felt protected by him once. We weren't together, but that summer, until it all fell apart, I felt like he had me. A feeling I'd only felt before with my grandmother. It's why since she died this year, I've felt like I was adrift.

Just before she died, Vovó told me that she'd send me someone who'd watch over me and love me like she did. And I asked her if she meant someone like my grandfather loved her. Who did she envision for me? I suddenly needed to know. Because they'd had a loving relationship, though Avô passed away when I was young. And she said that actually she was thinking of someone else. She got a faraway look on her crinkled face. I asked who, and she told me she was thinking about an old man with whom she once sat on a bench. That she felt like he was her guardian angel. She didn't explain more; she died hours later, and she used up her last bit of exertion on that story. We never spoke again, though she left the world holding my hand. So when I went to Lexa and Eli's wedding only a few weeks later, and saw Aiden again, I thought—hoped—it was a sign from my grandmother.

But I should have known better.

When Aiden turns back to me, he swipes at the corner of his eye, and I wonder if he just teared up. "Look, Jules, I knew Sydney was going through it. I mean, sure she had the popular girl energy. The confident, look-at-me thing down. But underneath it all, she was sick. She was struggling. That's why she grabbed me and kissed me, anything to distract her from herself. To make her feel more powerful. That's why I played it off. Didn't report it at the time. I didn't want to add to the kid's troubles. Don't you remember how she'd wander the campgrounds at night, when she was supposed to be sleeping? I caught her a few times, out there when she was supposed to be in her tent, in the middle of the night. She'd have her headlamp on, pacing back and forth. Sometimes writing furiously in her diary. I saw the pages over her shoulder a couple times. Really dark stuff. Like the whole world was on her shoulders. Like she was collapsing under the weight of all of it."

"I remember," I say quietly. "I always wondered if it would have been different, if the police had found her diary. Like, what was she writing? I wish we knew."

"Me too. I beat myself up for it a lot, after. I had her backpack, after all. I could have looked on my way back. I could have helped her. I could have stayed . . ."

"Had she looked in your bag?" I finally ask, steeling myself for the answer. "Did she know she had all the coke?" It's how I've imagined it—Aiden returning for his bag, and Sydney staring at him, with the kilo of coke on the ground.

"Yes. She did. But nothing happened. I apologized profusely

and told her it would never happen again. And she didn't seem overly upset. Even though I'm sure it was upsetting for her. But, look, the second I got there she was walking out of the sea and she told me she knew what was in my backpack."

"So that's it? Cocaine, rinse, repeat. Totally an ordinary interaction?"

"I mean, no, she was taken aback. I understood completely. I put her in a terrible position."

"She said she wouldn't tell."

He coughs, looks away. "She did."

"You didn't fight about it?"

"We—no."

I can tell he's not telling me something, and it pumps me with rage. "Nothing else happened? I find that really hard to believe. Really convenient. She didn't even try to kiss you again?"

"Okay," he relents. "Look, she did. She did tell me she liked me. But I swear, Jules, I told her not mincing words that trying to kiss me—"

"If I recall correctly, it wasn't *trying*. It was actually kissing."

"On her part! The second I got what she was doing I pulled away."

I'm quiet, because that's true, I guess. Even if his reaction was delayed.

"I told her it was not on any level okay."

"Right, because you had all the moral high ground."

He ignores that. "I said that we were camper and supervisor and if I'd led her on at all, she'd misinterpreted. She got it, Jules. The backpack switch—it was clinical. Short and sweet. Later, I replayed it all, every moment of it, trying to see if anything was a clue."

"And was there?"

"No. It—nothing sticks out. I grabbed my pack, she took hers, and I wished her luck, said she could do it. That I was proud of her. Told her not to swim, it wasn't safe all alone. Said I'd see her tomorrow."

"You'd see her tomorrow," I repeat, feeling sick. "You didn't tell the police that part."

"I didn't think what happened at the cove was relevant! And I wanted to get back home to my mom. If I told them, maybe they'd keep me in custody longer, and I needed to get back. Is this why you totally tuned me out after the wedding? It must be. You found out from Maria—put things together—and thought the worst of me?"

I stare at him disbelieving. "I mean . . . don't act like you pursued things."

"What? I did. You got my texts, didn't you?"

"Your texts." My heart clenches, remembering how brief and cold they were. "Yeah, I got them."

"Okay, so I don't get—can we please talk about what happened then? Can we—"

"Everyone into their harnesses and helmets?" Manuel asks, coming over toward us with a chipper vibe. "We'll be on our way shortly. My team has checked that the ropes are secure, but soon we will . . . how do you say, hook up to the descenders." He's totally oblivious to the searing tension he's gusted into.

"Cool," Aiden says distractedly, and I manage a nod.

"Jules," Aiden says. "I wish you knew how much I—"

But his words evaporate into the roar of a plane, flying low.

"What's that?" Manuel tips his head skyward.

Eli bounds over. "Guys, it's a surprise. Come see!"

We follow him toward the canyon's edge, and everyone gathers, all harnessed up, heads craned up. I'm perplexed, watching as the plane overhead begins to draw a big white smoke line in the sky.

"I thought—well, this is in honor of Sydney," Olivia says to us all, not taking her eyes off the sky. "The memorial thing is all my dad. It will be special, but—well, this is my way. When Eli and Lexa sent out the itinerary and canyoning was on it, I told them I wanted to plan this. Sydney loved canyoning maybe the most of anything we did that summer."

"More than singing?" Lexa brushes away—is that a tear? Lexa never cries; she's tough as nails. But I know she loved Sydney. Not just for Syd's social currency, like people have implied. They were true best friends. I remember seeing them once, how Sydney was sobbing that she couldn't sleep, and she hated her life, and how Lexa took her into her arms and whispered *I got you* over and over and over again. Lexa couldn't see me, but I could tell she was crying and holding her friend tight. Suspicion never really fell on Lexa, but when Sydney disappeared, I didn't think it could be her. And I was skeptical of Olivia as the villain. That's why ever since I met Maria and heard her story, it fell into place. Aiden.

But if he actually didn't kill Sydney, then who did?

Olivia's voice yanks me back to the present. "Even more than singing. I think—singing was a performance for Sydney. She got tons of praise for it—and she had an amazing voice—but it wasn't something she did purely for herself. It was wrapped up in our dad, and how much he loved singing with her on the High Holidays. Because she was—well . . . sick—she didn't get to do death-defying stuff. Our mom worried so much. It's a wonder they let her come on this trip. All her doctors had to agree. And Sydney was convincing. And then remember, Jules, they almost didn't give her the clearance to go canyoning."

"That's true." That was the conundrum of the summer, wasn't it? The thing I'm circling around in the documentary. Sydney was sick and weak—but also somehow the strongest one of us all.

"Well, I never saw her so happy. It's because of her we went rappelling three times that summer," Olivia says. "I'll never forget. She was behind me, so I looked down and saw the water and her smile. She was smiling so hard. So this is small, but it's for her."

My eyes flick back toward the sky. An *S* materializes in white smoke, stark against the crystal blue. Then the plane roars and spits out another letter. Letter by letter until at last it spells her name across the whole sky, like something out of a movie, brilliant white puffs, vivid against the blue and all the greenery around. It's like we're on the edge of the world, just us and her.

S-Y-D-N-E-Y.

It takes longer than I expect for the plane to get through all the letters, though again, I've never witnessed such a spectacle. The movies probably speed it up. I can say for certain that few Azoreans have Olivia's apparently sizable discretionary funds to pay for a plane to write out a message that evaporates into thin air.

What a perfect day for it, though. The microclimates here could easily have spat out fog and thrown a wrench in this plan. But there's not even a cloud to mar this utter perfection. It's almost like Syd is up there, orchestrating it herself, with her wide, mischievous smile. Laughing down at our sentimental selves. My heart stutters, and I look next to me to squeeze Olivia's hand, but she's gone.

CHAPTER TWELVE

Reuben

I DON'T WANT to go canyoning with this crew streams on a ticker in my head as I suit up in the harness. I hear shouts of glee from my former fellow campers and counselors, which I tepidly join in on, giving a half-hearted "Woo." I'm more a winery guy, or the lie-on-the-beach at a *White Lotus*–caliber hotel type. Risky, death-defying athleticism has always been my sister's realm. I grew up on the island, but this isn't my turf anymore, and I'm not sure I ever even enjoyed all that outdoorsy stuff. I only did the Azores trip—when I already lived year-round on São Miguel—to get away from that stifling home where I'd otherwise be stir-crazy all summer. It was a free trip, even if I didn't get to leave this claustrophobic island. Now, I've flown the coop, and I'm not quite sure at the moment that I should have agreed to come back. I fled at eighteen for a reason. In fact, a multitude of them.

But I'm used to doing things I don't want to do for a greater purpose.

Still, this trip is sheer torture. I'm counting down the minutes until I can leave. Back to my life in San Francisco, no matter how messy, both literally and metaphorically. Only a few more loose ends to wrap up here . . .

Before we begin our descent, after the whole skywriting

extravaganza, we convene for a quick photo, with Manuel telling us to say "on belay" instead of "cheese." He's already been fawning over Eli, calling him Senhor, asking if he needs a bandage for the minor scrape of his calf from some prickly plant—bowled over by this da Costa in our midst. On the island, the da Costas are akin to God. They own everything, from the diesel plants to the dairy farms, including some of the major national parks, like Terra Nostra with the hot springs, where we're going tonight. Eli shut it down a couple hours earlier than usual for us—the *entire* national park during peak tourism season. That's the da Costa power, and of course, it's not lost on Manuel.

I have to convince my eyes not to roll at this overly enthusiastic guide and his basic island ways. I give a covert glimpse to my vintage Rolex. Then as Manuel insipidly snaps away, I do some quick mental math. Twenty hours until my flight out. The rest of them are staying another day after the memorial, but I'm booking out of here tomorrow morning. No thank you to Eli's offer to comp another night. I committed to the memorial and to filming some of these dumb documentary sessions for Jules's sake. And to . . . taking care of my problem, once and for all. That's it.

Poor Jules. Frankly, she's seemed more unhinged than ever with how she spiraled over Aiden. I mean, was he dealing drugs that summer? Possibly. If only I could tell her what I know. Save her the trouble of going down the wrong route. But I can't, of course. I just need everything to pan out, tick into place, and then I'm outta here and likely never coming back.

After the group pictures, as everyone heads over to get hooked up to the descenders, I go to my station and pull out my phone. I click to my banking app and check. Dopamine surge, then a fast, swift plunge.

No, the money's not there yet. What's the fucking holdup?

What if—no. It will come. It must. Or else . . .

I close my eyes and all of it swims at me, the bills and the threats. I'm so deep at this point the shit's up to my neck. I can practically hear the clink of shot glasses with my so-called techy friends, all of us celebrating, a sea of one-upmanship. This one got promoted to C-suite, and this one cashed out a boatload of equity, and this one's start-up is about to be bought. Cha-ching. Cha-ching. Cha-fucking-ching.

All my life I've felt like I was in a race. But in my teens, we were all in a clump darting past the starting line, and the gun had only just gone off. Now, ten years later, I'm much farther back than I ever imagined I'd be.

Soon I'll be out of here, crowned a winner, I tell myself. I just need that payment to land. I swallow hard, my sweaty palms slipping on the rope as a guy assisting Manuel helps me start off. I begin the climb amid a whoosh of adrenaline. I twist my head and gaze down. Farther down than I thought to the waterfalls. I turn back, trying to steady my heartbeat. I can do this. I've done it before. No sweat. Plus, submerging in the water will be nice at the end. Refreshing. Cleansing. Both much needed right now.

I remember going to Salto do Cabrito with Mom and Cass when we first moved here. Not canyoning, but driving around and taking advantage of the free nature. When Cass got older, she and Mom always had jump contests, which I opted to watch. Off cliffs, into the ocean. Above waterfalls, down, down, down. Probably not the safest thing to do with your child, but ours was not a neurotic, careful mom. More like pushing things to the edge. Risking it all for the gold. Like mother, like daughter. Though they certainly go by it differently.

Twenty more hours. I can survive twenty hours, can't I?

———

I know something is wrong about one-third of the way into the descent, when I look up and notice the rope stretched in a way it shouldn't be. It's frayed, unbelievably hanging by only a few threads. I can tell immediately that the damage isn't merely to the sheath, but to the center too. My heart chills. How wasn't this checked?

I fumble around, managing to wedge my foot in a foothold, gripping onto a groove in the rock above.

"It's coming undone!" I roar and watch in stunned horror as the final threads make a sickening almost anticlimactic snap.

I scream again as the bottom of my rope suddenly drops out, swishing down toward the waterfall fifty feet below. I grip on with all my might, feeling my clammy hands start to slip on the rock face. I hear the plunk of the rope into the water, feeling more scared shitless than ever before in my life. The top section of the rope dangles there, still attached to the bolt above.

"Hold on, Reuben," Manuel is saying in Portuguese from my other side, on the same line as Maria, who opted to go down with him for her first time out. "My colleague is working the ropes from above, and he's going to drop you a new line. Stay calm, and don't move."

"What the fuck? How am I supposed to not move? I'm slipping! I'm going to die! I don't want to die!" Suddenly I am more sure of that than anything. This is not how I'm supposed to go out.

"*Agora, agora,*" Manuel says into his handheld speaker, his voice steady and controlled. *Now, now.*

"I'm losing—I can't—" I feel my face coated in a sheen of sweat, my bottom lip not so much trembling as vibrating.

"Hang on, Reub," Jules calls over, amid a chorus of other voices saying other things I don't register. "Manuel, there's no Prusik, right?"

"What the fuck is a Prusik?" I scream as a stream of sweat slips over my lips. My biceps are quivering, and the rock below my foot feels precarious, then begins to give way. "And where is the line? I need the new line!"

Jules says a Prusik is a type of knot sometimes used for

backup, but it's usually for technical or more challenging descents. This one was supposed to be standard and short. And no, Manuel says. No Prusik. The line is coming.

"Well, is it coming before I die?" I hear myself scream again, a terrifying guttural unceasing sound that now doesn't entail words. I feel like I'm outside my body, watching this primal creature. Begging for my life.

I'm hanging at the edge of the world, on this fucking island. It defies all comprehension. That this is happening. Now. That I'm managing to hang on.

"The line. I need the line!"

"Almost Reuben. Hang on," Manuel says.

Only these sweaty hands of mine. I feel them slipping, no matter how hard I try to stay anchored in place. And what I can report is that it's utterly terrifying to be hanging here all alone. Powerless against gravity. No leverage at all. It doesn't matter how loud I'm screaming, or that the safety rope is apparently on its leisurely way down, or that Jules is trying her futile sidestep over to save me.

Because I begin to fall.

———

I take back anything bad I thought about Manuel.

As I slide down the cliff, the rope slipping out of my grasp, Manuel has already anticipated what I'll need. In what feels like a flash, he's somehow scrambled down below me and now guides me into a new foothold. My heart slaps my chest as he steadies me on the rock face.

"*Você está bem,*" he says, switching to Portuguese. *You're okay.* He secures the new rope to my harness with a carabiner he's finessed out of nowhere and makes sure that it's properly adhered to my descender. Then, with shaky footsteps and Manuel's encouragement, I'm able to climb down the cliff. Finally, a few inches above the water, I unhook myself from the descender on purpose and release into the waterfall.

Everyone else jumps in after me, amid exclamations of relief that I'm okay.

I swim to the far edge of the pool, a strong desire coursing in me to be away from them all. I heft myself up onto a flat black rock, and Manuel does a brisk crawl stroke over.

"You okay?" he asks, propping himself up on my rock, causing me to inch over.

I wipe water from my face, my heart still pounding. "I'm alive."

"That could have ended very differently. That rope . . . I swear to you, we checked everything before. I don't understand how—"

"You saved my life."

He nods grimly. "I did."

"*Obrigado*," I say, still panting, as I watch the group of them gathering in the water beyond. I try to put an invisible energetic force field around me like I learned at one of my retreats, to repel them all from coming over.

One of them tried to kill me. There's zero other explanation for what happened.

"*Vou chamar a policia.*" Manuel reaches for his phone.

"*Deixe-me.*" I sigh, already imagining the energy and tumult all this is going to require. And I'm supposed to be out on the first flight tomorrow morning. I refuse to stay a minute later on this island. Maybe I should see if there's an earlier flight.

I can't believe this happened. I can't quite wrap my head around it.

I ease out my phone from the waterproof bag in my pocket. My mind races as I navigate to the contacts and locate Superintendent Flores.

She's going to be surprised to hear from our crew again.

———

"Well, this isn't what I thought my day had in store for me."

Superintendent Flores stands before us in the restaurant back at the resort, her back to the panorama of ocean. She pauses to glare at a server heading our way carrying a tray of juices clearly meant for another table. The server stops abruptly, her jerky movement sending beet juice sloshing over the side of a glass and the tray. I feel splatters on my skin and appraise the sleeve of my once pristine white tee, now dotted in red marks.

"*Sinto muito,*" she says, indeed looking very sorry. She catches another glare from the superintendent and scurries away, as I ponder the irony that my expensive shirt appears spackled in blood.

Superintendent Flores returns her disapproving gaze to the lot of us. She glances around, her puff of gray hair as parched and in need of conditioner as it was ten years ago. Her disheveled hair doesn't jibe with her stern navy uniform, her stiff jacket with rank markings composed of a variety of stars and bars and matching pressed trousers. She's lithe, with sharp brown eyes, a wide forehead that my mother would unkindly call a fivehead, and supple olive skin that is surprisingly smooth, belying her presumably sixty-some years. She's a wholesome Azorean though; I'm assuming the unlined skin owes to genetics, not Botox. The gray frizzy hair gives her an almost grandmotherly air, like she'd be at home in caftans versus starched polyester. And her accent is typical of São Miguel; like my mother's, also a native, it's softer and more melodious than that of mainland Portugal. But those are where the grandmotherly comparisons end. Because this woman can serve fearsome face.

"I'll say this," she finally says, "your accommodations have certainly upgraded in the past decade."

"That's down to Eli. And Lexa," I say. "None of us are paying for these rooms."

"Yes, the da Costas, I hear. So congratulations are in order. Very generous." She makes a notation on her pad.

I've showered and changed, which is why I'm even more irritated by my dirty shirt. Superintendent Flores met us initially at the scene of the crime, but I walked her through things, everyone was searched, and she left a team of officers to canvass the area. Then she directed us all to go clean up and meet her back at the resort. Including Manuel, who is now sitting at the table with us, everyone in varied degrees of trying to project calm, with frenetic energy beneath.

I was grateful for the time after, to think things through. But from the moment I spotted the frayed rope, I already knew what happened.

This scene reminds me, of course, of ten years ago, when Sydney didn't show up after our Survival Day. Only then, as the superintendent intimated, we were gathered at our campfire, sitting on logs surrounding our propane grill and ceramic cookware. From there she hauled us into the station. I'm not sure if that's where this is leading, but it's my rope that was targeted. So I'm the only one who can't be a suspect. And as soon as I can, I'm hightailing it out of Dodge.

"You," Superintendent Flores says sharply, and I follow the point of her finger to Maria. "You are new. Also Manuel. But him I know. Who are you?"

"*Sim.* Maria Machado, Superintendent; I am working with Jules, on the documentary," she says in Portuguese.

"The documentary? I understood you were all here for a reunion, for the memorial. I wasn't invited. I shall try not to be offended." She says it deadpan, so I don't know if she's being sarcastic or not.

"While they're here, everyone has agreed to participate in a documentary about Sydney's disappearance," Jules says, letting it out in a nervous burst.

"I see," the superintendent says, her face still impassive. "Well, if we determine that Reuben's rope was intentionally severed, I will need to see the footage."

"You—I don't know that I want to share that . . ."

"I shall compel it then. One way or another, you will cooperate. All of you. This will not be like last time."

Last time. The oxygen in the room feels like it needs a top-off.

"Was the rope . . . *severed*?" Eli asks. "That's what you think? That this was intentional?"

"That is how it appears, yes. But our lab will confirm it shortly."

I shake my head, then my shoulders, wishing I could stand up and do one of those full body shakes that looks manic, like I did on the Joe Dispenza retreat when I was flying high on meditation. If only I could return to that ecstatic place. I sift around for a breathing technique. I've learned so many over the years, but all I manage to remember is the stupid, standard box breathing. In, hold, out, hold. This situation definitely calls for something more advanced. I grip the crystal in my pocket that also managed to survive our fall.

"Reuben told me what happened, and of course, I will need to speak to each of you individually. But first I would like to ask about the skywriting. I understand a plane was hired, to draw Sydney's name in the sky. Whose idea was that?"

The superintendent taps her pen against her pad, and I notice a scratch by her wrist. It's scabbed over, but I immediately divine its source. I knew Superintendent Flores even before Sydney disappeared, after all. That's this island, suffocatingly small. She and Mom both volunteered at an animal rescue shelter in Nordeste together. I wonder if Mom still does. If she and Superintendent Flores are in touch.

Interesting. I file the thought away.

"The skywriting was my idea." Olivia flexes her fingers and draws them into fists.

"Was it now? How surprising." There is a distinctly sardonic note to the superintendent's tone.

"Why would it be surprising? That I planned something to honor my sister. Oh right—because you still think I murdered her." Olivia's voice sounds sarcastic, almost hostile. Not the most strategic way to approach the superintendent, in my opinion. But something about Liv seems off. Or else she's just highly triggered, understandably so.

"It would be surprising, or *not*, as the case may be, because what better way for someone trying to cut one of the ropes than plan an elaborate diversion for everyone to be staring at the sky?"

I suck in my breath, and I can feel Jules do the same beside me. I hadn't thought about that. My mind screws back to the airplane spectacle, Sydney's name in the sky. I grapple for any recollections, but all I remember is staring at the sky, feeling very sad. After all, I'm sure no one knows—including Jules— but Sydney and I fought before she disappeared. It was . . . *quite* a fight. Perhaps the worst I've ever had. No, not the worst. That came after. But I can still feel the shock reverberate in my body, the shaky breaths, squeezing my eyes shut and pressing my fist to my mouth so I wouldn't scream. How after we all arrived for our hike, Sydney and I went off to the side, alone. How we squared off, our individual anger and hurt a fire hose on the other. Even though I hated her in that moment, I didn't actually hate her.

I remember before that, sitting next to her on the bus on the way to Sete Cidades, to do our two-day backcountry trek around the area. We didn't intend to sit next to each other. We weren't friends, and she didn't like me and Lexa together. She thought I wasn't good enough for her best friend—*giving try-hard vibes*, I once heard her say about me, which deeply stung. Probably because she was right. I've always tried hard. So, so hard. But back to the bus—Lexa had wound up sitting with Eli; they were playing a card game, their mutual passion. And Sydney and I were last on, so we got stuck together at the front. And the whole time she was scrawling in her notebook, trying to hide the words from me, scowling when she thought I was looking. *I couldn't care less what you're writing,* I told her, and then she finally relaxed a bit and I did stare over.

I wish I could pull off my skin is what she'd written.

I snapped my eyes back, but I never forgot that. Of course, I have my suspicions about what happened to her diary.

"I don't care what you think, but I did not order a skywriter to commemorate my sister because I was trying to use it as a distraction to kill Reuben. What motivation would I even *have* to kill Reuben?" Olivia is trying to play this all off nonchalantly, but I can tell she's worried. That she knows her skywriting gesture doesn't bode well to advocate for her innocence.

"I don't know, but if it turns out the lab shows that the cut was intentional, you can be sure I will figure this out, once and for all. These . . . *manobras obscuras* . . . must come to an end." The superintendent looks to me to translate, and I have to admit, I'm relieved. It's almost like we are in cahoots, the superintendent and me. Because I am above reproach for my own murder attempt.

"You could say shenanigans, I guess," I offer. "But with a sinister connotation."

"Sinister shenanigans." Her lips are set in a hard line. "So no one saw anything. That's your party line?"

I notice Jules hesitate, but then she shakes her head, and everyone else does too. A chorus of no's.

"And who else knew about the plane Olivia hired?" the superintendent asks.

"Lexa and I did." Eli raises a hand, and I stare at him across the room, right smack in the midst of a beam of light striking in from outdoors. He's easeful, reclining back on his chair, legs crossed at the ankles. His white nondesigner sneakers are gleaming, almost taunting me. Like he doesn't need designer sneakers; he's Eli da Costa. His name is more than enough.

"I mean, we had to know everything, Lexa and I, to make sure we stayed on schedule. We've planned this whole itinerary. Paid for it, as you know. We organized around the memorial, of course. That was all on Isaac, Sydney's father. Olivia's father too."

"I know Isaac Azulay," the superintendent says dryly.

"Right. Of course."

In spite of myself, I glance at Lexa, sitting rigidly beside her husband, clearly on edge, and in contrast to her husband's perma-nepo-baby relaxed state. She's inches from me, but I feel like we're separated by continents. For the first time I wonder if it was the treasure that tore us apart—both of us blinded by the money, by the dangling temptation of the finer things in life, which had once been a unifying aspiration. Lexa and I broke up after Sydney disappeared, but if I'm honest with myself, the magic had already fizzled.

"Okay, so a whole lot of nothing is what you all are providing. I'd like to talk to each of you individually." The superintendent nods at a female officer standing in the corner beside a driftwood cabinet, who's been taking notes and probably observing us. "My colleague and I will take you each aside. Reuben, you'll be first."

"I already told you what happened."

"Yes, but we have more questions. If someone targeted you, we will need to figure out why."

I nod, even though I know this whole investigation is a farce. I need to get out of here as soon as possible. Get my head on straight. Figure out next steps.

"We'll be able to have the memorial later, though, won't we?" Olivia asks. "I mean, we'll all be able to go?"

"Unless I charge you with a crime, you're free to do anything. But don't leave the island."

"I'm leaving tomorrow morning." My anxiety builds. "I have to get back to work."

"We'll see," the superintendent says noncommittally.

"But I'm the one who was targeted!"

"This is an active investigation. Don't take this lightly, Reuben. You're not out of danger."

"I'm not taking this lightly. It's why I want to get the fuck out of here."

She ignores that. "After I speak to each of you, you need to be on the lookout. Not only Reuben. All of you. Be safe. Stick together."

"I should stick with these people, even though one of them tried to kill me?"

"There is safety in numbers. And, Reuben, you shouldn't be alone with any of them."

I nod, like I'm taking her seriously, even though I know who did this. I know there's only one person to fear. But they have to fear me too. Even more. They made a huge mistake today by failing at their plan. Showing themselves in the open. Leveling up this whole thing.

And for that, I intend to extract a heavier price.

CHAPTER THIRTEEN

Cass

"I CAN'T BELIEVE it. Someone actually tried to *murder* you?" I lean forward to grip Reuben in a tight hug, and my ice pack slides from my ankle.

"Yep," he says grimly. For someone who was nearly murdered a couple hours ago, my brother looks reassuringly well. He's wearing a terra-cotta T-shirt with slim, rumpled Levis, not even a scratch visible on his arms. He runs a hand through his dark hair peppered by grays. I always tell him I don't notice the grays. In truth, I do notice them. Since my earliest memory I've had a hyperawareness of, well, everything. It's a skill that comes in handy at the level of athleticism at which I compete.

But my brother is still devastatingly handsome. On that, I'm pretty sure all the ladies in his current rotation would agree.

"What are the next steps then? When will they get the results back from the—" My gaze catches on Jacintha, a talented ten-year-old launching into an admirable back handspring on a low practice balance beam. She wobbles a bit on the dismount, then steadies. Jacintha's eyes have been following me all day with an awestruck stare.

"*Bravo!*" I stand to clap, wincing as I put pressure on my left ankle. She sees me and smiles, and I wave her over.

"*Obrigada.*" She beams and walks shyly over to us.

"Keep it up, Jacintha," I say in Portuguese. "You're doing great. But next time make sure you're keeping your hips and shoulders squared to the beam throughout. You turned a bit midflight."

"Okay. Thanks so much, Cass. You're incredible. I watch your tapes from Paris over and over. I want to be just like you when I'm older."

"Well, keep training hard and you can be! You have amazing natural talent. Never let anyone tell you that it's impossible. You only have to put in the hard work. I expect to see you in the Ginásio Clube Português in Lisboa soon, okay?"

"Okay!" She beams, then trots off, and from across the gymnasium a woman I'm assuming is Jacintha's mother waves vigorously. Then she puts her hands together and bows slightly, her lips forming an *obrigada.*

"*Que querida,*" Reuben tells me with an easy smile, when I turn back to him. We speak English to each other and to Mom; we were both born in America, after all. But Portuguese also drips in. I sink back down to the pile of mats by the coaching offices, and I retrieve my ice pack and place it back on my ankle.

"She has a lot of promise. She's really good."

"Not as good as you were at that age. I mean, six years between us, but you came out of the womb already surpassing my athleticism."

I shrug. "You don't know at ten. You don't know how someone's talent will turn out."

"I knew it about yours. I always knew." He smiles and pats my arm. "I'm so proud of you."

"I'm proud of *you.* It's really inspiring to watch you go after your dreams and achieve them. I never want you to think I'm trying to eclipse you, Reub. That just because I'm—"

"An Olympic phenom? Portugal's only ever Olympic gymnastics medalist? And I'm a plebian wannabe trader?" He laughs, but I can tell it cuts. "I'm not jealous of you. I've always been incredibly proud. Like your success is happening to me too. Truly."

I know he's being genuine. I reach over to squeeze his hand. "I know you feel like that. And it really touches me. But you're so talented, Reub. I still remember when I was little and you were already trading bonds. Always on our one computer, so I couldn't ever use it. Should credit my medals to you. I had to find something to do with my free time."

He half smiles, and for not the first time I wonder what's really going on with him. He was more anxious than usual when I was in SF, always jabbing away on his phone, shoulders slumped, then the next moment almost manic, insisting he treat me to this new "it" KHAITE bag that I definitely didn't need. But he got the store to bring out champagne, and he toasted to my achievements. He was so excited about the production of it all, so I let him get the bag for me.

But something was off. *Has* been off. My sister radar is blaring. But I'm not sure now is the time to probe. "You're the best brother, Reub," I finally say, putting a hand on his knee. "You believed in me from the start. Even when I was Jacintha's age . . ."

"Even when our parents sucked, you mean." His bitterness is so raw it takes me momentarily aback. "And we were left to raise ourselves."

"Even then," I say lightly, preferring not to think back to that time at all. "But it all works out."

"It all works out," he echoes, not convincingly.

"Okay, so can we go back to someone trying to kill you? It doesn't feel real. Have you told Mom or Dad?"

"God, no. You think I'm going to them with—no. And please don't you tell them either. I don't want to ruin Sydney's memorial, okay? Everything aside, this has been planned for months. It's the reason I'm even here. And Mom and Isaac aren't going to do anything but cause more problems for me."

"The police superintendent—what's her name—she said the memorial can still—"

"Superintendent Flores. Yeah, it's a go. I mean, she said I should be careful, not be with any of them alone . . ."

"Which is really good advice. This is—weird, Reub. I don't get it. I mean, who would want to kill you? It doesn't make any sense to me."

He looks off mid-distance, toward a preteen working on a kip on the uneven bars. "I'm worried about you, Reub. Maybe— I don't think you should be around all of them now. Why aren't you worried? What am I missing?"

"Superintendent Flores being involved is . . . problematic, don't you think?"

"I mean, if she's going to reopen the investigation into what happened to Sydney, then yeah. I do."

"I know." He sighs and stretches his hands over his head.

"I thought you doing the documentary was bad enough. But this is—sorry, I don't want to minimize what happened to you. I'm just—" I remove the ice pack and stare down at my chalky hands.

"I know, I know. But I had to do the documentary. It would be suspicious if I didn't, and besides, I need to make sure no one knows."

We stare at each other, eyes darting in all the same ways. "No one knows," I finally say. "Only us two."

"And one other person. The person you gave an alibi to. Even though she had none the night Sydney disappeared. Our *fantastic* mother."

"Quiet," I plead, looking around, but no one's paying attention to us. A switch from the gymnasium in Lisbon where I train most of the year. But here, on the island, I've always been able to come and blend in a bit. Sure, I'm something of a celebrity here, but people leave me be.

"No one's listening. And, man, I'm so over hiding what she did. Coming back here is excruciating. I wish I'd stayed away."

"Well, I wish you had, too, given what happened today. When's your flight back?"

"Tomorrow morning. Not soon enough. I hope the superintendent lets me leave."

I grab my towel and mop at the sweat pooled on my forehead. "What's been said in the documentary so far? Give me the scoop."

"Honestly, not a whole lot. I mean, stuff about Aiden."

"What about Aiden?"

"He was apparently dealing coke that summer. And his backpack might have gotten mixed up with Sydney's. Jules is convinced he offed her."

"Shut up." I take that surprising information in.

"But we know that he didn't."

"Yeah." I sigh. "You didn't talk about—I mean, I'm sure you didn't, but—"

"No. Obviously not. But—" He pauses in a way that makes my heart still.

"But what?"

"No. Nothing." He bites his lip. "Fine, I've decided to tell Liv. Seeing her back here—she deserves to know. I still don't know why he's kept it from her all this time."

"No." My chest jolts. "You can't! You can't tell Liv. No, Reub. Abort mission. That's a horrible idea."

"Is it, though? Is it really?"

"It is."

He buries his head in his hands. "It's all so complicated, Cassie. Such a twisted mess. I'm tired of covering for her. For both of them."

"I know." I rub his knee. "Trust me, I know. We both grew up with Mom, but you got to get out."

"I have to tell Liv, Cassie."

I take that in quietly. He's serious. He's really going to do it. "Give it the day to think about," I finally say. "Don't be hasty."

"Fine," he relents. "But I'm not going to change my mind. Don't worry. It'll be fine. Whatever fallout there is. You're not here most of the time either. Plus, at least you got a brand-new daddy in the equation." He says the last part oozing sarcasm. But also pain, I know. Maybe some envy on top.

"Honestly, I know it doesn't make sense, but he was the best part of the equation."

"I can't believe you call him Dad. It kills me." He winces at the euphemism.

"I know. I know it does." There's nothing else I can say. I always wanted a real father, and I finally got one, present and attentive, all the time. I can't apologize for it. Even though I totally understand why Reuben left the island after Sydney disappeared and basically never looked back.

Reuben rubs his eyes. "I'm so dead. I mean, tired. Shit." He smiles sheepishly. "I'm manifesting funky stuff right now."

"Please stop manifesting your death. Don't even joke about it. It's not funny. Especially today of all days. I mean, it's Sydney's memorial."

"You're right. Sorry. I'm not going to die. Don't worry. Cass, stop." He laughs. "Really, I'm fine. I'll be fine. You're not getting rid of me."

"I better not be." But I feel myself relax. "Must be weird seeing Lexa again?" I finally ask.

"Weird? Yeah. *Weird*'s one word for it."

I decide not to press.

"And what about Eli?" I inhale sharply and immediately regret asking.

Reuben cocks his head at me. "What about him? Same old rich entitled asshole."

"All right." I force a smile. "I should go change before the memorial. What are you wearing?"

He looks down. "This."

"Shut up. You brought something to change into, didn't you?"

He smiles, then indicates a duffel off to the side. "Yeah. A suit. Mom will say I look like a movie star, guaranteed. But listen, before the memorial, we're doing an hour filming for the documentary." He checks his watch. "Actually, I should go. Jules rented out a room at A Tasca." That's the best family-style restaurant in PD, with traditional Azorean dishes, not far from the synagogue.

"You're not actually telling me you're still gonna do the documentary now?"

But Reuben's jaw squares. "Clearly one of them tried to kill me. And so I'm not bowing out. There are more secrets they're all still hiding . . ."

"Some of which involve our family," I remind him.

"Yeah, but I'm not giving up . . . well, you know what. Don't worry. But I need to be there. Trust me. I need to be able to manage how this goes."

I shrug. "Fine. So I'll meet you at the memorial. And then, after, you guys are going to Furnas, right?"

He looks surprised. "Yeah. How'd you know?"

"Aiden and Eli, actually," I say, trying to be casual about it. "They invited me. I said I'd come. I mean, you're in town, and now more than ever I think you could use a bodyguard."

He laughs. "You're my bodyguard, eh?"

I flex my bicep. "People would pay big money for these guns."

He smiles, but it quickly fades. "Cass, you're not, like—"

"What?"

"I don't know, I remember that summer. Don't kill me, but you definitely had a little crush on Eli."

"Please! You can't be serious, Reub. I was eleven." But my heart is racing now, and I can feel my cheeks heating up. Of course I had a crush on Eli. If I'm honest with myself, I still do. It's not the da Costa name, I could care less about that. It's him—sweet, caring, kind Eli. He's always made me feel valuable. Important. Maybe that's crazy, because I only knew him as a child really. Our sole interaction as an adult was last night. But I felt that same startling feeling, like he could see into me and like me even for my faults. He just feels like that kind of person. I shake my head, not wanting to entertain it within myself. He has a wife. I have no chance. Except—

"You were a kid." Reuben smiles, which makes me relax. "It was harmless, I know." His smile fades. "I'm only wondering if—"

"He's *married*, Reub. Even if I had a crush, which I don't, I'm not Mom."

"I know you're not Mom. I'd never say that. But still, you can have anyone you want, Cass. The sky is the limit. But Eli—I don't want you to get hurt. I only want—"

"You only want to look out for your little sister." I pat his hand, and suddenly my mind is filled with an image of me on the beam, perfectly executing the front handspring front tuck with a full twist named after Henrietta Ónodi. It's a mental visualization exercise I do with my coaches, and I can see myself in full Technicolor, sticking it to thunderous applause.

"Look, Reub, you can relax, I'm not coming to Furnas for Eli. The reason I don't have a boyfriend now is by choice. Gymnastics needs all of my focus. Los Angeles is only two years away. After the next Olympics, I can think about love."

"You don't have to get married. I just want you to have some fun."

"I *do* have fun. I love my life. I love gymnastics." I don't tell him how gymnastics *is* my love. It fills all the voids. Or it has, for the most part, until now. "And trust me, I have plenty of hot, eligible men lining up to date me, in case you were thinking I'm desperate."

"You? Desperate? Never." But he says it without verve.

"You okay, Reub?"

"You mean besides the attempted murder thing? Yeah, peachy."

"Yeah?" I scrutinize him, then finally ask. "Business stuff going well?"

"Really well," he says, but the way he says it, I suddenly know.

"You need money? Because if you ever do, say the word. Okay?"

"I'm fine. Plus, I'd never take money from you."

"I have way more of it than I could ever use."

"Still." He smiles, but I know it's forced. "I'm totally fine."

"What aren't you telling me?"

"Look, maybe I'm having a few business snafus, but nothing I can't work out on my own, all right? Plus, I'm in for a big payday soon. Once that comes through, I'll be golden."

"But if you need—"

"I don't. Please drop it."

"Okay." Now I'm really worried. "Look, after Furnas, you'll come back to the house? Maybe it's not a good idea to sleep at the hotel tonight, with someone who tried to—I still don't get it." I shake my head, because none of it makes sense. "Reub, is there something you're not telling me?"

He looks off toward the vault and the wall of windows that let in only a smidge of sunlight and probably haven't been cleaned since that summer Sydney disappeared.

"You know who cut the rope?" I probe.

"I know who cut the rope," he finally says, letting out a huge breath. "And I can't tell Superintendent Flores. I can't tell anyone."

"I don't—okay then, please tell me. If you tell me, I can help you."

He looks at me, teary-eyed. "Me and you against the world?"

"Always."

"Okay. Fuck." He brings his wrists up over his forehead, covering his eyes. Like if he doesn't see out, I won't be able to see in. "Don't hate me. Please—I don't want you to hate me."

"I could never."

"I want you to still respect me, though." He sounds desolate.

"I always respect you. That won't ever change."

He drops his hands, a circle mark on his forehead from where his Rolex dug in. "Fine. It's big, Cass. Honestly—I . . . I've gotten in way too deep."

"Reub, you're scaring me."

"I don't know what—fuck it. I'm gonna tell you everything."

CHAPTER FOURTEEN

Vanished from the Cove

Documentary Transcript

Jules: All right, so I don't exactly know how to start us off but—

Reuben: What, no script for the scenario when someone tries to off me?

Jules: No. None. Look, we've all sort of talked among ourselves about whether to film again now, and I know some of you wanted to stop, but I really appreciate that you all showed up. It seems like something in the documentary has struck a nerve, and maybe we're getting close—

Aiden: If you're talking about me—if you're implying that I tried to kill Reuben—I'm going to walk out the door so fast.

Jules: I'm not. Really. I don't have an agenda here.

Aiden: You did. You came in very hot earlier.

Jules: Look, you and I have agreed you'll film about the cocaine stuff separately. Right? I mean, you've told me, you've explained to all of us off camera, that you were transporting cocaine for money to help your sick mom. And that while you did inadvertently take Sydney's backpack, when you went back to switch it, she said she'd seen the cocaine but wouldn't tell anyone. You left her alive in the cove.

Aiden: I definitely did. And I didn't cut Reuben's rope.

Jules: So we'll cover all this soon, in a separate filming session. Maria—I'll have to insert some sort of monologue here, explaining what is happening in real time. Otherwise, it's going to get confusing.

Lexa: Look, Jules, I'm not trying to pinpoint you, but I have to raise something that's occurred to me. If someone actually did try to kill Reuben, who does that benefit more than you? More than this documentary?

Jules: That's ludicrous. I don't know what you're implying. I definitely didn't try to kill Reuben. Besides—

Olivia: Besides, I'm the one who set up the skywriting? So once again, all fingers point at me. No. I can't take it anymore. And by the way, I think we should all be mindful that . . . well, mindful that Superintendent Flores is going to . . . what's it called? Subpoena these transcripts.

Reuben: But if we have nothing to hide, it's not a problem. Whoever tried to kill me . . . whoever did . . . *whatever* . . . to Sydney . . . that's the only person who will be hiding anything. Maybe that'll help us sniff that person out. Right?

Jules: Look, this documentary is meant to get to the heart of what happened to Sydney. Right now, I don't want to add this extra layer, if someone actually did try to kill Reuben.

Reuben: Someone definitely did try to kill me.

Jules: Okay, but you're keeping your wits about you, Reub, and there's safety in numbers. We have the memorial shortly, and we don't want all this to eclipse why we're really here. For Sydney. If they're connected, then solving what happened to Sydney will also solve what happened to Reub. So can we go back to talking about that summer? Maybe we're actually unlocking something here. We can all get behind that, right? That's our common goal here. Okay?

Olivia: Okay.

Aiden: Fine.

Reuben: I think I'll clear the energy first. Otherwise, I can't stay. It feels like the air is, I don't know, toxic . . . heavy . . .

Lexa: Heavy? Heavy with what?

Reuben: Deceit. And lies dressed up like loyalty.

Aiden: Wait, you're not serious—you brought—is that incense?

Reuben: Palo santo. Never know when it'll come in handy. I need extra with this group.

Lexa: Jesus, Reub. Can you do your palo-whatever away from me? I'm allergic.

Reuben: Allergic to me.

Lexa: That too.

Jules: Okay, great, great. Now that we're good and palo santo-ed, let's move on. With any crime there are the elements of motive, opportunity, and means. Bottom line is we all had opportunity. Everyone was alone for twenty-four hours, but close enough together that any of us could have accessed Sydney in her spot in the cove. Aiden and I were mostly together, which gives us some alibi, but at certain times in the day, we did our own thing. Aiden went off up on a cliff to read his book, and I used the day to catch up on rest and, honestly, scroll Instagram. In terms of means, if Sydney was murdered, then there are any number of ways it could have happened. I don't want to speculate. So I think the most useful thing to talk about now is motive. We've covered Aiden—I don't see any need to rehash it.

Aiden: Great. Wonderful.

Jules: I want to admit point-blank—wait, strike that. I want to admit that we all could have motives imputed to us to kill Sydney, even if they're tenuous.

Olivia: Oh, really? I mean, I agree with you, actually, but I'm curious what you'd say for yours, Jules?

Jules: Okay, you want to start with me? Sure. That's fine. In doing this documentary, I've committed to being an open book. I'll tell the whole, complete truth. First of all, I was into Aiden that summer. We had something between us before the campers arrived. I'll be explicit: We slept together. Honestly, I was in love with him. That's not a secret, is it?

Olivia: No. We all knew that.

Aiden: It's news to me, actually. It's definitely news to me. What—you love me?

Jules: *Loved.* A long time ago. So don't get an inflated ego or something now.

Aiden: I can't . . . I don't think . . . that summer is kind of blurry to me, really.

Lexa: Well, you were always off in your own world. I mean, I love ya, Aiden, but you were. And the drug stuff, it tracks . . .

Aiden: I was preoccupied.

Jules: Sure. Go with that. Anyway, back to my motive. Sydney had a crush on Aiden. It was totally obvious, and Aiden flirted back in his mysterious, dry way.

Aiden: It must have been so dry I didn't even know I was doing it. Because swear to God, flirting with a camper was not anything I remotely intended.

Olivia: We saw you kiss her, Aiden. I saw you, and so did Jules and Lexa.

Jules: Look, even though I went hard on him earlier, I'd like to spare Aiden being the center of this session. He's already admitted to things that speak to his possible motives. But the fact that all three of us saw Sydney kissing Aiden goes to mine. I could be love-crazed, wanting to get rid of Sydney because I perceived her as a threat.

Lexa: I don't think any of us believe that's a legitimate thing that might have happened. I don't buy that you killed Sydney. It's not like you and Aiden were together after that summer.

Jules: No, but my plan could have backfired on me.

Eli: You're making me laugh, Jules. This is sort of outlandish.

Jules: I'm honestly trying to be objective. I want the same spotlight on me as I'm putting on all of you. I deeply, genuinely want justice for Sydney. Whoever did something to her is still out there, maybe even targeting Reuben now.

Reuben: Indisputably targeting me. By the way, on my way over, Superintendent Flores called and confirmed that the rope didn't fray by ordinary wear and tear. It was cut. By a common pocketknife, they suspect. But they searched all of us and found nothing. Someone must have disposed of it.

Jules: Now it's even more imperative that we get to the bottom of things. And granted that I had a motive to kill Sydney, but so did Lexa. And Olivia.

Lexa: Let's get this over with. Do me first.

Reuben: That's what she said.

Lexa: Shut up, Reuben. That's seriously gross.

Jules: Agreed. Gross. Maria—

Maria: I'll cut that.

Jules: So Lexa's motive—to address this we have to go way back to something Sydney told me on the trip. We were all hiking, on one of the Sete Cidades days. I distinctly remember we were hiking around the green volcanic lake, not the blue one, and there were kayakers, and Sydney had fallen behind. I think she wasn't feeling great. Aiden was up front that day, and I was bringing up the rear, and Syd and I talked for a really long time. I said she and Eli were cute together. I think I called them Barbie and Ken. And she confided in me that Lexa had actually liked Eli first. That Lexa had always had a crush on Eli. And I said to Syd something like, *So you wanted to have him?* And Sydney just nodded and said, *I'm really fucked-up.*

Lexa: God, that's messed up, to have it, like, confirmed. I mean, sure, I had always liked Eli. But I was embarrassed by my crush. I didn't think I could ever get a guy like him.

Reuben: So you settled for second place.

Lexa: That wasn't—you and I were a separate matter. My crush on Eli, that goes much farther back. I didn't even tell Syd, my best friend. But I always sort of suspected she knew. I never wanted to think she'd deliberately gone after him. Plus, everyone wanted Eli. I wasn't surprised when he chose Sydney.

Eli: I didn't *choose* Sydney. We were in middle school. It got back to me that she liked me, and so my friend said I should ask her out to the movies, and then I did. And then suddenly I was in a full-blown relationship with her that lasted years.

Jules: You got swept up.

Eli: I liked her, of course I did. But I've never been good at endings. We'd run our course. Frankly, if it wasn't for her being sick, I probably would have ended it already.

Lexa: You're not suggesting I killed Sydney because I was in love with Eli?

Jules: I mean, it's possible. Sorry, Lex. Just doing my job here. Maria, we'll cut that, okay? Sorry, Lex.

Lexa: You said that already.

Jules: Well, fact is, Syd disappeared, and you got the guy.

Reuben: And what am I, the chopped liver of this equation?

Jules: Well . . . I guess, yeah. No offense.

Reuben: That's nice. Because I loved Lexa. For the record.

Jules: Sorry, Reub. Really, I am. But if we're gonna finish this before the memorial, I want to close Lexa's motive by saying she also saw Sydney kiss Aiden. So she could have gone to Sydney and threatened to use that as leverage against her. Threatened to make her break up with Eli. And when she refused . . .

Lexa: And when she refused, I killed her? Is that how you're suggesting it happened?

Jules: Only speculating. And by the way, this all segues into Eli's potential motive.

Eli: Oh, *I* have a motive now? You can't be serious. I didn't hurt Sydney. I did nothing to her! She was my girlfriend.

Jules: You loved her, E. And she was kissing Aiden.

Eli: I didn't *know* she kissed Aiden. Not until much later.

Jules: Well, that's what you claim. But you could have known.

Eli: How?

Jules: You could have seen, or Lexa could have told you, or even Olivia or I could have. Although I don't remember telling you. But the info could have gotten to you any number of ways.

Eli: And so, what? I decided if I couldn't have her, no one could? You can't be serious. I already said that if I hadn't been a chicken and felt sorry for her, I probably would have broken up with her before that summer.

Lexa: I mean, really, this is sort of crazy, Jules. I love my husband, but he cries at *Bambi*. You think he murdered his girlfriend in cold blood?

Jules: I'm putting it all out there. That's what this is for, right? To get to the truth. It's all been piecemeal until now. Now, we're threading it together. All right, onward to Reuben.

Reuben: I'm sorry, but of everyone here, I'll point out the obvious. I had zero motive. Sydney barely gave me the time of day. I wasn't named Eli or Aiden. Wasn't rich enough or old enough for her. Sorry not sorry. She didn't deserve whatever happ—I mean, I didn't want *her* dead but—

Olivia: You guys fought.

Reuben: Huh?

Jules: You did. Right before she disappeared, maybe a week before, max. It was on the bus. You'd been looking in the back in her things—

Lexa: I remember it too. You weren't yelling at each other, but there was a lot of tension. She was furious, and you were furious too. You were with the duffels. Remember how the back half of the seats in the bus were taken out and it was a sea of duffels? We'd play euchre back there.

Jules: Yes, I saw Reuben looking through Sydney's duffel.

Lexa: I didn't see that, but I remember the commotion. You were both staring at each other in this really weird way. And then Syd ran to the front of the bus and burst into tears and wouldn't tell me what it was about.

Eli: That sounds vaguely familiar to me too.

Lexa: She wore her sunglasses the rest of the day, even on the bus. I asked you, Reub, but you played it off. But I could tell something had happened. Just, neither of you wanted to talk about it.

Olivia: I remember that. Syd was in such a bad mood near the en—before she disappeared. She wouldn't talk to me. Not that she would have confided in me, I guess.

Lexa: No, I know what you're talking about. It's not like Syd and I were on the best of terms then either, but she was almost . . . paralyzed. I could tell something was up.

Jules: Reuben, care to share?

Reuben: Honestly, I have no clue what you are all remembering. What a plot twist, I didn't realize I was auditioning for scapegoat today! I have zero memory of anything like that, and I certainly wasn't responsible for Sydney being in any sort of emotional state before Survival Day, if that's what you're implying. Sydney and I barely interacted. Probably I messed up one of her lip glosses or spilled Gatorade on her favorite shirt. Or I know—I'd get pissed that she'd pick out all the M&M's in the GORP. Was that it?

Eli: Wow, GORP. I'd forgotten all about that stuff. It tasted so good after—

Reuben: It was really fucking annoying that she'd pick out all the M&M's. Like, after she'd do that, it was all raisins and peanuts left. So maybe I was stealing some back from her bag. It would be pure Sydney to make that into a criminal infraction.

Olivia: No. I remember the M&M thing, but I know what Jules is talking about and that wasn't the vibe of it. There was a different fight you guys got in—something bigger, now that I think back about it, like—

Maria: Sorry to interrupt, but a heads-up on time. You guys have to be out of here in five minutes to walk over to the memorial. So, Jules, time to start wrapping up.

Jules: Okay, I think that's enough on Reuben's motive.

Reuben: Reuben's motive. Sure. Reuben's smear job. Whatever. I can't believe I agreed to participate in this crap.

Jules: Chill, Reub. Everyone's going through the wringer, even me as you saw. And I want to point out a side note, which is that we haven't even gotten into whether the treasure factored into motive. Because if Sydney happened to find it, and someone knew, maybe they took it from her. Maybe that's what happened. Somehow, I always felt like the treasure played into things.

Aiden: Based on what?

Jules: I don't know . . . call it intuition? I realize that's not anything to hang our hat on, so let's move on to . . . Olivia is left? Yeah, let's finish up with Olivia.

Olivia: Okay. Sure. Have at me. Again. But I can't imagine what new things you're going to unearth that haven't been written about in every major newspaper in the world.

Jules: Well, there is something, in fact, that I want to bring up. And it's slightly . . . *difficult*, but I hope we can all be adults about things.

Reuben: Well, I don't know about you guys but I still plug my nose when I take cough syrup.

Jules: What I meant is—most of us want to get to the bottom of things. Right?

Olivia: Most of us?

Jules: Everyone but the killer, of course. And we know that person must be among us because . . . someone tried to kill Reuben.

Reuben: Exactly. So the whole investigation in this so-called documentary turning toward me—all your fucking suspicion—is ridiculous. Because someone targeted me, and obviously I didn't cut my own rope. Right? Right?

Jules: I *hope* you didn't cut your own rope.

Reuben: Obviously I didn't! And for you to even suggest . . .

this is the last time I'm filming for this documentary, Jazz, if that's where you want to go. I'm so over this.

Jules: Fine. That's your prerogative. Like I said, I'm not letting up on anyone, including myself. I'm determined to get to the truth, and if anyone wants to leave, there's the door. I'm not holding you hostage here. I'm assuming everyone innocent wants to get to the bottom of things. So onward to Olivia. We've lightly touched on your fight with Sydney already, Liv, but—

Olivia: Fight? How about put an *s* on the end? I've never hidden the fact that we fought a lot. That we didn't always like each other.

Jules: Your fight in the synagogue. Near the beginning of the summer. You didn't say what it was about.

Olivia: Honestly, I don't remember.

Jules: I think you do. Because I heard you arguing about it later, by the tents, when you thought no one was around.

Olivia: If that's true, why didn't you ever say anything?

Jules: Because . . . because I didn't want to expose you. And I didn't think you killed Sydney. I still don't, I guess. Or— I don't know. Maybe I'm too biased. That's the whole point of this documentary. Let the facts stand for themselves. See where they lead.

Olivia: C'mon, say what you want to say, Jules.

Jules: I heard you and Sydney talking. Syd had read your own diary.

Olivia: I wouldn't call it my *diary*. Syd kept a diary. I wrote fiction.

Jules: Okay. Syd read your fiction then.

Olivia: It was a thing we both did sometimes, to annoy

each other. Read each other's journals. The police scoured my journal. I've never hidden it. Plus, I didn't write my personal thoughts. That was Sydney's thing. She was the tough cookie on the outside, but if you cracked her, she was dripping with emotion. She mostly let it out in her journal, or in person; as you all know, the girl didn't shy from a fight. Whereas me—I wrote fictional stories.

Jules: But there was one ripped page. One page that didn't contain a fictional story.

Olivia: How . . . how do you know about that?

Jules: Because I saw you that night, Olivia. I saw you and Sydney arguing about it, and then you ripped out the page and threw it in the fire and told Syd you'd deny it if she ever said it again. And I saw what was on it—

Olivia: You read my small handwriting as it burned in the fire?

Jules: No, I didn't read your writing in the lines. But in the top margin, there was a huge heart with someone's name in it.

Lexa: Liv had a crush? Ooh. On who?

Jules: Do you want to say?

Olivia: Fine. Whatever. It said Jules. It was a heart with Jules's name in it. I hadn't even realized I'd doodled it, to be honest. And it's, like, Syd was almost trying to force me out of the closet. It was the most awful thing she'd ever threatened to expose. But she was mad at me that I'd seen her kiss Aiden, and—let's say there was a lot of sisterly stuff between us. She was angry, often a raging bitch. Oh god, I shouldn't talk about her like that. I loved my sister. I know it's hard to reconcile all of this with love, but I did. Even if she could be awful.

Jules: Look, it *was* really awful, Liv. That's why I never said anything. I was appalled by the whole thing. Sydney had two sides to her. That's what I learned watching you guys that night. One side was sweet and bubbly and kind. She genuinely was.

Olivia: And another side was cruel. Yep. Okay, so there you have it. When I was in high school and grappling with all my feelings and identity—trying to figure out who I was and what I wanted—I had a crush on you, Jules. I don't anymore, if that's what you're worried about.

Jules: I'm not worried at all. I wasn't back then either. But I heard you fighting about it again right before Survival Day. I knew you didn't resolve it. That she was threatening you, in a way. Taunting you. And I also know you went to her, Liv. You went to her during Survival Day. Maybe you were even the last one to see her before . . .

Reuben: What? You can't be serious? You've known this for ten years and you've never said? That Olivia was at the cove too?

Jules: I really didn't think Olivia killed her sister. They both just had a lot of feelings and big, hard things they were dealing with. I thought I was doing the right thing. I didn't want to be the one to give the police the last piece of evidence that would enable them to convict her. They were so set on Olivia as the criminal that they were missing everything else. They missed Aiden carting drugs!

Aiden: She's right. As much as it pains me to admit that, she's right. They did miss that.

Olivia: Wait, back up. What do you mean—I went to Sydney? I didn't.

Jules: You're lying. You did. And I'm not trying to pin you as the murderer, Liv. I'm trying to get to the truth.

Olivia: Truth is that, if this documentary goes forward, if it's picked up by a Netflix or Hulu, it's going to make you millions, Jules. So don't act all benevolent, like you're the Mother Teresa in all this, trying to get justice for Sydney.

Jules: You're getting upset because you know I'm right. Because you saw Sydney before she died. And you don't want to tell us why. You don't want to tell us what happened. Maybe you're even afraid. Tell us, Olivia. We can help you figure this out. We owe it to Sydney!

Olivia: I wasn't there! You know what, I'm out. I'm going to the memorial, and I'm done with your documentary. Done with all of this bullshit. You're all acting like you're armchair detectives in some game—but this isn't a game to me. This is my life! My family. My mother took her own life. My sister *disappeared*. I still don't know what happened to her—where she is—if she's maybe even alive out there!

Reuben: C'mon, Liv, you can't think Syd's still out there, alive.

Olivia: Maybe she is! Maybe someone's . . . I don't know, after her, and she's had to hide out all this time.

Jules: I'm so sorry, Liv. But that sounds insane.

Olivia: Right, I'm insane. Never heard that before.

Jules: Look, Liv, I can't lie for you anymore. You were there.

Olivia: At the cove? Prove it.

Jules: I can. Because you had my bracelet. It's special to me. I'm wearing it now. My grandmother gave it to me.

Aiden: Right. You lost your bracelet before the overnights.

Jules: Actually, Aiden's the one who told me he'd seen Sydney with it. I must have dropped it, and Sydney found it, and put it on her wrist, knowing it was important to me. Aiden, you must've seen her with it at the cove, when you went to exchange the backpacks, didn't you?

Aiden: Yeah. I think so. It's hazy.

Jules: But then after Sydney disappeared, and the police had scoured the cove, the bracelet was on Olivia's wrist. You gave it to me, Liv. You knew it was special to me. You pretended you'd found it by our last campsite, but you didn't know that I'd already heard Sydney had it. So what happened, Liv? What happened when you went to the cove to see Sydney? And, please, this time—don't say you don't remember.

Reuben: Doesn't the bracelet give you an added motive, too, Jules?

Jules: What?

Reuben: It was your most treasured possession. I remember you saying that multiple times. If Aiden told you Sydney had it, maybe you went back to get it. And something happened . . .

Aiden: I was with her while you guys were on your overnights.

Reuben: The entire time?

Aiden: Well, I mean, we had separate tents.

Reuben: Okay, so—

Jules: I didn't do anything to Sydney! And I definitely didn't go kill her for my bracelet. I—okay? But, Liv, how did *you* end up with the bracelet? What's the story there? Sorry, Liv . . . oy, Maria. We'll have to cut the sorries. But I am. I truly, truly am, Liv. I don't want to accuse any of you. I care about all of you. But this is a necessary evil if we finally want the truth.

Olivia: I . . . I need some air. I think I'm done. No—I'm definitely done here.

CHAPTER FIFTEEN

Olivia

THE TINY SYNAGOGUE is packed, and I'm front row center where my father has insisted I sit, wedged between my stepmother and Cass.

We're family, Olivia, and for once we're going to look like it.

I know better than to argue when his eyes bulge out, stress fritzing off his olive skin as he pores over his speech, making a flurry of notations even at this late hour. But as I scan the synagogue on the lookout for her, my mind whirling with the documentary revelations, I feel something more than fury at my father, something closer to exhaustion. It's like I'm being pushed to the brink. Who the fuck cares how things look? What do appearances possibly matter anymore?

"You're going to be great up there," I finally tell him before he makes his way toward the bimah. *This is for Sydney*, I remind myself. I shift, trying to get comfortable, but it's impossible when we're all sardine-packed, and I'm trying my valiant best to scoot away from my stepmother and her perfume, which is probably a very expensive method of intentionally aggravating my allergies.

I was at the cove. After all this time, Jules has proved it. I didn't even remember having her bracelet . . . giving it to her . . .

If I did, then I was really there. Hundred percent certain. I feel rocked by the implications.

I sneeze a sequence of my loud, manly sneezes—three in a row. Just like my mother used to do. Sydney and our father would joke to no end about the two of us. *Here's a big one coming. A nine on the Richter scale.*

I rub my bare arms, wishing I'd brought a sweater. The place is over air-conditioned, and my butt throbs against the glossy wood pew.

"*Olá.* Hello, everyone. Today I'm going to speak in English, because of our large American contingent. And because my Portuguese accent, as my wife says, *é uma porcaria.*"

A few muted laughs to the joke that sails over my head. My father stands erect as ever on the bimah, but still, he's noticeably aged since the last time I sat in synagogue on the High Holidays, his melodic voice filling the room—and my head—for all those days on end. Ten years have passed since the last time I heard him sing, I realize.

He swipes his handkerchief over his brow and stares out upon the sea of us. I'm shocked at how many people are here, to be honest. The Jewish community doesn't exist on the island anymore, aside from my father and Daniella, though my father is a transplant. Well, and of course there are the da Costas, whose old familial estate still stands, even if they haven't lived here full-time for generations and, when they do come, opt to stay in their hotels. I don't recognize most of the people in the audience, but I imagine there are reporters. Superintendent Flores is here too. I haven't said hi, but she's sitting behind me, and I can feel her gaze bore into the back of my head.

Everything is such a fucking *mess.* Nothing has gone as I intended it to these past couple days. And then there's . . . her, of course. Syd. I've replayed my sightings of her ad nauseum—the little braids swishing by her cheeks. That necklace . . . I swear it had white beads, and a silver heart in the center.

I've tried to push it down, but I can't help the overarching sensation that's bubbled up. Hope. Fucking terrifying hope.

"If everyone could take their seat, we'll get started." Dad pages through his speech on the lectern where the Torah would ordinarily be spread.

I wonder if he knows yet that someone tried to kill Reuben. Not just someone, one of us.

"I want to thank all of you for coming to this memorial for my daughter Sydney. As you know, Sydney disappeared on this island ten years ago, when she was on a summer program in São Miguel, hiking the island with her friends and her sister, Olivia. It was a huge, huge shock when Sydney disappeared."

His face goes the same white I remember from the immediate days after. I was still dirty and sooty from Survival Day. I hadn't even showered and I was a shell of myself. They hauled me off to the police station, and excruciating flashes danced in my head like strange, old-timey films. As I waited in that awful interrogation room, an officer pointed to my feet and whispered to her colleague that he smelled something dreadful.

Of course, he did. We'd showered once a week at trucker stops. I remember, despite everything, thinking to myself that Sydney would really crack up at that comment.

"I happened to be on the island for a business trip while the girls were hiking. I didn't stop to see them. That's a huge regret I have now. I thought of it, of course, but I hadn't wanted to impose. Of course, it was hard for my departed wife and me to let Sydney go, especially. She had a very severe kidney disease all her life and was in pain and in and out of the hospital for years. She lobbied us hard to go on this trip, to treat her like an ordinary teenage girl, like her sister. And eventually we relented. We knew they had good medical care on the island, and it was only five weeks. Her doctors were supportive, she had all her medications, she'd be with Olivia . . ."

What I think of now is, bizarrely, that book by Jodi Picoult—*My Sister's Keeper*. It wasn't quite as desperate as that in my house. I wasn't conceived to save Sydney, and I wasn't being asked to provide my own tissues to do so either. But my life as a kid did revolve around Sydney's illness. Even when I had my own struggles too. The truths I was battling with inside, terrified to let out into the world.

Dad clears his throat. "I work for Sky Azores; I have for forty years now, hard to believe. And I've always traveled back and forth between the island and the States, where we have a satellite branch. I was in a meeting when they told me about Sydney. I thought it was nonsense—she was probably off with her boyfriend, making out in the woods. Turned out not to be the case, in the end."

Suddenly I hear weeping and realize it is my stepmother beside me. I fucking *hate* this woman, and even more do I hate her crocodile tears. Daniella's wearing black—like we're at a funeral. An expensive black silk skirt that tickles my bare calf, which I wish I could shove away. Shove her.

For a moment, I allow myself to envision that. The tabloids would go to town. So would all the gossip rags. My publishers would freak out.

Oh god—my publishers could find out about Reuben's accident. What if I'm actually arrested again? Ten years later, I have so much more to lose. I pinch my thigh with my fingers to distract myself from my thoughts, which loop off in too many directions.

"Of course, you all know what happened ten years ago. How Sydney's disappearance became the headline across the world. There were search parties. We tore this island apart. Everyone was questioned. While there were certain . . . suspicions, we still don't know what happened to her. Sometimes . . . sometimes I think I see her on the street. In a meeting. Once I ran after a girl at Starbucks, because I only saw her back, but she had those little braids like Sydney used to have . . ."

The world compresses into a single breathless pause. So Dad has seen her too? Has Syd really come back after all this time? Maybe she's been watching us all for years from afar?

I whip my head around to scan the pews once more. Could she be here, even, at her own memorial? I don't know anything anymore, but what I do know is that if my sister is actually alive, this is exactly where she'd want to be.

But I don't see Syd—no tiny blond braids, no beaded necklace. Maybe I'm just going crazy . . . again . . .

When I turn back, my father's face is still wrenched in a way that rips through me.

"But as you know, my Sydney never came back."

Now he is openly crying. I've always hated and loved that about my father. How he wears his emotions on his sleeve, like Sydney. Neither of them was of the camp of trying to bury them deep. That was just me.

"We waited for her to come home. I thought so many crazy things. Maybe a pirate had taken her. That was something I seriously pondered, if you can believe it. But after a year, we had a funeral. Of course, there was no body to bury. But we had a service. But I still—I know this sounds crazy—but I still thought she'd come back.

"Her mother and I were torn apart." I feel myself digging my nails into my dress so hard that I'm close to piercing my skin. "How do you mourn a child whose body you don't even have? How do you deal with your other daughter being accused of that murder and all the newspapers speculating? I was beside myself. So was June."

I want to put my hands over my ears to drown it all out, but I can't. I feel the thick heat of every eye in the place fixed on me.

Dad bows his head, and I rock forward and back, stirring with so much emotion that I'm afraid I can no longer contain. I try to take deep belly breaths like my therapist taught me, but it's not working. Breathing feels as elusive as it did this morning, when I ran up the path, frantic to find my sister.

"Sydney was—I want to tell you all about her, so you remember her the way I do. So you don't remember the spectacle and the tragic aftermath, how this took down my family. But so you remember her light. Sydney was my shining star. We used to sing together on the High Holidays at a bimah like this one, and she was an absolute angel in her white gown. She was often in pain, but she was the strongest person I knew. She didn't let her illness stop her. She could have stayed home and watched TV and had my departed wife cater to her hand and foot. We would have allowed that. Even encouraged it. But Sydney wanted to be normal. She didn't want to be defined by her illness. She wanted to do big things in the world. She was really into fashion and wanted to be a fashion designer like those . . . those two girls . . ."

"Mary-Kate and Ashley Olsen," I whisper.

"Those twin girls on TV who had made it big. And Sydney looked up to her big sister too."

At that, I suck in my breath.

"The girls are thirteen months apart, but the same year in school. They weren't best friends, no." He laughs nervously and then sips from a glass of water beside the silver yad that is used to read the Torah. "But they didn't hate each other like the media portrayed. I remember how Sydney was three, maybe, and in love with her shadow. She used to get such a kick out of her shadow, chasing it around, and noticing how the dress she was wearing was part of the shadow. And Olivia had outgrown that phase but was charmed by her sister's enchantment. She'd say, 'Go get it, Sydney! Go kiss your shadow.' And Sydney would. They loved each other. I know the girls loved each other."

My heart slows; my father's words roar in my ears. I didn't expect it—that he'd reference me in any positive way. Most of the people here probably think I killed her. And I suspect that my father does too. But he also knows that deep down I loved her. That if I did hurt her, it was an accident, or in the heat of the moment.

The shadow thing takes me back, a painful memory. Remembering Sydney—yes, but also myself. Because as a child, I was playful, despite how my serious adult self might disguise it now. I used to climb atop the rocks in our backyard, making up stories of far-off lands. But Sydney's illness and disappearance—and everything that followed—hardened me. I processed in the only way I knew how: with my pen. And allowing my childhood self to infiltrate now hurts, because it's a time I wasn't so withdrawn and angry. A time I had my mother in my life, and Sydney. Sometimes I see pictures from that time, and it's hard to believe that the girl with the infectious smile is me. She was reserved, sure, but she didn't plaster her walls in sketches of angry women. She could imagine so many wonderful worlds beyond her own. Her stories were vast and different, each one.

That Olivia wasn't writing murderous summers over and over and over again.

"Now I want to close by talking about the significance of this bimah, which has been restored in honor of Sydney. This synagogue was in ruins ten years ago. After Sydney disappeared, and all the . . . tragedy in my family . . . my *first* family—"

I wince.

"I mean . . . well, as you all know, I found love again. My Daniella." He smiles a wobbly smile.

Beside me, she makes a weepy emotive sound. My eyes feel itchy, a direct result of her perfume. She must have sprayed like ten sprays. The woman only knows one gear—full throttle.

He drums the wood with his fingers and gathers himself

back together. "As I mentioned earlier, the Jewish presence on this island has been nil for a long time, and this synagogue once lay in disrepair. After all that tragedy I already referred to, then marrying Daniella and moving full-time here, I was looking for a project. A place to which to devote myself, instead of sinking into all the sad.

"We're descendants of crypto-Jews, you see. Not to be confused with cryptocurrency." He pauses as if there might be a few laughs, but none come. "My family . . . others at Camp Zahav, too, in fact. Not many people know that Jews were among the first Azoreans. But in the fifteenth century, Portugal's Jews were forced to convert, leave the country, or be killed. And my family descends from a long lineage of Jews who clandestinely remained devoted to their faith in the face of persecution. Some of our ancestors refused to baptize their child, or deigned to wear a clean shirt on Shabbat, and were thus murdered in the Inquisition, or forced to languish in cells, or paraded in autos-da-fé in the town square.

"My ancestors are from this exact island, and one story passed down is that they had drawers in their dining room table. When visitors would show up while they were eating, they would hide their kosher food in the drawers and bring out different food, so as to avoid being discovered as Jews. They covered their Shabbat candles with jars so that no one could see the glow from outside. They had to hang a cross outside their doors but found ways to alter the cross design slightly to still represent their Judaism."

A crackle in the audience, some hushed conversation. I can tell the crowd is losing the connection to the memorial, to Sydney, but that's Dad—he's big on the stirring speech about persecution.

"Yes, this island is full of Jewish blood, even if most of them don't know it," he continues, paying no heed to the fact that his audience is growing restless. "It is estimated that more than fifteen percent of Azoreans have Jewish DNA. Crypto-Jews, or Marranos as they are also called, lived their lives with courage and conviction in the face of an ever-present threat of discovery. And I want to bring it back to my daughter now, because I think the comparison is very apt. Sydney, too, was sick, but she didn't let it stop her. She came on this trip! She wanted to suck the marrow out of life. Indeed, my daughter lived her short life with big heart and courage, and that does soothe my soul a measure. You know, after Sydney died, it provided me a lot of meaning to participate in the restoration of this synagogue. And the bimah is the pinnacle. The last piece, in Sydney's memory. I think she'd be proud. I think that she's here with me, singing."

His eyes close, and the pain etched in his blue eyes squeezes on my chest. "Yes, I can hear her. My sweet Sydney. She is here with us."

He flickers open his eyes, then rubs his knuckle against one of the corners. "Thank you for coming. You're invited to mingle now and join us for some refreshments outside the sanctuary."

I feel Daniella stand beside me, my left leg relieved of her presence, and now Cass rises too. All around me people are getting up, moving on. But I feel glued to this seat, the grief and anger a familiar fog that will swallow me alive if I let it again.

And I realize that I'm not only mourning Sydney, still, ten years later. I'm also mourning the person I used to be—the people we all used to be—before she was gone.

———

I'm beside a plexiglass display of a bronze Seder plate, riffling in my purse for a Xanax, when I feel a presence behind me. I turn, but by my spidey sense I already know that it's her. My step-mother.

"Olivia! You didn't take your seat until the very last moment, and then got up and escaped. If I didn't know better, I'd think you were avoiding me." She tinkles with a laugh and reaches toward me, but I sidestep and turn discreetly, placing the pill on my tongue. Then I grab a random water glass discarded on a side table.

I chug, fan my face. "Parched." I step backward, away from the scent of orange blossom and vetiver, which is a choking cloud emanating from her whole person. "Hi, Daniella."

I managed to avoid her at the dinner reception last night. Every time I felt her coming, I dodged and went to the bathroom. Once, she was blocking the main door into the hotel, so I snuck down to the beach with my wine and read a chapter of the new Abby Jimenez. No one even noticed I went. But now this woman is unavoidable.

I meet her eyes, wholesome brown. A mirage, like the rest of her plastic, Stepford wife vibe.

"How are you, Olivia? We didn't get to catch up last night. Your father is always going on about all your accomplishments, rightly so, but I know he wishes you would visit. Our home is always open to you."

"Well, that's . . . honestly, I don't plan to come visit you guys," I finally say, hearing and liking how authentic I sound.

"I can understand that it's been hard for you. With Sydney, and your mother . . . your father marrying me."

"It's not that. And you know it."

"I know? I know *what*?" Daniella wields her faux innocence like a weapon. "Then what is it, Olivia? Why do you hate me so much that you've avoided the island for ten years? You are your father's only remaining child—and you deny him seeing you."

"I deny him? He sees me in New York. And obviously I don't enjoy coming back here after everything that happened."

She swallows but doesn't move her eyes from mine. "I don't know what you're talking about. But I understand the anger, honey. I've had—well, I understand loss. It's unbearable when someone is taken from you, and you're searching for someone—anyone—to blame."

I'm steely, but my hands are trembling. She thinks she can get to me with sympathy?

Then her face softens, like she realizes she's gone too far. "You miss your sister. Of course, you do. It will always hurt. But I'm not to blame, Olivia. Neither is your father. You've punished him enough. Come home."

"Home? Home is New York." I laugh and hear how it sounds, like a crazy person's laugh. But that's exactly this conversation—conversing with a lunatic, only it's not me. "And you know why I don't come here. You know exactly why."

On this point, I'm gambling a bit. But I can tell I've shaken her.

"Oh, really? Why is that? Why don't you be clear?"

"Yes, why don't I finally be clear?" I say, hating that I've resorted to mocking her, but now I can't contain what is a geyser inside. "You hated my sister."

"Sydney?" Her startled face juts back, acquiring a slight double chin, which gives me a fleeting hit of satisfaction. "That's absurd."

"Oh, really? I mean, it's why you don't want to do the documentary—why you and Dad and Cass have refused—"

"We're not doing the documentary because we have nothing to share. Nothing to hide. We weren't on the trip! And your father doesn't want to make Sydney's death into a national spectacle again."

"Please! *As if* you have nothing to hide. You weren't uninvolved. You were a part of our trip."

She sputters with a laugh, like what I've said is outrageous. "A few hikes I led you guys on. A few times I took you to some secluded spots."

"You were there. And my sister drove you crazy. You wouldn't give her water from your spare Nalgene when she needed it. You kept chiding her to keep up, but she was sick! That time we were up by the geothermal plant?"

She looks at me dumbly. "The old thermal baths?"

"My sister was having trouble breathing that day. And you couldn't have given two shits. You forged ahead. Does that ring a bell?"

"Oh, honey." She pats my arm, and I whip it away. "You miss your sister. But your silly memory—it's a bit mixed-up, we all know that. You're inventing stories in your head that I hated her, but sorry to say, none of that happened. Though I understand why I'm an easy target of your sadness."

"You're gaslighting me. You once muttered *fucking slut* under your breath at her. I remember that crystal clear."

"I did no such thing!"

"I heard you. And when you brought us treats, you always gave Sydney less. *Oops, must have told them the wrong number of pastries!* You wouldn't meet her eyes. She noticed, and I noticed. Every time. She even told me—"

"She told you what?"

I square my shoulders. "She said you were dangerous. Days before she disappeared. So explain that."

For the millionth time, I wish I'd pressed Syd on what she'd meant. But we were in the midst of a blowout fight, her threatening to expose my crush on Jules, me retaliating with the fact that I knew she kissed Aiden, and it all exploded. We never revisited the Daniella conversation, at least not that I remember.

"That's offensive!" Daniella's face contorts in a fierce way. "That's deeply offensive, and disrespectful, and actually slanderous, and I won't stand here and take it. Maybe you should look in the mirror, Olivia. Because you're the one who everyone thinks killed your sister—and I wouldn't point this out if you weren't being such a bitch, because I try to keep the peace for your father's sake. But maybe that's exactly what happened—you murdered Sydney and dumped her off the cliff like that man saw you doing—and now you're pointing the finger at me to take away your—"

"Your only alibi is Cass," I whisper.

"What?" She stills. "How dare you? How dare—are you implying that I—"

"You could have. You live right by the cove. Easy enough. Your daughter was sleeping . . ."

"That's preposterous." Instead of projecting anger, Daniella smiles at me sadly. "Really, that's ridiculous. You need help, honey. You need serious help."

"Everything okay here?" Dad suddenly asks, startling me. His eyes waffle uncertainly between us. "Are you—what's going on here?"

"Nothing," Daniella says and stalks away without looking back.

I reach for a donut-looking thing on a tray, with a placard in front of it that reads *Malassada*. I chew but don't say anything, can't muster a single word. I was going to try to be the bigger person now, praise Dad on his speech, on the memorial, because I know he needs it. But now I can't. I'm too angry. Too . . . so many things. If I say anything more, I might actually regret it.

"Livvie," Dad says, with a warning tone.

"Don't *Livvie* me! Not now. Just tell her to stay away from me, okay? Tell your wife to stay the fuck away from me."

And then I run down the stairs, desperate for fresh air. Desperate to be alone, and to think about all the incomprehensible things. But as I round the bend at the bottom of the stairs, I nearly crash into someone.

"Oh, sor—" I begin to say, until I realize whom I've barreled into.

"Oh." I stop. Inside I'm screaming, *Fucking hell*. But I keep my face blank.

"Hello, Olivia." Superintendent Flores stares at me with a

similarly emotionless look to her creased face, with its pitted cheek divots that signal a long-ago battle with teenage acne. She's wearing a beige pantsuit and she smells of cigarette smoke. Her whole vibe gives harmless grandmother, other than the cigarette smoke, which I can tell she's tried to mask by a spritz of floral perfume. "On your way out?"

"Yes." I stand up straighter, trying to act like I have nothing to apologize for. "Need some fresh air."

"Well, don't go too far," she says lightly, though it sounds like a warning.

"I'm aware of the rules."

"Right. We'll have more questions for you in due course, Olivia. My guys are looking for fingerprints on the rope."

"Great. If that's all—"

"Liv!" I swivel, surprised to see Reuben coming down the stairs, looking flustered. "I was looking everywhere for—I really need to talk to you." He registers the superintendent and runs a brash hand through his hair. "Oh. Didn't realize you were in the middle of something. Hello, Superintendent Flores."

"Hello, again, Reuben," she says. "Anything you'd like to say to me, as well?"

"No, it's—not that important. Just . . ."

"Just sort of important?" Superintendent Flores asks.

"No. It's not—no." He shakes his head, but I can tell there's something off with him, and I can't discern if it's the near-death experience, or more. Maybe he's seen Sydney too. Could that be it? Reuben and I aren't close. I mean, we're stepsiblings, sure, on paper, at least. And we went to camp together for ages as kids. But we don't have much else in common, even back to that summer. Of everyone on the trip, I was the least close with him. And since I hardly spend time with my father and his new family, and Reuben doesn't seem to, either, it's not like our paths have had the occasion to cross.

"Can I—" I glance at the superintendent.

She shakes her head. "We're not done here."

"I'll find you back at the hotel, okay, Reub?" If he's seen Sydney, too, we shouldn't talk about it here. "Jules canceled the documentary filming for tonight, given . . . given what happened to you. So we have some time before Furnas."

"I'm not going back to the hotel now. I need—I need some space from everyone, is all." His eyes dart toward the superintendent. "I'm gonna spend time with Cass in the city. And then we'll meet you guys at Terra Nostra."

"Oh, I didn't realize Cass was coming tonight. Okay . . . well, we can talk at Furnas. Is it—it can wait?"

"Sure." He waves a hand, but I can tell he's only miming a casual affect. "We'll talk at Furnas. It's—all good. *Até mais*, Superintendent." He quickly escapes out the door, shuttling a whoosh of fresh air inside. I watch him disappear from sight, feeling a new layer of disoriented.

I face Superintendent Flores once more. She looks at me thoughtfully. I hold my breath, wondering if she's going to probe that interaction, but instead she says, "Book eight, chapter twelve."

"Wha—huh?"

"Book eight, chapter twelve of the *X Marks the Spot* series. The book you published two years ago. Hit number two on the *New York Times* bestseller list. It's called *Death in the Depths*."

"I wrote it, so yeah, I remember."

"Well, in it, the group goes canyoning, and Dashiell is murdered because someone cuts his rope."

"You read my books?" I ask, my brain one giant scramble.

"Of course." The superintendent doesn't break steely eye contact. "This case—your sister—I've never let it go."

"I didn't do anything to my sister. Or to Reuben."

"So the book—it's a coincidence? A coincidence that in it, Serena stages a firework display so everyone is distracted while she cuts Dashiell's rope?"

"You literally think I'm so stupid that I'd imitate my own book to try to kill Reuben? As if no one would read it and realize? As if I don't know there aren't legions of armchair detectives who study my books as if they are manuals to actual murder? Maybe one of the others read my books and got an idea. Have you thought of that?"

I'm practically screaming, I realize, while the superintendent is perfectly calm. Simply taking me in. I force myself to take a few deep belly breaths. *Jesus, get it together, Olivia.* I'm hardly helping my case.

"Where did you go during the skywriting?" the superintendent asks.

I back down a step, to the landing, itching to finish this and get away from people. Get back to the hotel and call Tomika so her sweet, soothing voice washes over all this absurdity. Maybe even confess to her that I've seen someone who looks just like Sydney, twice.

"If you're going to arrest me, then do it already," I finally say.

"We're simply talking now. I'm not trying to be hasty. I already excused you, but new information surfaced in interviewing your friends—"

"They're not all my *friends*," I say, before instantly regretting it. I need to keep my emotions in check, now more than ever. Until I can get home to Tomika. *If* I can go home to her again. The realization that I'm probably now a prime suspect in a new crime spikes a chill down my spine. What if I made a huge mistake coming back here? What if this calculated risk I took, joining the reunion, is the one that finally does me fully in?

Suddenly all I want to do is run after Reuben. It's important what he wants to tell me, I know that in my bones. What if he can finally explain why—

"In talking to the rest of the people who aren't your friends, then, they couldn't account for you during the skywriting." Superintendent Flores cocks her head, like she's conducted some intricate assessment of my guilt or lack thereof but isn't going to fill me in yet on what she's deduced.

"Great," I hear myself mumble.

"Jules said you were beside her. But then she reached over to grab your hand for emotional support, and you were gone."

"I went to the edge of the canyon! A little farther down, off to the side. So I could be alone to take it all in."

"I see. That's certainly a convenient explanation."

"I didn't cut Reuben's rope. Just like I didn't kill my sister. Though I know those neat explanations for things would work out for you quite *conveniently*," I say, trying and probably failing to keep the licks of fury at bay.

"We'll see," she says thoughtfully as she begins to walk back upstairs. "There's only—" I go rigid at the note of uncertainty in her voice. "There's something going on here that I can't quite make heads or tails of."

"Join the club." But as soon as it's out, I regret it. I know I'm letting my emotions spill out in a way that could be to my severe detriment. How is this happening? Again? I had started to make some peace with what happened ten years ago, but this trip? None of it adds up.

To my surprise, Superintendent Flores smiles faintly. "This time, Olivia, I promise I am not going to let up until I get to the bottom of things."

CHAPTER SIXTEEN

Lexa

TERRA NOSTRA NATIONAL Park, on the southeast swath of the island, is where I first fell in love with my husband.

Now, ten years later, Eli holds my hand as we traverse the silent park, dusk descending, the trees cresting against the sky and the park's nonhuman inhabitants engaged in their pleasing whistling and chirping. Everything is awash in greens and blues, punctured by the muddy yellow-brown thermic pools. There is the large famous pool—the Iron Water pool, comfortable for bathing, encased by stone walls. But other smaller pools and fumaroles are surrounded by ropes, steam rising up from geothermic vents, warning signs cautioning that the water is scalding.

I've always felt the whole vibe here is *Jurassic Park* on steroids. The walkway is lined with camellias and azaleas, ferns and Japanese cedars, pine and eucalyptus. Blackbirds and bullfinches swoop and chirp overhead, darting among the trees and then skittering over to the valleys. The soothing sound of water streaming through the brooks fills the backdrop, and I will it to uproot my thoughts from their conjoined place in my brain, to send them rushing away.

Eli smiles a lopsided smile at me that shoots me right back

to the memory of us. Truth is, the story we often tell people—
a story people love to cheer on—is that I was in love with Eli
since I first saw him in third grade. But that was a childish love
and unreciprocated for a long time. And besides, a few years after
that one-sided love story began, Sydney asked Eli to dance at her
bat mitzvah, and then he invited her out to the movies, and the
rest was history. But on our summer trip, a couple weeks into
it, we came to Terra Nostra, and same as now, Eli had the park
shut down just for us. It was kind of hilarious tromping in here
all muddy, reeking of that particular stench of sweat whose layers have baked on over days, like a congealed lasagna. Reuben—
I think it was Reuben—pointed out a potential twelve on one of
the plaques, and we all investigated until concluding that no, that
didn't jibe with the "twelve tribes of Israel." None of us had showered in a week, and the park staff gently suggested we go through
the bathhouse before entering their pure pools.

We did, a shower so delicious I remember we all discussed
how much we would have paid for it had it not been free. *A million dollars* was Eli's declaration—and I think he actually meant
it. We were in awe of our brand-spanking-freshness, sniffing our
armpits and even sniffing each other's. As we all left the bathhouse, Reuben rushed ahead, always wanting to be first. I was
walking on the side of the Iron Pool when I nearly slipped—and
then I felt Eli's hand reaching out to catch me.

Zap. That was the feeling when our hands touched. Thunder-
bolt. The sensation that the earth has shifted in a seismic way,
and in doing so, it's plopped you onto a new planet.

Eli squeezes my hand now. Zap.

We arrive at the terrace of the hotel that abuts the park (which
Eli's family also owns, of course) and approach the table that's been
set up in the waning sun, with lanterns dangling from the trees.

"Whoa, quite the setup," Cass says.

Thick silence and then chairs scratch against the stone and

bodies ease onto cushions. Dread coats my throat as I get out my phone to check if there are any updates. Sure enough, I spy a flurry of texts. I angle subtly away from Eli and rattle off a response.

"Everything okay?" Eli asks.

"Yeah. Work." I slip my phone back into my purse and give my husband a small, hopefully encouraging smile.

"Dad needs to give you a raise." Eli laughs, taking my smile at face value like he takes everything else. "All those people who think you only got this job because you married me are so ridiculously wrong. You're the hardest worker of us all."

You have no idea, is what I think but don't say. My heart drums in my chest, reminding me of that drug lord who tied the cocaine onto the barrier rocks, not expecting the sea to thrash so hard and dislodge it.

"Wow," Jules says. "This is totally magical."

"Magical and ripe for a murder," Reuben says cheerfully, sitting at the head of the table and motioning Cass, who is still standing, to sit beside him. "I mean, amiright? It's like *Knives Out*, but make it jungle. Only throwing out ideas, in case any of you were planning on finishing the job. Try not to get my blood on the caviar, though; I hear Eli's had it imported."

"Oh, shut up, Reuben," I mutter.

"Seriously, though," Reuben says cheerfully, ignoring me, "if murder's on the menu tonight, I hope you brought your A-game. Seems I'm hard to kill." Reuben stares directly at Eli and me. Then he laughs gruffly and unfolds his linen napkin. "Man, attempted murder does work up an appetite."

"I'm on guard too," Cass says. "For Reub, I mean. Just so you all know." But she says it pleasantly, looking stunning, even though it irks me to admit it. She's wearing loose white silken low-rise pants, paired with a floaty white crop top that shows off her insane chiseled abs and layers of silver jewelry, including a cool silver pendant with black loopy engravings. It's a chill look that doesn't scream designer like her brother's Ferragamo loafers and Saint Laurent linen shirt. (I saw the tag and felt perhaps more incensed than called for; even Eli doesn't buy such high-end clothes.) Cass's relaxed style is more cool girl, highlighting her glowy, Olympian strength and beauty. She must get men hitting on her constantly. I watch Eli staring at her, and when he sees me notice, he coughs and averts his eyes.

"Thanks for letting me join you guys while Reub is in town," Cass says, as a waiter fills her glass with the frosty bottle of local Lombadas sparkling water. I've noticed she doesn't drink, which I assume owes to her strict Olympic training regimen. "Especially after . . . what happened today. You can imagine, I don't want to let him out of my sight. I just hope the police were wrong . . . that someone didn't actually—"

"They're not wrong," Reuben says. "I was there. Someone tried to murder me."

"Superintendent Flores agrees," Jules says. "That's why I hope you guys will still be up for filming more of the documentary tomorrow morning, before our Sete Cidades hike. I understand why you didn't want Maria here tonight—"

Jules throws an obvious glance over at me, which irritates me. I only said to her in confidence that after what happened to Reuben, and the memorial, it would be nice if we could all relax with one another. Eli and I put so much into this reunion—time, money, not to mention effort. We don't want to be filmed and scrutinized at every moment. But now they're all going to know I didn't want Maria here. It makes me look suspicious.

"I feel like we're onto something—we're going to flesh out what happened to Sydney. We're close. I can feel it," Jules says, teeming with Jules-level can-do spirit, which I'm happy to see, even if I find it improperly placed. Jules has been so depressed lately, and with her grandmother's death, it's felt like nothing can go right for her. I'm glad we can give this to her, the documentary. I want her to succeed. But I also want us all to come out on top. Which for the first time feel like incompatible aspirations.

"I don't know that I want to film anymore," I finally say.

"Probably what an attempted murderer would say, eh?" Reuben says, eyes boring into me.

"That's ridiculous. How can you say that about her?" Eli asks.

"Because it's what I'm thinking. Anyone who backs out of the documentary now looks guilty. And possibly *is* guilty. So is that what you're doing, Lex? Backing out? I bet Superintendent Flores will find that interesting too." His eyes rove around the table. "Anyone else?"

I swallow hard. "I have nothing to hide."

"Oh, don't you?" Reuben asks.

"I'm staying in the documentary. Until the end," Olivia says, with more ferocity than I expect. Then she flicks her eyes back toward the entrance, as if she's expecting someone new to pop out from the gate. Man, Liv has the paranoid energy of a twitchy squirrel this trip. A twitchy squirrel who nonetheless looks stylish, I have to admit. She's wearing baggy cream barrel jeans and a pale blue oversize button-up shirt that she's done a half tuck with and paired with black clunky crisscross sandals that perfectly encapsulate the wrong shoe theory. On the table beside her cutlery is a tiny yellow bag with cream polka dots. The whole ensemble is shockingly chic, like a Copenhagen girl, far different from the Liv of our summer trip whose wardrobe consisted of oversize tees and baggy drawstring basketball shorts. Her outfit now is as stylish as mine, perhaps more so, and certainly less obvious. I look down at my own ensemble, suddenly feeling entirely too naked for this whole situation. I'm wearing navy trouser shorts with a chartreuse linen crop top that felt powerful when I hit Soho before this trip. But now, here with all of them, I feel an unsettling lack of armor.

"Well, good then." Reuben slaps his palms on the table. "Glad no one's backing out. Other than Lex. I'm sure the superintendent will be interested to hear it."

I swallow hard. "I'm not backing out. I was just . . . voicing a concern."

"Great, then," Reuben says.

"Great," I echo.

"In fact, in order to be here for the filming tomorrow, I've moved my flight," Reuben says.

"You have?" I ask, trepidation slinking up my spine.

"Yep. How do you feel about that, Lex?"

I'm quiet for a beat. "I don't have any feelings about it," I finally tell him.

"Sure. Anyway, tomorrow is Sete Cidades. How could the prodigal son come home without at least stopping by the most magical spot on the island? I need to get the full measure of this trip, planned meticulously by our esteemed hosts." His voice oozes sarcasm, like he's trying to goad Eli and me. Or just me.

"I wouldn't call us the hosts," Eli says. "Isaac is the one who planned this."

"You simply made it all fiscally possible," Reuben says, managing to sound magnanimous instead of snarky.

"Thanks, Reub," Jules says. "I'm really glad you're staying, for one. And I really think we're onto something. If the police don't figure it out—which they didn't ten years ago—then we can. All of us together, again."

"The cozido!" Aiden announces, sounding as desperate as I am for a conversation swap, and we all turn. Muted cheers as the great black pot is carried in with its usual fanfare by a couple of waiters. The dish is unique to Furnas, this eastern part of São Miguel, prepared by lowering the pot into a local hot spring heated by volcanic steam. It cooks slowly for about five hours, and the hot springs underground work magic on the meat and vegetables.

As the top is peeled off the pot and the contents unveiled, the waiters heap stew onto plates. I slip out my phone again and glance at it beneath the table.

My heart sinks at another message from him.

I can't do it anymore, I stab off this time, my hands shaky, messing up the letters and garnering wonky spell-check suggestions that further infuriate me. *It's too dangerous.*

He writes back quickly. *You have to. No other choice.*

I shove my phone back in my purse and stare at my plate, steaming with beef, cabbage, carrots, potatoes, and chorizo.

"You're never off your phone these days, Lex," Jules says.

"Work," I say, trying to be bright about it. "Constant fires to put out. You can't imagine the stupidity of some people. Everyone needs hand-holding."

"You must be employee of the year, though. You're so dedicated."

I love Jules, but something about what she's saying strikes me as . . . combative. I'm contemplating a response when Eli says, "Try employee of the decade. Trust me, the Da Costa Group could not chug along without my wife."

I smile again, but this time I know it must look as tightly wound as I feel. I only hope that the darkness masks things.

"Everything okay?" Eli whispers as everyone goes back to eating, and I remember one of my favorite things about my husband. That he needs me. Ever since I was a child, I've been used to being needed. By my mother, when my father left us in a spectacular way, incinerating our savings. And now by my husband. People think the opposite—that I need him. For his money and prestige and the da Costa name. I do love those things, absolutely and completely. Since I've been with Eli I'm finally secure, on solid ground that won't just open up into an unforeseen sinkhole. I never have to worry where my next dollar is coming from, never have to scrounge or beg. I can support my mom, pay for my great-aunt's nursing home. I would do anything to protect this life. Anything. But even with all that said, Eli still needs me more than I need him. He relies on me. I take care of all the invisible things, so he gets to be the Happy Baby. I don't resent him for it, but for the first time I do wonder whether my entire adulthood is one extended trauma bond.

Eli is still looking at me expectantly, his Happy Baby smile beginning to falter.

"Yeah." I squeeze Eli's thigh under the table. "Everything's good."

———

The main thermal pool is filled with volcanic water from the hot springs at a balmy one hundred degrees. Steam sizzles off the surface and evaporates into the now-cool air. It's massive—an Olympic-size swimming pool, large enough to fit a thousand, it feels. But it's only Eli and me.

"Where did they all go?" I ask Eli, glancing around, nerves rattling in my chest.

"Dunno. Jules and Aiden had both come out of the bathrooms, last I saw. He was trying to talk to her but she acted like she had to make a phone call and walked away."

"Hmm." The sky is black now, the stars bright like they were that summer. Sydney was obsessed with them, I remember. The girl never slept. I'd nudge my foot over to her sleeping bag, poking around to get a solid leg—but nothing. She was always roaming outside during the night. Said the stars were in solidarity with her. That she felt smaller when she looked at them.

I remember feeling astounded, that anything could make Sydney Azulay feel small.

Eli's leaning against the wall, eyes closed. "You think Jules and Aiden will ever realize they love each other?" I ask, resting my head against his shoulder.

Eli laughs but doesn't open his eyes. "Yeah? You think they do?"

"I know it."

"Could have been a wedding fling."

"It wasn't."

"Sometimes, I . . . no, never mind."

"What?"

"Being back here, I don't know. Sometimes I think Sydney is going to waltz out from behind a corner. Smile and say it's all been a huge prank or something. That she's alive and fine. That she had to leave for a reason that will finally make everything make sense."

I'm quiet.

"You know what I mean?" He opens his eyes and stares at me with such intensity that I blink. "Do you ever wonder that too? If she's still alive somehow?"

"No. I don't," I say firmly. Then, "I don't get where they all are. What about Reuben and Cass? And where's Liv?"

"I saw Liv come out of the bathrooms—she was looking for Reuben."

"Oh? Why?" Those two aren't close.

"Said something about how they needed to talk."

"Huh." I ponder that, sift things around, but come up with nothing illuminating. "How didn't I see any of this? Everyone . . . dispersing."

"You were touching up your makeup," he points out diplomatically.

"Oh." Inside I curse my vanity. I should have been on top of things, from the moment the dinner ended. Now it's all unwieldy.

"And Cass?"

"I don't know where Cass is," Eli says lightly, snaking his hand into mine. "Wasn't paying attention. But probably with Reuben."

"You sure about that?"

"Sure she's with Reuben? No, I told you. I only saw Liv."

"No, sure you weren't paying attention to Cass?" I immediately regret it as soon as it leaves my lips.

Eli laughs like I've said something ridiculous. "I'm paying her as much attention as anyone else, Lex. And honestly, most of my mind's been on today. Everything that's been said. Reuben's . . . near-death thing. The memorial. It's been . . . a lot. Can we relax for a bit?"

He wraps his arms around me, but I can only stand frozen in his embrace. Everything is wrong. It all feels deeply, deeply *wrong*.

I detach myself from his arms and turn toward the stone side, pushing myself up out of the water. I fumble up and stare out at the grassy hillside where, during the days, people spread out on the lawn and picnic and enjoy the springs. The pungent scent of sulfur stains the air.

"Where are you going?" Eli asks. "C'mon, Lex. They'll show when they show. It's nice to be just us for a little."

"No, I have to—I need to go to the bathroom. I'll be right back."

"Lex, come on. We just got out here."

"It will only take a few minutes. Back in a sec."

By the sulk of his usually serene face, Eli is frustrated, but he doesn't argue anymore. He flips onto his back and begins swimming a choppy backstroke toward the center of the pool, where a puff of shrubbery sprouts in the midst of all the murkiness. I look longingly at him for a moment, all alone in that big pool, but then I stiffen with resolve and walk away.

———

I don't see anyone when I grab my phone in the bathhouse, which is sort of eerie. I know we're the only ones on the property, but I want to ensure total privacy for this call.

Where is everyone?

What am I going to do?

What the fuck am I going to do?

I walk aimlessly down dim paths amid the croaks and creeps of god knows which animals and insects, but none are as scary as the situation in front of me. Eventually I stop in the sanctuary of a massive tree and get out my phone and dial.

He answers on the first ring.

"I've been thinking about you. What's going on?"

"What's going on is I can't do this anymore. I wasn't kidding when I wrote that."

"I understand," he says, his tone irritatingly soothing, "it's not a normal situation."

"Normal? It's the opposite of normal." I take a deep breath, needing to be firm. "Today—it could have gone so differently. They could have caught on."

"But they didn't."

I feel like I'm at my wit's end. "I love you, but I can't do this. I'm done. *Done.*"

"Lexa, listen to me—"

"Lexa?"

My heart shoots out of my chest. Two people saying my name. One in my ear, one . . .

I turn very slowly and see Jules sitting on a bench in the darkness.

"Jules?" I press end on the call and swivel. "You scared the shit out of me."

How much did she hear? What does she think?

I paste a smile on my face. "Sorry. Work stuff. What are you doing here anyway? Are you okay?" It hits me that Jules and I have barely spoken this trip, very odd for us. We normally text a few times in a week, catch up by phone once a month or so. I guess now that I think about it, I've been the one scurrying away.

Jules did say she wanted to talk to me, didn't she? Shit, I really dropped that ball.

She's quiet, just looking at me.

Did she hear? I was speaking softly. Maybe she didn't.

"I gotta get back. Eli will wonder where I was. He hates me taking work calls on vacation, but I can't help it, you know? I'm sorry I've been so MIA. I really want to talk. How about coffee in the morning, just us?"

I'm babbling. Shut up, Lexa.

"Oh." She nods but doesn't smile. "Sure."

"Coming?" I ask her.

"No, you go. I'm gonna stay here a little and enjoy the peace and quiet."

"Okay, coffee in the morning, I'm excited," I chirp, and then walk away very fast.

CHAPTER SEVENTEEN

Jules

I'M SITTING ON a bench beside a bubbling brook, my mind rattling with what I just overheard, when an itch worms up my skin. Another signal I'm no longer alone. But this time it's not Lexa, seemingly cheating on Eli. Instead, I look up, and Aiden is standing there.

Aiden folds down beside me on the bench and looks at me, really looks at me with those intoxicating gray eyes. Wind whirls through the overhanging ferns, and the nearby shrubs quiver with a series of croaks. For the first time since this reunion, Aiden and I are quiet together, and I'm not trying to run away.

"What are—what are you doing here?" I finally ask.

"Looking for you."

They're words I both want to hear and don't. I open my mouth but don't know what to say in this moment that could turn either magical or dark. The carpet of stars feels heavy above, and the sweet flowery perfume of this island like a suddenly suffocating embrace.

"Jules, can we talk?"

"We already talked, Aid. I'm tired."

"Really talk. You know what I mean."

I do. He smells of leather and musk, his intoxicating cologne that he's worn since that summer. I feel how hungry my body becomes, how much I still buzz with wanting him when I'm not denying it to myself. But then my body tenses when I consider what he did. Not only abandoning and deceiving me—but I more than anyone know that when you're desperate, when you're pushed to the brink, you will become another person in order to untangle yourself. Is that what happened? Did Aiden become another person, one who killed Sydney? I don't know what to believe, but I still want him. I feel it in the thrum of every one of my cells, when he's this dangerously close.

Or maybe I don't want Aiden fully, but I certainly want the deconstructed dish version of him where I can take what I want and leave the rest. As I look at him, I catalog all the good parts. The way he held me the whole night after the wedding, not escaping to his own side of the bed like other ex-boyfriends. The passion with which he talks about sharks, and the way his front teeth are slightly different lengths but like a perfect puzzle in his mouth. He would be a great father is what I think, the type who respects that his child wants to be a sculptor and not a computer scientist.

But amid all that good, I'll pass on the part of Aiden that made him run away after Sydney disappeared, how he left me to deal with the aftermath on my own. And that he might have killed Sydney. Because of all the motives we went through today in the documentary, I still can't help but feeling that Aiden's drug admission remains the most likely of them all.

"Fine, if you don't want to talk, I will. I don't understand— Jules, *this* is why you've frozen me out since the wedding? Because Maria told you I was involved in some drug thing back when I was a kid, which literally is not connected to anything. I thought—"

"*I* froze *you* out?" Anger geysers inside me; I could rip a scream right through the whole park. "When we slept together at the wedding, you said it was special. You said it meant some-thing. You said you'd missed me."

He gapes at me, like he's confused. "It *was* special. I meant all those things. I texted you right after."

"Yeah. *I had an amazing night.* And then a day later a blue heart with a bird emoji."

"I had an amazing night," he parrots me, blinking rapidly, like he's confused about my sarcasm. "I did. I really did."

"And a blue heart. A *blue* heart. With a *bird*."

He runs a hand up his forehead. "I'm sorry, but what's wrong with that? Anyway, you never responded. I got the hint."

"*You* got the hint?" I hate how I'm getting riled up, but he's not going to gaslight me here. "*I* got the hint. You had an amazing night. You came like, what, three times?"

"I wasn't counting. I don't think you were lacking in that de-partment, either, if I remember right."

"Okay, well, I got it. Point taken." I've been called amazing in bed, too many times, by men who subsequently leave me. But I'm not sharing that shame with him now. "After I came home, I was—ugh, I don't want to be that girl."

"What girl?" He tips my chin up gently, and I get lost again in his eyes. "Jules, I really don't understand."

"The girl who wants you more than you wanted me! And then you texted. *I had an amazing night.*"

"I still don't get why that was so bad. I did. It was the most amazing night of my life."

I blink through my tears. "Mine too. But I want more than that, Aiden. That's the problem. I've always wanted so much more than that."

"Well, I do too. It was only the start of a conversation, Jules. You were supposed to respond, say something like you had an amazing night too. And we'd take it from there."

"We'd take it from there?" I'm trying to process. "You sent

me a blue heart the day after. And a bird. It felt like a clear goodbye."

"A goodbye?" His eyebrows shoot up. "Literally, Jules, you hadn't responded. I wanted you to respond, give me something to work with. It was a heart."

"A blue one."

"Blue's my favorite color."

"Blue's your favorite color," I repeat. I almost want to laugh. Maybe it really is true, the whole men are from Mars, women are from Venus theory. "What about the bird?"

"What about it?"

I point to his arm. "Ten years ago, you told me about the birds. That they meant freedom to you. That where you grew up in America felt so small and constraining. That all you ever wanted to do was take flight."

"Oh . . . so you—"

"I thought it was a message that the night was fun, but you're a free bird." I try to smile, but it doesn't quite pan out. And it occurs to me that maybe it wasn't Aiden's text that was out of line, but my own reaction. But I realize I've never really trusted him, not since that summer. And certainly not since what Maria confided to me.

"You thought . . ." Suddenly he peals laughter, deep and bois-terous. It's a totally unexpected, un-Aiden-like sound. "Jesus, Jules. I'm not writing code. I sent you a bird emoji because I love birds. And, yes, birds signify freedom to me, but they mean other things too. Did I show you my new tattoo? I got it *two* months ago," he says, so I get the import. He turns over his forearm, and I see two birds, beaks curved inward toward each other. He shrugs. "A pair of birds is better than one. Don't you think?"

"Huh," I finally manage as everything he's said settles like sunlight in my body.

I cycle through all my prior grievances, wondering if I overreacted. I've been so emotional the past few months. I thought it was my grief over Vovó dying. And then I met Maria, and I told her my sob story about Aiden, and her eyes went wide and she told me what she knew. I decided it was destiny that Aiden and I hadn't worked out. Because he'd murdered Sydney, and I was going to prove it. Maria and I conceived this documentary. It all spiraled. But also—

I force myself to look away from him, and I rub my stomach gently. How much is truth, and how much is me having drawn conclusions from thin and fearful places?

Apparently, pregnancy hormones are not a joke.

Truth is, my whole life, I thought that when I'd get pregnant in the future, it would be like in the movies—the girl bare legged, wearing just an oversize button-up shirt askew off a shoulder, leaping toward her husband and whispering *I'm ovulating* seductively against his lips.

When I look up, Aiden's still staring me straight in the eyes. Normally, I find prolonged eye contact abrasive, but maybe that's because I've been scared of looking into my own eyes, my own self. Not wanting to face how my whole life has narrowed to this pinprick existence. How stifling it's getting closed in on by my studio walls. In the quiet, endless nights, if I'm honest with myself, I can admit that I'm tired of lying in bed listening to the noises outside, trying to tell whether the agitated, anguished cries I hear are my neighbors having sex or the street cats in yet another squabble. That's the excitement my evenings have taken on. I used to spend them with my grandmother, but since she's gone, since the wedding and seeing Aiden, all the Technicolor in my life is gone.

Is this why I decided to do the documentary? Even if only subconsciously, have I chosen to play with people's lives to enliven mine?

Reuben was nearly killed today. What if that's my fault?

"I didn't do it, Jules," Aiden says, and his face is so open and earnest it hurts to look at. "Honest to god, I had nothing to do with Sydney disappearing. And it's been killing me—*killing* me that you could think that. I've been thinking about you day and night for months." He points between us, and my heart glugs down to my toes. "This means something to me. *You* mean everything to me."

"Don't say it if you don't mean it."

"I *do* mean it. But we can't start talking about us, about where we go from here, if you still think I'm a murderer. I swear to you I'm not. I swear on . . . I don't know what. I swear on the thing I most hold sacred."

"Sharks," I say quietly.

"Sharks." He looks solemnly at me and spreads his arms, palms open. "I promise to you on all the sharks I've known, tagged, and loved. I didn't do anything to Sydney."

I nod and bite my lip and admit to myself that in my depths, I believe him.

"Aiden, I'm pregnant."

———

"Wow," he says, about five million times, in various iterations of staggered. "And it's . . . ?" The question mark lingers in the air.

"Yours." I don't bother to hide my irritation. "Yep. The last time I slept with anyone else was nearly two years ago." My cheeks flush with shame as I realize how that sounds. Like no one else wants me. Like he is special, just because we drank a lot at a multimillion-dollar wedding in the south of France and landed in bed together.

"We used a condom." His face screws in thought.

"We didn't. Remember? You didn't have one. You asked me when I'd last had my period, and I said it'd just ended. So we said, *Ah, should be fine.*"

"*Should be fine,*" he says slowly.

I shrug, holding my breath, waiting for more.

"How do you feel about it, though, J?" he asks suddenly, so tenderly that it wipes my head of fears. "You must be, what, three—"

"Three months. Yep." I gather the courage to meet his eyes again. "Honestly, I was terrified when I found out. Vovó had just died, and I get back from the wedding and show your picture to my friend in my film class, and the whole sordid drug story pours out. And then days later I realize I'm pregnant. It's not the fairy tale a girl dreams about. So if I reacted a bit . . . rashly and emotionally to your texts, that's where I was coming from."

He nods, his face crinkled in thought, like he's putting the whole timeline together and understanding things better now.

"But I'm happy," I tell him, surprising myself. "I'm scared—terrified really—about doing this alone. But happy. Excited."

"Who said you have to do this alone?" He looks angry. Or sad. I'm not sure.

"When I thought you killed Sydney, I was definitely planning on doing this alone. But now . . . well, maybe things are different." Hope swells in my chest, and I hate it, and am scared of it, but there's nothing I can do about it. It's simmering there. Undeniable any longer.

"Yeah. We really need to talk." His face softens. "This is . . . wow."

I smile slightly. "It's a girl, by the way. I just found out."

"A girl, that's . . ." A shadow passes over his face, and then suddenly he bursts to a stand. "Look, I want to talk about this, I genuinely do, but I need a beat. To take it in. Is that okay? I promise we'll talk. I only need a—I need a sec."

I rub the swell of my stomach and let out a shaky exhale.

"I'll find you later. In the pool. We'll talk. We have all the time in the world now to talk, don't we?"

"Not all the time in the world, no." I point to my stomach,

"We'll talk." He kisses my cheek.

"Not a blue heart kind of talk."

"Not a blue heart kind of talk," he agrees. "Never sending you a blue heart again. Never sending *anyone* a blue heart, in fact. A baby. God, Jules, a baby girl."

Then he walks off into the night, and I replay his words, trying to decipher if he meant them in awe, or in terror.

I think awe. How much I want this—him—us—squeezes my organs.

I'm not sure how long I sit on that bench, my mind running the likelihood of future scenarios with the perceived precision of a mathematician.

At some point, Lexa and Reuben pass me. They're tense—immediately I can tell that, by their raised voices and choppy hand motions. Why aren't they back at the pool? Why is Lexa here again? Lexa's conversation earlier flings back at me. God, she's cheating on Eli. I rub my temples.

"If anyone's the puppeteer, it's you," Reuben's saying, his tone so vicious my head jerks. "Was this your plan all along? When we slept together that summer—my first time by the way, and it meant something to me, at least—were your eyes always closed because you were imagining it was him?"

"That's fucking ridiculous!" They're feet from me but haven't yet noticed I'm here. Becoming a pattern on this bench, shrouded in shadows. I rub my hands against my arms, chilled by Lexa's tone. I've almost never heard her voice so charged. She's usually difficult to rile up. If I recall correctly, the paper-plate award Aiden and I had made for Lexa—which we never got to dole out, because Sydney disappeared—was Most Likely to Not Give a Shit. Because Lexa has always done her own thing and is fairly unbothered by anyone else. Except for Eli, and Sydney too. I *know* Lexa gave a shit about her best friend.

"Are you really trying to imply that—take some responsibil-ity, Reub! I'm warning you—"

"What? That you'll try to kill me again? Or send your lackey husband to do it?"

"How dare you—how fucking *dare* you—" Suddenly Lexa's eyes flitter my way, and she shrinks back, wide-eyed. "Oh, hey, Jules," she says, back to her flat monotone. "We have to stop run-ning into each other like this." She feigns a smile, but her affect of normalcy doesn't fool me. She's afraid.

Why is Lexa afraid? Why would she possibly be afraid of Reuben? And is this connected to her call before? She's clearly not having an affair with Reuben. But I'm totally confused, and completely wiped. I'm likely missing signals that are right in front of my face.

"You guys . . . okay?" I ask, a sentiment that immediately seems entirely mismatched to the situation.

"Yeah, fine." Lexa heaves out a breath. "Look, we're almost done here. We just need to cover a couple more things. Meet you back at the thermal pool soon?"

"Sure," I say, dazed.

As they walk off, forking onto a new path that takes them farther from the main gates, I rewind the conversation, try to pinpoint what it could mean. Reuben thinks Lexa tried to kill him? But that's utterly ridiculous. The two of them have a zero relationship all these years later. And Lexa has no motive. Unless Lexa killed Sydney? And Reuben somehow knows?

No. I shake my head. This reunion—it's doing things to me.

When they're gone from sight, my mental gymnastics re-turn fully to the central question of my Baby Daddy. Of what will happen with us, if anything at all. Of whether I can truly put to bed the question marks flittering in my head, of whether Aiden was involved in Sydney's disappearance. Can I trust him—rely on him—if he decides he wants to do this with me? Be a father, maybe even a partner? Or is all this a pipe dream I've held for ten years that's bound to burst into flames?

I'm not sure how long I sit with my tangled thoughts, but finally I rise and decide it's time to return to the Iron Pool. A van is due to retrieve us at eleven, and I fumble in my pocket for my phone before I realize that, shit, we all left our phones in the bathhouse lockers. I stare up at the sky, at the bloated moon, remembering that the full moon is today; Reuben mentioned that earlier, saying he was going to do a ceremony or something. The moon is high in the eastern sky, nearly overhead, so not yet midnight, but close. Maybe ten thirty, which means well over an hour and a half has passed since I wandered here. I need to get back before everyone else kills me for making them wait.

I begin to tread the narrow path torched by sparse lampposts. It's the same path that Reuben and Lexa used, one side of it a grassy knoll that looms high, menacing even, slanting over me in the dark. I pass a koi pond studded with lily pads, moss clinging to the pond's stone border. I'm surprised that I wandered this far, that Aiden, Lexa, and Reuben were out here too. I know where I am though, from many visits here, and so do the rest of them, more or less, but it's eerie being alone in this massive, vacant park.

As I round a bend and step over a fallen cedarwood branch, I notice a roped-off bubbly hot spring—but something's odd about it. I stop abruptly, trying to make sense of what I see. My eyes focus, refocus in disbelief. What is that—

Suddenly, I find myself dashing, leaping up the stone steps and slipping under the rope, staring in abject horror at the distinctly human shape in the pool. I want to go right in, to help, but I hesitate. These pools are forbidden for a reason. Scalding waters that can incapacitate a person. Subject them to chemical burns. We're indoctrinated in this stuff, growing up on the island. When I used to lead tours, I always warned tourists that some of the thermal pools are fine to swim in, but others are dangerous. Composed of water that can cause a fast death . . .

As the seconds pound along, my life force returns to me, and I begin to scream. I scream and scream, because there is a body in the pool, face up, and I've now recognized him.

Reuben.

I realize quickly that he's already dead. Not only because of the burns blistering his skin, his limbs slack in the seething water, but his eyes—wide and gazing up skyward, like he's seen something unspeakable.

I clutch my stomach—perhaps an instinctual clinging to life. And then I dig in my pocket for my phone, to call 112. The police. Until I remember again I left my phone in the bathhouse. So I start to run.

CHAPTER EIGHTEEN

Olivia

JULES HAS FOUND Reuben dead in a hot spring, and one thought buzzes in my brain now. The same exact thought that looped my mind ten years ago, when Sydney disappeared:

What do I say when I can't say what really happened?

We've gathered in a conference room in the Terra Nostra hotel where we had dinner, adjacent to the gardens. The lights are stark and confronting in the middle of the night, but not as confronting as Superintendent Flores's grim stature as she stares us down, each in turn.

"I cannot believe that I am standing here today—tonight—with all of you, yet again. And Reuben Bensabat . . . dead."

Wrenching weeps come from the other end of the table. Jules has an arm wrapped around Cass's quivering back, but other than that, no one's touching or looking at one another. Outside the world is black, and I wish I could evaporate right into it. The pressure in my forehead builds. I want another Xanax, but I don't dare reach for it, lest I look even more twitchy and guilty.

"Who wants to tell me what happened? Obviously, we will need to talk to you each in turn again. But first I'd like to hear from you, collectively."

Superintendent Flores gestures at two officers—one older male in his early sixties with dark, shoe-polish-like hair, and a younger woman, early thirties, with prominent, bushy brows that skew unkempt, not fashionable.

"I want to construct a timeline. Who last saw Reuben, and when? Because I understand you were all meant to be in the main thermal pool, but some went off into the park. Convenient place for a murder. Closed off to tourists by the almighty da Costas." Her eyes linger disapprovingly on Lexa and Eli. "No cameras monitoring the section of the park where Reuben—well, we know now what happened."

"How were there no cameras that show anything?" Eli asks.

"This is a small island, Mr. da Costa," Superintendent Flores says. "As you well know. This isn't New York or Boston. And we are fortunate that crime rates here are exceedingly low. Except when you folks show up."

The shoe-polish-hair officer says, "Senhora Superintendente, *posso falar consigo um momento?*"

Superintendent Flores strides to the corner where he is standing to consult, and my curiosity is piqued as he hands her a clear baggie with a few small things.

Now she returns to us and holds the baggie up. "These were found in Reuben's pocket. Perhaps you recognize them."

I hear a gasp that mirrors my own heart racing. It's Eli, his boyish face stark white.

In the baggie is a small tiger eye crystal, which is not responsible for my shock. But next to it, plain as day, is a gold coin. A *fake* gold coin, I presume, whose plastic or plating is congealed, deformed by the high temperature of the hot springs.

A gold coin that looks like the ones outside the terrace that first night.

———

"The treasure hunt again. *Meu deus*, I thought we'd finished with this." The superintendent rubs her eyes. "Tell me, does anyone know how this coin ended up in Reuben's pocket?"

Many heads shake briskly, including mine.

"Right. Well, perhaps he simply pocketed it the night you all saw them. Or maybe there is a different explanation. It sounded like a childhood prank when I was informed of these coins earlier. But now—well, we will certainly get to the bottom of this."

The young, female officer walks up to Superintendent Flores and whispers in her ear. After muffled consultations, Superintendent Flores nods. "I understand that each of you was seen on the cameras covering the Iron Pool and the bathhouse between the hours of 9 p.m., when you finished dinner, and 10:38 p.m., when Jules found Reuben dead in the hot springs. Some of you were in the Iron Pool for a length of time, but all of you—it happens— at some point in that time frame are seen on camera walking the path that ultimately led to the hot spring where Reuben was murdered."

My breath hitches at that.

"Unfortunately, that's where the trail stops. As I've said, there were no cameras outside of the Iron Pool area. My officers are still combing the footage, but from preliminary analyses, it seems that any of you had the opportunity to murder Reuben. Of course, we will need to get a full picture of where each of you was in that time frame. And I'll tell you something right now: I have my suspicions, I certainly do, but I promise you that this isn't going to be a repeat of ten years ago. You aren't all walking out of here scot-free, without someone paying for Reuben's murder. It seems fairly obvious his murder is connected to what happened to Sydney, and I won't rest until I unravel it all. I'll be needing the documentary footage, Jules. I know I said so earlier, but that's become top priority now."

"Okay." Jules nods.

No one else speaks, just the occasional puff and spurt of the central air and Cass's low, desperate cries, which stab at my brain. Then Superintendent Flores says, "Olivia, why don't you tell us what happened tonight?"

"Me? You want *me* to tell you what . . . happened?"

I can't stop thinking about Sydney. If she's alive, how she plays into all this. But of course, I can't say that.

"Yes. I'll rephrase. Where you were during the hours leading up to and after Reuben was murdered?" The question is strategic—and so is the fact that she queued me up first—but her tone isn't sarcastic. She just looks at me thoughtfully, which is even scarier. I like to know what I'm up against. And now I can't tell if Superintendent Flores is friend or foe. She desperately wanted to charge me with Sydney's murder ten years ago. Does she resent that she couldn't do it or does she have a new line of inquiry? She's smart. I still can't decide if that works in my favor or against. I remember her astutely pointed questions from our interrogations when I was younger, and earlier today after the canyoning incident.

Was that actually only this morning? This day is one long mind fuck of a nightmare. Well, I suppose the day is over, actually. My phone tells me it's 12:46 now.

"Olivia," Superintendent Flores says, staring at me expectantly.

But instead, Eli says, "Maybe Reuben wasn't murdered . . . maybe he just . . . slipped." He looks around at us all, as if to galvanize support. "I mean, it could have been an accident."

"An accident?" Superintendent Flores scoffs. "Doubtful. Of course, there will be an autopsy. But a spry young man went up to a roped-off boiling spring and fell in? Hours after an attempt on his life? No, I don't think so. Olivia, please—"

Jules interjects. "Look, before you question Olivia, I have to say—I saw Lexa and Reuben fighting. Sorry, Lex. But I feel like I need to . . . I want to tell the truth."

"You did?" I try to slot that information into place.

"When was that?" the superintendent asks.

Jules shrugs, keeping an arm on Cass's back, still stroking her tenderly. I remember how kind and protective she was of us that summer.

"I don't know. None of us had our phones, so I really can't say. Maybe ten, ten fifteen, I guess?"

"Well, what were they fighting about?"

"We weren't fighting," Lexa says, but almost sounds . . . relieved? As if she thought Jules was going to say something else. But maybe I'm imagining things.

"You were fighting," Jules says simply. "About, oh . . ." Her eyes roll back, like she's trying to summon it amid all the horror of the night. I think about her finding Reuben in the springs and shiver. "I guess about how you guys used to date. And . . ."

"Yes," Superintendent Flores prompts.

"Reuben said something about Lexa being the one who tried to murder him. Or else . . . Eli."

"I can assure you I didn't kill Reuben," Eli says. "I was waiting in the pool for my wife. For all of you guys. I thought that was the plan."

"You did leave the pool at some point," Superintendent Flores says. "We've confirmed it on the video footage from the Iron Pool."

"I went to find Lexa!" he shouts, with uncharacteristic anger. "To see where everyone was."

"And did you find your wife?" Superintendent Flores asks.

"No," he admits. "But—"

"But it's a big property," Lexa says. "The grounds are massive, and I haven't been here in a decade. Not that I knew my way around from back then. I got lost after I talked to Reuben. And I certainly didn't kill him. That's preposterous."

"You dated him when you were younger," Superintendent Flores says.

"So what? I broke up with him. And you can ask anyone—ask his sister, I'm sure she'll vouch—he's had a steady stream of model girlfriends. He's not pining after me. Or he wasn't," she corrects herself with a slight wobble. "And I certainly wasn't pining after him."

"I think he did always pine over you, actually," Cass says, the first words I've heard her speak since her brother's body was found. She lifts her face, her eyes now racoon-looking, smudged with black eyeliner and tears.

"Well, I certainly wouldn't have murdered him for it," Lexa says.

A quiet blankets the room, and then Superintendent Flores says what I'd been hoping she wouldn't. "Olivia, do you have anything to add?"

I've been playing this thing I will say over and over in my mind since Jules ran to the Iron Pool, screaming about Reuben, after I'd just slipped into the hot, sulfuric waters.

"Honestly, I needed some time alone. After we changed in the bathhouse, I wandered aimlessly a bit and sat on a rock somewhere and stared at the springs. Aiden passed by at some point, if that helps."

"Yeah, I saw her," Aiden says, and I nod gratefully at him.

"You sat by yourself for an hour or an hour and a half?" Superintendent Flores says. "Reuben wanted to speak to you. That's what he said when you and I chatted in the stairwell earlier. What was that about?"

I exhale slowly. "I don't know. At some point, I decided to walk around and try to find him, but I didn't see him or anyone, and I came back to the same rock."

"The same rock," Superintendent Flores repeats. "A *rock*. That's your story."

I feel all eyes boring into me. But I'm so fucking done with this. I sit up straighter. "It's not a story. It's what happened. I don't know what happened to Reuben, but I know I had nothing to do with it."

"Uh-huh," Superintendent Flores says, and she opens her mouth to say more, but then I hear commotion out the door. Hysterics, really. I brace my hands against the table as the door opens and my father and Daniella enter, my father rubbing his eyes with his handkerchief and Daniella's haunted cry, eyes darting around like a hunted animal. Or like a vicious predator—I'm never entirely sure. Cass leaps up and into their arms.

CHAPTER NINETEEN

Cass

I **WAKE TO** my mother sitting at the foot of my bed. "What time is it?" I ask, feeling fuzzy and unreal, before it slams me again in the chest.

Reuben's dead. How can it be? How—

"I don't know." She convulses into sobs, the same familiar staccatos of misery, of desperation, of incomprehension, that have punctured my world, punctured our home, since my brother was found dead in a boiling hot spring. Last night I thought, perhaps unkindly, that Mom was the most beautiful mourner I've ever seen. She was made for the role of Bereaved Fifty-Something, willowy and elegant. But now I think I was wrong. Now she's small and sad and the shadows play on her skin, which looks sallow in the moonlight. She is deeply sad, a sad that is not a put-on affect like it certainly was when Sydney disappeared.

"I know, Mom." She grips me to her in a viselike hug and weeps against my chest. "I know. It's . . . I haven't begun to process it yet. It's—"

"Not real." I can feel the wet on my shirt from her face.

Now I'm crying again too. "I know."

"He's—such a good boy! Such a success. So happy. So brilliant."

I stroke her hair, perfectly silky. "I know." Of course, I don't tell her the truth. What Reuben told me. He wouldn't want her to know about his business failures. Even if he sort of hated her, he wouldn't want me to sully her image of him.

Suddenly she pushes me back, jarring me enough that I knock against the cabinet beside my bed that holds all my childhood medals.

"Casia, you didn't—"

"Of course not." I exhale and rub my elbow where it poked the wood.

"Sorry. Oh, thank god. But—"

"I know. But of course, I didn't."

She nods and stands and I watch her long silk robe swish behind her as she leaves. I press the side button on my phone. 4:24. I crick my neck back and forth. We got home around a quarter past two and I sunk into bed, fell into a turbulent half sleep, half nightmare. But that's it for rest. For now, I ignore the gazillion messages lighting up my WhatsApp and instead go to the news, force myself to scan the articles. Unsurprisingly, Reuben's death is being covered worldwide. The headlines range from "Brother of Olympian Casia Bensabat Dead in Suspected Murder" to "New Development in the Disappearance of Sydney Azulay" to "São Murder Island."

The news crews are bound to descend, I realize. It will take them today to get over here, to this island in the middle of nowhere, smack-dab in prime tourist season, when all flights and hotels are booked. But by tomorrow or the day after, they'll arrive. This is too big a story to let go. And it's different from ten years ago; now true crime podcasts proliferate even more, and twelve-year-olds are armchair detectives. Reuben's death is bound to be dissected, to become a lot of people's Super Bowl.

I lift a pillow to my mouth and scream.

————

I pull on shorts and a tee and consider whether to go right to the gym. It's not open, of course, but I have a key. I don't want to be indoors alone, though. I feel myself itching to run, explode into the wilderness. My coach will kill me—the roads are concrete around here, until you get to the trails, and it's bad for my knees and my shin splints, which are currently kept at bay. But I don't care. I need to clear my head.

I check my messages, scroll through the myriad expressions of sympathy from friends and acquaintances. I'm about to close my phone when I see a message from an unknown number, but with a face in the little profile circle that I recognize.

It's Eli, and he's written to me an hour ago: *Hey, Cass. I got your number from Jules, hope that's okay. I know I said it already, but there aren't enough words for how sorry I am. I won't pretend I was close to Reuben, but he was a good guy, and I know how much he loved you. He talked about you all the time, even back then. He was such a proud big brother. Anyway, I know the funeral won't be immediate because of the autopsy, and I'm sure you have a million people who are supporting you right now, but if you need anything—anything at all—I'm here. Lexa, too, of course. We'd love to see you today, if you're up for it. Eli*

And he's put a red heart at the end.

I smile, my first smile since Reuben died. And then I lace up my running shoes, slip on a headlamp, and tuck my phone into my pocket. I hear voices in my parents' bedroom, cries and the sound of something clanging. I linger there at their room door, listening, but can't make out anything distinct. I take a deep breath, then open the front door and sprint out of the house.

I race like I'm being chased, down the cobblestone street with its whitewashed houses in blue and yellow trim and all the basalt stonework around windows and doors. No one's afoot as I pass by the fifteenth-century Catholic church with its looming bell tower, then on through Praça Bento de Góis, a charming piazza adorned with statues and a fountain but otherwise empty now. The moon still looms heavy overhead. How can this possibly be the same splendid moon I looked up at only hours ago, when Reuben was alive? The minutes have this dreamy, floaty sensation that make me feel like I'm gazing down on myself from outer space.

I run harder, faster, sweat now dripping down my face and soaking my shirt. Past the town buildings with vibrant azulejos, depicting historical scenes and religious icons. Down toward the ocean, where I can see rocky outcrops and coves, fishing boats bobbing in the distant harbor, and beyond, the famous islet of Vila Franca do Campo with its distinctive circular shape, where in daylight, people swim and dive and snorkel. After a stretch of coast, I swerve inland again, heading toward the dense forests and babbling streams of Serra de Água de Pau.

As I run, I think only of Reuben. I picture my brother in his ridiculous red-light glasses that he wears at night, because he swears they're better than weed gummies at improving his sleep.

I'll never see him again.

The grief is buried, though, beneath the rage. I feel it bubbling up, like I could actually combust.

What am I going to do?

I'm not sure how long I run until I can't run anymore, but when I reach a field of wildflowers, I tear off my headlamp and explode into a whip back with a double pike. It's one of my signature moves—a low, fast back handspring where my hands don't touch the ground, followed by two backflips in a pike position. In the second I'm in the air, I am so highly present that nothing else exists. But when I land, it all thuds back, making me launch up again into another pass. And again. Again.

I don't know how long until I'm done. Absolutely spent. I crash into the flowers and stare up at the awakening sky. The memories flood in. All of them containing my brother.

When we moved to the island when I was four, I remember how Reuben came to my preschool classroom during lunch and ate with me. One of my very first memories. Even though my teacher told him he wasn't allowed to, he said he wasn't leaving. How we'd collect seashells on the beach and Reuben would walk with them in his hands, adamant that he liked the feeling of something from the earth against his skin—the early precursor to his crystal obsession. How we'd play in the Ghost Hotel, the old abandoned hotel on the same property as the Ananda. Mom worked as a waitress at the Ananda when we first moved here, so when Reub and I sometimes went to work with her, we would trot the half mile down there to play.

I still remember traipsing through the dilapidated rooms and halls, hearing eerie echoes and unexplained noises. Reuben would tell me ghost stories that he learned at camp about the island. He'd spin tales about phantom ships that sunk off the coast, whose sailors and crew now wander the island, and about the ghosts of early settlers who perished during the island's colonization. I didn't get to go to camp because I was always training all summer, so I lapped that stuff up. He said that at camp there was this tradition where a counselor would sneak up to a campfire in the midst of a ghost story, dressed in one of those Handmaids-style traditional Azorean capes—*capote e capelo*. They're gray, with a massive hood that, from the side, fully eclipses a person's face. And Reuben always threatened that he was going to wear one to scare me, but he never did. Still, sometimes he'd burst out of the dumbwaiter we discovered at the Ghost Hotel and would shake my shoulders and scream. He never actually scared me, but I'd pretend and shriek with glee.

I remember how Reuben spotted me the first time I landed a

back walkover, how vigorously he cheered, pride radiating off his face. What Eli wrote me earlier has lingered. My brother never resented the attention I got for gymnastics, never cared that I was famous and he wasn't. He struggled and wanted things for himself he never attained, but he didn't begrudge my achievements. He was genuinely happy for me. And he loved me more than anyone else on earth.

I don't just assume that. I know it. He told me it all the time.

God, I'm so fucking angry. I look out on this quaint, pastoral scene, with the dramatic mountains and the heady scent of the flowers I was raised on, and all I feel is rage.

What am I going to do?

I get out my phone and thumb back to Eli's text. I type out a reply: *Thanks. Means a lot. It's shocking . . . I haven't processed it at all. But I need to get out of the house, and like you said, we can't have the funeral today. It would be really nice to see you.* I add a red heart at the end, too.

Suddenly I know exactly what I am going to do.

CHAPTER TWENTY

Sydney

Ten Years Before

THE FIRST THING I do after Aiden drops me off and I bound down to the cove, finally stepping atop the black sand deliciousness, is kneel down to open my backpack.

Then I remember that the pack isn't mine. Which is entirely my fault.

I start to spiral about the fact that when I took Aiden's backpack, I didn't remember my journal. I twist my thumb around his zipper, stress-scrolling my thoughts. Even though it's the same requisition black backpack that everyone gets from the assigned camp store in Newton, of course Aiden's pack doesn't have the green lanyard Olivia made me at camp like seven years ago that I've always sentimentally kept. She doesn't even remember making it for me—which is good because I don't need to give my sister the ego boost. I mean, we love each other. She's literally my favorite person in existence. But it zings me how I often tell her the opposite. Once I even called her the human embodiment of a Monday, which at the time I was pretty proud of. We fight so often that our parents have said we're like feral toddlers with a vocabulary.

But I mean, we're sisters; ever since I came down the birth canal and onto the scene, we've been competing for the bigger share of the finite parental pie. I usually win—I'm sick. Trump card. Plus, Dad is team *me*. Always has been. But Olivia is smart and a genuinely good person and quiet and loves to read, and Mom is an introvert, so Liv is edging me out into favorite zone.

I shove off all these uncomfortable feelings that crawl down my spine. Emotions on steroids. I seriously can't deal. All I want now is my journal to spill them out into. I picture Liv, writing her stories around the campfire, face scrunched in concentration. I should be nicer to Liv. I should never have threatened to tell the rest of them about her crush on Jules. That was savage and unnecessary. I wish she was here, and I could apologize, and then tell her what I just found out.

Tsunami-level devastation. It affects us both.

I was going to tell her last night, but then she called me "an awful person" after she saw me kissing Aiden. And then it was on. We went at it. I rub my shoulder, where she scratched me hard. I said things I didn't mean. We both did. And then I trauma-dumped it all in my journal until the fire within me had somewhat subsided.

The fire is back. What if—

No. Aiden won't read my journal. He has integrity.

Unlike me—and the shame bubbles up again. Because, yes, I deliberately took Aiden's backpack, knowing he'd have to come swap his back. I kissed him by the woods, but clearly nothing can happen between us when everyone else is around. I've given him the perfect way in. My medicine is in the backpack I've left behind. When he figures it out, he'll have to come switch them back. And now we've got this whole slice of paradise. Just us . . . alone.

I know he wants me. I know it.

I imagine us making out next to a waterfall. Or on the flatbed of rocks, him pinning me down, my back slippery so he has to lock me in place.

I close my eyes and picture him: sexy and mysterious and

tanned forearms, all those bird tattoos lining them. How he issues orders, confidently, and everyone snaps to attention. He's not boy-next-door sweet like Eli. He's a man. And he's off-limits. And the fact that he hasn't given into me yet makes me want him more.

Even though I've noticed how he sometimes flirts with Jules (Aiden's version of flirting is offering to carry her pack, or fill her water bottle back up, or take boxes from her arms, like she's some kind of invalid—when, hello, *I'm* the invalid!). He looks at Jules when she doesn't notice with this piercing, pensive sort of gaze, like he's drinking her up, everything about her. I low-key burn with envy when that happens, to be honest, even though I know it's not rational. Jules is nothing but sweet to me. It's actually cute, how much she wants my approval, how she asks me to teach her how to braid her hair like I do mine. But when Aiden stares at her all sappy, it makes me despise Jules. It's why when I found her bracelet by the campfire last night, I took it instead of giving it back to her. She was freaking out, but I still didn't tell her I had it. In the car with Aiden, I put it on my wrist.

I'm probably a monster for this, aren't I, that I want to make her suffer a little? Harmless suffering. But I know the bracelet is special to her. She was straight-up crying over losing it. It's a family heirloom, apparently, passed down by her grandmother. It's very heavy, compared to my gold-plated stuff, which makes me think it's real. It also just looks real. Old. I stare at it, the arrows below the cross. It feels kind of wrong to be wearing something with a cross on it. It's not like it's even that cute of a bracelet or anything. I'll give it back to her after Survival Day.

I keep messing with the zip on Aiden's backpack. The waves rip and roar, and the air is that briny beachside whip that brims with promise. I stare out from my little cove hideaway, feeling at peak curiosity over what might be inside his pack. Finally, I can't handle it anymore. I unzip it and am kinda shook at what's sitting right on top. Bundles wrapped in cellophane. Holy shit—is this . . . ?

I spin one around in my palm. Yep, yep it certainly is. I set it down, digging beneath the bundles to take stock of the other items—a thick cloth-covered *War and Peace*, black boxer briefs, a Dopp kit with a smudge of blue toothpaste on the vinyl lip. My brain scrambles to make sense of things.

Okay, so Aiden's dealing drugs or is, like, a mule—so *that's* what his secret phone chats have been. Now it all clicks. I was thinking it could have been a girlfriend back home but, nope, guess I was wrong.

I feel this, like, crushing sadness all of a sudden, which I can't even really explain. Because I've put Aiden on a pedestal of integrity, but apparently, like every other man I know and love, he is such a complete letdown.

I know, of course, about the cocaine saga on the island fifteen years ago. There've been stories about campers on heritage trips back then who got mixed up in it. But I've lived a pretty sheltered life, I guess. No one I know does drugs. Okay, maybe some weed, but that's it. I might talk tough, but deep down, I'm basically a Goody Two-shoes. I still sing in the synagogue choir, like, come on.

There's a crunch in the shrubs behind, and I whip around, heart racing. But then the sound is gone, and all I hear is the churn of the ocean. There's no one but me.

Chill, just chill, Syd. I've been counting down the minutes for this—to be alone and free. To think, make a plan of what to do next.

Make out with Aiden when he comes to swap our backpacks.

The town isn't far, so I know it's possible that I'll see other people, even though this beach on the inlet is a secluded one, because to reach it you have to travel over a hundred stone steps down the steep mountainside. And I know, logically, that I have the emergency radio, in case I need it. But what if Aiden's drug lord buddies come looking?

No way, that's totally insane. Still, these twisted fears won't leave me alone. Of everything I've been stressed about this past week, I didn't expect to add a couple pounds of drugs in my possession to the list.

Aiden reminded me not to swim when he dropped me off here. That it's not safe without a lifeguard. That riptides can appear no matter how calm it looks.

But this is a cove, after all, and the waves are little kitten licks. And also, like, doesn't he know that telling me not to do something is only going to make me want to do it ten times more?

I pull my T-shirt over my head and catch a whiff of my smelly armpits. Back home, I'd be grossed out, but here? The smell is kind of like a trophy. This summer is so delicious and awful, both at the same time.

I cram the drugs back into Aiden's backpack and zip it back up, then I run at full speed toward the ocean, screaming like a maniac.

———

I've been floating like a mermaid, tanning it up, when I spot movement on the steps. Instant drug-lord-size heart attack. But then—those arms. Those familiar, stupidly hot inked-up arms.

Oh, thank literally *every* deity. It's Aiden.

I rise to greet him on the sand, trying to walk in a sultry way like they do on that old-school *Baywatch* show where they pair Speedos with Ugg boots. Lexa and I were watching reruns once and dying at the fashion, and she grabbed the Ugg boots that my mom wears in the snow and one of my Speedos and went to try them on and then put on this dramatic fashion show, serving face. It was hilarious, and by the end we were both crying-laughing on the floor. Lexa is the best, if you don't count the fact that it's obvious she wants my boyfriend so bad. Actually, I kind of like that part. That I have something she wants. Maybe it's even why

I've stayed together with Eli so long. To make her jealous. I'm the literal worst.

I flip my hair in Aiden's direction.

"I told you it's not safe to swim" is the first thing he says, not smiling.

"I know." Heart: racing even faster. I clock Liv's lanyard swinging off his backpack and I exhale. "But I've never been much for following rules."

I squeeze out my dripping hair, proud of my audacity. But then I gaze down at my protruding stomach in my Speedo, a product of too much GORP and Spooey (this delicious chocolate gooey thing we concocted). You'd think a hiking trip would make you drop the pounds, but nope. The opposite. And boom—I'm suddenly so aware of standing in front of my counselor postkiss, all half dripping and weirdly breathless. Cool cool cool. I remind myself he's seen me looking far worse—dripping sweat at the top of Sete Cidades, sitting next to me on day six after not showering. But this is different.

He tosses my backpack down. "Did you even realize you took the wrong one?"

"Well . . . yeah."

"Oh." His eyes are hidden behind his Wayfarers, but I can tell by his rigid stance that he's nervous. "So you saw . . ."

"I saw."

"I'm sorry." He exhales heavily. "You shouldn't . . . wow, I'm really ashamed, Sydney. It's a long story. I'm not doing drugs, by the way. Look, my mom's sick and we need money for her treatments and—"

"You don't have to explain," I rush out, feeling all kinds of awkward. "I didn't know your mom was sick."

"Yeah." The word is full of emotion, heaviness.

Then he says, "The second I realized I had your backpack, I came back. Wanted to make sure you have your medicines."

"Oh. Yeah, it'll be fine."

"Okay, well . . . we're okay?"

I know what he's asking. "I'm not going to tell anyone what I found, if that's what you mean."

He smiles, his lopsided Aiden smile that I think about at night when I manage to close my eyes. "Thank you. Thank you so much, Sydney. I can't tell you how much—well, I really appreciate it. This is my last drop, I promise. I've made enough. I'm done. I can't believe I nearly put you—honestly, I'm angry at myself. Really angry."

"It's okay." It feels like the wrong time to try to kiss him, but I want him so bad. Eli and I have been a thing forever. But lately it's like . . . he just doesn't get me. Not my mood swings, not my whole "tomorrow might literally be my last day" spirals. I'm trying to live loud, chase what I want, make each day really count. Because I'm not guaranteed a tomorrow. That's the sucky truth.

"Aiden, I like you," I tell him, trying to be bold like Queen Esther. *What would Queen Esther do?* is something I ask myself often. Even though I know comparing myself to her is totally dramatic, especially in this situation. But still, when I think of how she legit saved the entire Jewish people from genocide back in ancient times, I feel this weird surge of bravery. "I know that we're not allowed to—"

He reddens, backs away. "Sydney, you're underage. And also, you have a boyfriend—"

"Yes, but it's a high school thing. We're basically done. I'll end it. I'm going to end it."

"I . . ."

My whole body is buzzing. I'm just standing here—like, kiss me already! Scoop me up in your arms and reassure me that it's going to be okay. We'll sit on the rocks by the water, and I'll tell him everything—literally everything. What I found out this week. And he'll help me. Suddenly I'm certain of it; he's the person who won't bail, who will help me figure out how to deal with all the shit hands I've been dealt.

"Sydney, look, I'm really sorry if I've somehow unintentionally led you on. You're amazing. An amazing kid."

Kid? Instant stab to my heart.

"But I—we can't. I should have said so explicitly the other night."

My insides are twisted up like pretzels. "Is it because of the camp rules? Because I'd never tell. I wouldn't—"

"That and, honestly, I have feelings for someone else."

"Oh." Jules. I knew it. I twirl her bracelet around, wrapping my fingers in the jangly charms.

His eyes travel to my wrist. "Is that Jules's? The bracelet she was looking for?"

"Yeah." I flush and put my hand up like a visor on my forehead, pretending the sun has gotten in my eyes. "I found it by the campfire this morning. She'd already left to drop off Lexa, Reub, and Eli, so I put it on for safekeeping, to give to her tomorrow."

"Here." He puts out his hand. "I'm going to see her now. I'll give it to her."

But the bracelet feels glued to my wrist. I literally can't deal—the rejection, and the fact that he's gonna run back to Jules with her dumb bracelet like he's in some Nicholas Sparks book. Bet she kisses him right then and there.

"I'll give it to her tomorrow," I say firmly. "It will be safe on my wrist until then."

He opens his mouth like he's conflicted but eventually closes it, not protesting. I know we have a silent understanding, one like others I've made in the past.

It's: *I know that you know I'm doing a sort of shitty thing, but I also know your secrets, so let's call it even.*

"Okay, I'm gonna go," Aiden says. "Leave you to your Survival Day. Sorry to start it off so . . ."

I wait, curious about the word he'll use to describe this whole trainwreck exchange, but nope. Radio silence. He gives me an awkward half salute, half wave, no hug, and then turns and walks briskly up the stairs. I rub my foot into the gritty sand, hoping it will ground me, but all I feel is this big echoey hollow feeling. Like the Ghost Hotel inside me. Even though the drugs are outta my hands, and I'm no longer worried about getting popped by some cartel guy, I'm suddenly freaking out for the rest of Survival Day, and regretting that I insisted on getting assigned the beach spot. It sounded romantic and fun, to swim here alone. Plus, most importantly, the old abandoned da Costa estate is right above. Potential treasure up for grabs, if I'm in the mood to go looking for it. How sick it would be, to casually walk back after Survival Day and be like, *Hey, guys, I found it. We're fucking rich!* But more than that, my secret reason for why I want to find the treasure more than anything is that I believe in the legend. If I find the treasure, all my problems will be turned to gold. I'll be cured. Healed.

I'm not being sappy, I know that being healthy is the OG treasure chest.

We didn't find the treasure the day we all went to look at the old da Costa estate, but I figured being a stone's throw away, I could go, climb the gate, poke around. But now I'm realizing, even if I do that, I'll have to sleep here later. And the beach is so open. Wild. Exposed. And, yeah, that's kinda terrifying.

Maybe I should have taken Liv's spot, a mile from here and snug in some meadow. I could have been chilling in a cute little field with wildflowers and birdsong. But no, I had to pick the "adventurous" beach. This isn't cozy. It's savage. And so isolated. I'm not going to actually find the treasure. Let's be real. Honestly, the treasure's probably fake. A glorified campfire story.

I stare at Aiden, getting smaller as he mounts the steps. He turns abruptly. "Syd?"

My heart does a horrible fluttering thing. For a full beat,

I think he's gonna sprint back and grab me, like full rom-com mode.

"Yeah?" I manage to sound bored and uncaring, but inside the hope is combusting.

"If you go swimming again—which I highly advise you do not, but if you do—take Jules's bracelet off before and put it in a safe spot. It's an heirloom. Her grandmother gave it to her. Please, Sydney. Take good care of it, okay?"

CHAPTER TWENTY-ONE

Lexa

"REALLY? MORE WORK?" Eli asks me as we get in the elevator. "Who are you texting this time?" He tries to look over my shoulder, and I angle to the side, blocking his view.

"What?" I stuff my phone in my purse. At least I was allowed to keep that, when we were finally herded back into the hotel and given new rooms. I look at myself in the mirror as we lurch down. Definitely a fat mirror, and I don't look my best, to say the least. Leave the bluish crescents beneath my eyes that I didn't have my concealer to cover up. I'm in Eli's shirt, a pair of denim shorts, and Vejas, all of which were retrieved in a rush under the watchful gaze of the *polizia*. If only I had sunglasses to put on, but nope. Those are in our suite. We weren't even allowed to take our suitcases when we got back last night after being interrogated, and the officers kept hurrying us along like we were presumptive criminals. I don't even have fucking deodorant. I'm going to smell as bad as I did ten years ago on our heritage trip.

"Who are you texting?" Eli repeats. I can tell he's irritated but trying not to unleash it. "I mean, even for you, it's a lot. You're, like, glued to your phone. And it's the weekend now."

I rub my shoulder. "I slept like shit. The bed is rock-hard. They have nicer ones in the suites."

"They're the same beds. Lex, what's going on? Who were you texting?"

"My mom," I finally explode. "Not work. My mom was texting. Is that okay with you? The news is all over the place at this point. It's like . . . international."

"Shit." He rubs his forehead. "Sorry. I'm—"

"She's obviously worried. And . . . upset."

"Oh." I see it dawn in his eyes, that my mom knew Reuben. I mean, he didn't live in the Boston area like the rest of us, but he grew up going to camp. And we were dating.

"Sorry. I-I—"

"I know." I squeeze his hand. "We can't lose it. They're going to tear us apart now, try to get us to implicate each other."

"We didn't do it, though."

"Well, I know that, and you know that. But Superintendent Flores? Pretty sure she doesn't know that."

"We had no motive. I literally have barely thought of Reuben Bensabat in ten years."

"They're out for blood," I say quietly as the elevator dings at the lobby. "We have to be a united front, E. And on guard."

———

We've all written in our text group, arranging to meet in the lobby to debrief after the horrific night, but the first person I see is someone surprising. A person not in our text group. Cass Bensabat.

The even more surprising thing is Eli striding over to greet her like she's come from a daring desert island rescue. "Cass! Oh god, I'm so glad you came. I'm so sorry. We're all—words can't express. It's unreal. Absolutely unreal."

He wraps her in a hug, and I hate the feeling that overtakes me as she rests her perfect, poreless, filtered-in-real-life face on his shoulder and flutters her eyes closed. When she opens them, she is racked with a sob, and then Eli pulls her in again. I stand awkwardly beside them, like a personal assistant.

"Lex, do you have a tissue?" Eli doesn't look at me, only extends his hand and flexes his fingers a couple times.

"I didn't realize Cass was coming," I say, loud enough for her to hear. I know I should be one million percent sympathetic right now. Cass lost her brother, in a truly horrifying way. But she's also a stunning Olympian medalist currently sobbing on my husband's shoulder. My husband, with whom she's been subtly flirting the past few days.

"Lex . . ." The hand-flexing thing again, as he gently pushes her hair out of her eyes.

"I don't have a fucking tissue! When have I ever once carried a fucking tissue?"

At that opportune moment, Superintendent Flores appears from behind the massive banquette that houses the coffee and tea station.

"Ah! You're all here." She fixes her gaze on me. "I have some further questions."

———

As the rest of them file in, Cass parks herself right beside Eli on a couch, leaving me in a stuffed chair to his other side. Superintendent Flores informs us that there have been some discrepancies in our interviews. They will want to talk to us all more, but later in the day after more evidence has been gathered, our suites been thoroughly searched, the documentary footage pored over, and further investigations made.

"But I do have one immediate question: Why did all of you lie to me?"

Eli reaches over and puts a hand on my thigh. It chills there like deadweight.

"Why did you not tell me that someone else was at Terra Nostra with you? Maria . . . Maria—"

"But I wasn't."

I blink a couple times and register her, this Maria girl who is always with us, popping out of corners. The one who saw Aiden with her drug-addict father and pieced together his deceptions. It's suspicious, isn't it? Or at least, suspicious enough to throw the suspicions off the rest of us. Off me. I relax a smidge.

"I didn't go to dinner with them," Maria amends. "They didn't want it filmed."

Affronted murmurs—everyone balking at the implication they have something to hide. Except all of us do, which is increasingly clear to me. And which I think can be used to my advantage. If I can sit by myself with a coffee—a very, very strong coffee—for a beat and think. Think without all of them, including Eli, in my ears—

"It's not that we didn't want it filmed," Jules says carefully. "But we had the memorial for Sydney earlier. We simply wanted to be together. Friends who hadn't seen one another in a long time."

"Friends—one of whom murdered another," the superintendent says.

"Touché," I say under my breath.

"You're still calling it murder," Aiden says, "but couldn't it have been an accident? Like, maybe Reuben went up there . . . and somehow fell in?"

"No. We're treating it as murder," the superintendent says. "We've identified bruising on Reuben's upper back consistent with him being shoved."

Deafening quiet, as everyone takes that information in.

"But he was found face up," Aiden says, then reddens. "I mean, wasn't he? That's what Jules said."

"He was found face up," the superintendent confirms. "But

there was water on the ground next to the pool, as though he'd struggled but then succumbed. So our working theory is that he was pushed from behind. Moving on to . . . Maria. Tell me, please, why did my *inspetora* inform me that you were seen on the grounds of Terra Nostra? By the cameras around the Iron Pool. Shortly before Reuben's murder?"

All eyes snap toward Maria. I notice that for the first time her blood-red lips are smudged onto her yellowish front teeth, confirming it's been a shitty night for us all.

I have to give it to her, though, she's calm as a cucumber. "I had a rough cut of the documentary filming. I was starting to put it together, and I got excited to show Jules. I thought she'd want to see it as soon as it was ready."

"At ten in the evening?"

Maria shrugs. "This project has been our whole lives the past few months. It's felt like . . . life or death." She pinkens: with her red lipstick and shoes she looks even more like the girl from that fairy tale. The girl who bites the apple. Or the one with the cape? I never went gaga for fairy tales as much as the other girls did.

"And . . . you saw Jules?" the superintendent asks.

"No." Maria pauses meaningfully, making me wonder whether she saw something else. But she quickly says, "I didn't see any of them, honestly. None of them were at the Iron Pool. I checked the bathhouse quickly, but Jules wasn't answering her phone. I figured they'd all left."

The superintendent cocks her head. "Even though the guard told you they were still there?" She turns to all of us. "He only let her in because she was already on the list."

"I literally only met Reuben this week! I certainly didn't kill him," Maria says.

"Well, we'd like to ask you some more questions. So please don't go anywhere."

"And what about the rest of us?" Aiden asks.

"The rest of you . . . like I said, we'll want to talk to you later. And don't leave the island, that goes without saying. Stick together. There is safety in numbers."

"Can we go back to our suites?" I ask. "I have a few things I want to—"

"No. We're still searching them."

"So twiddle our thumbs in the lobby then?" I try to sound jokey, but I can't excise the anger that comes through.

No one laughs anyhow, and I can tell Eli is irritated with me. He has an arm slung around a white-faced Cass, who is staring out in mid-distance toward the sea, looking like she's somewhere very far away. I notice that Eli's stroking Cass's shoulder with his thumb, and I pinch my thigh.

"What were you all planning to do today?" the superintendent asks, surprising me.

"Hike Sete Cidades. Like, nothing intense, a stroll up top for a couple hours, for old times' sake," Jules says. "Obviously we won't do that anymore. Not with Reuben—"

"Well, you should go," the superintendent says, standing abruptly and slapping her thighs. "Yes, off with you all. You will go!"

"Go . . . hiking?" Aiden asks. "Isn't that—"

"Yes. You will all be together, so there should not be a safety concern." Her eyes rove among us and suddenly she says, "Senhora Casia."

"Wha—yes?"

The superintendent's whole face softens. "I've already expressed my condolences, but I want to do so again. I promise you, we will find out what happened to your brother. And in the meantime, you are here because . . . Why are you here?"

"Oh, I don't know." Cass wrings her hands together in her lap but doesn't look up. "I didn't want to be alone. And frankly, I didn't really want to be with my parents. They're . . . distraught. You can imagine. My friends are mostly on the mainland. I train in Lisbon, so I haven't lived on the island since I was much younger. And Eli invited me here so—"

"Yes. Good." The superintendent nods. "So you will all go hiking. And since Senhora Casia is the only one among you cleared of all suspicion—because she was not on the infamous canyoning trip—then she will alert me if anything goes awry. Senhora Bensabat, are you up for the task? *Talvez o ar fresco te faça bem.*"

Cass lifts her head, gives the superintendent a weary gaze. "Hiking? You want me to go hiking?"

"It is only a suggestion. You are free, of course, to do anything you like."

"Hiking." To my surprise, she nods. "Okay, it's a weird thing to do the day after . . . the day after he . . . but we can't bury him yet. There's the autopsy to wait for. So—yes. I'll go."

No one moves. I think we're all stunned. Hiking . . . now? It's the last thing I want to do.

"*Tá bom?*" the superintendent says. "Out of my hair then, all of you."

I look down at my feet. I was able to grab my sneakers last night, but not socks. "I don't even have socks," I say quietly, not expecting her to hear.

The superintendent cocks her head at me. "I'm sure Senhor Reuben would wish for his only problem today to be a lack of socks."

CHAPTER TWENTY-TWO

Jules

SETE CIDADES IS on the western side of the island, famed for its twin lakes situated in the crater of a dormant volcano and separated by a narrow isthmus. I used to come here with my grandmother. Vovó grew up across the island, and for her, a trip to Sete Cidades was the special, rare equivalent of, say, a trip to Paris for kids here nowadays. Even when she stopped being able to walk, I used to take her in her wheelchair, push her by the overlooks onto the two lakes.

Now, I stand at the slat-wooden fence and peer out, over the meadow of cream and pale blue hydrangeas slanting down into the green lake, with forests hugging the shoreline. Beyond the green lake lies the blue one, but today the fog crowds it out of sight.

A few feet over, I hear a tour guide explain the legend of the lakes to a couple. How they are different colors because once a green-eyed princess and a blue-eyed shepherd were forbidden to be together. They both cried so hard that their tears filled the crater, creating the two lakes.

Aiden is a few feet away, listening too. We haven't spoken much since Reuben was found murdered. I mean, of course he hugged me and tried to console me, said he was there for me, but

I couldn't let him in. I've felt so numb ever since finding Reuben in that awful way. When we finally got in last night, and I got assigned a new room, I nearly crawled to my bed with exhaustion. And I stared at the ceiling, rubbed my stomach, and cried. Not only because Reuben was murdered, but because it solidifies the fact that one of us is a murderer and killed Sydney all those years ago. No matter how much I suspected that was true, I realized that I've held on to a shred of deeply subconscious hope that Syd disappeared for her own reasons and would pop up out of nowhere one day when the timing was right. And then I fell into a startlingly deep and dreamless sleep.

I awoke to a fit of nausea and barely made it to the bathroom before throwing up the entirety of my cozido. Then I crawled back in bed, and all my problems cascaded back. I felt an overwhelming sense of guilt for even thinking of myself and my relative minutiae when Reuben is gone. For contemplating how this is going to affect the documentary—but I can't deny that I am.

"The shepherd and the princess." Aiden comes up behind me. "I always loved that story." I have a powerful urge to lean back against his chest, but I suppress it.

"If you've come here to make a comparison to us, I don't think it's really the day for it."

"No, only that it made me think about what color eyes our baby will have," he says softly, stunting me of breath.

"I hope blue like yours," I finally say. "Mine have been called muddy brown."

"Well, I hope beautiful muddy brown then."

"How can he just be gone, Aid?" I feel my eyes burning, and I fumble for my sunglasses in my bag.

"I don't know. But they're going to get to the bottom of this."

"They didn't last time."

"No. That's true."

We stand in quiet for a while, and I notice that Aiden still hasn't asked me if I did it. If I killed Reuben. I wonder if he's thought it at all, if even a small part of him entertains the idea that it could be me. Because I can't deny that a small part of me has wondered if it could be him. Not for any specific reason, but because I can't understand why someone would murder Reuben in such a vicious way. After one daring, unsuccessful attempt already. It's just—why is everything still so opaque ten years later? Why can I still not see things clearly?

I spot Lexa some ways over, staring out into the misty day, seemingly having the same idea as me, waiting for a lightning bolt of understanding to spike down. Her eyes flick over to us and she smiles tentatively, eases back from the railing like she's about to walk over. But suddenly I am keenly anxious to escape that interaction. Get my thoughts straight before I confront Lexa about what I heard last night.

"I'm gonna walk with Liv for a bit, okay?"

"Sure." Aiden pats my shoulder. "I'm here, Jules. I'm not going anywhere."

I nod and stride briskly ahead along the gravel patch to catch up with Olivia. Eli seems to be leading everyone, along with Cass, down the path through the forest that leads to Lagoa do Canario.

Olivia almost leaps from her skin when I barrel up next to her.

"Sorry, didn't mean to scare you." I touch her arm. "How you holding up, Liv?"

"I don't know. Shocked? My dad is beside himself."

I wince, remembering Isaac from last night, when he and Daniella came to collect Cass. I always thought Isaac was so handsome, like a tanned, blue-eyed George Clooney. He always seemed vigorous, but last night he looked like a shriveled raisin version of himself. Frail. Elderly, even, as he tried to console his wife, to prop her up, but I saw his knees buckle. How he collapsed down into a chair, buried his head in his hands.

"I can only imagine. It . . . doesn't feel real. And you were . . ."

I decide to take a stab at it, no matter how clunky it might sound. "Sitting by yourself on a rock the whole time?"

She swallows, then says something surprising. "Yes. Reuben wanted to talk to me, did you know that? He tried to pull me aside at the memorial, but I was with the superintendent."

That's news to me. "What did he want to say?"

"I don't know. I tried to find him. He was murdered before he could tell me."

"Shit." I find myself surveying her, trying to see if she's telling the truth. I don't want to feel suspicious of Liv, but honestly, she's been twitchy and weird since she arrived on the island again. Liv and I aren't close, but I've always thought her heart was pure. And I've never truly thought she murdered her sister, or else I would have told the police about her having my bracelet. But now they're going to find out when they get through the documentary transcript. Maybe today, maybe tomorrow. It's going to be suspicious. For Liv—and for me—that I kept it secret.

"Liv, you know they're gonna find out about my bracelet."

She nods, a shadow passing over her face. A chill descends as we enter the forest, and I pull on my grandma's cardigan, the one thing I made sure to grab from my suite last night. The trail to the lake branches off to the left, leading us through the dense cryptomeria and cedar trees. The path is moss-lined and shaded, lending an otherworldly aura to this otherworldly conversation.

"I told you," Olivia finally says. "I found it on the cave floor after the police swept the place. When we all went, it was there."

"I don't believe you."

"Well, that's your prerogative."

"Liv, if there's anything more you want to tell me, I'm here. I really want to know. I've never thought you killed your sister. And I don't think you killed Reuben. But I'm worried the police might draw different conclusions. If you tell me, maybe I can help."

"You can't help," she says, sounding . . . desolate. That's the word that comes. "No one can help. Only my sister." She whispers the last part so quietly I barely make it out.

I know it for certain now. She's keeping something big inside. "Tell me. Just tell me, Liv. Two heads are better than one. You can trust me."

She stops her brisk pace and spins toward me, her face ashen, her green eyes dulled.

"Okay, fine, but it's going to sound . . . insane."

"I can do insane." I gesture around to all of us walking down the path. "This is all already insane."

"What would you say if I told you . . . I think I've seen Sydney twice since I got here."

"Your sister?" I finally manage to say. "You're telling me you think your sister is alive . . . and watching us?" I spin around, chills budding on my arms. "Are you joking?"

"It's not a joke. And honestly, that's not all. There are things I haven't said—because I'm afraid—but I need to tell someone, Jules. If I don't, I feel like I'm gonna—"

But she's interrupted by Cass letting out a curdling scream ahead. I rush forward out of sheer instinct as Cass crumples to the ground, clutching her ankle. Aiden rushes past me toward her. Eli is already bent down beside Cass, examining her ankle in his hands, as Cass swivels it and says stuff about how she thinks she's all right, that she must've tripped. I'm not needed—the guys have got it. I stride back toward Olivia.

Olivia just stands there, unmoored.

"Liv? You okay? What were you starting to say?"

But I can already feel the moment sliding away. And honestly, will I even believe whatever comes out of her mouth? Maybe everyone was right back then, maybe Olivia *is* a little cuckoo. Because Syd being alive . . . and somehow stalking her . . . it's totally impossible.

Right?

Olivia smiles sadly. "Nothing. Honestly—it was nothing." She walks ahead, past Cass and the guys, not even looking at them, toward the marshy, ethereal lake in the distance. And then she's engulfed in the fog and gone.

————

Back at the hotel, Superintendent Flores is waiting for us. She announces she has more questions, starting with Aiden. He meets my eyes from across the lobby. I shrug, and he shrugs back. I imagine we are communicating with these shrugs, but I'm not sure what we're even saying.

All I know is I'm spent. I'm exhausted and queasy and also ravenous. I'm eating a sleeve of crackers Aiden bought me, but I'm desperate for a real meal. We've all been told to stick around the hotel, so my plan is to go collapse in my room and order room service.

I join Lexa at the reception counter, because this is the type of überfancy hotel I only learned about at Lexa and Eli's wedding, with wooden keys you have to leave behind on your way out the door, that the front desk gives you back when you return. I still don't get the appeal. I'd rather have a key card that I don't have to drop off and collect again. Rich people—can't say they're not skilled at finding ways to complicate things.

I tell the receptionist my new room number—24—and Lexa says hers, and then the receptionist's face sparks.

"You are Mrs. da Costa?"

"Yes," Lexa says.

"Mrs. da Costa," I repeat, remembering what I overheard last night.

Lexa gives me a sad sort of smile, and part of me is hoping she'll confide in me without me having to ask.

"I was given a message for you. It's . . ." The receptionist rummages in her drawer, then she slides out an expensive-looking cream envelope. "I was told specifically to only give it to you. Not to Mr. da Costa." She smiles broadly, but when Lexa doesn't react, the woman's smile immediately fades, like she understands she's said something indiscreet.

Lexa stares expressionless at the envelope, then slips it in her purse. We both accept our keys. Lexa begins to stride off toward the elevator bank.

"Lex . . ."

She looks wearily back. When I catch up to her, she says, "It's fine that you told the police you saw me with Reuben. We might have fought, but I didn't kill him, Jules."

"I know you didn't. Of course, you didn't."

"Oh? Okay, good. And I'm sorry we didn't get that coffee this morning, given the circumstances—"

"I don't want to talk about that. I want to talk about your phone call I overheard last night."

Lexa goes very still. "What do you think you heard?"

"What do I think—I mean, I heard that you're having an affair. That you're cheating on Eli. And I don't—"

"An affair?" Lexa laughs, a startling laugh. "Oh god, Jules. I have so much to worry about right now, but that's the least of it. That's fucking hilarious. An affair? *Hilarious.*"

"You're not having an affair," I repeat uncertainly.

"No. Definitely not."

"Okay . . . what's the note then?"

"That?" She waves a hand. "I don't know. My mom probably. Look, J, I love you, but I need to go rest before they want to talk to me again." She gives me a paper-thin hug, then dashes off.

I watch her disappear into the elevator. The doors close quickly—like she jabbed at the close button to escape me instead of waiting for them to naturally shut. Finally, I start toward the elevator bank, scrolling absently to my email. I click on a spam auto insurance message, and then an email from an unknown sender. I scan the email incredulously.

"Holy fuck," I say, as Eli comes up next to me and presses the up button.

"What's that—Jules, did you see Lex?"

"Yeah, she already went up. But holy fuck, Eli." I show him the email as we step into the elevator. "Does this look legit to you?"

He reads, then whistles. "The vice president of documentary features at Netflix. This is wild, Jules. How did you even get to them?"

"I had a contact for a content executive and was cold emailing them, but they didn't seem interested. She told me when I had the full footage to let her know, but she couldn't make promises. And she couldn't buy it on spec. I never really thought—never dreamed, to be honest. Netflix. Fuck."

"Well, things must have changed after Reuben's murder made international news."

I'm silent, because he's right. That must be it.

"Wow, you couldn't have planned that more perfectly." Even though I know he doesn't mean it as a jab, it stings.

But it's true, isn't it? I loved Reuben, and as torn up about his death as I am, I can't deny the documentary has become a hell of a lot more marketable with another of the Fab Five dead.

"It's really great, Jules. They *should* make the documentary. They'll pay you a boatload, I'm sure."

I hate myself, that I too am already seeing the dollar signs.

"They'll want us to film more. I don't know if everyone will be up for that at this stage."

"They'll probably take what they can get," Eli says. "Be happy with what we've already filmed. Any morsel will be something for the rabid fans."

Fans. He's right, but it feels gross to imagine there are fans, cheering on this grisly story that doesn't yet have a culmination.

The elevator dings, and Eli motions for me to enter first. I do, feeling chilled even though I'm snuggled in Vovó's cardigan. Eli scrolls his phone, clearly trying to detach, and that's fine with me, because I don't have the bandwidth to cheerily engage anymore. To pretend that his wife isn't having an affair, and that this isn't the new worst day of my life. The email is incredible—unreal, really—something I would have died to receive just a day before, but I can't forget that I'm still trapped in this new old nightmare.

Even if Netflix does buy the documentary, does want to pay me to see it through, we're still very much in medias res. And I have zero clue what comes before The End.

CHAPTER TWENTY-THREE

Sydney

Ten Years Before

WHEN I'M BORED with baking on the rocks and staring out at the ocean, I decide to venture toward the steps hewn into the cliff face, leading up from the cove. I sling my smaller knapsack around my shoulder, with my journal, a bottle of water, and my medicine, just in case, and I begin the trek up in the boiling sun. I look up at the sky, trying to decipher what time it is from the sun's position. They used to teach us that shit at camp, but I was never paying close attention, either midflirting with some guy, or midrehearsal for a camp play, or midrotting in bed, feeling sick and writing angsty journal entries about how tragic my life was.

I don't understand how Liv spends all her time writing these fake stories about fake people. I could spend my whole lifetime writing about myself and still not be done. But Livvie's life isn't as scary or interesting as mine, I guess.

The steps take forever. By, like, step thirteen, I'm already regretting my life choices. I have to really pep-talk myself up, and once I'm on top, I'm completely out of breath. I stop to gulp water. Then I unscrew the top on a little orange bottle and pop two of my pills. Crap, I'm starting to get sick again. I can feel it all creeping in—swollen ankles, weird nausea, and that tired-in-my-bones feeling. I know I should get my blood pressure checked. I probably shouldn't have convinced them to let me do Survival Day. But I wanted to! Just to feel fully normal, for once. I need to hold it together till I'm home. Fake it till I make it. Yes, some of this summer has really sucked, but it's also been sort of epic too.

And maybe I'll still find the treasure. The da Costa estate isn't far, I know. Down the path, hang a left, then another left. But I'm so wiped now, I can't even imagine making it there. And scale the gate? Laughable. I can't even scale my own life right now.

I'm never gonna find the treasure. I'm never gonna get healed.

I walk slowly over to a bench looking out over the cove and plop down. I don't even know how long I'm on the bench, with the ocean hypnotizing me. And then—BOOM—a voice. I nearly jump out of my skin.

It's in Portuguese, so I don't understand it, but I realize it's coming from an old man who's sat down beside me. He's tall—I can tell by his long legs in ugly brown cuffed pants—and old, definitely old, with a face that looks like someone's left it out in the sun too long, like a dried-up fruit, but not in a cute way.

"Uh . . . *hola. Desculpe, não falo português.*" I know enough to say I don't speak Portuguese, but that's about the extent of it.

"Ah." His face gets weirdly excited. "*Inglês?*"

I nod and get out my journal, hoping that if I open it, he'll get the hint that I don't want to chitchat. Or maybe he'll simply smell me and hightail it away. I can't be too pleasant to be around given that I haven't showered in a week. But I did just go swimming, so maybe that's masked things.

I stare at the page I've opened to, which I started earlier in the cove. I've written: *I'm so stupid. I can't believe I ever thought Aiden wanted me. I hate myself so much. So much so much so much so FUCKING much.*

My eyes blur with the words and the rejection that sling-shots back. But then I feel the man on the bench shift over, his gaze heavy on me. I move to the edge, and he moves closer still.

Feeling a heavy dose of the creeps, I start to stand, but he tugs at my wrist.

"I always knew you come back."

"What?" I try to yank away my wrist, but I can't. For a very old person, his grip is shockingly strong.

He shakes my wrist gently, the one with Jules's bracelet.

"The girl with the bracelet," he says, almost in awe. "I always knew you come back."

———

"Come back?" I totally don't get what's happening.

"I waited for you. I wait for you . . ." His brown eyes are rheumy, rimmed in red. "Eighty years?"

"I'm only sixteen." I finally manage to detach my wrist from his grip.

"No. Twenty years? Sixty? I don't know." He gets a far-off, starry-eyed look. "I wait a long, long time. And I never tell. And I never, never tell anybody. I tell José, I never tell *anybody*, only the girl with the bracelet." He zips a finger across his lips. "Only you, only you, only you."

Now I'm really creeped out. And who the hell is José? This guy is a few fries short of a Happy Meal, as Dad would say. "Just leave me alone, okay? I'm gonna go, and don't follow me or else I'll scream."

I stuff my diary back in my bag and start to dash away when he says, "Twelve tribes of Israel point to Fortunato. Said you know what that mean. He told me, sit on the bench with you. So many times, I look at bracelet on women. I try to find girl with bracelet. I never find her until you."

I stop in my tracks, my heart yammering my chest. "What did you say? The twelve tribes . . ."

I know the letter by heart, of course. The one Eli found in his great-grandfather's papers.

Twelve tribes of Israel pointing to Fortun . . .

"Twelve tribes of Israel." He pronounces Israel in the Portuguese way, like *Ees-rah-ale*. He reaches for his cane, propped up against the bench, and stands with some effort. He stumbles toward me slowly, and I freeze as he takes my wrist again. This time I let him. I can't even process this. I literally can't form words. He's quoted directly from Eli's letter. How would he know the contents of that letter unless—

He runs his finger over the arrows below the cross on Jules's bracelet. I've noticed Jules doing the same thing. It's like her tic, what she does when she's nervous. For the first time, I recognize how the bracelet is intricately carved, with all these little grooves and curves. It's hefty, made of pure silver. It even looks old-timey, like an artifact in a museum.

He counts, "One, two, three, four . . ."

All the way up to twelve. The twelve tiny arrows on this bracelet that I've definitely never noticed.

"Twelve tribes of Israel pointing to fortune," I say breathlessly. "Wait—you know where the treasure is? The fortune?"

He laughs, displaying a mouth that makes me wince, too many spaces where there should properly be teeth. Then he stabs a finger out in the air, an inch from my chest, and circles it back to point at himself.

"I Fortunato Sousa. The fortune you talk about, it's me."

———

I stare at him, taking everything in. So there actually is a treasure? And Jules had the bracelet that unlocks it? How does that make any sense?

Or is he trying to say *he* is the treasure? Because the letter says *Fortun* and then abruptly stops, like someone got cut off in the middle of writing it.

"Sorry, what did you say—your name is Fortunato? That's, like, a real name? So *you* are the treasure?"

"I Fortunato. I lead you to treasure. And you are the girl with bracelet. The girl I wait for long, long time." He laughs again and takes my hand. I flinch but don't pull away. His hand is shockingly smooth but veiny and, to be honest, I don't really like old people. Lexa is always going to her great-aunt's nursing home and asking me to come to run the bingo games, but I just can't.

Old people remind me of death. And every second of my life already does that.

"Come with me." He starts walking, pulling me with him.

"Come with you? Where?"

Every fairy tale I've ever read or seen and every kidnapping story my mom is riveted to on *Dateline* tells me not to follow this old man.

"Not far," he says. "My house . . ." He motions toward a little alleyway around the bend.

"Why?"

"Why?" He laughs again, and I look away from his revolting mouth. "Why? Because I take you to the treasure."

———

His house isn't quite *Hansel and Gretel,* but a bit too close to it for comfort. It's more shack-size than house, made of the island's standard basalt stone with yellow trim, stunning blue and white hydrangeas all around, and a dewy garden with a wrought-iron table I'm currently sitting at. Fortunato went into his house and promised to be back soon, and thank god he didn't ask me to tag along. Because, let's be real, I was gonna say no. I've already followed a stranger to his home on Survival Day, and absolutely no one in the world knows where I am. So yeah, I'll chill out here in the garden, thanks.

Dad would kill me that I even came this far. He's totally overprotective. Just thinking about Dad makes me want to explode. Like, angry doesn't even begin to describe it. I'm livid, and honestly, devastated. He tried to call me a few days ago, through Aiden, but I got on the line and said, "I hate you" and "I don't want to talk to you ever again." And hung up.

I've said stuff like that before, overreacting, but what he's done—it's beyond words. I can't even process it. I called him back, though, when I realized I could leverage things. Make him let me go on Survival Day.

It's all too . . . much. Life is way too much. I'm not dealing with it well, huh? I look back toward the shack-house's open door and wonder what Fortunato has gone to get.

Fortunato. I still can't believe that's a real name. That the letter is real. That the treasure is real.

I mean, okay, this part of life is finally fucking cool.

For the first time in years, I tip my face to the sky and decide to talk to God. I used to believe in him, used to belt my heart out at synagogue, but after my kidney disease flatlined me, it was harder to have faith. If he exists, though, well, he's done something cool for me this time.

Heal me, God. I don't care about the money or gold. The rest of them can keep all that. Just give me back my health. And help me be a good person. Help me forgive Dad, somehow. Fix my family. Make us okay. Help me be nicer to Livvie. Help me protect her when all of it comes out. Or maybe she doesn't need to find out. Help us be okay. Let me be happy. Or at least . . . give me some peace. All I want is to feel healthy and at peace.

When I finish, I feel a wash of calm. Then I realize Fortunato has returned and is sitting across from me at the table. He's placed a super worn-out brown leather portfolio on the table. It's the type that an old-school businessman would use to stash papers. I scan the space, wondering if the gold bullion was too heavy to carry or something.

"This is the treasure?" I ask as he slides the portfolio closer to me. "Where's the gold?"

"Gold? No gold. Why you think gold?" He opens the portfolio and with trembling fingers unveils yellowed papers. "I no open. No open. No tell. Only girl with bracelet. Only she. She take papers and do right thing with them. Only her. Only you."

"Okay," I say, but I can't totally stop my heart from sinking. Papers. Fucking papers are the treasure? Maybe they're bonds or something, I think, heart slightly lifting, but when I stare at them, it's only handwritten words. A letter, all in Portuguese. Definitely not bonds.

"I help you, okay. I translate to you."

"Okay." I'm trying to keep my disappointment in check that this is the actual treasure. Even if there's no gold, it's still epic that I found it. And maybe there really is a secret healing property in it, like a potion or something. I remember that I have my diary in my bag. "Oh!" I get it out. "I'll write in this."

"Good, good. Now letter from José. You know José?"

I laugh in spite of myself. This whole situation is ridiculous. "I definitely don't know José."

"José, he the big papa. José da Costa."

"José." Come to think of it, it actually does sound familiar. "My boyfriend is Eli da Costa, and his great-grandfather recently died. He's the one we found the clue in—" I see the man isn't following. "Vasco. Vasco da Costa."

His eyes torch up. "Vasco is son of José. He start the family business in America. Already successful here, in Azores. But he go start American branch."

I do the math. "So José is . . . like, Eli's great-great-grandfather."

Fortunato shrugs.

"He must be." Suddenly I remember something. "Wait, is José the one who was murdered in his office? Stabbed with a letter opener in his neck? One of his staff members was trying to steal his fortune?"

"Yes. Stab in neck." Fortunato's eyes go misty now. "Very, very sad. No understand. Vasco no investigate. Never understand."

I'm confused. I knew I remembered that story, I just didn't know if it was on Eli's mom's or dad's side. Eli sometimes whips the story out as a party trick when he's nervous. *Dude, get this: my great-great-grandfather was murdered by a letter opener by someone who worked for him.*

"Okay," I say slowly, "so read me the letter."

I'm not sure how long it takes for Fortunato and me to go through everything, word by word, with our ramshackle communication, my barebones Portuguese and his better but still poor English. Hours, maybe. He's pretty good at translating, but I can tell he has dementia or something, because every so often he looks at me like he doesn't remember who I am, and then his eyes sparkle when they catch on the bracelet. He mumbles sometimes, rabble babble stuff, but eventually we get through it, and it makes sense. Some wild kind of sense. I stare at my translation, jaw basically on the floor.

"Holy effing wow."

———

To the girl I sat with on the bench, to whom I gave my family heirloom bracelet:

    I don't even know your name, but I do know where you live. In our one meeting, I am thankful I had the presence of mind to inquire. Immediately, after writing this letter and giving it to my secretary for safekeeping, I will write and send to you a brief letter, directing you to come find me because I must speak to you urgently. My life is in danger.

If something happens to me, then you will still receive my short letter and understand my instructions. I will write it a bit cryptically in case it drops into the wrong hands. But you will understand.

When you come with the bracelet to my secretary, Fortunato, the twelve tribes of Israel represented in the arrows beneath the cross will signify to him that you are the one. My treasure, to whom I bequeath the rest of my treasure. I've instructed Fortunato as such.

My treasure, you might wonder? Why didn't I simply write all of this in the second, shorter letter I'm about to post to you? Why the cloak-and-dagger treasure hunt? Am I exaggerating?

Well, this is quite a sordid tale I am about to unload on you. Forgive me if you don't understand at first, but I promise you eventually will.

Now, to start, I would like to tell you that sitting next to you on the bench all that time ago was a highlight of my elder years. My only son had gone to America, or so I thought. And my wife had died many years before. I was lonely. I used to sit outside my estate on a bench looking out to sea. And you sat there one day, beside me. When I looked at you, I couldn't believe it. You looked exactly like my son, Vasco. The spitting image, like my son in female form. And you had the exact same sprinkling of freckles across your right cheek as he had on his left cheek. It was uncanny. A mirror image.

We got to chatting, and I found you delightful. Smart and clever and full of life. I did something very spontaneous that afternoon, not in my character at all. You see, I am renowned for being a keen businessperson. A person who thinks with his head and not with his heart. But sitting next to you on the bench—I acted from my heart. I have no other descendants aside from my son, and spontaneously, I gave you the bracelet I always kept in my pocket. My wife wore it during her life, but it originally belonged to my mother and came from her mother, all the way back to my ancestors who escaped the Inquisition. The bracelet, as you know, is silver with a cross, with twelve arrow-tipped arms beneath. I explained to you that this was a symbol that Jews who were forced to convert and display their Christianity used to maintain their Jewish identities in secret. I told you how the twelve arrows represent the twelve tribes of Israel. That by wearing this bracelet, my ancestors were able to proudly proclaim their Judaism under an ostensibly Christian cover.

I didn't know exactly why I was giving you the bracelet. I didn't even know your name. But I felt compelled, like someone else sifted inside my pocket and handed it to you. Hashem. That's what I think. Perhaps you thought me a bit mad, and you did try to decline the gift, but I insisted hard enough that eventually you accepted. I remember that my hands shook as I fastened it around your wrist.

We had a beautiful conversation that day, one of the most memorable of my life. You told me how you loved to explore the island, that you enjoyed collecting pretty rocks at the beach. That you grew up without a father. When I inquired further, you only said he had died before you were born. You said your mother was wonderful, though, that you were very lucky. And you said that mathematics was your best subject in school. That you would love to start a business, perhaps, even though it was unlikely, because women were meant to have children.

Then I shared with you, in a moment of self-pity, the fact that my only son was abroad and never visited. I shared that my only friend was my young secretary,

Fortunato, and I pointed down toward the little street, where he lives. You said with that name he must be my lucky charm, and I said that indeed he was, the only person in the world I really trusted. I told you I had no one else, no one who would care about my possessions and family history when I was gone. And then you—who looked so much like my son—took my hand and we sat silently and looked at the ocean. I can still feel your touch, the smooth metal of the bracelet now on your wrist, brushing against mine.

Before we parted ways, I asked you where you lived, and you told me the address. I hadn't meant the number, merely what village you lived in, but I filed the information away. And I am most grateful that I have it now, so that I may post you a letter. We didn't even hug.

I don't know if it meant anything to you, but meeting you, I must tell you, meant everything to me.

I hope I will see you again, I hope it with all my heart. But even if I do not get the privilege, ever since I sat with you on the bench I have reflected on the subject of love. And I have changed my view on it because of you. I've decided that perhaps what matters in life is not how long we are given to love someone, but how big is the love we feel in a moment. It makes no sense, but in that moment on the bench with you, I felt love as big and deep as I've ever felt in my life.

After, I very much regretted that I had not asked your name. I thought about finding you; after all I knew where you lived, but I did not want to interrupt your life. And I didn't even know what else I had to say. If I said you reminded me of my son, you would have thought me an old kook. Or maybe something worse.

Now, in order to explain the rest of the story, I must

return back to said son, Vasco. My only child. Vasco was always a wonderful, loving son. He doted on his mother and me. He was smart—brilliant, really. But kind. That was the thing I was most proud of. On the weekends, he used to go out to more remote villages and help the elderly there. I knew he would take our company to new global heights. He was the only child with which we were blessed, and we were so happy it was him. I loved Vasco deeply. You will understand soon why I speak of him in past tense.

You didn't know it, almost certainly not, when we sat together, but I am José da Costa. Perhaps you have heard of my family. And my Vasco wanted to capitalize on our success, to expand our real estate empire and various business enterprises to America. America was the new frontier, was it not? Making it in America—the pinnacle of success. But that I sent my son so readily to America is something I have long regretted.

Nonetheless, so it was. We decided Vasco would go and run the American operation from Boston. Not to live there forever, but for some time. He wanted to take his best friend with him. Solomon. Solomon was the only bad decision Vasco ever made. He was a malandro. *[Sydney note: Fortunato says he doesn't know a good English equivalent. He says it is a no-good person.] Solomon never could pay attention in school. He courted many girls. He gave his mother endless worry. But my son loved him. Solomon wasn't smart like Vasco, but he was going to be Vasco's secretary. Like Fortunato has done for me. It is relevant to point out that the boys looked enough alike that people always wondered if they were brothers.*

Now, in the first decades of the twentieth century, many Azoreans were going to America for business opportunities. Before Vasco left, he confided in me that he was having second thoughts about going. His mother had died only a few years before, but I felt that wasn't it. He had met a girl—I saw it in his eyes. I said, son, go, and you will soon come back.

How wrong I was.

Vasco and Solomon were flying Sky Azores, the national airline that I in fact owned. But as it reached American soil, the plane crashed, and Solomon and a few more crew members died. My son survived. Or so he informed me in a letter. I was so relieved. So incredibly relieved.

Thereafter, our business thrived, both on the island and in America, but I didn't see my son for almost twenty years. This was a source of much sadness in my life. At first, I was happy for him, that he was making it in America, but I have to admit, I was sad and lonely. Money does not have anything to do with happiness. It is important that I tell you so. But it can indeed cushion life's blows. That is for certain.

As the years passed, suspicions began to creep into my head and congeal into something bigger. Why were there never pictures in the papers of my son when he went to events? Articles, yes, but no photos. Why hadn't he come back to visit in years? Why were his letters so perfunctory, with the tiniest bits of often irrelevant information?

Sometimes, in dark times, I wondered if it was really my son who had died in the crash, and if it was Solomon who had survived. I imagined it—a plane crash, the heir to a fortune dead, and the other alive. Would a nonprivileged man leap to jump into the life of the privileged one? Would airline employees help him cover it up?

I needed to know. It was eating me up inside.

I decided to send word to my son that I was dying, and

that I had become fully blind in my old age. I wanted to go over business matters with him, including my last will and testament. I thought that might entice him to make the trip. I had asked him to visit many times over the years, but he always had some excuse or another. I did not think my real son would have abandoned me so. But if Solomon had taken over my son's life, then perhaps he would be assuaged by an invention of my blindness.

Sure enough, Solomon arrived. He came into my office, and I immediately knew. I was devastated, of course, that my suspicions had been confirmed. That my beloved son, Vasco, was dead. I hadn't wanted to truly believe it. But I had also sat with the gnawing suspicion for a long time. Especially after I met you, the spitting image of my son. In some ways, I had already mourned Vasco years ago.

I erupted—of course I did. Solomon was startled; he'd really thought he would get away with it. Stealing my son's identity. Nearly stealing my entire company and wealth. He must have been foaming at the mouth that I was seemingly on my deathbed, and he was about to inherit everything. What a coup he nearly pulled off.

Then Solomon surprised me. Instead of cowering in fear now that I knew the truth, he demanded to know the location of the treasure chest: Where is the remaining treasure?

There was always lore, of course, that our family wealth had its roots in a long-ago shipwreck. That we'd retained some treasure in a hidden place in case an emergency were to brew. I knew of these rumors, but they were not true. I had plenty set aside for an emergency, stashed away in safe institutions, banks being far better receptacles in this day and age than a treasure chest buried in the ground. Still, I was startled by Solomon's inquiry and refused to answer. In that moment, I thought about you. I always wondered, and now I knew. I told Solomon he owed me the truth. I asked him if Vasco had been in love with a woman on the island. If he had possibly impregnated her. Solomon's face said everything I needed to confirm my suspicions.

Solomon fled my house. When he left, I tried to reach my lawyer, but I have not yet succeeded. I will soon call the police, but first I want to aggregate my proof, so as not to appear like a kooky old man with wild, unfounded suspicions. I am still trying to wrap my head around the fact that you are my granddaughter. However much I hoped—or even suspected—it's a different thing to know that it's true.

I have to admit, I am afraid. I am afraid of Solomon. Even though I have warned my staff that he is not to enter my estate, I haven't yet informed them why. As Solomon left, I overheard him trying to bribe my staff, to convince them that I am going insane. I've told my staff to have nothing to do with him, but money talks. Oh, it talks. And the truth is, I am old and perhaps sometimes I do forget things. Solomon could use this to his advantage. So I am barricading myself in my office, and I am writing out everything I know to be true: The man who purports to be Vasco da Costa is not my son. My son is dead. And you, dear girl, are the true heir of my estate.

You are my treasure. And everything that is mine is now yours.

I hope we will be able to embrace. I hope I can tell you the story of your father. He was wonderful. It is a wonderful legacy that he has left for you. I must make everything right. I will make everything right.

I will send you the brief letter with the cryptic direction first, in an abundance of caution, in case Solomon finds you and tries to intercept the letter. You are the threat standing between him and my fortune. I know you will remember—the conversation about Fortunato, and where he lives. I want him to be with you when you receive the revelations contained in this letter. I trust Fortunato with my life. He doesn't know the things described here, for his own protection now, until I can deal with Solomon. But if I am gone, he will protect you. He will introduce you to the right people, who will help you find your way. You excel at mathematics; my intuition tells me you will figure out how to run a company too. You can do anything you set your mind to. You, my dear, are a da Costa, and now you are our future.

I only sat with you for the briefest of times, but I am certain I leave my legacy in the most capable of hands.

With love, your grandfather, José da Costa

———

It's getting dark when I say goodbye to Fortunato and return to the cove. He is confused about where I'm sleeping, and I try to explain about Camp Zahav and our summer trip and Survival Day, but this is where our translation groove glitches, because he doesn't really get it. I mean, fair. Eventually I just stand on my tiptoes and hug this old man, and honestly, I wish I could stay in his bony, musty embrace. Maybe sleep in his garden instead of by myself at the cove. But he doesn't understand when I ask—trying to explain Survival Day to him feels like giving a TED talk to a cat.

So I force myself to pull away from his arms and give a little wave, like "I'm fine, totally fine." And then I clutch the portfolio in my hands, because it doesn't fit in my knapsack, and set back off for the cove.

———

It's the middle of the night, and I shoot up like a toasted Pop-Tart in my sleeping bag at a rustle outside. I've found a cave to sleep in, about the size of my bedroom at home, tucked behind the black sand beach. I scoot back on the hard rock floor, my brain running through every worst-case scenario. There aren't rats at the beach—are there? Or something fierce, like wolves? Actually, there aren't dangerous animals at all on this island. I relax a bit, remembering. Then I remember how Daniella phrased it, when she told us that.

Don't worry, kids, she'd said, and I swear she was full-on staring at me. *The only thing dangerous on this island are the humans.* And then she laughed her obnoxious, giggle-laugh, like she's starring in a shampoo commercial.

"Hello," I call out, holding my breath. But—nada.

I settle back on the cave floor, and as I shift, my body crunches over a granola bar wrapper. I ate it last night, ravenously, as everything that happened during the day scrambled my brain. My stomach's growling for something more substantial. I have more granola bars and nuts and stuff, but that's bird food. I wish I could have a big, juicy steak.

I found the treasure. Of course, I can't sleep. It's actually bonkers. Like, what even is my life right now? And those yellowed papers that look worthless are actually worth everything. Eli's dad is going to *flip*. He's obsessed with their private jet. Obsessed with talking about how many homes they have. Eli's actually not even into their wealth that much. Sometimes I think the da Costa name is heavy for him, that he'd prefer doing something with his hands, like woodworking. He's really into shop class at school and makes gorgeous stuff. Like a little jewelry box he carved my initials into. He'll be okay, I suddenly know. And Jules . . . wow. I'm actually so happy for her. Okay, fine, maybe I'm kinda jealous too. Sometimes I feel like Jules is the sad puppy dog who needs you to pet it and feed it, and maybe this will help her now, help her stand on her own two feet. She's told me about her family situation; I know she doesn't come from much. This will change everything for her.

Lexie is going to be green with envy, for sure. This would be Lexie's absolute dream—to find out she was a secret heiress.

And even though I am truly happy for Jules, it's kinda crushing too—like, the treasure isn't going to save me. It doesn't exist, after all. The legend of turning your life to gold was always an illusion.

But then something else occurs to me: I have the power now. By virtue of the portfolio, which I've slid into a hole across the cave. I tore out my journal pages with José's translated letter and stuck them inside too. And I've put my backpack on top, for safe-keeping. I don't know why, it's only me here. But better safe than sorry.

I have the power to change lives, Eli's and Jules's, but for the better for them both, I think. For the first time it hits me that maybe it isn't a treasure I actually need. Maybe *I'm* the one who needs to turn my life to gold. To be a good person. Sometimes it's so hard, and easy to complain, because I've gotten dealt a shit hand. And this past week I've learned another layer to the shit. Dad.

I shove that away for the time being. I'm going to be a good person now, I resolve, especially to my sister. Things will get better.

I hear that rustle again, and for the first time I feel excited. "Livvie?"

It's possible, isn't it, that she could have come? She's pissed at me, yes, furious, honestly rightfully so, but she loves me more than anyone. I know that for sure. And she's protective over me, makes sure I'm taking my medicine and resting when I push too hard. She would have had to put her headlamp on and come here from a mile away, which is beyond scary in the middle of the night, but of anyone I know, Livvie doesn't scare easily. My sister is literally the bravest person I know.

My heart's on the verge of leaping out of my chest. "Is someone there?"

But I wouldn't hear footsteps, I realize, because if someone's out there, they'd be traipsing on sand. I flick on my flashlight, scanning the cave walls, feeling superexposed. My heart kicks into overdrive, and then there it is. A human-shaped shadow at the entrance.

CHAPTER TWENTY-FOUR

Lexa

I KISS ELI'S cheek and whisper, "Good night, sweetheart," but he's already out, even though it's only seven in the evening. Slack-jawed, lightly snoring, serene, the nighttime version of his daytime Happy Baby. It's not only the day's stress that has done him in. I put two sleeping pills in his whiskey. That definitely did the trick.

We're back in our suite, and I brace myself on the desk by the window, trying to give myself a pep talk, trying to ease my hammering heart.

I can't believe I've drugged my husband.

I can't believe I've done any of the things I've done this trip.

I'm living in a nightmare, and it's not over yet. Not even close.

I stare at my phone as a message blinks in. My entire body lurches. But it's only him again. Eli's father, David. The man I chose to call Dad. The man who took me in as his daughter ever since I got together with Eli nearly a decade ago. The man I looked up to, until he confided his dirty little secret. A secret Eli doesn't even know. Because Eli is too weak for all this, David told me, as he passed a cigar my way, and we sat side by side drinking whiskeys out on the Adirondack chairs out back at their summer home on Martha's Vineyard. The blackmailer knew to bypass Eli. To go straight to the power center.

I don't think I've ever in my life felt as important and special as I did when David took me into his confidence. But I made a deal with the devil. I realize that now.

"You, Lexa. You are exactly like me." And then he proceeded to tell me things I wish I could burn from my skull.

I scan through the messages now. More upbeat nonsense about how everything's going to be fine. We'll pay up. At this point, just cut our losses. Get out. No harm, no fail.

The last sentences: *I love you. Make me proud.*

Fuck him. Fuck him. Fuck this man I've come to think of as my father. It's the first time I feel like that. Tears sting my eyes.

He's left me all alone here, to deal with this. A real dad wouldn't do that. But I've never known a real dad. An upstanding man.

Well, except Eli. I stare at him sleeping in the bed and bat the tears from my cheeks. I don't deserve my husband. That's the truth.

I thumb the message away, which is my version of a screw you to David. Because he's drilled it in me that I can't only dismiss the message. I have to go into the app and delete our conversation train.

Leave no trace.

Sure. No trace. Huge lol.

A new message appears on my screen, right as I've closed out the app. Not from him, though, which gives me a start. Until now, David's the only one with whom I've communicated on Signal.

My limbs feel shaky as my mind re-loops the message on the notecard the receptionist handed over.

I opened it in the bathroom, sitting on the toilet, as the water ran in the shower. Staring at the words over and over again in disbelief.

Reuben told me. Download Signal if you don't have it already. It's on tonight. Love ya, xoxo

I sat there numbly, feeling like my life was a train that has completely moved away from me. Left me screaming after it whizzed out of the station.

Love ya, xoxo. I imagined the desk clerk, transcribing this message, completely oblivious as to its import.

The new Signal message is from a person calling themselves "Reuben's Ghost." I grip my phone hard as I read it.

Ghost Hotel. 10 p.m. sharp. Don't be late. Don't be early, either.

Figure out a way so you don't rouse Eli's suspicions, because he's not involved in this. I know that for sure. Sleeping pills seem the easiest route; if I know you, you've already done it. You're nothing if not a planner, Lexa. At 9:45 p.m., leave from the back door of your suite to the path. You know the one. Reuben told me you once went there for some romantic alone time. Walk at a normal pace. Don't attract attention. Pretend you're out for a stroll. The police are stationed in the front of the resort, but they're not monitoring the back. I'll bring the proof. It's yours, for the price of two million dollars. That's right, the price has gone up, and there will be no further negotiations. Get ready to make the transaction in front of me. I'll give you the bank account information in person. We'll never speak again after this night, I promise you that. I'll give you the papers. I have them. The originals. Or else—and I won't hesitate.

A second message: *When you arrive at the entrance of the building, there will be two gray Azorean capes on the landing. Put one on and pull the hood up over your head. This will ensure we're concealed in case anyone is watching when we meet for the exchange. Wait inside on the first level, by the broken window that looks out onto the ocean.*

A final message: *This will all be over soon, and we'll both walk away happy. Don't do anything stupid.*

———

In the hours until I have to leave, I pace our suite, feeling the walls closing in. Of course, I've communicated with David. *Dad.* It's all set. This reunion has been a colossal failure. Now I need to salvage things. For me, for my family. For my future.

I stare out at the inky night, the ocean black as the sky in the distance, impossible to demarcate the line between. Then I draw the curtains, stamping out the night, and dress in black leggings and a black tee. I'm mostly avoiding my Google search engine, not wanting to leave any incriminating trace, but I can't help but google "Azorean cape." Not gonna lie, the instruction in the message that I'm going to have to wear a cape, besides feeling incredibly unnerving, triggered some sort of recollection. I thumb through Google Images to confirm that, yes, there is an Azorean traditional cape that I must have heard about at some point on the island or at camp, and it's creepy as fuck.

It's called a *capote e capelo*, and the black-and-white images that pop up are like *Handmaid's Tale* porn. Staid women draped in heavy dark cloth, all the way to the floor, and the hood part is a broad head covering supported by a bow made of whalebone and a hemp lining.

Do we really need this to conceal our identities? Or is my blackmailer requiring it for some other malevolent reason? I consider the scenario, how I would do it if I were her or him. The Ghost Hotel is, I acknowledge, a genius meeting point. It's on the massive grounds here, so the police won't clock me leaving. And no one's monitoring the back grounds, especially not the path along the ocean, which then curves into the forest. It's late. I can't imagine anyone will be at that abandoned hotel. Who would possibly be around to see us? But I guess the blackmailer is thinking better safe than sorry. There's a route to sneak into the Ghost Hotel through the woods, if you park your car on the other side of the dirt road. Teenagers do it sometimes, go to make out there. At least that's what Reuben said ten years ago, when he pushed me up against a dusty wall at the hotel and kissed me.

I feel a lump in my throat. No matter everything that happened, I'm still sad that he's dead. He was weak and a blackmailer, with a ginormous ego to boot, but he also could be sweet. I picture him with that crystal in his pocket, and my chin trembles.

I turn back to the task at hand, tell myself to buck up. This isn't the time to go soft. This is the end of the road, and then it will all be over. I stare at my husband, sit beside him, and stroke his hair. I study him, the rapid flicker of his eyelids, how he occasionally spurts with a snore so apocalyptic I think he might have sleep apnea. Then I smile at how he always sleeps with his left leg straight, the right one bent at the knee, in a triangle, right sole hugging his left knee. He's so dependable. So sturdy. Sleeps so soundly.

Truth is, that hasn't been my lot in life, to sleep soundly. And I expect after tonight it never will be again. But I'll be able to go back to my happy life, and Eli will never know. And I'll continue to sleep on my thousand-thread-count sheets. As many sets as I like.

That's something, isn't it?

I stand and return to my feverish speculations, the ones in which I've been engaged ever since I got the note. My new blackmailer has to be one of us. Staying here. In the suites right beside me. Perhaps already at the Ghost Hotel, staking it out.

I keep running through them all. Liv. Jules. Aiden.

Who is it?

Reuben killed Sydney—that's been obvious to me for a very

long time. It's the only thing that makes sense. Sydney must have found the treasure: the proof that Jules is the true heir to the da Costa fortune. And Reuben went looking for the treasure on Survival Day. Somehow he must have realized Sydney had it, killed her, and has been blackmailing Eli's father ever since.

So far David has paid up. But the blackmail has been angering him, especially as Reuben's threats have accelerated and his monetary demands increased. And now someone's taken over his blackmail scheme. Someone found out what Reuben knew. I can't imagine it being any of the three of them, but it has to be. I'm close to Jules and Aiden; it makes me sick that one of them could be threatening me. I don't think it's Jules; wouldn't she go right to the authorities? She's the true heiress to millions after all—the blackmail money is relative peanuts. And Aiden's never struck me as a guy who is out for riches. I'm leaning toward Olivia. She's been so odd and distracted, and there were always inconsistencies in her story from when Syd disappeared. Plus, critically, apparently Reuben wanted to talk to her before he died.

Liv says he never got to, but I wonder. Is she capable of blackmail? Of killing Reuben? She didn't kill her sister, though—Reuben did—so I always felt bad about the whole Sister Killer stigma. Everyone staring, dissecting her books. But that doesn't mean Liv doesn't have at least one devious, self-serving bone in her body. I remember those panic attacks she used to have, how she could erupt in anger at her sister, say skewering things with more venom than you'd think could live inside her otherwise soft, sweet exterior package. And she writes insanely dark stories, which must come from dark places inside of her. Still, she doesn't need the money. She's a mega bestseller. So then . . . why?

That's what I keep coming back to. None of it makes sense.

I look at my phone. 9:40. Well, I guess I'm about to find out.

———

I navigate the narrow, winding path with an assist from my iPhone flashlight. The path nearer to the resort was lit up by lampposts, but now I'm off the main property, deep into the forest, surrounded only by the silhouetted trees. I run my hand along the ancient stone walls that used to be agricultural boundaries. A slick flurry overhead, and I gaze up as a few bats swoop into the trees. There are distant animal sounds, but mostly what I hear is the roar of my heart in my ears.

I recall the glint of that knife in the minibar and regret my decision not to pocket it. The blackmailer killed Reuben—what makes me think he or she won't do the same to me? I scan the area for a weapon, but all I see are snapped twigs. I draw my shoulders back—maybe if I project confidence, I'll feel it. Bottom line: This person wants money. If they kill me, they won't get it. So I'm safe. I'm safe. I'm safe.

The Ghost Hotel spurts into view, the massive, multistory building wild and untamed with overgrown foliage. I remember it, of course, but in daylight. Traipsing through the rooms overgrown with greenery. It was like something out of a storybook, but it's different in the dark. Many of the windows are shattered or missing altogether, and jagged edges of the glass glint in the moonlight. A faded sign over the door hints at the hotel's former grandeur, and out front a once-luxurious swimming pool stands empty and cracked, collecting rainwater and debris. The surrounding vegetation has reclaimed the area, now growing right up to the hotel's front stoop, and as I approach the first lichen-covered step, I see the robes to the side, stacked one atop another.

I pause, my bare arms prickling. There is an eerie, almost palpable silence, broken only by the whisper of the wind, and I know instantly I'm being watched. Of course, I am. Whoever Reuben's Ghost is had to have come here first, to leave the robes. And now he or she is lurking, waiting for me to follow instructions.

I bend down and unfold the top robe. It's enormous and cumbersome, and it takes me a bit to identify the back, which I assume is the longer of the sides. I swing the cape part over my shoulders, like a coat, and then I pull the hood over my head. It's bizarre, like being completely shrouded. The whalebone bow keeps it sturdy and upright, so I can just see out the hood. Strangely, I don't hate this thing. On a night that I'm feeling very exposed, it gives some sense of security. False security, surely, but I'll take what I can get.

Here goes nothing.

I step into the main lobby, with its once grand staircase ahead, the decorative ironwork now rusty. There are wooden fittings and faded floral furniture that hint at the hotel's once-opulent past. As I walk slowly through the lobby and into what was once a dining room, I presume, I recall the hotel's history. It opened in the early fifties, a five-star resort that was modern and ambitious. But it faced operational challenges from the start, and the financial instability of the times was its nail in the coffin. It was forced to close its doors after only five years of operation and has laid abandoned ever since.

When Eli's family bought the property, they decided to build the Ananda closer to the sea and left the old hotel as is. I run a hand along a wall that has been decorated in graffiti, with Portuguese words I don't understand but can tell by their red splashy typeface are angry. Then in a spontaneous decision, I prop my phone on the dusty fireplace mantel, aiming the light so it sort of illuminates the room.

It's ironic, I realize. Eli's family owns this place. And by extension, so do I.

Suddenly I hear footsteps, and I swivel to see a shadow back by the entrance. I hold my breath, remaining by the once-window onto the ocean like I was directed. Because the window no longer exists, the cool breeze fans my face, the only part of my body exposed to the elements. If I crane my head to the right, I can see the distant lights of the town.

The footsteps are getting closer, and now I turn and brace myself. It's the most surreal sight: this creature approaching me in a robe.

I start a tentative walk to meet my blackmailer. It feels, quite honestly, like I'm walking the plank. *This person is ruthless*, I remind myself. I grapple for steady breath, but it is currently eluding me.

Neither of us says anything. There is just the creak of the old wooden floorboards as we close in on each other, the occasional nail or bolt that I feel even beneath my soles.

Suddenly, I'm near enough that I can see.

"Oh my god. Olivia?"

CHAPTER TWENTY-FIVE

Olivia

"LIV? IT'S *YOU*?" Lexa says, her face framed by the ridiculous cape, mouth agape in the moonlight.

I switch off the light on my phone, since Lexa's propped her phone on the mantel, the flashlight beaming out. "I—"

"You're the blackmailer? I don't get it—I didn't really think it could be you. Why would—"

"The blackmailer . . . ?" I'm trying to make sense of her words, of her presence here, but nothing computes. I thought it was going to be—

"Olivia, how could you?"

"Lexa, I don't fucking know what you're talking about."

I grip the knife at my side. I should have put it under my cape to conceal it, I realized outside, but I'd put on the robe already and had a prickly sensation I was being watched.

"What I'm talking about? All those messages on Signal. Arranging this meeting. It was you. You killed Reuben?" Her robe is covering her forehead, but I can make out a sheen of sweat on her cheeks.

"I definitely didn't kill Reuben." I look around.

Where is she? Is she hiding? After all this time, did she not call me here to reunite, but to lay a trap?

Lexa's gotten messages from Sydney on Signal too? My brain is working rapidly, but I'm still missing pieces.

That's the problem. I've always been missing so many pieces.

"You had to have killed Reuben," she says. "You wrote me as 'Reuben's Ghost.' You're the blackmailer."

"Lexa," I say, trying to say it nicely but feeling like I'm about to let out a massive scream. Why is Lexa here fucking this up? Literally—why?

"I don't know what you're talking about. I'm not 'Reuben's Ghost.' I didn't send you any messages."

Lexa's gazes bounces around the room, then lands again on me. "Then why am I here, in this absurd getup? Who the fuck sent me those messages?"

"I should tell you someth—"

But footsteps through the door make the words die on my lips. I turn, watching a third robed figure make its way toward us. My entire body is clenched and I feel like I've forgotten how to breathe.

Sydney. I can't believe it. She's alive.

"Syd, oh my god, it's really y—" I lunge toward my sister, but then I flinch and stop. Because I can finally see properly who it is.

I blink my eyes, wondering if I'm seeing right, and then realize I am.

Finally, it appears, after all these years, I am.

Lexa gasps, and I do, too, as it shatters and dawns through me. Because it's not my sister standing here. Not Syd.

It was supposed to be Syd.

Then I notice the gun in her hand, trained at us both.

"I don't believe it," Lexa says. "Cass?"

CHAPTER TWENTY-SIX

Sydney

Ten Years Before

THE ABSOLUTE LAST person I expect to see in the middle of the night outside my cave is you.

"Sydney?" you call.

"Cass? What are you doing here?"

I wriggle out of my sleeping bag and take a few hesitant steps toward you, this small girl wearing a pink button-up pajama top with yellow daisies and matching pants, a purple cloth knapsack slung over her shoulder.

"I thought you might be scared here at night. I live nearby, you know?"

"You do?" I'm not sure what to do, what the protocol is for when a little girl shows up in my cave at like four in the morning.

"Yeah. Reuben and our mom and me. We live in Vila Franca do Campo."

"Eli's family lives here too," I tell you. "Or they used to."

"A lot of people do." You give this solemn nod, then suddenly you fling your arms around me. Your hug surprises me. I don't know at all what to make of all this. You're muscular for a little girl. Of course, I know you want to be an Olympic gymnast, and I always nod and am supportive when you talk about your dreams. I keep my mouth shut about the odds. But good for you, you're really working at it, if your little kid biceps are any indication.

We separate. "How did you even know I'd be here?"

"Survival Day," you answer matter-of-factly.

"Yeah, but . . . how did you know?"

"I heard everyone talking a couple weeks ago. How Survival Day was taking place on the southern part of the island, and my mom gets all the emails, you know? She's on the list with the counselors."

"She is? Uh . . . okay."

"Yeah." You brighten. "So I saw it in her email. The list of where everyone would be. There was a second email, where they switched people around. You got put here. It's really close to my house."

It still doesn't explain why you're here. The only thing that computes is that you *know*. And clearly, you want to talk. To be honest, ugh, hard pass. I don't feel like being the designated listener-slash-amateur shrink. But I can't just turn you away.

"Can I sit down?" you ask.

"Uh, I guess? I mean . . . free cave." I force out a laugh.

"Great!" You plop down and sit cross-legged across from me.

"Cass, it's the middle of the night. I still don't get why you came," I admit, joining you on the cold rock floor.

"Don't you?"

I forget to breathe for a second. "No, I really don't."

Okay, you definitely know, kid. Fuck. I'm so freaking pissed at Dad, that he's put me in this position. I wanna scream my lungs out at him. But nope. Instead, I have to handle this dumpster fire.

There's something stubborn in your stare, but you don't say anything else.

I try another tactic, my heart going berserk. I'll say something gentler, to perhaps make you spill. Otherwise, we're gonna be here all night. And I'd really like to get a couple hours of actual sleep again before morning. Tomorrow's gonna be a whole *thing*.

"Does your mom know you're here?"

"My mom doesn't care where I am. She only cares about herself."

It feels like the saddest thing for a kid to say. I suddenly feel very lucky that I have parents who never made me feel that way. Although I also realize the extreme irony in my thinking so.

"Cass, I think I know why you're here," I finally say.

"You do?"

"Yeah, and I want you to know, you can talk to me."

"Really?"

"Yep. We can talk or do anything you like." My heart breaks a little for you, whose life has been all cracked up like mine. Like Reuben's too. Only you're eleven. So small and innocent and way too young for this crap.

I'm surprised Reuben told you, though. That was shitty and honestly selfish of him.

"Really? We can do anything I want?"

I reach over to pat your arm, feeling awkward. "Yeah. Sure."

"Okay!" You leap up, surprising me. "Can we play that game then?"

"Game?"

"Yeah, that treasure hunt game. The one we've played before."

"Oh. That's not exactly what I was talking about. I thought you might want to confide in me. Really, you can tell me anything and I won't judge. Maybe I can help."

"But I don't want to talk." You're almost pouty. "I want to play the game."

I sigh. "It's late, Cass."

"Come on, only for a little."

"Okay, fine. We can play the game."

You clap your hands in excitement, then grab your knapsack

and circle behind me. You sit, arrange yourself, and scoot close against my back. I'm hit with this huge, aching need for Livvie, like it's all-consuming. I wish it was her who was here. I wish so badly that my sister would burst in, hug me, and I could tell her everything. Absolutely everything. I wish I could twitch my nose like Samantha in *Bewitched* and make you disappear. Like, poof, you're gone, and Livvie's here in your place.

Your fuzzy pink pajamas brush against my arm, and it sends this weird wave of unease through me. I try to push all my worries and what-ifs away. All my futile fantasies. I shut my eyes. This will all be over soon.

You draw the circle on my back to mark the start of the game.
We're going on a treasure hunt
X marks the spot

CHAPTER TWENTY-SEVEN

Cass

MY GAZE BOBS between Lexa and Olivia, and I feel a surge of exhilaration, like right before I step out into a floor routine to rousing applause.

"Cass . . . you're the one blackmailing me?" Lexa looks at me dumbfounded, in a way that feels very, very satisfying. "Reuben was my original blackmailer. But you've replaced him? So that means—oh god, you killed your own brother?"

Lexa looks funny in her cape. Olivia too. Like women in vintage photos. I imagine a satellite looking down on us. Three witches around a cauldron. Even though this isn't that. I am not just some witch bitch. I'm me. Finally, honestly, me.

Thing is, I wasn't playing when I told Lexa that we needed to wear capes in case anyone were to be in the vicinity, somehow see in. But this cape thing, it only adds to the surreal ambiance of the Ghost Hotel at night. I had to scramble this morning, come up with the plan. But there's something perfect about it, when I survey my handiwork now. Something that feels true. Fitting.

Since I was a kid and we moved to the island, the Ghost Hotel is where I've come when I need some peace and quiet, in later years, where I can be practically guaranteed that no one will come up to me angling for a selfie and autograph. For me to dazzle them with Olympic stories. Instead, I can sit on the top floor, legs dangling off the side of the hotel, and stare out at the ocean.

Or I can finally bring what started a decade ago to a fitting conclusion.

I steady the gun, still training it right on them both. I can see by the shock in Lexa's eyes that she hasn't quite processed this. Olivia, too—she came expecting her sister. Though I can almost see her brain working, shuffling memories around, appraising some of them in a new light. Am I a genius for all of this or what?

And clearly neither of them expected the gun. Now it's game over.

"Yes," I finally say. "I killed Reuben. I didn't intend to! We were fighting, and it got heated. He wasn't seeing reason, and so . . . I almost don't know how it happened, but suddenly I realized I'd shoved him into the hot springs."

I wince as the memory shoots back—the crack as he fell, hitting his head on the cement rim of the pool; the haunted look on his face in the water as he thrashed around. Reaching out an arm, some tepid splashing, all the while his eyes boring into mine, pleading, and then . . . And then gone.

"Honestly, I'm really fucking angry I had to kill my own brother."

"You're angry you had to kill your brother," Lexa repeats, slack-jawed. "I . . . I don't understand any of this."

"No, you wouldn't. You think you're so smart, but truth is, everything's gone right on over your head."

A flicker in Lexa's eyes. Anger. I've challenged her, and she wants to fight. Well, I knew she would. And I've actually looked forward to this encounter all day.

I couldn't fight with Sydney. It had to be fast. Clinical.

And Reuben—I didn't relish doing it one bit.

But this . . . this can be a little fun and messy.

"Where's my sister?" Olivia whispers. "I don't get it—where's

Syd? Sydney wrote me a letter. She said to download Signal, and from there she told me to meet her here. That she'd finally explain everything."

"Oh, Olivia." I laugh. "You fell for it, hook, line, and sinker. Syd's not alive, sorry to say."

"I saw her." Her voice is hoarse. "Near the synagogue, and then again by the sea. I saw her."

"You saw a woman I paid to wear her hair in tiny braids and put on a white beaded necklace with a silver heart charm. You saw a woman I paid to scare you a bit. I'm sorry about that. I guess you're—you've always been collateral damage in this whole thing."

"You killed my sister?" Olivia falters, and Lexa reaches over to steady her. "So those memories I have . . . you were actually there too. I wasn't imagining it. It wasn't my medication messing with me. I wasn't going crazy and it wasn't grief twisting things in my mind. You were there, too, in the cave. I don't understand. I—"

"You will," I say, even a bit kindly. "This night is meant for understanding. Reckoning too."

"You're a monster." Olivia grips onto Lexa's hand, a little stronger now. I have to give it to her—she meets me, eye to eye. "I can't believe you hired someone who looked like Sydney to fuck with me. I can't believe she's actually dead." She whimpers now, and I endure her cries for a bit, pitiful sounds pinging off the musty walls.

"I'm sorry, Lex," Olivia finally says. "I'm really sorry you're getting roped into this."

"Lexa's *roped* into this?" I say, or maybe I yell it. "She tried to kill my brother! *I* didn't go canyoning with you guys. It was Lexa. He told me. She cut his rope and tried to kill him."

By the nonreaction on Lexa's face, the only part of her not shrouded, I am served up confirmation that I'm right. But of course, I knew it. Reuben knew it too. It's still crazy; I only just found out from Reuben what the papers Sydney left in the cave contained—the papers that at the last minute I took home ten years ago, in case my DNA had gotten on them. How it all devolved—Reuben finding the papers, discovering the true heir to the da Costa fortune, and blackmailing Eli's father with the information. Eli's fucking father, who turned to his minion, Lexa, to take care of his dirty work and make their little *problem* disappear.

"I . . . I couldn't figure out what went down," Lexa says, and I can tell she's trembling.

"What went down—that's a quaint phrase for attempted murder. Your father-in-law told Reub he was going to transfer the funds, but he was stalling to give you the window for murder."

"Like you can talk!" Lexa says, trying to sound strong but unable to hide how she's bug-eyed staring at my gun. "And I came here intending to transfer the money. You told me we could just do the transfer. That this would all be over. I don't understand what's happening. I don't get why Liv is here. I don't . . ." She keels over suddenly, head to her feet.

I watch her carefully. "Don't try anything. You know what I'm capable of now. This gun is fully loaded. And I promise you, I won't hesitate to use it."

I see her eyes flicker toward her phone, which she had the unfortunate luck of placing out of arm's reach, using it as a flashlight. I look at Liv's hands and nearly laugh. She's trying to maneuver to make a call, and she's also fumbling with a knife.

"So you brought a knife just in case, I see. Just in case Syd actually came and tried something crazy." I smile, contemplating the irony in that statement. I walk up to Olivia and jab the gun into her chest. "Give them to me. The knife and the phone."

Her breath sucks in, and there is something very satisfying about how easily she hands them over. I place them behind me on an ancient table.

This—this here right now—I feel on top of the world. In

perfect control. I haven't felt in perfect control this week. Things have blindsided me left and right. Reuben telling me he knows what the treasure is and that he's been blackmailing the da Costas over it. Especially him confiding that he was going to finally tell Liv. I tried to convince him not to. I wish I could have said, *You can't! I've taken care of things, even paid a Sydney lookalike to confuse Liv and get us through this memorial trip without anything real being revealed. We're almost on the other side. You'll ruin everything!*

But I couldn't convince him. Not without telling him the truth about that morning with Sydney—and I couldn't do that. And so I had to kill him instead. Or kill Olivia.

I should have killed Olivia first, but what happened at the hot springs was a self-preservation reaction in the heat of the moment. I really didn't intend to kill Reuben. I stare at Olivia. This woman who has come back and ruined everything for me. I lost my brother because of her. Now, she's going to pay.

"If you're going to kill me, fine," Olivia says, so resigned that I actually feel disappointed.

Fight, goddamnit, I want to say! *It's only fun this time if you fight.*

"If you're gonna kill me, then please tell me why. I only remember bits and pieces. And I've never even been sure those memories were real."

"What do you remember?" I ask Liv, curious.

"I remember standing over Syd, and she was face down, crumpled on the floor of the cave." Lexa makes a strangled sound, and the pitch of Olivia's voice rises. "I turned her over and—her eyes. Syd's eyes. They looked so . . . dead."

Olivia's eyes roll back, like she's back there again, and she begins to cry. "You were there, wearing pajamas, I think? They had daisies on them? You said something about how you'd just come down for a morning swim with Sydney, once you learned how close she'd be to your family's house. You said you'd come across Syd's dead body, and you didn't know what to do. I don't know, so much of it is a black hole. I know you said something about Daniella. I can't remember what."

"You really do remember a lot," I tell her.

"I thought I'd dreamt it, to be honest. I never trusted the memories. They're patchy and strange. You're saying . . . all of them are right?"

"They're right," I tell her. "I mean, there was more. The second you showed up, I realized I was in trouble. There was blood everywhere, and Syd had a knife in her back."

Olivia makes a sharp sound, and I can tell she didn't remember or know that part.

"I told you I had no idea what had happened, and I begged you not to tell my mom I was there. I said she'd been mad at me for tagging along with the teenagers all summer. Like, the terrain is dangerous for a kid and she worried I'd hurt myself and lose my spot at nationals. You were freaking out, having a full-on panic attack, and I told you that if you said you saw me here, I'd tell everyone you did it. But then you said, like, *oh my god, how could you have done this, you're a tiny child?!* And so I felt like I was fairly safe. You were such a mess. I'm the one who had to put Sydney in a bag and toss her off the cliff. I made you help me. If we'd slid the body into the cove, it could have washed up back on land. You brought Syd's diary, you don't remember this part?"

What comes out of Olivia is like the sound of a wailing animal, telling me that she does.

"You didn't want anyone to be able to read her diary. You were mumbling something about how she'd be embarrassed, and so you threw it over while I threw her body into the ocean. After that, you were, like, collapsing. But I did the hard part. Honestly, how strong was I for an eleven-year-old?"

I almost expect them to express admiration, but nope.

"Anyway," I continue, "I knew to take a more secluded route back home, so no one saw me. I ran ahead and left you behind. But I guess you took the normal route, Olivia. That must be where the old man saw you coming up from the path. Worked in my favor in the end."

"I never knew—all those flashes—snippets of conversation—I thought I was going crazy. Sometimes I thought I might have killed her myself!"

"You never told anyone about seeing me there?" I ask, genuinely curious. "I knew no one would believe it, but still, I did worry. It's why I had to make sure you were . . . *distracted* this trip. And what better distraction than your sister resurrected from the dead?"

"You're disgusting," Olivia spits. "I wish I had shouted it from the rooftops, all the flashes and snippets. I can't believe . . ." She heaves out a breath and now seems to shrink and shrivel to a smaller version of herself, any vestiges of fight expunged. "I told Dad only once I thought you might have been there, and he immediately shut it down. We never spoke of it again. Please tell me why you killed Sydney. Please."

Her voice is weak, her face pallid. She wavers, almost like she's faint, and then lowers herself to a clunky seat on the floor. She reminds me of Sydney, actually, when she was sick. How sometimes Sydney would have a dizzy episode—maybe she'd even fake it for attention—and everyone would rush to her side.

"Just tell me," Olivia says.

"Fine, I'll tell you." I take a few steps back and ease atop a floral chaise. The chaise coughs up dust that storms my nostrils, makes me feel on the precipice of a sneeze.

I try to sneeze, but it eludes me. I hate when that happens.

"I'm your sister," I finally tell her. "By blood. Your father isn't my stepfather. He's my birth father. Reuben's also. He's had two families this whole time."

CHAPTER TWENTY-EIGHT

Olivia

CASS'S REVELATION THUDS through me. It's like I've been wandering through a haze for ten years, an impenetrable fog, and suddenly it's lifted, and before me is terrain whose contours suddenly make perfectly terrifying sense.

"I knew he was having an affair with Daniella," I finally say, breathless, as it all converges. "She was hideous to Sydney. So when they got together, after my mother—"

I look up at Cass in horror, suddenly wondering if she had something to do with Mom's suicide.

"Your mom killed herself. Don't come at me for that one."

I nod, a throb in my chest. "But she killed herself," I say through clenched teeth, "because you fucking killed her daughter. I can't believe it—this whole time I didn't know. I didn't know if I'd actually killed Sydney and caused my mom to—"

"Wait, Liv, back up." I look over at Lexa, my partner in crime in this nightmare. The hood has fallen down over her right eye, so I can only see her left one. I reach up for her hand, squeeze.

She turns her face to me, and I can see tears welling in her eyes, both of them visible now. *I'm sorry*, she mouths.

My lips quiver. All I can do is nod.

I can't believe I came to the Ghost Hotel hoping my sister was still alive and had orchestrated our reunion. What the hell was I thinking? Deep down, I know it's not my fault I was so manipulated by Cass, but right now I'm irate at myself. I'm irate at the truth that was staring right at me, only for me to explain it away and make it my own fault. I knew I was missing pieces, important pieces. But I couldn't have fathomed this.

I thought I was coming to this island again to get closure finally. Figure out what happened, once and for all. When I saw those glimpses of a girl who looked like my sister, I thought it was all going to finally make sense. And it does, I guess, but in such a deeply sad, disturbing way. After Reuben's death—oh my god, Reuben is my brother. If what Cass said is true, then he's my actual blood brother. Sydney's too.

And Sydney must have known. Reuben also. Their fight, I realize. The fight on the bus the week before she died. Maybe they found out. Reuben went home for a day that week. I remember he missed one of our hikes. What if he went home to confront Daniella, and Cass somehow found out too?

Everything locks into place with chilling clarity. And now I realize, staring at my psychopathic sister, her gun trained on us, not a grain of remorse on her face, that I've made a huge mistake coming here. Lexa and I are defenseless, in the middle of the woods. I didn't tell anyone I was coming, because who would I tell? And what would I even say? They'd think I was losing it again.

I've never even told Tomika what happened, all the questions I've had, including about my sanity and my own potential guilt. I've pushed it down, written my pain and shame into the pages of my books. But it hasn't helped. Not even being with Tomika, whom I love, has helped. Nothing has helped close the chapter on what happened ten years ago.

And now I realize, Cass is blackmailing Lexa for reasons I don't yet understand, but that means Lexa probably didn't tell anyone she's here either.

"Does Eli know you're here?" I whisper to her.

The woeful sag of her face makes my stomach sink.

"Stop chitchatting. Move apart." Cass thrusts up from her seat, walks over, and waves her gun in my face, so close I can feel the breeze the barrel generates.

Reluctantly I slide my hand from Lexa's and inch a couple steps over.

"Now that we've covered the basics, we can proceed," Cass says with a wide, psychotic grin, so different from her graceful Olympic smiles. There are two versions of Cass, I've always suspected, I suppose, subconsciously. The one she presents to the world, and the one I was unlucky enough to stumble upon that day in the cave.

"By next steps, I mean, why I've invited you both here." Cass points the gun right up at me, miming a pop in my forehead.

I flinch.

"I think you can both probably use your imaginations."

"We haven't covered things at all," Lexa says. "You've only explained bits and pieces. Cass stabbed Sydney to death? And, Liv, you found them? Can someone please fill in the blanks?" Her eyes flit at me, and I know she's playing for time. That we need to stretch this out. Keep Cass talking. So that we can figure out how to overpower her. She's an Olympian with a gun, unfortunately for us. But we're also two against one. We have to be able to play that to our advantage in some way.

Cass smiles with a wide, eerie smile, the true-her smile. "Yes. Do tell her, Liv. Everything you remember."

Lexa clears her throat, and I flick my eyes over at her. I immediately know what she's communicating by her gray features, the swollen slump of her lids. She loved my sister. And vice versa.

They might have both liked the same guy, or had typical best friend squabbles, but they were two peas in a pod. Best friends forever. And for ten years Lexa has lived not knowing what happened to Sydney, the same as me.

"I was in the meadow," I say, taking a deep breath, "on Survival Day."

"I know. I wasn't far," Lexa says. "In some pasture, on the top of a hill."

"Right. But I was supposed to be in the cove. That's where I was initially assigned, and Sydney got them to switch us. Maybe she did it to spite me, or just because she loved the beach. Aiden dropped us both off. Syd first. She elbowed me—for sure intentionally—as she climbed over me, and then she went around back to get her backpack. She didn't even look at me, didn't even say goodbye, and neither did I. Those memories are, for better or for worse, crystal clear."

I stare down at the weathered wood floor. Even in the dim night I can see that planks are ripped up, others rotting down.

"Anyway, my Survival Day is a blur. I don't remember a lot of it. That got me in trouble in police interrogations. I probably should have made stuff up, but I was in such a bad way, not thinking clearly. I was furious with Syd when she left for the cove. We rehashed this in the documentary filming; she'd threatened to tell everyone about my crush on Jules. And that was a big deal to me then. But I was also worried about my sister. Sydney was sick. She milked it sometimes, sure, but it was a real thing. And I didn't even think our parents should have let her go on Survival Day. Actually, they'd said no, but something happened in the last week that Sydney convinced my dad. Maybe it was finding out—"

I can't say it yet, not aloud. Still can't fully process what Cass has revealed.

"Maybe she used what she found as leverage to make Dad say yes," Cass says.

"Yeah." I shrug. "I don't know. But I knew Syd was having a hard time. I'd seen some stuff she'd written in her diary. Of course, we looked in each other's stuff because we were being bitchy sisters, but I also read her journals because I was worried. I hated to see my sister in pain. All this stuff about how she hated her life and wanted to rip off her skin. It was terrifying. I didn't know—what if she did something to herself? Or what if she fainted? I remember I couldn't sleep. It's hazy, I get flashes, and I've always questioned them, but now, I guess, they all must be true. It wasn't a dream, or the medication warping things. I had to make sure my sister was all right. I've always been fairly good with directions, and I knew where the cove was, because we'd dropped Sydney off first."

"That's brave, Liv," Lexa says quietly. "To walk over in the night by yourself. I was scared shitless. Every noise I heard I thought was an animal about to pounce."

I smile weakly. "I wouldn't call it brave. I wouldn't say that anything I did was actually brave. But I got to the cove and, yeah, I remember going down the steps. It was only starting to get light. At first, I didn't know where Sydney was, but I saw the cave back behind the beach. I went to investigate. This is when my memories kind of . . . float off. The rest . . . I've never been able to trust what I did or didn't see."

"You did see," Cass says proudly. "I can attest to that. You saw me. Well, me and your sister. Your *other* sister."

"The scene—it wasn't computing," I say, as it all roils back. "My heart started racing and it was like I couldn't get enough air. I felt dizzy, like I was watching myself outside my body. Well, it wasn't my first panic attack. From there, I think I blacked out for a bit."

"You screamed and ran to Sydney," Cass says. "You were heaving. I thought you were going to faint, or have a stroke or something. You kept telling me to do something, help, call someone. You were frantic."

I close my eyes as those hideous moments—the worst of my life—are retold. I don't remember them with clarity, but I feel them somehow, like bruises beneath the surface that won't ever heal.

A new memory crystallizes. "I think—were you even wearing gloves?"

"Yep," Cass says, perking up with pride. "I thought of everything. And I was only eleven." She gazes at us almost expectantly, as if we'll gush over with admiration. "I knew that your fingerprints were the only ones on the knife, because you'd tried to pull it out."

I shudder, still not remembering that part. Maybe for the better.

"And I planned to wash my pajamas at home so there'd be no bloodstains, and there would be absolutely no evidence that I'd ever been to the cove."

"Did you—did you think Cass had killed her, Liv?" Lexa asks.

"No, she was just a kid!" I only look at Lexa now, needing her to understand. Needing her not to forgive me, but to validate me. Tell me I'm not crazy. Or that even if I am, I reacted the only possible way I could have.

"Later, I wondered, of course, if those memories were real, but I couldn't come up with Cass's motive. Plus, it was all so ensconced in what-ifs. I couldn't trust a single memory I had. I thought maybe I'd invented Cass being there—or murdered Sydney myself! Sometimes I'd even—I wondered if Daniella had done it and Cass had covered up for her."

"No," Cass says. "But you're not the only one. Reuben thought our mother killed Syd, too, all this time."

I swallow and try to stave off a wave of nausea. "But I don't understand," I finally say. "How did you know we had the same father?"

"Oh. That." Cass grimaces. "Sydney and Reuben fought the week before she died."

"Before you killed her," I say through gritted teeth.

"If you want to be descriptive. I guess Sydney had a picture of your family in a little frame in her backpack."

I nod, remembering that. I had the same one. Our mom gave them to us, so she and Dad would always be close.

"Reuben found it." I exhale and it clicks into place, confirming my earlier suspicion about the general contours of what happened.

"Yes. He was looking for something in his backpack but checked in Sydney's instead. The second he could he left the trip and came home, to confront our mom. I'd gotten back early from gymnastics that day, and when I walked in, they were fighting. Reuben was screaming. They didn't see me, but I heard everything."

"You heard . . . what exactly?"

"Our dad had two families." *Our* dad, it rings around my head. I still can't quite reconcile it. "They met at synagogue, of all places. That's when we were living in Massachusetts. You weren't even born yet. That's what I heard her say. And Mom got pregnant."

"Reuben," I whisper.

"This is some crazy *Parent Trap* shit," Lexa says. "The photo, Massachusetts—sorry, sorry."

"Mom was on a tirade," Cass continues. "I think Oprah could have walked in and she wouldn't have noticed. She told Reuben the whole timeline, though she didn't know I was eavesdropping in the hall. Their affair continued their entire marriage. Mom said she and Dad wanted to be together, but Dad needed time. There was something about money. Your mother had money?"

I feel so empty, like my whole body is organ-free, only skin propped up by bones. "Family money. My grandparents."

"Well, he could only get it after twenty years of marriage. It had just been twenty years—that summer."

I remember how we all went to dinner at a nice fish restaurant to celebrate their anniversary, and the waiters brought them out a carrot cake. That must've been a month or two before the Azores trip.

"So under their prenup—I didn't understand exactly what that was, but even at eleven I got the gist. Anyway, under their prenup, Dad got a huge payout after twenty years. When the twenty-year mark came and went, my mom was really angry that he wasn't leaving your mom. He'd promised, and she'd moved back to the island when I was little so that our family wouldn't threaten yours. But Dad swore he'd join us and be a real present father to me and Reub. As it was, he only popped in for a couple weeks every few months. But the reason he said he couldn't was Sydney. Sydney's kidney issues had gotten worse. He said he couldn't leave her. And Mom was *pissed.*"

I find myself piecing together my life in such a new way. Like when you get a fresh eyeglass prescription, and suddenly you can't believe you were looking out at all the smudginess before, thinking that was clear. Dad always traveled; he and Mom used to fight about it. But he worked for the airline, and the island was always special to him. He had to be gone a lot, he insisted. It was for our family. But now I know that was all a lie. He had another family.

"Mom was lashing out at Reuben. Reuben was so angry. I mean, after that he never called our father Dad again. He was always Isaac to him. I think Reub—he couldn't go there. It was different for me. I was younger. I wanted my father. I still needed him so much. The whole thing was . . . horrible. Mom kept saying that Dad had promised, but Sydney ruined it. Twenty years had passed, so he'd get the money, but Sydney was the missing piece. She was sick, and he wouldn't leave her. Mom said, *I wish that girl would fucking die already.*"

I flinch.

"Yeah." Cass nods, almost sympathetically. "Look, she's a piece of work, my mother. I always knew Dad traveled for work, but I felt—shattered. I crept to my room. I couldn't believe you and Sydney were my sisters. An idea occurred to me, and I started to imagine what it would be like if Dad could actually be here full time."

I shake my head, having a hard time taking it all in. "I know how it happened," I finally say, "or at least the end result, but will you—at least tell me about . . ." I can barely say it, and I hate that it feels like I'm begging. "Sydney's last moments."

Cass is pensive. "Look, I didn't relish it, if that's what you're asking. I knew it was the only way, and—the idea came from that game . . ."

"Game?"

"The treasure hunt game."

"Oh god," Lexa breathes beside me.

I can't speak. I know exactly what she's talking about, and it stabs me in the gut.

"You remember it?" Cass asks.

"*We're going on a treasure hunt,*" she starts, and then Lexa joins in with her for the second part. "*X marks the spot.*"

Those now-sinister words rattle through me, and I feel like I'm about to choke on the stench of dampness and decay.

"*Knife in your back,*" I finally say, but I'm not sure if it's even audible. "*Blood gushing down.*"

Cass shrugs. "It got the wheels turning. The rest was actually . . . fairly easy. I asked Sydney if we could play, and I sat behind her, and well, you can imagine. I'd taken the knife from a restaurant. Not from home; even as a kid I knew I needed to cover my traces. It was quick. I don't think she suffered. She made some noises . . . but then—well, it was over quickly."

"What were you going to do if Liv didn't come then?" Lexa asks. "Who were you going to pin it on?"

"I knew no one would ever suspect I did it," Cass says, like she's offended. "They'd blame someone on your trip. One of the counselors or campers."

"Your brother," Lexa says.

"No. He was the farthest from the cove on Survival Day."

"What if it came out about your father's two families? Then Reuben could have been the prime suspect?"

"But it didn't!" she erupts. "It went how I intended that it would go. Dad didn't want anyone to know about the two families. Said it had nothing to do with Sydney's disappearance and would only look suspicious. But even if he'd wanted to tell, my mom would have convinced him not to. He'll do anything she says."

A laugh scuttles through me, sad and spent and biting too. "Except leave Sydney for her. And so you had to make sure of that."

I look at her—my *sister*—really look at her, for the first time since that morning in the cave. This evil monster, with the same blue eyes as Sydney and Dad, I see now. And suddenly, I realize, I've been afraid of her ever since that day. Cowering from her. Hiding from the shadows, from what may come out. Finally, I know the truth. Syd's not alive, like I hoped. But I have nothing— absolutely nothing—to be ashamed of.

I grapple up to a stand and thrust my shoulders back, an onerous task in this oppressive, sweaty cape. I refuse to be afraid of this weak, spineless girl any longer. She took my sister from me. She took my mother from me. My entire family. If these are my last breaths, I'm not going to spend them kowtowing to her.

"And your mother knew you killed Sydney, Cass? And

suspects you could have killed Reuben? And Daniella just lies down and lets you commit these crimes?" Lexa asks.

Cass looks moodily off, and I can tell that cuts into her in some place. "My mother is really good at seeing the world as she wants it to be," she finally says.

Lexa grasps my hand again and looks over at me with teary eyes herself. She squeezes my palm once, nodding her chin subtly toward the table where Cass has placed my phone and the knife.

With my other hand, I swipe my palm against my cheek to catch a wayward tear. I look at her quizzically.

Cass glances back at us, looking fully recovered from whatever triggers the mention of Daniella roused. "I have to say, hearing it all retold only proves my point: I was such a genius. Such a fucking genius. Unfortunately, besides the both of you, no one's ever going to appreciate my genius, so I'm glad you can. At least for as long as you're alive." Cass chuckles and lifts her phone up to read a text, her gun still trained on us.

"You grab the knife," Lexa whispers. "I'm taking her down. If we don't come out of this alive, I'm sorry, Liv. I'm so sorry about everything."

Then it all happens fast—Lexa lunging for Cass, me toward the knife. Cass reacts quickly. She explodes into a backflip, keeping a grip on her gun, as Lexa gets close. As my fingers curl around the knife, and my Olympian sister twirls in the air, I can't help but wonder if I'm actually in a dream.

But loud curdling screams bring me back down to earth. One of them is mine. And then I feel the knife knocked out of my hand. I dash, running purely on instinct, toward the stairs.

A single shot pops into the air.

CHAPTER TWENTY-NINE

Lexa

"IT'S ONLY YOUR leg, Lexa," Cass hisses as she drags me up the stairs. "You can live without your leg. Lots of people do."

With every jerk of my body as she hefts me up a new step, I writhe with pain like nothing I've ever felt in my life. Each stair brings fresh stabbing sensations in my calf and a renewed, rough drag of my cape against the wound.

"What are you wailing about? Would you like me to amputate it? Maybe that will help. Because I have a knife here. Good thing your friend Olivia left that behind." She pricks the knife against my neck, and I scream harder.

This is it. I'm going to die. And god, maybe I deserve it.

"Olivia," Cass calls out, almost singsong, blessedly moving the knife away from my skin. As she lifts me onto the landing, she lets me drop onto the floor, and I crumple inward, reaching down to my leg, unfurling the cape. I heave at the sight—my ankle is almost dangling from my calf in the most unnatural bent angle.

"Olivia, come out, come out, wherever you are. You're not getting away alive this time. I promise you that."

My vision blurs with the creped wallpaper, the dark, dank space. "Don't listen, Liv," I scream through clattering teeth. "Save yourself. She's going to kill us both no matter what."

I am racked with sobs. It's the shock of what's happening, the very real pain, but also everything Olivia said. I can't believe she's been living with that for ten years, alone. We were never close friends, but I grew up with her. She was always nice to me. After Sydney disappeared, Liv and I didn't fall out exactly, but we drifted. Liv was going through her hell, and I was going through mine. And we weren't close enough that either of us could lean on the other. Once I found out about Reuben's blackmail—and thus believed he was the one who'd killed Syd for the "treasure"—I felt too guilty to reach out to Liv. Because I knew information that could clear her name, but I couldn't volunteer it.

And now I think about Liv finding Sydney in such a brutal way. Watching an eleven-year-old psychopath heave Syd's dead body off over a cliff. Questioning her own memories, wondering if she'd killed her own sister. Poor Liv. Poor, poor Liv. Poor all of us.

Suddenly Cass is back, hefting me up from my armpits. "Let's go. Time-out is over. I need you to walk."

The butt of her gun rubs my temple. I try to hobble, but every time I put weight on my leg it feels like it's being ripped out at the ankle socket. I stop and fold like Gumby over the banister. "I can't."

"You're clearly not an athlete. Your pain tolerance is, like, zero." Cass grabs me again. "C'mon. We haven't even talked about you yet, Lexa. Only Olivia's sordid tale."

"What is there to even say?" I manage, digging my fingernails into my palm to stave off the pain as my leg bumps along the floor. The needle stabs have radiated all over now, down the tips of my fingers, up to my head, but I am aware that adrenaline is coursing, too, blunting the brunt.

"There's a lot to say. You tried to kill my brother."

I actually laugh. "You're the one who killed him! And he was blackmailing me. Blackmailing my husband's family. *My* family.

For ten years! He's not innocent in this. He thought your mother killed Sydney, and he could have turned her in. If he'd brought it to the police, the papers you took from the cave, the police would have figured things out."

Cass continues to drag me across the dusty corridor leading to old, forgotten rooms. I'm gasping now, but I need to get out.

"Sydney's fingerprints would have been all over the papers, probably yours, too, and the whole thing would have unraveled. Reuben isn't blameless. Not even close. And I thought he killed Sydney! This whole time, I thought he murdered my best friend."

"Oh sob, sob," Cass says, almost distractedly, continuing to yank me across old, dusty carpet runners. But she doesn't say anything more. She appears to have lost interest in me, and I'm terrified now that I'm running out of time.

Where's Liv? I know she didn't get the phone, either—Cass was quick. Backflip, grab, shoot. Didn't even break a sweat. Fucking hell that we have to be up against an armed Olympian. I half hope that Liv will suddenly leap out from somewhere, but a more realistic part of me says that maybe she'll go. Back down the stairs, now that Cass isn't guarding them. Run away from here. Save herself, at least.

I wonder what I would do and hate that the answer isn't immediately clear. In fact, I detest the feeling that crops up—that I want Liv to save herself, but not at my expense.

I want to live! Finally, I have such a beautiful life. And I don't want to forsake the chance to live it.

I decide to attempt a different tactic with Cass. "If you try to kill us, how do you think you'll get away with it?"

"What do you mean?" she asks, peering through holes where doorways hang on hinges, trying to sniff out Liv.

"I mean, for instance, I have your notecard in my room. They'll find it. Liv probably does too."

"So? Nothing can be traced to me. And I have an anonymous

notecard too. Sent a message to myself. The rest of our communication was on Signal. I'll say that I told you what I knew at Sete Cidades, about the blackmail, and that you wanted to meet me, make a deal. I'll say I went along with it, because I wanted to catch you red-handed. I was planning to record your confession, but you brought a gun, and everything dominoed from there. Oh! Actually, speaking of . . ."

She halts, plunking me to the ground. She kneels beside me and jabs my fingers into the trigger of her gun. It's so fast, in and out, that I don't even process. She rips the gun away and returns to a stand.

"Now your fingerprints are on the gun, too."

"But so are yours."

"Yes, but I had to use it in self-defense. You're the one who met with some shady guy by Sete Cidades to get the gun. I showed him your picture. Gave him instructions. For a lot of money, he's agreed that if anything's traced to him, he'll cut a deal. And he'll claim it was you."

"That's insane."

"Or brilliant. Anyway, I don't even think it will be needed. Because maybe the police haven't zeroed in on you yet, but they will." She sounds smug, triumphant. "They won't need to dig that deep. The evidence will be crystal clear."

"What about Olivia?" I try to push down my fears, sound strong. Not like I'm losing it. Losing all hope.

"What about Olivia?"

"If you're pinning this on me, trying to act like I orchestrated it, why would I possibly lure Olivia here?"

"You didn't lure her; she saw you through the window, heading down the back path. And she followed you, suspecting the worst. Her death—" My breath catches at that word, thins out to fumes. "Olivia just got caught up in your crosshairs. Unfortunate, really."

"I don't understand." I'm crying openly now. "How could you do this? Maybe I could understand why you killed Sydney. You were only eleven, and it was so unfair for you to lose your father all the time to his other family. But Reuben? Your own brother? He loved you so much. And I know you loved him."

I realize the irony in what I'm saying. I tried to kill her brother once. I did. But I was so relieved that the canyoning thing didn't work. It's what made me realize I couldn't do it. That's why I've been having these awful conversations with David. That's why I tried to make Reuben see sense in the park. I wanted him to give it up, his increased extortion attempts. He'd gotten enough money out of the da Costa family through all his blackmail, all these years. His fault he squandered it. If he wanted to live, he needed to let it all alone.

Only Cass got to him first.

"I did love my brother." She scowls. "But love has nothing to do with anything now. He was going to tell Liv about how our dad had two families. What a time to grow a conscience. If Liv knew the truth, her memories would make more sense. She'd tell someone. The police. As you can imagine, I couldn't let that happen."

"So you just killed him? So brutally like that?"

"It was quick," she says distantly. "And like I said, I didn't plan to. I thought I could make him see sense, but at a certain point, you know when to admit defeat."

"You took him up to the spring. It was roped off. That doesn't sound unpremeditated to me."

She pinches my leg, and I scream in pain.

"We already covered this, you fucking bitch. Anyway, you're the one who will go down for it, in the end. Not long until the cops zero in on you."

"What about the coin in his pocket? Did you put it there?"

"No! Are you kidding? What, like as a calling card? It was

enough to figure out how to get him up to the roped-off spring—telling him to let me just test out the temperature, I've always wanted to. So that he'd walk up past the rope with me. You think I could slip a coin in his pocket and shove him in simultaneously? I'm not Houdini. Although." Now she chuckles, a terrifying sound. "A calling card. Not a bad idea."

"Reuben was the one who put the coins outside on the terrace, isn't he?" I ask, playing for time, because he already confirmed it to me right before he died. When I tried to convince him to stop blackmailing us. Back when I was oblivious to the fact that I was still missing so much of the picture.

"It was smart." Cass nods. "He knew how to get what he wanted. And intimidating you was part of that."

"He was hemorrhaging money. Do you know how much we gave him over the years to stay quiet?"

"He wasn't great at business," she admits. "But everyone has their faults. If it wasn't for you and Olivia, I'd still have a brother. Less talk, more walk."

She jerks me up again.

"Ow! Oh my god, that hurts so bad." I hate myself that I'm crying. Hate that I'm at her mercy, breaking down, pleading for my life. "And what did you mean before, that the police will zero in on me? Did you do something? Plant evidence?"

"Besides the gun? No, nothing. I didn't have to. I heard the lieutenants speaking to each other in the hall, after my follow-up interview with the superintendent earlier."

"Oh." My heart sinks. "And what did they say?"

"That they found a Swiss Army knife on the riverbank below the canyon, on the other side from where we rappelled. It's lucky they found it, not submerged. Otherwise, it wouldn't have fingerprints on it. But it did. And it's only a matter of time before they identify those fingerprints. And link them to you."

"No . . ." A wave of dread crashes in.

"Yes." She's taking pleasure in this. "I knew when I heard this that we could have a fruitful meeting tonight. You've made it so simple for me to take Reuben's place as blackmailer. To get rid of you and Olivia in one fell swoop and pin it all on you."

"No." My heart is beating so fast, and yes, I'm fucking furious at myself, for not concealing the knife better. David had told me to dispose of it well, not to keep it, because the police would search us. I'd planned to dig a hole beneath a tree or something, but then I didn't have enough time, and I thought it would be better to throw it off the other side of the canyon. Who would hunt there?

Stupid me. But right now, I have bigger problems than being found out by the police. Namely, my life in this sociopath's hands.

"I'm losing patience, Olivia," Cass shouts. "If you don't come out soon, I'm going to kill Lexa. You have sixty seconds. Don't test me."

Cass's breathing has become heavy, labored, or maybe that's my own. "Ow! Ow ow ow," I cry as she hauls me up a mini-stairwell toward what must have once been a sitting room. The windows are smashed, and moonlight pours in, dancing shadows on the dusty parquet. It's gusty outside, and the fresh air feels good against my face. I can see out onto the front of the property, the vacant swimming pool, the path I walked upon only a little while ago.

I can't believe I fell for this.

"Olivia! Come the fuck out!"

"She's gone," I say dully. "She'll save herself."

Suddenly I get a burst of optimism. "How will you explain things if Olivia survives? She has to die to make your plan work."

Cass stomps down on my injured calf in reaction, and I rip out a scream.

"Olivia, if you don't fucking show your face in the next ten seconds, I'm gonna shoot Lexa in the heart, and then I'm going to come hunting for you. Don't fucking test me."

The wind whistles, and the floor seems to grunt under our weight, but I hear nothing else. No footsteps. This is the end. And I can't even tell Eli that I love him. It strikes me with panic that if Cass gets away with things, he's going to think I'm a monster. He'll think I killed my best friend for him. To lure him in for myself and preserve his family's grip on the treasure.

He won't know that in a warped way I've done all of this for us. Because I really, truly do love him. But in the pit of me, I know that I'm also weak. A person with integrity wouldn't have signed up for the role as his father's minion. I wanted to bring Eli into the circle of trust, to tell him what I've been going through, for the good of our family. But Eli is a good simple person. It's what I love about him. He'd want to be honest, make things right, even at our own expense. It's probably why Reuben never issued the blackmail ultimatums to Eli, but bypassed him directly in favor of his dad. And also why David never clued his son in. Eli would never in a million years agree to get his hands dirty like I have. And for the da Costas to survive with our assets intact, I've had to get my hands dirty AF.

Cass is the menace here, though, I remind myself, trying to focus, my mind spinning on how I can possibly turn this situation in my favor.

"You're . . . you're like whatshername," I finally whisper. "The figure skater who tried to have her competitor killed or something."

"Tanya Harding." She smiles. "Her husband paid people off to take down Nancy Kerrigan before the Olympics. Allegedly."

"You're just like her." I try to wiggle back away from her, but it's futile. I'm going to die. Without telling my husband that I'm sorry. That I haven't done most of the things that will be said about me. That loving and being loved by him these last ten years has been the highlight of my life.

"I'm not Tanya Harding." Cass laughs. "Trust me, I'm so much worse than Tanya Harding."

And then she cocks her gun right at my heart and pulls the trigger.

CHAPTER THIRTY

Olivia

"NO!" I SCREAM, bursting into the room. "I'm here. Don't kill her!"

But it's too late. Lexa's gone. I know it right away, by the vacant way her eyes stare up at the ceiling, by the unnatural loll of her head.

Same way Sydney looked.

In an astounding swell of rage and shock, I fling myself at Cass. And this time she doesn't backflip away. Maybe it's her surprise at me showing up, or the exertion she's now expended, but I manage to edge her up against the open window and bend her back, wrangling the gun from her hands. I'm shaking, staring at it dangling in my hand. I don't even know how to operate it, is the thing. My hands jiggle, as I aim it at her. I try to summon all that research I've done for my books, but it feels like sifting in sand for one elusive kernel. Do I have to pull something first, load a bullet—or just press the trigger?

Suddenly, a familiar voice cuts through the night.

"Cass!"

"Dad," we both whisper at the same time.

She uses the distraction to her advantage and drives her knee forward, sending the gun sprawling from my hands. For a split second, we both look wordlessly at each other as it slides across the floor, stopping up against Lexa's motionless body.

"Daddy!" I scream with all my might.

"Olivia?"

But before I can say anything else, I feel a powerful thrust at my hips, and then there's a startling weightless sensation as I begin to fall backward out the space where there once was a window. Into nothing nothing nothing.

CHAPTER THIRTY-ONE

Isaac

AT FIRST, I think my eyes are playing tricks on me when I pace up toward the Ghost Hotel. I see two figures up on the second floor, both cloaked in those strange capes that I immediately recognize as the traditional island garb, *capote e capelo*.

My eyes have progressively deteriorated, and I need glasses for practically everything, so I blink a few times, thinking I'm imagining this peculiar scene. Who are these figures, and what the hell is happening?

"Cass?" I call, because that's why I came in the first place. Cass hasn't been home all day, and she wasn't answering her phone, which is odd. She usually answers for me, or at least calls me back shortly. Olivia wasn't answering, either, which is more par for the course. But on the day that my son was murdered, I wasn't going to be able to sleep until I knew they were both okay. But I couldn't find either of the girls, and I didn't know what to do. So I came here. Because I know this is where Cass goes to be alone.

"Daddy?" I hear, and everything inside me goes still, brittle.

"Olivia?" I haven't heard her call me that in over a decade.

I start to run closer. Why the hell are they up there? And dressed like that? I can't tell who is who, and I don't like the look of this one bit. And then suddenly one of them falls backward through the window that I now realize is open.

I scream, racing forward, but I'm too late and too slow, as always, to catch her.

———

If there is any miracle on this night, it's that Olivia's fall was cushioned some by her landing in overgrown bushes.

It's a blur, to be honest. Twenty-four hours after my son was murdered, there is another dead body, and my daughter nearly falls to her death out of a second-story window.

The police arrive, and then the paramedics, or maybe it's vice versa. Cass is frantic, of course, after the gruesome things that apparently went down at the Ghost Hotel. When the police arrive, Cass gives the superintendent an old portfolio full of yellowed pages, and others that look more recent. And then Cass proceeds to state the most fantastical claims, but that nonetheless seem to actually make sense in the context of, well, everything.

I am really only half listening, though. Half processing. I stay with Livvie the whole time, stroking her hair, saying the *Shema* over and over and over again as they load her onto a stretcher. Then I sit with her in the ambulance and tell her that I love her so much. I tell her she's going to pull through this. Even though I have absolutely no clue if that's true.

I tell the same to Cass, too, of course, before I go. Hold her tight to my chest. My other daughter, who has mercifully made it out of this murderous rampage without even a single scratch.

———

Daniella goes with Cass to the police station, because they need Cass to give a formal statement. And I don't leave Olivia's side. The doctor tells me that her condition is serious; Livvie has sustained a head injury and has several cracked ribs and extensive bruising. She's being monitored for internal damage, and her vital signs were completely unstable when she was brought in, but they're starting to stabilize with intervention. He informs me they're going to put Livvie in a medically induced coma to reduce brain swelling and allow it to heal.

That sends me spiraling into sobs, but the doctor tells me it's actually a good thing. That this is not the worst possible outcome, and that I have reason to hope.

At some point in the night, Superintendent Flores arrives at the hospital to check on Liv and fill me in. Cass and Daniella are already home, I know, from texts, and I feel gratified at least, to know two members of my family are safe and secure. And that the murderer has finally been apprehended.

Lexa da Costa. Lexie. Little Lexie.

How unbelievable. I never would have thought. I remember her and Sydney together, doing their fashion shows, watching trash TV, giggling.

"You know, I work with dogs," Superintendent Flores says, after fully briefing me. She's a sturdy woman, about my age, probably, six years older than Daniella, although with her cropped gray hair, she and Daniella appear to be from wholly different generations. She actually reminds me of my first wife, June. June was solid like that. I guess that's why I stayed with her so long. She wasn't the fun, shiny, fancy, latest model to which I've now gravitated, or fallen prey, however you look at it. But she made me laugh, and she was a great mom, and a great partner.

"Isaac?"

I shake my head. "Sorry, you were saying—dogs?"

She looks at me sympathetically, but thankfully doesn't offer any further platitudes. "Yes. I volunteer with them. And often times when I walk a dog on his short leash, I think somewhat sadly about how the leash keeps the dog from experiencing the whole world. How it keeps him tethered to a small sphere. The dog can only see what's around him, not any farther. And I need to tell you—well, I want to apologize for my shortsightedness ten years ago, and this week too."

I smile sadly. "That's unnecessary."

"I should have tried harder, though. Look, I don't keep the dogs on their leash because strangers pose a legitimate threat, but simply because the dog fears what is unfamiliar. And I realize that's what I did here. I was so convinced it was Olivia—because of Mr. Sousa's testimony and the blood under her fingernails— that I ignored the broader landscape. I ignored Lexa, and how desperate she was for Eli and his fortune. Desperate at any cost, as it turned out, to keep Jules from knowing the truth about her family legacy. I thought the theory that the treasure had something to do with Sydney's disappearance was absurd. But I thought wrong."

"You couldn't have known," I finally say and think about what I haven't told her. How I kept Livvie on my own small leash too.

"No." She gets a far-off look on her face.

"What?"

"Nothing. For a moment I felt like maybe I'm still missing something. But it all fits."

She gives me a sad smile as she leaves, and then her words turn and turn in my head.

———

I get back from the hospital at noon, having spent the night and early morning consulting with the doctors and sitting over Livvie at her bedside, talking to her. Telling her how special she is to me. How sorry I am that I didn't fully, one hundred percent believe she didn't kill Sydney. How I'm going to spend the rest of my life making things up to her.

The doctors tell me she's doing well, that her vitals are improving. They're even starting to take her out of the medical coma now. They say I can return later, and that I have reason to hope for some progress.

So I came back to shower and get some things from home. I slip into our bedroom, the room cloaked in darkness in this midday.

"Sweetheart." I can see Daniella's shape on the bed, staring at the wall. I sit beside her, but she doesn't look at me. "Can I bring you something? Do anything?"

"Bring Reuben back."

"I know. I wish with everything in me that I could." A pain shoots down my rib, and for a moment I wonder if I'm having a heart attack. How can this all be . . . I still don't understand . . .

"Leave me alone, Isaac," she says dully. I continue to stroke her back, and she jerks forward.

"You're angry at me."

"Of course, I am."

"You have every right to be." What shitty timing, that Daniella found out about my recent little . . . dalliance with a local girl who works at the bar I frequent.

"I'm sorry," I say for what feels like the millionth time. But that's why I had the affair, I suppose. In our relationship of late, it feels like *I'm sorry* is all I ever say. I know it's passé to blame my wife for my cheating. But still, it doesn't feel like I can ever do anything right.

"I don't forgive you. So we're clear." This sucks the breath out of me. Because if one thing has been true for me and Daniella, it's that she has always, always loved me. Doted on me, waited for me. Stood by me. Forgiven me. Her patience has been a marvel. Sure, she had boyfriends. We had an arrangement. But she always said I was her endgame.

"Leave me alone, Isaac."

I stand and go, what else can I do? I close the bedroom door, feeling like an interloper in my own house. A stranger in my life.

My son was murdered, and my daughter was murdered, and another of my daughters is in the hospital, and who knows if she will make it. My body thrums with the heavy, impossible weight of it all. And the feeling, perhaps worst of all, that I'm missing something.

I'm a dog on a leash, and I can't see the bigger picture.

My breath hitches as I replay the memory I've shoved deep down, of a distraught Livvie after Sydney disappeared. I was on the island, after all, working, and of course seeing Daniella on the side. I knew Reuben and Sydney had found out they were half siblings, and that I had two families, and I was beside myself with grief about Sydney disappearing and feeling responsible for the suffering I had surely caused her.

When Livvie told me that in her splintered, piecemeal memories, she thought she might have seen Sydney lying dead on the floor of the cave—and that Cass was there, too—I lost it. I was furious at Olivia for inventing such a bald-faced lie. She could have said she saw anyone else on the trip—and I would have believed her. Of course I would have. But she said the name of my only other living daughter. I convinced myself it was her meds. She'd imagined something or was even protecting someone. Anyhow, Cass didn't know until later that I had another family. We only sat her down after Sydney's disappearance was broadcasted on the news and our family became famous for all the wrong reasons. Cass was bound to find out. But she only knew after the fact, so even leaping over the enormous obstacle of an eleven-year-old child murdering someone with a knife, Cass would have no motive to kill Sydney. That assuaged any fears I had at the time. Plus, there was the reasonable explanation of Olivia's antianxiety medication. Messing with her memories, no fault of her own. She just couldn't repeat her memory flashes to anyone; I drove the importance of that home to her. I never fully believed she was capable of killing Sydney herself—or I thought that if she had, she hadn't intended to. And thankfully she was never charged. I tried not to ruminate on it all too much. There was far too much tragedy as it was to add to it one of my daughters having murdered another.

I resolved then and there—Olivia would never know that I'd started my affair with Daniella when June and I were only engaged. That I was the true father of Reuben and Cass. It was easier to keep my families separate when one was on a faraway island. It was why I strongly encouraged Daniella to move to the Azores when Cass was little. Dealing with my two families in the Boston area was far too messy. I promised I'd move to the Azores eventually. I told Daniella I wanted her the most—and I did. But I also loved my life with June and the girls, and there was June's family wealth to consider and the twenty-year condition on our prenup. Five million dollars was what I got after that anniversary. The money tempted Daniella, too, and so she was willing to wait. I was working for the airline at the time, because I loved it out here. It's always felt like home. But I didn't make nearly the kind of money my first wife's family had.

I'd long ago promised Daniella that after the twenty-year payout I'd move to the island to be with her. At one time, that deadline loomed far enough out in the future that I felt comfortable with my safety zone. I liked having both my families, my two worlds. And as the twenty years came closer, Sydney's kidney disease worsened, and there was no question. I had to stay for my girl. Sydney needed me.

Maybe Livvie was right. She always said Sydney was my favorite, and I denied it. But there was something to it, I guess. Sydney worshipped me. Maybe that was it. I was her hero. And I'll never forgive myself that she found out. I warned Daniella it was playing with fire to have the kids at camp together, especially when Reuben, Liv, and Sydney were all in the same grade. I worried Daniella was even trying to force things to a head. But Daniella insisted she wasn't, said Reuben had just as much a right to go to camp, and since he was offered a scholarship, he was going. Then, years later, I tried to rail against them being on the Azores trip together—that felt like a disaster in the making, especially with Daniella involved herself. But Daniella wouldn't budge. Said Reuben wasn't getting short shrift, and she wanted him out of typical teenage trouble for the summer. Said the Azores trip would be good for him, make a man of him, and that I didn't get to take that from him. I understood where she was coming from, so I relented. I figured there was no way the kids would ever put it together. What teenage kids even talk about their dads? Worst case they'd say something like, "Oh, your dad's named Isaac, mine is, too."

That's not how it turned out, in the end.

In the early days, every time there was a knock at the door, my heart would lurch that it was Sydney, having swum across the Atlantic, made it home.

Absurd. Yes. I knew it on the surface, but my heart didn't want to accept it. And with all the horror that spawned from that awful summer, I couldn't go there, to what Livvie had claimed. And Daniella swore to me up and down that Cass didn't know.

And thankfully, Livvie was never charged, so I didn't have to dwell on her imprecise memories too deeply. But of course, if I were to appear in a court of law over this, they would say: *But you didn't tell Olivia about your two families. You pretended you fell in love with Daniella after June killed herself. You kept her half siblings from her—all because you knew if you told her, it could bring the Cass memory to the surface.*

You are a coward. You let people all over the world call her the Sister Killer. And you protected your other daughter in her place.

What if Daniella lied? Cass is her baby. The pride and joy of her life. Wouldn't Daniella protect her no matter what?

I wonder if it's grief, doing funny things with my brain. My anger, or the intense fear thrumming my chest. Maybe . . . maybe I'm imagining things that don't exist. Drawing thin conclusions from the past. But I know I can't let it go this time.

Cass is sprawled on the love seat by the window, staring listlessly out into the garden. Absently, I go over and kiss her forehead.

"Thank god you're okay," I whisper.

"I'm tough." But her voice sounds raw, like she's been crying. "Plus, those weird robes Lexa made us wear protected me from getting cut on the window."

Her phone vibrates and she stares at it. She doesn't smile, but the texts are like sparkplugs, bringing her face alight.

"Who's that?"

"Just Eli. Eli da Costa. It's terrible for him—what happened to Lexa. And his whole family business—it's like, not even his anymore. They've implicated his dad too. You know that the police found a Swiss Army knife with Lexa's fingerprints on it that she threw over the canyon?"

"Yes. I heard."

"It's crazy. And she drugged Eli."

"Lexa did?"

"Yeah. Sleeping pills in his whiskey. So he'd sleep through everything. She figured he wouldn't notice. So crazy. She was such a sociopath."

I nod, exhale deeply. "So you and Eli—"

"Dad, no. No." She grimaces. "I'm only being a friend."

"Okay." I pat her shoulder and begin to walk toward the door.

"Where are you off to?" I turn, and from this farther vantage point, she looks so small and forlorn that I have to remind myself she's an Olympian. I've seen her strength displayed countless times.

Again, I replay Cass's explanation to Superintendent Flores, the fragments that I caught. The two of them in the capes Lexa made them wear, facing off in some strange way at the window. I can't put my finger on why it was strange—it just was. Or maybe I can work into it: Lexa was dead; Cass managed to kill her. So then why were Cass and Olivia at the window, struggling? Why did Olivia fall backward?

Cass says Olivia stumbled back after she tried to grab for the gun, and the superintendent seemed to accept that at face value and didn't press for details. But I've thought through this, trying to imagine it like a movie, and yet it still doesn't wholly make sense. The two girls in those massive gray capes, looking . . . tense by the window.

I flinch, remembering how it looked like . . . if I didn't know better . . . how one of them pushed the other over. Livvie is the one who fell. Lexa wasn't at the window. So if anyone pushed anyone, it was—

"Dad?"

"Oh yeah." I manage a small smile. "I have a meeting, incredibly important, otherwise of course I'd move it."

"In PD?"

"No. The satellite office." That's our smaller office on the eastern coast. I'm lying, about all of it. But it's wild how automatic lying is for me. It comes naturally. Lying is an inextricable part of my DNA.

"Okay. How's Liv?"

"Hanging in there. Her vitals are a bit better, actually. There's less swelling, too, in her brain. They put her in a medically induced coma last night, but she's having positive responses to stimuli, like light, so they're going to start taking her out of the coma soon."

"Really? Is that good?"

"Very good. As best as we can hope for, in her condition. I want to be there later, when she starts to wake up."

"Good. That's really good to hear. I'm so relieved," Cass says, sounding heartfelt. "Stop home after your meeting, and I'll come with you to see her, okay?"

"Sure, baby, that sounds good." I pause. "When this is all over, when Liv is good and can come home, I'm going to tell her. It's time, don't you think?"

I study Cass's face for any flash of anything, but she's my sweetheart, chin trembling. "Yeah, Dad. It's time. I never understood why we had to keep it from her."

"It would have looked bad, with the investigation. They might have made suspects out of you and Mom," I tell her. I don't say what's on the tip of my tongue. That I really did it for her. Bottom line is that I chose to protect one daughter over the other.

Cass rises to hug me. I squeeze her tight, savoring the feel of her head against my cheek. I couldn't be with her all the time—most of the time, if I'm honest—when she was a child and for not the first time do I contemplate the effect of that. But this child—she couldn't have done the unspeakable things that are circulating as question marks in my mind. She just couldn't have. It's like the superintendent said—I'm still somehow ignoring the broader landscape. I'm missing something, but it can't be this. It can't be my baby girl. My champion. My star.

Sydney was my star too, I realize, feeling like my heart's on fire. It's been ten years. Sometimes I'm starting to forget. That, maybe more than anything, is the worst purgatory of all.

"It's going to be okay. It's all going to be okay now," I whisper into Cass's hair, not even knowing what I'm promising exactly, but aware deep down that I'm going to abide by the vow.

CHAPTER THIRTY-TWO

Jules

I DON'T FIND out what happened until the morning. Because in the evening after that awful day, once I've spoken again to the superintendent, Aiden knocks on my door and leans against the doorframe and I let him in. Really, finally let him in.

We shut out the world, turn off our phones, and spend the whole night talking. We talk about Reuben, what might have happened, running through the timelines but not settling on anything that makes sense. Then we start to talk about this baby. Aiden tells me his ovaries have been screaming lately, which makes me giggle, but also I feel touched, because he seems genuine about it. His last long-term girlfriend was a few years ago. He wants us to really try to make a go of things. Of us. I say I can work on the documentary from Terceira for now, but that I still dream about giving Hollywood a chance. Filmmaking, perhaps doing some intensive courses there too. Aiden says he's open, lucky that LA has sharks, too. We talk about our hopes and wishes for our baby girl. About how crazy it is that Netflix wants the documentary, even though we have no clue how the whole thing will shake out. He says that when he saw me in that emerald dress on the first night, I took his breath away. I ask if that means he doesn't like my Jessica Fletcher outfits, and he says he doesn't know what that means, but he likes me in everything I wear (and also in nothing). Spontaneously, I rummage in my suitcase for the dress and put it back on to model it jokingly for him. And then he stands and comes toward me with the most serious face and reaches for the zipper to take it slowly, agonizingly slowly, off.

Later, when we're lying in each other's arms, I tell him I'm still scared. He says he is, too, but that life is a never-ending exercise of stepping into the unknown. And that he thinks our unknown is a friendly one.

Our friendly unknown. It makes me smile so big my grin might shatter my cheekbones.

And then we wake up to a world that's shifted on its axis.

My phone lights up with calls from the police, lawyers who apparently want to represent me, representatives of Eli's family. Eli himself. Eli's father, David. Cass, too, sending screenshots of the craziest letters, one in Portuguese, the other on ripped-out notebook paper, in Sydney's handwriting.

Lexa is dead. She murdered Sydney and Reuben, all in the name of money. It was always about money for her—apparently *mine*. Our whole relationship was a lie. She's dead. My close friend is dead.

Myriad texts filter through the transom, from friends and also people I haven't spoken to in years. Media requests. Maria calls nonstop. Eventually I power off my phone again entirely.

We check out of the Ananda, thankfully managing to avoid Eli. Suddenly all I want is to be home in my little studio in PD and sit at my wicker table in the garden and absorb things without anyone who wants or needs something from me.

It will take a lot of time to process. And I'm nowhere near close.

Lexa—she—no, I can't go there now.

I am actually the heiress to the da Costa fortune.

Olivia is in the hospital, fighting for her life.

I can see the reporters already outside. Aiden's ordered a cab, and it eases in through the throngs.

"I've got you," he says, and I believe him.

———

When the cab pulls onto my street and stops outside my pale blue cottage, to my shock, there are more reporters clamoring outside the gates.

They stick microphones in my face and ask abrasive, intrusive questions to which I haven't the faintest idea how to answer.

What will you do with your millions? Will you let the da Costas keep any of it? Will you still do the documentary? Did you ever suspect Lexa?

Thankfully, Aiden ushers me inside and says, "*Sem comentários, sem comentários.*"

When we're safely ensconced with the gates, we stare at each other wide-eyed.

"These are only the local reporters," he says grimly as I slide a chair out in my garden and sink down. "Can you imagine what it's going to be like when the international ones arrive?"

We decide we need food for hunkering down here, and Aiden says he'll go out to grab it. I give him some instructions on the best spots and then have him read the list back to me from the note he's written on his phone.

"Rotas da Ilha Verde, for salad-y stuff. And Lan's Pizzeria—"

"For the decadent, carb-explosion stuff," I fill in, in a cyclone of thoughts and hormones and feelings. I'm glad, actually, that I'll have a little time alone now.

"You'll be okay until I get back?"

"Sure. I'll be better when I can stuff my face with pizza. By the way," I call after him, and he stops. "In the chaos this morning, I forgot to tell you—I'm really glad it's been confirmed you're not a murderer."

"Oh." His gray eyes spark up. "Well, I'm happy to say I told you so on that front. I think baby's probably happy about that fact too."

In spite of everything, I laugh. "She is. Oh, she's already told me—she is."

———

He's only been gone twenty minutes when I hear a series of rapid knocks at the gate, and I realize Aiden doesn't even have a key to my place. I walk over but when I peer through the peephole, I'm surprised that it's not Aiden.

"Isaac?"

I open the gate and shoo him in. "Quick, it's nuts out there."

"Nuts."

I take in his unkempt hair, his pallid face. "Isaac, I'm so sorry."

"Yeah, thanks, look—I need to talk to you, Jules."

"I've heard. I've heard it all. And there are no wor—"

"No. You haven't," he says, his face strained, perplexing me. "I need to tell you *everything*, Jules. And then I need you to tell me if I'm crazy."

———

Isaac proceeds to unload a collection of the wildest speculations I've ever heard. And I thought I'd heard it all this morning. I shake my head, trying to reconcile what he's saying with what I'd only begun to process.

"I don't know, though," he tells me. "I might be going crazy. I probably am. I needed to come here, Jules. You see why I needed to talk this out with you. I need you to set me straight. To help me make sense of it all."

"I get it," I say slowly, trying to let the puzzle pieces settle. "So they have hard evidence Lexa is the one who tried to murder Reuben when we went canyoning?"

"Yes. So I understand."

I've now pieced it together, that the conversation I overheard her in at Terra Nostra wasn't with a paramour, but with Eli's father. I still can't believe Lexa knew that the da Costa fortune was actually my family's and kept it from me all these years. Killed Reuben over it. And Reuben knew too. I thought they were my friends. It's too much to take in for a morning, and I know it will take me a long time to accept, let alone forgive. And yet the overarching thing I feel is sadness, that both of them are gone. But especially Lexa. No matter what she did, she was my friend. Or maybe she wasn't. Maybe my problem is that I've never quite been standing up for what I deserve.

"Okay, right, so Cass is your daughter by blood. I still can't believe it."

"I know." Redness creeps up his neck. "I know I've done so many things wrong."

"Now isn't the time for recriminations. Now we need to get things straight."

"That's all I want to do. And have Livvie wake up, and be okay."

"Yes." I pat his hand, feeling very sorry for him, but not able to shake the part of me that also feels like he's brought some of this on himself.

"Okay," I say, my brain hurting from all the twists and turns I'm making it take. "There are a few things I'm still cloudy on."

"Good. What?"

"Well, first, Lexa agreed to do the documentary. To be honest, when I proposed the idea to everyone, I never expected it to actually happen. I mean, sure, I figured they could be cajoled to help me. Because . . ." I gesture around, at my very simple abode. And I tense, thinking of my debts, even though I'm fairly certain I will have enough money to settle them now. That part is still wild. I push all that to the side. I need to focus.

"Like, I needed the documentary. And they all knew that. But I figured whoever murdered Sydney—and she had to have been murdered, we're positive on that?"

"Yes. She was murdered with a knife in her back. Well, according to Cass, who said she heard it from Lexa."

"Right. So whoever murdered Sydney wouldn't have agreed to the documentary, don't you think? That's why when everyone did agree, I was a bit shocked. More relieved than shocked, I guess. I pushed my doubts away. Look, I understand why everyone would agree, but Sydney's actual murderer? No. I mean, everyone had secrets, it turned out. But all those secrets didn't have to do with the murder. If all Lexa did was participate in blackmail, well, she could have rightfully thought that would never come out through the documentary. So why would she sign up for a documentary centrally meant to expose Sydney's murderer?"

"Why, indeed," Isaac says, "unless she didn't kill Sydney."

"Unless someone else did. Unless Cass did, according to your theory."

"Olivia said Cass might have been there," he says, repeating what he's already shared. "That's what she told me, and I was angry at her! I was so angry. I thought she was lying. I even thought she might have done it."

He stares at me, stricken. "There's still one thing that doesn't make sense."

"What?"

"Well, if there's proof that Lexa tried to kill Reuben in the canyon, but failed, then she could have tried again at Terra Nostra. And she did have motive after all. So did Lexa actually kill Reuben? Or could . . ." I can tell he can't bear to say it, but it rips out of him. "Why would Cass kill her brother? That's what I don't understand. She loved him!"

Suddenly something occurs to me, and I gasp. "Wait. Reuben

wanted to talk to Liv before he died. She told me—she said he told her he needed to talk to her."

"What could he have wanted to tell her?"

"Maybe the fact that they were half siblings," I venture. "Maybe after everything happening this week, he thought it was finally time Liv knew the truth. After all, it's his half sister. And . . ." I exhale deeply as I play this through. "Maybe he told Cass he was going to tell Liv. He didn't know Cass killed Sydney. He must have thought Daniella did."

I see it dawning in Isaac, the heavy sorrow in his eyes. "Reuben never comes home. I thought he resented me, and I understood, but I never got why he didn't come home to see his mother. It affected her deeply."

I don't say that Reuben wasn't innocent in all this. He could have told the police about the portfolio with the treasure. He could have said he found it at home. It would have had Sydney's fingerprints on it. Maybe they would have found bloody clothes in the laundry. Maybe so many things would have been different.

"If Reuben thought Daniella killed Sydney, then coming home probably triggered a lot for him."

"And the documentary."

"And that." He looks at me wide-eyed. "If he told Cass he was going to tell Olivia about my two families—"

"Then Olivia would know exactly what Cass's motive would be to murder Sydney. She might finally have the last piece of the puzzle to substantiate her memories and go to the police with."

"*Madre mía.*" He stumbles up. "I have to get to Olivia."

I take a deep breath and put a hand to my stomach. "Yes."

I trace the arrows on my bracelet, and for the first time since all the revelations descended, I piece something together. The letter from my great-something-grandfather José, in which he talked about the girl on the bench. It just occurs to me what Vovó said before she died. How she said she'd send me someone who'd watch over me and love me like she did, and she told me about an old man she once sat beside on a bench. How she felt he was her guardian angel. I've clung to that, like she's been helping me up above, and as I move my fingers across the arrows, I realize that maybe she has. And maybe she and José are together up there, happy that things have finally been revealed. Vovó was so sharp, so brilliant selling her homemade cheeses when I was a little girl. She would have gotten such a kick out of owning a huge company. I shake my head, because it still feels absolutely unreal that I now do.

"You know, Isaac, before you go, I have to tell you that Olivia had my bracelet after Sydney disappeared. And now I understand why she couldn't tell me how she got it."

"What's that?"

"You'll see, Liv will tell you. And it's in the documentary transcript. But this bracelet—"

"I know about the bracelet." His face sags looking over at me, his white hair wild. For the first time, I don't see a magnetic businessman with hypnotic blue eyes. I see an old man ravaged by life.

"I've read the papers. The superintendent sent me the screenshots of the papers. It's wild, about the treasure. Your inheritance. It's absolutely wild, Jules."

"Wild," I agree. "But so Sydney had my bracelet during Survival Day. That's how Fortunato Sousa recognized her, to give her the portfolio. But then, after she disappeared, Liv is the one who gave it back to me."

He's silent, absorbing. "You never said anything to the police."

"I didn't want to implicate Liv. I never really believed she did it. And she told me she found it in the cave, that the police must've missed it on their sweep."

"Plausible, I guess."

"Yeah. But then this week, with the documentary, I felt like

I couldn't *not* bring it up. We were all putting everything on the table. That was the point of this thing. To dredge it all up. And I guess why I'm telling you this is because I understand now why Liv couldn't tell me the real reason. I mean, maybe she didn't even remember this herself. But she must have taken it off Sydney's wrist, after she was already dead. She did that for me, because she knew how much this bracelet means to me. Your daughter—Liv—is a wonderful person."

His eyes fill with tears. "She is. I have to go see her."

"Yes. Go. But Isaac." He pauses by the gate. "You know, this bracelet is in the da Costa family—my family, I guess—as a crypto-Jewish heirloom. I know you have the same history. And I was thinking how . . . I don't know . . . our ancestors had to hide their identities, you know? Hide who they really were."

"Yes," he says, but I can tell he's not getting what I mean.

"Cass had to hide who she was too. Look, if everything you've said here is true, and if we're right on our suspicions, then—"

"Then my daughter is a sociopath," he says grimly.

I nod. I don't want to finish this for him. He needs to go finish it himself.

"But also I did this. I made her hide who she was." He wipes his eyes.

"You didn't do this. Not per se. Oh—wait—" I suddenly put something together that I overheard at dinner on the first night we all reunited. "Cass said she was named after her birth father. I figured someone whose name starts with a *C*. But—Casia is an anagram of Isaac, isn't it?"

"Yes." Isaac hangs his head.

"She wanted you," I say softly, so beyond heartbroken. It hits me that if all this is true, and Cass is responsible, then maybe Lexa isn't the demon I've started to think of her as. Maybe our friendship—some of it, at least—was real. "Cass was a kid, and she thought by killing Sydney, she would have you. It's so messed up. So broken."

"And it worked." Isaac looks at me distraught. "It worked."

Suddenly Aiden walks into the garden, holding a paper bag full of the food I sent him out for. His eyes flicker with surprise when he sees Isaac. His face grows solemn.

"Mr. Azulay," he says. "I'm—" I see him falter, not knowing what to say. "I'm so sorry about Reuben. It's . . . there are no words. I really hope Olivia will pull through."

"Me too. And thank you. In fact, I'm on the way over to see Olivia now."

Aiden bends down to kiss my cheek, and I try to smile at him, but it's an effort. "I just ran into Cass. She was heading to the hospital too."

Isaac makes a sharp sound, and my heart spasms. "You saw Cass? When did you see her?"

Aiden looks perplexed at my urgent tone. "I don't know. Fifteen minutes ago? By the church, I'm not sure what it's called—"

"The Church of São Sebastião?" I ask, panic rising in my chest.

"Fuck!" Isaac says, which visibly startles Aiden.

The church is practically next to the hospital. Both are a ten-minute walk from here. Five if they run.

"I'm going!" Isaac launches toward the gate. "I'm going there now. Call the police, Jules. And the hospital, tell them—"

"I will. I'll call them. Just—go! It will be okay, Isaac." *God, please make it okay.*

"What's—" Aiden says, eyes darting between us. He drops the bags on the table.

"Go with Isaac." I grip his wrist. "Cass is dangerous. Really dangerous. Please, trust me and—"

But Isaac is already bursting out the gate, with Aiden following close at his heels.

CHAPTER THIRTY-THREE

Cass

"OBRIGADA," **I SAY,** smiling at the nurse who led me to Olivia's room, thinking it's nice she's a fan. Though most people are.

"You make our island so proud," she tells me in Portuguese, practically vibrating adulation. She's clutching the surgical mask I've autographed, because she was so nervous when I asked for directions to Olivia's room that she couldn't even locate a piece of paper at the nurses' station.

"God bless you. God bless your family," she says.

She looks at me with reverence, and I have to admit, it feels great. Every time it happens. But especially today, when things didn't exactly go as planned last night and I need to right them.

"Obrigada." I plaster on another smile. My mouth is used to stretching these unnatural ways.

She's already seen the headlines, of course. I imagine most of the world has.

"Handmaid's House of Horrors"

"Grisly Murder at the Ghost Hotel"

"The Disappearance of Sydney Azulay Finally Solved Ten Years Later"

She wanted to know how I was doing but said, of course, how

could I even begin to answer? She was effusive with condolences over Reuben. I actually saw a tear drip out her eyelid. No doubt she'll tell everyone about how she met the Olympian. The hero. The one who brought the case to a resolution. Who fought against evil and prevailed. Who restored peace to our island.

I slowly shut the door to Olivia's room, maintaining my smile, even as she keeps babbling on.

Click. Ah. Finally alone. Well, not alone, but with my sister. Just the two of us at last.

I glance over at her, lying peacefully amid the *beep beep beeps* of the machines. I walk over to her bedside, taking stock of the room, the little picturesque window onto the broccoli-bunch branches of a few trees. My hand reaches into my purse, clutches around the syringe. The nurse has told me they've started bringing Olivia out of her coma. Apparently, she's not out of the woods yet, but there's reason to be hopeful.

Of course I smiled and gushed relief.

On my way over here, I turned on my burner phone to use ChatGPT, asking how to take care of Olivia before she wakes up. They won't tell you how to murder someone, but I did figure out a good workaround. You simply tell ChatGPT that you're an author of crime thrillers, and that one of your characters is in a coma, and you need a way to kill her in the hospital. And then ChatGPT serves it all up.

My sister, the real author of crime thrillers—irony of ironies— is lying there, so peaceful, not an obvious bruise on her, other than her head injury. So not the plan, but plans can be amended. I stand up straighter. I am resilient. I remind myself that I know how to adapt and adjust in order to stick the landing.

I've come this far. I close my eyes and visualize, like I've done countless times. I can see myself now, at the Kia Forum in LA, standing on the platform, the roar of the crowd in the backdrop.

Mom and Dad waving, tears cascading freely, telling everyone in the vicinity that I am theirs. I can feel the heft of the medal as it is placed around my neck.

Beep beep beep.

I slip toward the machines. Olivia's off the ventilator, which has been good news for her, and not so good for me. Dad had an important meeting that he couldn't move, and so I knew this was my opportunity. By tomorrow, Tomika will be here, and I'm sure the doting girlfriend isn't going to leave Olivia's side. Add to that the whole taking of Liv out of the medical coma happening now. And so I knew I had to act fast.

I'm just the loving stepsister, come to pay a visit. I considered donning scrubs and sneaking in, but quickly nixed that plan. I'm famous—aside from Eli's family, the most famous islander there is. If I were spotted in a disguise, there would be questions, and someone would make the link when Olivia dies. As it is, I'll slip out before she's found dead. It will be perhaps a bit odd that I was the last one to see her, but the case is all wrapped up, the evidence overwhelming. I've already given statements to the effect that Reuben murdered Sydney for the treasure. We have the treasure papers to substantiate things. The police have subpoenaed records from Eli's father. I'm sure it's only a matter of time before skads of proof surface as to the whole blackmail and payments that have spanned a decade. And Lexa *did* actually try to kill Reuben when they went canyoning. The knife with her fingerprints attests to that.

Fairly perfect, isn't it? If only I weren't the solitary soul to appreciate my brilliance. The only loose end is Mom. She knows what I did to Sydney. And by now she probably has figured it all out. But I'm fairly certain she will never tell. Not even Dad. She may hate me for killing her precious son, but she would never ruin her pretty life over it. Anyway, if she threatened to tell, there are ways I could spin things. Implicate her. We're in this together, she and I. We made our joint bed a long time ago.

She wanted Sydney gone. I just did her dirty work.

I hover over the bed, my sister's heart thumping an infuriatingly steady beat. If only I hadn't lost control over the gun; one bullet would have made this cleanup unnecessary. I stare down at her, so seemingly innocent, with a blond tendril curling over her forehead.

It's possible her memories are all jumbled again, just like ten years ago when she surprised me in the cove. It's possible that if she wakes up, she'll have blacked some parts out, even question what she remembers. She's still on those antianxiety pills, I know. They could save me, yet again. But this time, I'm older. Smarter. And with much more to lose. I can't risk it.

"I'm sorry it has to be this way," I tell her sleeping frame. Then I turn back to my mission at hand.

ChatGPT and I had an involved conversation about how to make sure no one suspects me after this is done. Some of the ways the chat suggested—like injecting a toxic substance into the IV— would flag suspicion. And Olivia's no longer on the ventilator, so I can't just remove it.

An air bubble into her IV line. That's the solution we settled upon. Fitting end, for the author of murder mysteries. I smile to myself, because it's genius. Everything I've done, to get to this point. And now it's over. Finally. Now I can enjoy the fruits of my labor. Even though, I have to admit, something in me wishes my father could appreciate the full breadth of my genius. Of all his children, look at what I've achieved.

The Olympic medals will have to suffice to earn his love and adoration. Those, and the fact that I'll be his only child left standing.

I get out my syringe, and I clasp the line. I look over at Olivia one more time. My sister. I feel nothing toward her, though. An emptiness. Strange, that. We're blood, after all.

Her eyes are closed, I notice suddenly, but fluttering. Like trying to open.

Then at once Olivia's eyes are fully open. I am acutely aware of the moment her eyes focus on me. Intense, startled.

Fuck. This was not in the plan. What if she starts screaming? Anyone can come in. Even though Dad's at his meeting, and Mom wouldn't come here. But a nurse could, or one of Olivia's friends. It's okay—I'm family. Her stepsister. This of everything can be explained. But not if someone sees me injecting the syringe. I need to finish this now.

"Dad," my sister whispers.

My heart beats wildly, not the exciting entrance-onto-the-Olympic-floor beat but an erratic one. Like in a few moments, nothing will be predictable or controllable or assured. Olivia's whispering now, but what if her voice returns at full force?

Olivia says it again, louder now. Emotive. "Daddy." As if he's walking through the door, about to save her. Her eyes go strangely slack, almost relaxed.

"Daddy's not going to save you. Shut up."

I could use a pillow to suffocate her, if need be. My breathing returns as the semblance of a backup plan forms. It always works out for me, I remind myself. In this too I shall prevail. And then it will all be over, forever.

I ready the syringe.

"She's talking to me, Casia."

ACKNOWLEDGMENTS

FOR A LONG time I've wanted to write a "camp" book. I grew up attending sleepaway camp in Michigan, the pinnacle being a five-week trip for the fifteen-year-old campers in the Western United States. We slept in tents each night, cooked our own food, hiked and explored national parks, and showered once a week at trucker stops. The water ran out as soon as our couple of coins did, so I learned to take very efficient showers. That and many other life lessons were instilled, though I did subsequently retract my exuberant declaration after the trip's culmination that I saw no reason to ever shower again more than once a week. Plus, fun factoid: Survival Day was inspired by a real camp tradition for the oldest campers. As a teen, I was also fortunate to join several trips to explore my Jewish heritage in international locales. When I stumbled across the fascinating Jewish history in the Azores islands of Portugal and imagined a group of teens on a rugged heritage trip, this book was born. And what a fun, murder-y trip it took me (and I hope you) on!

I have so many people I'd like to thank. First, my wonderful agent, Rachel Ekstrom Courage—eight years and counting, and I feel endlessly grateful for your sharp eye, astute guidance, and friendship. And a huge thank-you to Nick Courage, Heather Baror, and Tara Timinsky. To my amazing editor, Lara Jones, my heartfelt thanks for believing in me and my books and for editing them so brilliantly. I love our brainstorm sessions and the twists you helped me come up with for this one! And my deepest gratitude to the spectacular team at Atria/Emily Bestler Books: Emily Bestler, Libby McGuire, Dana Trocker, Megan Rudloff, Aleaha Reneé, Hydia Scott-Riley, Karlyn Hixson, Morgan Pager, Chelsea McGuckin, James Iacobelli, Paige Lytle, Shelby Pumphrey, Sofia Echeverry, Jason Chappell, Laurie McGee, Davina Mock-Maniscalco, Vanessa Silverio, Nicole Bond, Abby Velasco, and everyone on the sales, audio, and education/library teams. I always feel pinch-me lucky to be working with such talented and kind people.

I am very grateful I was able to visit the gorgeously restored Sahar Hassamaim Synagogue, including its moving museum, in Ponta Delgada. I learned a lot there that was invaluable in shaping this book. And to Diana Lisboa, Silvia Miles, and Susan Burkat Trubey, thank you for sharing your insights into the Azores islands, São Miguel, and the Jewish communities there. I am also indebted to Jake Realejo, who led me on a fabulous tour of São Miguel and answered my myriad questions. The Jewish history represented in the book is all accurate according to my research. And I tried to be as faithful as possible to the realities of the island, but occasionally took a few liberties. For instance, you won't find the Ghost Hotel where I've placed it, but it is based on a similar abandoned hotel that exists on the western part of the island.

I am thankful for the friendship and support of so many in the creative community, especially Lisa Barr, Nicole Hackett, Jill Salama Handman, Barbara Peters, Allison Hill, and Linda Sivertsen. And a big thank you to the wonderful booksellers, librarians, bookstagrammers, and podcasters who champion and host me and my books.

Thank you to the very best family: Mom, Dad, Bubs, Suz, Jas, Nadav, Arica, Uncle David, Aunt Nancy, and Uncle Jeff. And Suz, a massive thanks for being the first brainstorm partner and editor for all my books; our voice notes from afar mixing thoughts on life and our creative processes are nearly as soul-fulfilling as sister-ing while living in the same place. (One day again!) I am also particularly grateful for my local creative community and beloved friends who support and nourish me: Tracy Alexander, Natalie Blenford, Dani Faitelson, Zo Flamenbaum, Lexy Grant, Jaclyn Mishal, Rinat Spivak, Shani Zanescu, and (honorary local) Eden Adler Pearl. I wish there was sufficient space to list my other wonderful family and friends who cheerlead me all the way—please know I cherish you all. And finally, a special thank-you to my nephews and nieces who are such lights in my life: Liad, Reagan, Griffin, Noa, Archer, and Ari. It's fun imagining which one(s) of you will be able to read your name in one of my books for the first time when this one comes out!

And finally, to you, my readers. Thank you for buying, borrowing, and reviewing my books. Thank you for spreading the word and sending me the loveliest notes. I wish I could leap through these pages and hug each one of you.